tales from
the crib

tales from
the crib

risa green

 NEW AMERICAN LIBRARY

New American Library
Published by New American Library, a division of
Penguin Group (USA) Inc., 375 Hudson Street, New York, New York 10014, USA
Penguin Group (Canada), 90 Eglinton Avenue East, Suite 700, Toronto,
Ontario M4P 2Y3, Canada (a division of Pearson Penguin Canada Inc.)
Penguin Books Ltd., 80 Strand, London WC2R 0RL, England
Penguin Ireland, 25 St. Stephen's Green, Dublin 2, Ireland (a division of Penguin Books Ltd.)
Penguin Group (Australia), 250 Camberwell Road, Camberwell, Victoria 3124,
Australia (a division of Pearson Australia Group Pty. Ltd.)
Penguin Books India Pvt. Ltd., 11 Community Centre, Panchsheel Park,
New Delhi—110 017, India
Penguin Group (NZ), cnr Airborne and Rosedale Roads, Albany,
Auckland 1310, New Zealand (a division of Pearson New Zealand Ltd.)
Penguin Books (South Africa) (Pty.) Ltd., 24 Sturdee Avenue,
Rosebank, Johannesburg 2196, South Africa

Penguin Books Ltd., Registered Offices: 80 Strand, London WC2R 0RL, England

First published by New American Library, a division of Penguin Group (USA) Inc.

First Printing, April 2006
10 9 8 7 6 5 4 3 2 1

Copyright © Risa Green, 2006
Readers Guide copyright © Penguin Group (USA) Inc., 2006
All rights reserved

■ REGISTERED TRADEMARK—MARCA REGISTRADA

Library of Congress Cataloging-in-Publication Data:

Green, Risa.
Tales from the crib/Risa Green.
   p.   cm.
ISBN 0-451-21769-1
1. Motherhood—Fiction.   2. Domestic fiction.   I. Title.
PS3607.R445T35 2006
813'.6—dc22   2005029696

Printed in the United States of America

publisher's note
This is a work of fiction. Names, characters, places, and incidents either are the product of the author's imagination or are used fictitiously, and any resemblance to actual persons, living or dead, business establishments, events, or locales is entirely coincidental.

   The publisher does not have any control over and does not assume any responsibility for author or third-party Web sites or their content.

For Davis—
My beautiful, beautiful boy

prologue

As the car pulls into the driveway, my heart starts to beat wildly as my anxiety kicks in.

Okay, Lara, I tell myself, taking deep breaths. *It's time.*

When we're safely in the garage and the car has come to a halt, I turn to Andrew.

"You take the baby," I command, opening the passenger door and stepping, carefully, out of the car, first one foot, then the other. *Ow.*

I hunch over, placing one hand on my abdomen in the hopes that this will somehow prevent my fresh purple incision from splitting open, and I book it inside, if *booking it* could be defined as taking approximately three steps per minute. But when I walk through the front door, my speed walk is interrupted by Zoey, my dog, who promptly jumps up and places her front paws squarely on said fresh purple incision.

"Ow!" I yell at her. "Watch it, Zo!" Confused by the lack of mommy love after four days of separation, she lowers herself down and begins frantically sniffing my legs, trying to determine where I've been for so long. *Hmmm,* I think. I wonder if I still have my special I-can-hear-my-dog-talk power, or if that was just a pregnancy thing, like the ability to smell body odor from four miles away.

"Zo?" I say, trying to catch her eye. She cocks her head and looks at me, but if she's saying anything, I can't hear it. Oh, well. She was starting to get on my nerves anyway.

I give her a quick pat on the head as a consolation prize, and then move on into the foyer. I focus my gaze on the flight of stairs that is looming in front of me, and I steel myself.

All right, I think. *Let's do this.*

As the theme song from *Chariots of Fire* plays in my head, I lift my right leg, place it on the bottom step, and begin my ascent.

Ba ba ba ba baaaaah ba. Ow. Ba ba ba ba baaaaah. Ow, ow, ow. Ba ba ba ba baaaaah ba. Holy shit, this kills. Ba ba ba ba baaaaah.

By the time I reach the top, I'm sweating from the pain, and the hallway leading to my bedroom might as well be the Arabian Desert, it seems so long. I pause to rest for a moment, and give myself a pep talk.

Come on, Lara. It's just a few more steps. You've been waiting nine months for this moment. Get yourself together, woman.

And so I take a deep breath and push on. By the time I reach my bedroom door, I've found my second wind, and I am now singing out loud, at the top of my lungs.

"Ba ba ba ba ba da da da da"—I rip off my shirt and toss it on the floor as I head toward the bathroom—"ba ba ba ba baaaaah"—(weird flapping noise that I don't know how to re-create in writing). Then off comes the bra. "Ba ba ba ba ba da da da da . . ." The pants are slightly more difficult. There's no way that I can bend down, so I have to use my left foot to pull down my right pant leg and vice versa, and then I step out of them. "Ba ba ba ba baaaaah." I remove my watch and my rings and place them next to the sink. "Ba ba ba ba baaaaah ba." Oh, what the hell. I take off my earrings, too. "Ba ba ba ba baaaaah." I hesitate for a second, but then I figure that I might as well be completely thorough, so I reach up and pull the elastic ponytail holder out of my hair, hitting the final crescendo. "Ba ba ba ba baaaaah ba. Ba ba ba ba baaaaah."

And here I am. Completely naked except for a sanitary pad the size of Texas and a pair of white mesh, hospital-grade panties that are specifically designed to accommodate the Great State. Trembling, I say a silent prayer.

Please, please be kind.

With that, I close my eyes and step onto the scale.

When I open them again, I hold my breath and look down.

No, I think. I rub my eyes, just in case they've developed cataracts or glaucoma or some other vision-impairing disease in the last ten seconds, and then look back down again. But the number is the same.

Okay, I think, trying not to panic. *Let's think about this rationally.* I close my eyes for a moment to calm myself, and then I have a thought: *The panties. It's got to be the panties.* I pull them down, pad and all, fling them across the floor with my foot, and quickly step back on the scale. Nothing. *Oh, my God. Oh. My. God.*

I hobble over to the toilet and sit down, my eyes welling up with tears. "Andrewwwww!" I yell. "Andrewwwww!"

"What?" he yells back, and then I hear heavy footsteps as he runs up to our room. "Hold on, I'm coming," he shouts. He bursts into the bedroom. "Lar? Lar? Where are you? Are you okay? Did your stitches open?"

"I'm in here," I say, my voice breaking. He runs in, holding the baby in his arms.

"Honey," he says, sounding concerned. "I told you not to try the stairs yet. I told you that you should just sleep downstairs on the couch for a day or two. Are you all right?"

"I'm fine." I sniffle. Just then he notices the giant pad lying bloody-side up on the floor, and he makes a face.

"Why are you naked?" he asks me.

"I had to know," I say, lifting my chin in the direction of the scale. Andrew turns his head to see what I am talking about, and then looks back at me and rolls his eyes.

"You *weighed* yourself?" he asks. "We've been home from the hospital for three minutes and you've already weighed yourself?" I nod, and in some deep place inside of me, it feels like a tsunami is gaining momentum, getting higher and higher with each breath that I take. I try to steady myself.

"I only lost six pounds," I say, holding my hands up in confusion. "How is that even possible? The baby weighed seven pounds, two ounces when she was born." I shake my head to myself and look up at the ceiling. "You're telling me that I actually *gained* a pound?"

I feel the tsunami peak, and then, out of nowhere, I am crying. Huge, uncontrollable, heaving sobs; they're about nothing, yet somehow they're about everything, and as they flood through me, I have the frightening sense that they're washing away whatever shred of sanity that I have left.

I stare at Andrew. He's holding Parker in his arms and she's fast asleep, her tiny, four-day-old mouth sucking away at the air. I want to think that's she's adorable. I want to be overwhelmed with love for both of them. I want to feel elated by the fact that we've just become a real family. But all I feel is hostility. Hostility, anger, and maybe a little bit of resentment, too. I look Andrew in the eye.

"I'm going to be a big, fat cow for the rest of my life, and it's all your fault," I say, my voice quivering. "And hers," I add, nodding at Parker. Andrew shakes his head.

"Oh, God," he mutters to himself. "Here we go again."

one

All right. I'm just going to come right out and say it: Having a baby sucks, and it is not at all how I thought it would be. Now, look, I didn't have any delusions that I would be some granola freak who just *loooooooves* motherhood, but I had no idea that I would be crying all day long, and that I would be having regular fantasies about sending her back, either. And I've gotta tell you, it's a good thing that they made it so hard to figure out where "back" is, exactly, because if I ever do, this kid is *gone*.

Now, I know what you're thinking. You're thinking, *What is it that's so horrible? What is it that could possibly be so bad?* Well. There's the total lack of sleep, for one thing. I thought that I was prepared because I have insomnia every now and then, and because I used to pull all-nighters when I was in law school. But that was for two or three nights in a row, tops. That was amateur hour. I mean, I would give my left arm for this to be two or three nights. Please, I would give my left arm for this to be two or three *weeks*. But we're going on five weeks here, and there isn't even an *inkling* of an end in sight. And it's not like you ever get a break. It's not like you're up all night and then you get to sleep all day to recover. No, this is *relentless*. You're up all night, and then you're on duty all day, at the beck and call of this little screaming person who could care less that you're completely exhausted, on the brink of total collapse, and a little too sympathetic to the kind of people who walk into post offices and start shooting. And it certainly doesn't help that she's colicky and that she cries all fucking day long for no reason whatsoever; or at least, not for any reason that I can figure out.

Then there's the breast-feeding, which is more or less hell on earth to begin with, but becomes more like burning-in-flames-for-eternity-hell when you to add to it the fact that I'm an anal, type-A, must-be-on-a-schedule, scary control freak, and my baby is Sleepy the Dwarf, who can't suck for thirty seconds without falling into a coma, but who then wakes up starving twenty or thirty or forty-five minutes later, and thus ends up not even remotely in the vicinity of the pediatrician-recommended, eat-every-three-hours plan, but instead snacks all day long, making me feel like a crazed, out-of-control, human bowl of all-you-can-eat popcorn.

But there's something else, too. It's something bigger than the crying, and the getting up at night, and the scabby, sore nipples, and the inability to get on a feeding schedule. It's difficult to articulate, but that tsunami that's inside of me—oh, yeah, it's still there; big-time still there—I think it comes from the fact that, when you have a baby, and when you're the unlucky soul who gets to be the mother, life as you know it comes to an abrupt, screeching halt. You see, there is no *you* anymore. There is no *us* anymore. There is the baby, and there is, simply, nothing else.

Here, let me see if I can explain it to you in a way that makes sense. Okay. Just a few short weeks ago, a typical day for me went something like this: Every morning, at six thirty, I was roused by the sound of Howard Stern interviewing porn stars coming over my clock radio. After hitting the snooze button a few times, I got up, took a shower, slathered my face with two-hundred-dollar-a-bottle antiwrinkle cream and twenty-dollar pink lip gloss, and spent thirty minutes blowing out my hair. Then I got dressed, put on a pair of gorgeous-yet-totally-impractical stiletto heels, and ate a bowl of cereal while pondering where in the world Matt Lauer was. I then went to my office, where I spent eight hours talking to a bunch of overindulged teenagers about where they should go to college, assuaging a few angry, overindulged parents whose kids didn't get into the colleges they were hoping for, chatting on the phone with my friend Julie, and, if I had some real downtime, doing the day's *New York Times* crossword puzzle online.

At four o'clock, I headed to the gym, spent an hour in some type of high-intensity cardio class (lower intensity while I was pregnant, of course) with really good music performed by really cool, obscure musicians who just happened to be really close, personal friends of the really hip fitness instructor/actor who happened to be teaching that day. I then came home, where I plopped down on the couch, elevated my aching feet on a pillow, and read a book or watched TV until Andrew arrived with a meal cooked by one of the four chain restaurants from which we ordered takeout five nights a week. After that, I got in bed, watched *Oprah* or *The Sopranos* or whatever else was on my TiVo, had, if it happened to be a Wednesday night, very solid, midweek, married-couple sex, and then drifted off into a deep sleep for eight full hours, complete with multiple REM cycles.

And then there's now.

Now, at four o'clock in the morning, I am roused by a noise that sounds very much like what I imagine a banshee sounds like, coming over the baby monitor. I jump out of bed, throw on my bathrobe, and run to Parker's room, which has, inevitably, been overwhelmed with the sickly sweet smell of breast-milk poop. Because I am not wearing my contact lenses and have forgotten to put on my glasses, I get breast-milk poop all over my hand while I am changing her diaper, and, after I wash it off, I sit down on the rocking chair and stick my boob, which is about the size and firmness of a large, unripe cantaloupe, into her mouth. After four minutes Parker falls asleep, and I very gently, very quietly, stand up and try to lower her into her crib without waking her up. But of course, the second that I slide my arm out from under her, her eyes shoot open and she is screaming again, so I sit back down, stick my other boob in her mouth, and start the process all over again.

When she starts crying after I put her down in the crib for the second time, I resist the overwhelming urge to run away and never come back, and I instead carry her around the room and sing "Old MacDonald" thirty or forty or seventy times, because I have somehow figured out that this is the only song that calms her down, *e-i-fucking-e-i-o*. When, finally, an hour and a half later, I do manage to get her to sleep, I run back to my room and dive into bed, where I immediately crash until maybe twenty minutes later, when I am again roused by the banshee noise.

By this point, Andrew has woken up and is getting ready for work, and I spend the next hour hysterically crying and pleading with him to stay home and help me, which he does not, and when he leaves, I call him on his cell phone and scream obscenities at him and curse him for ruining my life until he reaches the spot on Beverly Glen Boulevard where he loses reception and I realize that I am crying into a dead telephone.

I then spend the next eight hours alternately nursing the baby, sobbing, pacing up and down the den with the baby over my shoulder while she screams, sobbing hysterically, and cursing the people who make bouncy seats and infant swings for causing me to believe that my baby will actually sit quietly in them while I eat my breakfast and read the paper, instead of screaming her head off until I take her out and start pacing again. Oh, and did I mention sobbing? During all of this, mind you, I am still in my bathrobe.

At four o'clock, when I simply can no longer stand my own filth, I strap Parker in her car seat and put it on the floor of my bathroom, and I take a thirty-second shower while she screams. I then throw on sweatpants, a T-shirt, and tennis shoes, stick my dirty hair into a ponytail, and spend the next hour pushing her around my neighborhood in her stroller. When people pass me and smile and ask me questions about the baby, I just nod at them and keep going, because I can't form sentences without bursting into tears, and I really don't feel like having multiple breakdowns in front of strangers who will then go home and talk about me to their spouses and point at me when I walk past their windows the next time that I am out on one of these strolls.

When I return home, I try to sit down on the couch with her to watch one of the zillion *Oprah* or *CSI* episodes that have backed up on my TiVo over the last month, but that never happens because Parker screams until I stand up and pace some more. After an hour or so, when the pacing stops working, I nurse her again, and about a minute into the feeding, she falls asleep. I then spend the next half an hour employing various techniques to wake her up so that she can finish eating, and just as I am contemplating whether it would be wrong to hold her by the ankles and swing her around my head, she finally opens her eyes. But when she's finished sucking me dry and she realizes that there's no more milk coming out, she immediately starts to scream again, so I stand up and continue to pace with her until Andrew arrives with a meal cooked by one of the four chain restaurants from which we now order takeout seven nights a week.

I take three minutes to scarf down my food while Andrew paces with her, and then we switch. Then I nurse her again, and then I run, crying, into our bedroom and lock the door behind me, leaving Andrew to deal with her until it is time for her to eat again, at which point he timidly knocks on the door and informs me that Parker is hungry. I then spend fifteen minutes informing him, through both tears and the locked door, that I don't care, and when he finally manages to pick the lock, I nurse her *again,* and, at about ten thirty, finally get her to sleep. At ten thirty-one I drop into bed, and then I am up again at midnight, at two, at four. I manage to clock a total of about twenty-seven minutes of sleep the entire night, while Andrew lies in bed next to me, sleeping so soundly that he's practically in a coma. And, according to everyone in the world, I am, as a mother, supposed to blissfully enjoy this new life of mine, day in and day out.

Well, guess what? I don't. The truth is, I miss my old life, I want it back, and I am furious with the world for not telling me that this is motherhood. Well, actually, I am mostly furious with *People* magazine. And *Us Weekly.* Oh, come on. They snap those pictures of Kate Hudson and Gwyneth Paltrow, out on the town with their brand-new, three-day-old babies, and they make it seem like the kid is nothing more than just a trendy fashion accessory. Like it's the new purse that *all* the stars are carrying this season. I swear, I always half expect to see a letter to the editor that's like, *Dear* In Style: *In your September issue, Courteney Cox had the cutest little baby with her. Can you tell me where I can find one just like it? Thanks, Amy Smith, Knoxville, TN.*

You have to admit, it's terribly misleading. And very irresponsible journalism. I mean, based on those publications, I just assumed that I would get home from the hospital and go on with my regular life, albeit with an extra piece of luggage to tote around. How the hell was I supposed to know that the piece of luggage would howl all day long, and that it would require my constant, undivided attention? Really, those pictures should be run with disclaimers. Something along the lines of this, maybe:

Attention, real people: Just because Gwyneth and Kate are seen here shopping at a farmer's market or having brunch in Santa Monica in full hair and makeup within days of giving birth, do not be fooled into thinking that you, too, will be able to get your shit together enough to even leave the house for ten minutes at any point in the near future, because you won't.—Ed.

And you know, magazine people, if any of you are reading this, you'd be doing women around the world a huge service if you'd print some shots of the stars in *their* bathrobes at four o'clock in the afternoon, all fat and puffy from crying for weeks on end. Now those are some pictures that I'd like to see.

But anyway, the moral of this story is that I'm miserable, and I have been ever since the day that we came home from the hospital. Part of it, too, is that I'm just lonely. Aside from a trip to the pediatrician and a dash to the local drugstore to get some infant Mylecon drops (on day six I was positive that the cause of all of her crying was gas. But, of course, I had no such luck. After I gave her the Mylecon she just cried even harder), I haven't seen a living, breathing adult in five weeks (and Andrew doesn't count because I currently hate him and his stupid penis for getting me into this mess). I desperately need to talk to someone who understands what I'm going through, so today I have broken down and called my friend Julie, who is both the only person I know with a baby and the only person I know who does not work and is available to come over and bring me lunch in the middle of the day on a Tuesday.

When Julie comes bursting through my front door, carrying salads and a gift for Parker, I hug her so hard that I almost break her ribs. I swear, I don't think I have ever been happier to see another human being in my life, and coming from someone who is three steps away from being a full-fledged misanthrope, that is saying something.

I put Parker in the swing—of course, she doesn't cry when there's someone here to see it—and as Julie dumps the salads onto paper plates, I sit at the kitchen table and watch her.

"Jul," I say, trying to conceal the fact that I am at about T minus three seconds to a total nervous breakdown, "you know I love you, but I can't believe that you didn't prepare me better. You should have told me that it would be like this."

"Like what?" she asks, looking around the kitchen and surveying the mess.

"Like, horrible. Like, never leaving the house. Like, total sleep deprivation and constant feedings. And the crying. Why didn't you warn me about the crying?"

She cocks her head and looks at me. "Lara, I assumed you knew that babies cry. It's not such a news flash." She walks over to the sink, which is overflowing, and starts loading the silverware into the dishwasher. She leaves the dishes, though, and I can't say that I blame her. They've been there since before we left for the hospital, and they have some kind of a fungus growing on them. But I refuse to touch them because, aside from the fact that I have no time to do them, I'm using them to test Andrew. I'm waiting to see how long they will have to sit there before he realizes that I am not going to be the one to clean them up. Apparently, five weeks is not enough time for him to get the hint.

"I didn't mean the baby, Julie; I meant me. You didn't tell me that *I* would be crying every thirty seconds."

She turns around to face me, her brow furrowed. "You are? Really?" Julie blinks. "But why? You're a *mommy*. You're not working, and all you have to do all day is take care of that precious little girl. What could be better than that?" She looks over at Parker, and, as if on cue, Parker begins to scream. I sigh. I knew she wouldn't last in that thing for long. I stand up, but before I can get to her Julie has lifted her out of the swing and begun to smother her with kisses. Parker cries louder, and Julie beams.

"God," Julie shouts, so that I can hear her over the screams. "I forgot how sweet they are when they're this little." She puts her face close to Parker's head and deeply inhales. "Mmmmmm," she says. "You are so lucky. I can't wait to have another one."

I stare at her, feeling like a robot that's encountered a situation it wasn't programmed to handle.

"Well, you can have her," I say matter-of-factly. "Just give her back when she can talk and sleep through the night." Julie makes a *tsk* sound.

"La-*ra*," she says. "You're terrible." She shakes her head at me, as if I've just made a silly pun. "You'll see; she's going to get big so fast, and then you'll wish that she was just a little newborn again."

"I highly doubt that," I tell her, as I try to hold back the tears that are swelling behind my eyeballs. At this, Julie makes the *tsk* sound again, and I feel a pang of insecurity hit me in the heart. *What is wrong with me? Why don't I feel the way that Julie thinks I'm supposed to feel?*

Suddenly Julie lifts one finger and points it up in the air, as if she has just had an epiphany.

"Hey, have you told your doctor how you feel?" she asks. "You know, you might have postpartum depression or something." She taps her chin with her index finger. "I think that they can give you something for it even if you're breast-feeding."

"Please," I say, feeling a lump form in my throat. Oh, here we go. Here come the tears. I walk over to the counter to get a tissue, and I start dabbing at my eyes. "There isn't enough Xanax on the planet."

Actually, the possibility of postpartum depression has crossed my mind. I mean, there's no question that I'm depressed. I spend about twenty hours a day in tears, and the lump that forms in the back of my throat every time that I open my mouth to speak has become so familiar that I've named it. His name is Luthor. Luthor the Lump. And the feelings that I'm having; do you remember that movie with Molly Ringwald? The one where she's, like, sixteen, and she gets pregnant and marries her boyfriend—it was called *For Keeps*, I think. Anyway, there's a scene where, after the baby is born, she lies in bed all day while the baby screams, and then when the boyfriend/husband gets home from work, he does everything and she just stays in bed with her head under the covers, while the neon sign from the bar across the street flashes in through the window of their run-down studio apartment, and she refuses to hold the baby or feed the baby or even look at the baby.

Do you remember that? You do? Okay, well, that's exactly how I feel. But I don't really understand it, because I'm not sixteen, and I'm not living in a crappy apartment, and this baby wasn't an accident that derailed my plans for college and Paris and the rest of my life. No, I, of course, am almost thirty-one, I live in a four-bedroom house near Beverly Hills, I've just embarked on a six-month, paid maternity leave, and this baby was so intricately planned that I can tell you the exact minute that she was conceived. And so, yeah, it kind of makes me wonder if maybe there isn't something a little off-kilter going on in my brain. But the problem is, I'm too scared to ask. Not because I'm afraid to have postpartum depression. No way. I would be thrilled if there were a medical reason behind all of this. The truth is, I'm scared to death that that if I call my doctor and tell him what's going on, he's going to tell me that it's *not* postpartum depression. He's going to tell me that it's just me, and that people like me are not meant for motherhood.

"So really," I say to Julie, my voice breaking, "you never cried, and you never had one moment where you hated Lily?"

Julie gasps. "No," she says, flatly. "Never. I didn't cry once, and I loved Lily from the moment she was born." (For the record, I find this very hard to believe. The first moment that a kid is born is not all that it's cracked up to be. I fully expected the whole weepy, dramatic kind of thing that you see in the movies, just like every woman does. You know, I envisioned that the nurse would hand her to me, and as I gathered her up in my arms, our eyes would meet and I'd start to cry, and then I'd say something sappy and totally out of character for me, like how she's the most beautiful thing that I've ever seen. And then I figured that I'd spend a minute or two just holding her, and daydreaming into the future about all of the Saturday afternoons that the two of us would spend together, lounging on the couch and eating fat-free yogurt straight from the carton while watching a chick-flick marathon on the Oxygen channel. And in the background, as this first moment was taking place between us, I imagined that I would hear the Beatles singing "In My Life," and, if the moment was long enough for two songs, Stevie Wonder's "Isn't She Lovely.")

But what really happened is that the nurse handed her to me, and since I was paralyzed from the spinal block and couldn't feel my arms, she just sort of lay on top of my chest while I strained to lift my head high enough to see her eyes, which was pointless because they were smeared with something that looked like Vaseline anyway. So I just kind of stared at her, and then I announced that she looked just like my grandfather, who is not one I'd describe as particularly attractive. My first thought was, *How long do we have to wait before I can get this poor kid a chin implant?* And then, when I inspected her a little more closely, I saw that she had dark hairs sprouting from the tips of her ears, a nasty white blister on her bottom lip, and her entire body was the color of a grape Popsicle. Overall, she was kind of gross, and all I could think about was giving her back to the nurse so that I could get up to my room and go rest for a few hours, since I had gotten up at the butt crack of dawn that morning in order to make it to the hospital by five A.M., even though my surgery was scheduled for seven. And in the background, as this moment was taking place between us, I heard my obstetrician stapling my stomach back together, and the nurses counting the number of bloody towels on the operating table, just in case one inadvertently had been left in my abdomen.)

I make a face at Julie as if to indicate that I think that she's full of shit, and she shakes her head.

"Really, Lar, I didn't have any of . . . of this." She waves her hand in the direction of the sink. Oh, that is so low. And by the way, I just remembered that a certain person named Julie had a twenty-four-hour baby nurse for the first six weeks after her daughter was born, so it makes perfect sense why she didn't hate Lily. She didn't have to take care of her.

I walk over to the counter and grab another tissue. I blow my nose and look up at Julie, who is staring at me. With pity.

"What?" I ask her, feeling defensive. She's pacing around the kitchen with Parker, who has finally toned things down to a slight whimper, supplemented by random yelps every few seconds.

"Nothing," she says, shrugging her shoulders. "It's just . . . I don't know. I feel like you're only focusing on the negatives, and you're not thinking about any of the good things. I mean, having a baby is such a miracle. You and Andrew created *a life*." She glances down at Parker and smiles beatifically, like she's the Virgin Mary looking down at baby Jesus in a Botticelli painting. "Do you realize that you made her out of thin air? Do you realize how totally amazing that is? Really, Lara, you should be happier than this."

Oh, okay. First of all, I did not make her out of thin air. We made her out of an egg and a sperm. It's not like a stork flew by and dropped her on my doorstep. And second of all, could she be more judgmental? *God*.

I give her an I-am-so-annoyed-with-you-and-all-of-your-miracle-made-her-out-of-thin-air-bullshit look, and I snort.

"Well," I retort, "I'm sorry that I'm not meeting your expectations."

"Oh, come on," Julie says, brushing off my sarcasm. "When I called you this morning and asked how you were, you said that you were, quote, 'fucking miserable.' You've got to admit, that's not really normal."

Oh, yeah. I guess I did say that. But I'm just being honest. I start to cry again.

"Well, I *am* miserable," I sob. "I haven't left the house in weeks, I barely get two hours of sleep a night, I can't get Parker on any kind of a feeding schedule, my nipples are killing me, Andrew and I are fighting all the time, and I haven't watched TV or read a newspaper or checked my e-mail or had any kind of human interaction since the baby was born. And what am I supposed to do? Lie and tell you that it's the greatest thing in the whole world? Because it's not." I am in full-blown crying mode now, snot bubbles and everything. "You know," I say, pointing my finger at her, "maybe you're the one who's not normal. Because I don't see how it can possibly be normal to think that any of this is fun."

Julie shakes her head at me, ignoring my assault upon her normalcy.

"Okay, okay," she says. "Then why don't you just hire a nanny? Everybody else in LA has one. Well, I don't—I could never leave Lily with a stranger—but it's different for me. I have my mom here to help. Anyway, it's not a big deal. You don't have to be a martyr."

"I'm not tr-trying to be a m-m-martyr," I say, attempting to talk through my tears. "Believe me, I want to have help. We tried to hire someone before Parker was born, but Andrew was so cheap about it. He wouldn't use an agency because he didn't want to pay the fee, and he would only interview people who were illegal and didn't speak any English because he thought they would charge less, and it turned into this big fight, so we decided to just wait until after we had the baby." I take a deep breath and sniffle. "But now I can barely get dressed in the morning, let alone interview people and try to make a decision. . . ."

Julie has completely stopped listening to me and is fishing through her purse. "Just wait a second," she says, holding up one finger. She takes out her wallet and pulls about fifty business cards from one of the compartments, and begins to go through them one by one. "Here!" she exclaims, when she finds the one she wants. "Here it is." She hands the card to me, and I reach out to take it.

The Happy Nannies Agency, Inc.
Because happy nannies make happy mommies.

(310) 555-6438

I sniffle again and wipe my nose.

"What's this?" I ask.

"A girl from my Mommy and Me class gave it to me, in case I ever need someone. She said that it's the greatest nanny agency in LA. You don't have to do anything. Just tell them what you want, and they'll send someone fabulous over to you the next day. No interviews, nothing."

I stare at her. "Are they really expensive?" I ask.

Julie shrugs. "Probably," she says, "but this is your *baby*. You don't want to leave her with just anyone. I'm sure that all of their people are great."

She's right. Of course she's right. I don't know why I listen to Andrew and his ridiculous ideas. It's my money, too, and if I want to spend it on an astronomical agency fee and a nanny who pays taxes, then I will, damn it. I turn the card around in my fingers and take a deep, unsteady breath.

"Okay," I say, nodding at her. "Thanks. I'll talk to Andrew about it." Julie picks up her things and gives me a hug good-bye.

"It will get better," she says as she puts her arms around me. Then she pulls back, puts both of her hands on my shoulders, and looks at me earnestly. "Just try to think happy, baby thoughts," she advises, dead serious. "It works."

I bite the inside of my cheek to keep myself from laughing in her face, and I walk her to the door.

"Bye, Jul," I say. "Thanks for bringing lunch."

"Of course," she says. She turns to go, and as I am shutting the door behind her, I hear her call my name, so I swing it back open again.

"Make sure you tell them that you want someone who will wash dishes," she instructs. "Because your sink is revolting."

two

DO NOT TURN ON THE DEVICE UNTIL AFTER THE SUC-
TION CUPS HAVE BEEN PROPERLY POSITIONED ON THE
NIPPLES OR SEVERE INJURY COULD OCCUR.

Oh, God. I can't believe that it has come to this. I can't believe that I
am actually about to use an electric breast pump. Luthor is sitting
in the back of my throat, just waiting to burst through my tonsils.

No. I am not going to make this worse by crying. I am not.

But just as I am thinking this, I catch a glimpse of myself in the mirror, and it's all over. I start blubbering like a third runner-up in a West
Texas beauty pageant. But really, you can't blame me. If you saw yourself
sitting on the floor, naked except for a hands-free pumping bra and a pair
of lime-green, cotton, full-butt underpants (size L), believe me, you'd
start crying, too. I mean, the bra alone is enough to send you over the
edge. It looks like a poor man's S and M getup. Imagine a white cotton
bandeau bikini top that zips up the front, with two round holes cut out of
it for your nipples to poke through, and then imagine ten pounds of back
fat hanging over the top of it on all sides.

I take a few moments to compose myself, and then I sigh.

Just forget how it looks, I tell myself. *Think about the big picture. Think
about sleeping tonight, while Andrew gets up and feeds her. Think about
revenge.*

I muster up all of the anger and resentment that I've been feeling toward Andrew for the past five weeks—Andrew, who gets to go to work all
day and sit in a chair in peace and quiet; Andrew, who gets to sleep for

eight hours every single night; Andrew, who seriously asked me this morning if I would mind if he played golf this Saturday—and Luthor slides back down my throat like a turtle that's retreated into its shell. I exhale, and then I quickly stick the suction cups inside the holes of the bra and flip the switch on the pump to on. *Thwick, thwick, thwick, thwick.* The air starts pumping through the hoses and I watch as my nipples get drawn outward.

All right. It's not so bad. At least I did it this time. The last time I tried to pump, about three weeks ago, I couldn't even get past the bra. I cried so hard when I put it on that I actually broke a blood vessel in my left eye. And the giant red spot in my sclera made for an attractive ten days, let me tell you.

After about ten seconds, I feel the strange, burning sensation of my milk letting down, and then, suddenly, streams of it start squirting out of my nipples and into the bottle. *Oh, gross.* I take a deep breath, trying not to start a fresh round of tears, and an image of myself in my favorite outfit pops into my head. It's my perfect black, plain-front, straight-leg Theory ass pants, a slim-fitting, gray cashmere sweater with bell sleeves, and my black Zanotti slingbacks with the single white flower attached to each toe strap. Oh, if the salespeople at Barneys could see me now. I've gone from beau monde to bovine in less than two months. But then I picture Andrew, pacing around Parker's room at three o'clock in the morning while I sleep—oh, beautiful, delicious sleep—and I smile. Fuck the Barneys salespeople. This is worth it.

When Andrew gets home from work, I don't say a word to him. The poor guy didn't even do anything, but I got myself so worked up about him while I was pumping that now I'm furious with him, and I'm feeling the need to lash out at him just for being alive. I swear, sometimes I feel so sorry for Andrew. I don't think he had any idea what he was getting himself into the day that he married me.

"Well, hello to you, too," he says, putting down his briefcase. I take a deep breath to steady myself, and I hold Parker, who is, of course, screaming, out for him to take. As he adjusts her over his shoulder, I glare at him.

"I'm done," I announce. Andrew looks at me, confused.

"Done with what?" he asks.

"With everything," I say. "With being the only one who takes care of her. With letting you do absolutely nothing while I wither away in this house, losing my sanity."

"I don't do nothing," Andrew shouts. "I pace with her for almost an hour every night when I get home. I change her diapers all the time. And if I'm home early enough to give her a bath, I always do it."

"Great," I yell back. "But I get up with her all night, and you *never* get up with her. I'm exhausted, Andrew. Exhausted. And I can't do it anymore." Luthor is there again. I give myself about three more words, four max, before I lose it. Andrew throws his hands up in the air.

"I can't breast-feed, Lara. It's not my fault. And by the way, you should thank God that you're with me, because I do a hell of a lot more than most husbands do."

I narrow my eyes and try as hard as I can to shoot fire out of them. "What does that m-mean?" And there go the tears. Like I said, four words. "Let me remind you that you're fifty percent responsible for her existence! More if you count the fact that you talked me into having her in the first place. You do more than most husbands do? You should be doing half, at least."

"I have to work!" he yells. "If I don't go to work, we don't make any money, and we need to make money. We've had this discussion a hundred times now."

I roll my eyes at him, tired of hearing his we-need-to-make-money speech. Hey, I never said that I was rational. You try not sleeping for five weeks and see how rational you are. I take a moment to hyperventilate into a tissue, and for a split second, I expect him to come over and put his arms around me. But he doesn't, and I suddenly remember that this is because Things Have Changed.

You see, in my old life, if I so much as hinted that I was about to cry, Andrew was like putty in my hands. I could get anything out of him when I turned on the tears. *Anything.* For example, a few months after we got married, I started to cry because I found a china pattern that I liked better than the one that we had registered for, and even though I've never cooked a meal in my life and would certainly never cook one that would require fine china, Andrew was so distraught over my unhappiness that he went out and bought me the whole set. Twelve place settings *and* all of the serving pieces. It must have cost him a small fortune. Meanwhile, we've been married for four years and, of course, I haven't used it once. In fact, I think it's still sitting in boxes in the garage. Anyway, that's how much of a sucker he was. He got upset because I cried over a friggin' *china pattern*. Even I would have told me to just shut up about that one.

But ever since the baby was born, my crying doesn't even faze him anymore. It's like he's built up a tolerance to it, the way a frat boy does to beer. I swear, if I cried an entire ocean, Andrew would just go buy a raft and row himself to work in the mornings.

Well, if the tears won't do the trick, I'll just have to resort to Lara Logic. Which, as we both know, is not all that logical. But maybe he won't notice.

"Fine," I say. "Then how about *I* go back to work, and you stay home and take care of her. Huh? How about that?" Andrew snorts. As we've been having this discussion, he's been holding Parker against his chest and taking slow, heavy steps across the kitchen, bending each knee and then bouncing up and down once before straightening it. He looks ridiculous, like one of the zombies from Michael Jackson's "Thriller" video. But it's working, because Parker has finally stopped screaming. Now she's just kind of whimpering, the way that Zoey does in her sleep when she's having a nightmare and her little paws start moving really fast, like she's running away from a giant vacuum cleaner or whatever else dogs have nightmares about.

"Okay, Lar," he says sarcastically. "You go back to work. And the next time you want to spend five hundred dollars on a pair of new shoes, you can pay for it with *your* salary." I pluck another tissue from the box on the kitchen counter and I blow my nose.

"Well, Andrew, I don't think I'll be needing new shoes anytime soon, seeing as how you've got me running around barefoot and pregnant all the time."

He closes his eyes and grits his teeth, as if he's trying to keep himself from saying something that he'll regret.

"And by the way," I announce, "you *are* getting up tonight." I walk over to the refrigerator, open it up, and take out the six-ounce bottle that I pumped this afternoon, holding it up in the air for him to see. "This," I say, "is for you. Tonight, when she wakes up at two o'clock, *you* can go feed her."

Then, without another word, I close the refrigerator, run back to my bedroom, and slam the door shut behind me. I fling myself onto the bed, sobbing, although now I'm sobbing because I feel bad for yelling at Andrew like that, and because I hate this person I've turned into—this person who yells at her husband for no reason whatsoever—and then, finally, because, even though I know that I was wrong, I still can't bring myself to go out there and apologize to him.

But then, out of nowhere, I hear Andrew's voice.

"You're mean," he says. I look around, but he's not in the bedroom. It's like God is talking to me, or Orson from *Mork & Mindy*. "You're really mean."

I follow the sound of his voice, and then I realize where it's coming from. It's coming from the baby monitor. He's in Parker's room, and he's talking into the baby monitor. I sit up and look at the television screen that is on my nightstand. Andrew has put his face right in front of the camera, and I am staring directly into his nostrils. Okay, remind me to buy him a nose-hair trimmer for Hanukkah this year.

I smile though my tears at the sheer absurdity of the situation, and I watch him as he continues to talk.

"But I'm letting it slide because I know you're tired, and I know that you're hormonal, and it's not your fault. A client of mine told me that he thought his wife had developed Tourette's after their baby was born, because all she did was curse at him. So I guess I should consider myself lucky."

I laugh at this. I can't help it.

"Anyway, I'll be glad to get up with her tonight. Believe me, there is no one on this earth who wants you to get some sleep more than I do." Then he walks away from the camera, and the room goes quiet again.

Yeah, yeah, I know. Thank God I married Andrew. A lesser man would have killed me by now, for sure.

At ten P.M., I nurse Parker and manage to make it into bed by around eleven forty-five, which is a new record. I swear to God, if you even saw what I go through every night to get her to sleep, you would die. You know, that's another thing that I'm pissed about. Nobody told me that there's no such thing as just putting her in the crib and leaving. It's a whole friggin' ordeal. It starts with her "falling asleep" in my lap while I rock on the glider, but, as the quotation marks indicate, it's actually not really sleep at all. It is, rather, a state of consciousness that *looks* like sleep, but that is disrupted by the quietest sound, the slightest movement, or the tiniest shift in pressure. Therefore, holding her in *exactly* the same position in which she "fell asleep," I very slowly, very gently, get up off the rocking chair while simultaneously moving my body back and forth to try to simulate the rocking motion so that she doesn't notice that I've moved.

I stand like that for a few minutes, rocking back and forth, and when I am convinced that she is, now, actually asleep, I slowly walk over to the crib. Then, still keeping her in the same position, I lean over as far as I can, lowering her down until she's resting on the mattress. Then, to trick her into thinking that she's still asleep on my chest, I stay parallel to her, with my upper torso resting ever so slightly on top of her. From there, I gently pull one hand out from under her butt, and then I count to twenty. With Mississippis.

Once I am sure that this has not woken her up, I ve-e-e-ery slowly slide my other hand out from under her back (still parallel to her, by the way), and count to twenty again. Then I begin to straighten up, one vertebra at a time, while at the same time resting my forearm on top of her so that she doesn't notice the change in pressure or temperature. When I get all the way up, I freeze. If she moves, I go right back down on top of her and start all over again. If she doesn't move, I drop to the floor and crawl out of the room on all fours, so that, if she does happen to open her eyes, she doesn't see me tiptoeing out.

I would say that I'm successful about twenty percent of the time. For the other eighty percent, she starts screaming as soon as I get out into the hallway, and I have to go through about six more tries until I finally make it out of there. But tonight, I made it out in only two, and I am salivating at the thought of Andrew having to suffer through this in the wee hours of the morning, while I sleep away, oblivious to his pain. In my head, I laugh a deep, wicked, bad guy, ha-ha-ha-ha-ha-the-world-will-be-mine-all-mine laugh, and then I close my eyes and pull the duvet over my body, settling in, at last, for a decent night's sleep.

*   *   *

As if on cue, the banshee noise begins just a few minutes after two o'clock, and I gleefully kick Andrew in the leg.

"Get up," I say, perhaps with a tad too much sadism in my voice. "It's *your* turn." He grunts at me and rolls out of bed, and I lie back down, smiling in the dark. He goes into Parker's room and picks her up, and then I hear him walk into the kitchen with her while she screams.

Stupid, I think. *He should have heated up the bottle first.* Oh, well. Not my problem. I settle into my pillow. *Okay, Lar. Go back to sleep.*

But I can't sleep. The screaming in the kitchen is too loud, and now Andrew's started singing to her, and I'm getting distracted because I can't figure out what song it is.

"Bomp bomp bomp bomp, bomp bomp ba-ba-ba-bomp, bomp bomp bomp bomp, bomp bomp, ba-ba-ba-bomp."

What is that? I think. It sounds vaguely familiar. I listen to him, trying to match the tune to real music. . . . Wait, I've got it. It's "Safety Dance." He's singing "Safety Dance" to a five-week-old. Okay. Fine. Now I know what it is, now I can go back to sleep. I close my eyes and try not to listen to him.

"S-S-S-S-A-A-A-A-F-F-F-F-T-T-T-T-Y-Y-Y-Y . . . safety . . . dance. Bomp bomp, bomp bomp, bomp bomp, ba-ba-ba bomp, bo—"

Oh, my God. I slam my hand down on the mattress, trying to control myself, but I can't. I just can't. At the top of my lungs, I yell out across the house, "E! *Safety* is spelled with an E!"

"Thank you," he yells back sarcastically. "Do you think she'll stop crying if I spell it right?"

Oh, screw him. I close my eyes again, and I start counting backward from one thousand. *Nine hundred ninety-nine. Nine hundred ninety-eight. Nine hundred ninety-seven.* I get to seven hundred and fifty-six when I realize that I'm not going back to sleep. *God damn it.*

Twenty-one minutes later, Andrew is back in bed.

You've got to be kidding me.

As he rests his head down on the pillow, I sit up, fuming in anger.

"What are you doing?" I demand. He rolls over to look at me.

"I'm going back to sleep. What are you doing?" I don't want to tell him what I have been doing. I have been lying in bed, wide-awake, my eyes glued to the baby monitor, anxiously waiting for his suffering to commence. And I have also been practicing, in my head, exactly how I was going to word the I-told-you-she-was-an-evil-terrorist-now-do-you-understand-why-I've-been-so-miserable speech that I fully intended to deliver once he came back from her room and put his fist through the wall out of sheer frustration with her.

But the suffering never came. And neither did the fist, or even the frustration. No, it went just about as well as could be expected. He gave her the bottle, hummed "Rock-a-Bye Baby" to her, and practically dropped her into the crib. And she didn't so much as move a muscle.

"I don't understand," I yell. "How did you do that?"

"Do what?" he asks sleepily.

"That," I scream. "How did you get her in the crib without waking her up? *How. Did. You. Do. That?"*

Everything in the room looks red. Oh, my God, I am seeing red. I had no idea that that could really happen. I always thought that it was just a figure of speech. In a far corner of my mind, I can hear Andrew barking at me.

"Lara! Calm down. *Calm down!"*

I am startled to hear him yell like this. He's never used a tone like that with me before. I start to cry.

"Why are you yelling at me?" I whimper. He looks bewildered, and lowers his voice back to normal.

"Honey," he says, "you have got to get it together. Seriously. I don't know how much more of this I can take."

"How much more *you* can take?" I shriek. "Do you think I'm *enjoying* this? Do you think that I *like* crying every five seconds? Do you think that it's *fun* for me to hate my own child? Do you think that I *take pleasure* in feeling completely and totally out of control? Do you?" I am near hysterical now, and I am afraid that he's going to try to slap me out of it. I swear, I will slap him right back. But he doesn't move. He just stares at me like he's never seen me before in his entire life.

"Lara," he says, talking though his teeth, "what is it that you want from me?"

Oh, please, where do I start? Let's see . . .

I want you to fly backward around the world and turn back time to before I got pregnant, the way that Superman did in the first movie, when Lois died in the earthquake.

No. Too sci fi. How about:

I want you to grow mammary glands and produce estrogen, and I want you to breast-feed and cry all day long.

Yeah, yeah, I know. Too vindictive. Okay. I've got it:

I want you to acknowledge that taking care of a baby is miserable, and that if you get to have a wife to stay home and do it, then I should get to have one, too.

Perfect.

"I want you to let me get a live-in nanny," I say. "Immediately."

He throws up his hands in frustration. "Fine," he says, sounding exasperated. "Get a nanny. I wanted to hire someone before she was born, remember?"

Yes, I remember. He wanted to hire a woman whose only word of English was *table*. Oh, and *grandmother*. Let's not forget that she knew how to say *grandmother*.

I reach across the bed to my nightstand, and I pull the card that Julie gave me out of the top drawer.

"From here," I say, waving it in front of him. Andrew sits up and turns on the light next to his side of the bed. He takes the card out of my hand and studies it, and I brace myself for round two. But, to my surprise, he just sighs.

"You know what, Lar?" he asks, handing the card back to me. "If they can make *you* a happy mommy, God bless 'em."

And with that, he turns off the light, rolls over, and goes back to sleep.

three

Two days later, promptly at nine A.M., my doorbell rings.

Woo-hoo, I think. I run down the stairs with Parker flopping over my shoulder, screaming as usual, and as I try not to trip on the bottom of my bathrobe, I make up a song in my head.

My nan-ny is he-ere, and I am so ex-cited, because I am getting my life back. La la la, la la la. La la la la la la.

Despite my excitement, however, I've got some serious butterflies flapping around in my stomach, because other than the cleaning crew who come twice a month, I've never had a domestic employee before. And a live-in? I have no idea how it works. Am I supposed to eat meals with her? How late will she stay up with the baby? Will she want to hang out and watch TV with us every night? I'm not that social. I don't want to have to make small talk in my own house.

And then, of course, I'm also nervous because I have no idea what to expect. I mean, I didn't interview this woman or anything. I just called the agency and told them that I want someone who has experience with newborns, who is willing to do laundry and light cleaning, who speaks excellent English, and who can start right away. And then, two hours later, I got a call back that they had found the perfect person; she's worked for three families over the last twenty years and started with all of them when the kids were born, she cleans, and English is her first language. *Great,* I thought. But when I asked if she could tell me a little bit more, just so that I had some idea of who would be coming to live in my house, the woman said that she doesn't meet the nannies, she's just a receptionist, and the guy I would need to talk to had just left for the day to go get a root canal. And so, I've spent the last twenty-four hours trying to picture what my savior might be like, but the only picture that I've been able to come up with is one of Mary Poppins.

Oh, come on. What else am I supposed to think? Doesn't everyone think of her when they hear the word *nanny*? It's like trying to picture a daytime talk show-host without thinking of Oprah Winfrey. Impossible. It's an automatic association. But even if she weren't branded into the American culture, my mind would still go there anyway, because I kind of have a thing about *Mary Poppins*. You have to understand, when I was a kid, I was obsessed with that movie. I must have watched it five hundred times, and to this day I know every single line by heart. I don't know what it was, exactly; I mean, at the time I thought that my parents were great. But for some reason I yearned for a British nanny who could take control of my life, keep me on the right track, and somehow manage to solve all of my problems with a clever, if somewhat Pollyanna-ish song.

It's funny, too, because it's stuck with me into adulthood. Not the obsession with the movie—I haven't watched it in years—but more what the movie represents for me. I mean, I've noticed that sometimes, when I'm particularly stressed out, I'll have dreams about chimney sweeps and dancing penguins. It's like my subconscious is trying to tell me that I need to go into Mary Poppins mode and get back in command of things. Needless to say, the dreams have been exceptionally vivid lately.

But now that I actually have a real, live nanny coming . . . I just can't help it. It's like I'm ten years old again. I'm dying for someone to just swoop in here, take over, and make everything all better. You have no idea; when the woman at the agency asked me what I was looking for in a nanny, it took all of my restraint to keep myself from telling her that I want someone who can fly and jump into chalk drawings. Anyway, I know that it's ridiculous, but there's just a small part of me that's hoping that when I open that door, Julie Andrews is going to be standing before me with a carpetbag in her hand.

As I approach the front door, I put on my warmest smile, smooth my hand over my hair, and swing it open. A large black woman carrying one of those hard, leather, avocado-green suitcases from the 1970s is standing on my doorstep. She's got to be six feet tall, maybe two hundred and twenty or two hundred and thirty pounds, and her chin-length hair

appears to have been freshly set in rollers just this morning. She is wearing jeans, a red T-shirt, and Reeboks.

Okay. So she's no Julie Andrews, and it's not exactly a carpetbag. But
that's fine. Nobody said that Mary Poppins can't be black. She can be updated for the twenty-first century. The nanny smiles.

"I'm Deloris," she says, trying to make herself heard over the din of
Parker's screams. She has a strong Jamaican accent. "Happy Nannies said
that you needed some help."

Yeah. That's the understatement of the year.

Deloris places her suitcase down on the ground and reaches out toward me, taking Parker out of my arms. Immediately Parker stops crying
and closes her eyes.

"That's right, sugar," she coos. "You don't need to cry no more; Deloris
is here now."

She walks past me into the house, leaving me standing in the foyer. I
grab her suitcase and run to follow her, catching a glimpse of myself in
my bathrobe, with my glasses still on and no makeup, as I pass the mirror
in the entranceway.

God, I think. *I look horrendous.*

"I'm Lara," I say, calling after her. "And that's Parker. She's almost six
weeks old, and she's really colicky. She only quiets down if you pace with
her. Otherwise she just cries all day long." I hurry into the den, and I see
that Deloris has already plopped herself down on the couch. Parker is
staring up at her and not making a sound. I shake my head.

"I don't know how you did that. She never lets me sit." Deloris looks
me up and down and smiles.

"Babies are smart, Mrs. Lara. She can tell when you're stressed out,
and from the way you look, I'd say you're pretty stressed out most of the
time."

Feeling self-conscious, I reach my hand up to smooth out my hair
again. "Well, today happens to be a particularly bad day. . . ." She cocks
that eyebrow again, as if to say that she knows its not just today. I sigh.
"Yeah, I guess so."

"Listen," she says to me. "You go do what you need to do, and Deloris
will watch little Miss Parker here." She looks back down at the baby.
"We'll have some fun, won't we, sweets?"

"Really?" I ask. "Are you sure? Because she gets hungry a lot and I'm breast-feeding, so I can't really leave her for very long—"

"When was the last time she ate?" Deloris asks me.

"About an hour ago," I say. "She ate for ten minutes on one side, but she fell asleep after only four and a half minutes on the other side, so she'll probably be hungry again soon—"

Deloris cuts me off. "You go on. She won't need to eat again for another two hours, I promise."

I raise my eyebrows. This woman has no idea what she's talking about. Parker hasn't gone more than forty minutes between feedings since she was born. But whatever. Deloris will see for herself.

"Okay," I say skeptically. "I'll be in my bedroom if you need me. By the way, your room is just at the end of the hall. It's not quite ready yet, but I promise I'll get it together this weekend. I'll just put your suitcase in there."

"Okay," she says, putting her nose in Parker's face and smiling at her. I start to walk toward her room, and then I turn around and go back.

"The diapers are in the changing table in her room," I say, pointing upstairs, in the direction of Parker's room. "We don't use wipes—my doctor said to just use gauze pads with water for the first three months—and I use the filtered water in the sink because the tap water has some kind of white residue in it that looks a little sketchy to me, and—"

"Mrs. Lara, no offense, but you need to relax. We'll be fine."

I put my hands up as if to say that I will bother her no more. "Okay," I say. "I guess I'll go take a nap."

I place her suitcase on the floor of her bedroom and then retreat upstairs. I lie down on the bed and click on the television, but I can't concentrate on watching it. *You need to relax.* Mary Poppins would never say anything like that. I mean, how condescending. She's not the one dealing with a screaming infant who wants to nurse all day long. She's not the one who is constantly bickering with her husband and who hasn't had sex in almost four months. She's not the one who's spent the last five and a half weeks in a bathrobe and who hasn't shaved her legs in the same amount of time. Relax, my ass. I'd like to see her relax if she had my life. I take a deep breath and exhale.

Okay, I think. *Just let it go. You have some time off here, so try to enjoy it.* I close my eyes and start counting backward from one thousand. . . .

An hour and a half later, I wake up with a start, and I am totally confused.

Wait, I think. *What happened? Where's Parker?*

But then it all comes flooding back to me. The nanny agency. Deloris. The green suitcase. The Jamaican accent. I stretch my arms up above my head and stand up. God, it felt good to sleep. I wonder how Deloris is doing. I wonder if Parker is starving. I put on a pair of sweatpants and a tank top—no bathrobe!—and, as I walk down the hallway, I get the feeling that something isn't quite right. It seems different . . . quiet. That's what it is. The house is quiet. And then, suddenly, I realize that this is because Parker is not crying.

Oh, my God, I think. *Deloris killed her. She couldn't take the crying and she smothered her with a pillow.* I run out to the den, but they're not there. *Oh, my God. Oh, my God.*

Just then, I hear a noise coming from Parker's room. It sounds like singing. I rush in, and I see Deloris sitting on the floor in front of Parker, who is resting on top of a red-white-and-black fabric mat. Rising up out of the mat are two crisscrossing fabric-covered bars from which various toys are hanging, including something that I think is supposed to be an octopus but that looks more like a red bell pepper with eyes and legs. The whole contraption is called a gym-something, I think. A Gymini. That's it. *Huh.* I forgot all about that thing. It's been sitting in the closet since the day that Julie schlepped me to Babies "R" Us to buy baby stuff when I was nine months pregnant. And that's not all that Deloris found. She also pulled out the classical music CD that someone gave me as a baby gift but that I keep forgetting to open. The songs on it supposedly stimulate infants' brains, and it must work because Parker is kicking her feet and waving her arms and making little cooing noises, just like the babies that you see in diaper commercials.

What the hell . . .

I narrow my eyes and glance at Deloris, then back at Parker.

"Hi," I say from the doorway, with just the slightest hint of surprise in my voice. "It looks like you two are having fun." Deloris looks up at me and smiles.

"She is such a sweet girl," Deloris says. She leans over and gently pinches Parker's thigh. "Aren't you just a sweet little girl?"

This time I'm the one cocking an eyebrow. "I don't know if I'd call her sweet, exactly. All she does is eat and cry."

Deloris looks me straight in the eye. "Not with Deloris," she says. "She hasn't cried once since you left."

There's something in her voice—judgment? sick pleasure?—that tells me this is less of an observation than an implication. I pause and look down at Parker, who seems more content than she's ever been in her short little life, and I can't decide if I should hug Deloris or fire her.

"Well," I say, choosing to do neither. "She must be starving by now."

"Yes, it's probably about time," Deloris says.

I pick Parker up off of the floor, and she immediately starts wailing. I glance at Deloris. I guess I expect her to be laughing at how much my own baby hates me, but if she thinks that this is funny, she's not letting on. I am feeling an overwhelming, competitive need to pretend that I am loving and maternal, and that Parker and I have a close, special bond, so I raise my voice about three octaves.

"Shhh, shhhh," I say. "Oh, it's okay, sweetie. Mommy's here. It's time for lunch, that's all." I sit down in the rocking chair and position Parker in my lap, but Deloris is still sitting on the floor, staring at us. Okay, I am not going to nurse with her sitting there watching me. Uh-uh. When it comes to breast-feeding in public, I am firmly in the No Way, José camp. It's just not something that other people need to see. And draping a scarf over the baby's head doesn't make it any better, okay?

"Um, I'm not really comfortable breast-feeding in front of people," I say. "It's nothing personal, it's just how I am." Deloris nods and stands up.

"That's okay," she says. "But I don't see how you'll ever manage if you won't do it in public. You'll never be able to leave the house for more than an hour or two at a time." *Yeah*, I think. *I kind of figured that one out already*. I decide to let her in on my secret plan.

"I know," I say. "I'm actually thinking of stopping. It's just not really working that well for me." Deloris's eyes go wide.

"You're going to stop after six weeks?" She *tsks* at me. "That is a big mistake. Breast milk is God's food. That formula, it sours them from the inside out. They get bad breath, and their poop starts to smell. It's just not natural. You ought to do for it at least three months."

I grimace at her. Oh, great. So now she's going to judge me for that, too. Well, she can get in line, because Andrew's pretty much got the market cornered on this one. I swear, the man is a breast-feeding Nazi. You'd think that he was a founding member of the La Leche League, the way that he talks about it.

You see, it all started with my stupid pediatrician. (By the way, if this were a television sitcom, this would be the part where the screen would get all fuzzy, and the characters would reappear in bad eighties wigs, with the girls decked out in turquoise socks pulled up over their leggings, and the guys wearing Van Halen T-shirts or *Miami Vice* outfits, so that the audience is sure to understand that this is a flashback.) The day that Parker was born, I was lying on the operating table, getting my stomach put back together, when the nurse who was preparing her bassinet yelled out to me across the OR.

"Hey, Mom," she shouted (and it took a second before I realized that she was talking to me), "are you breast-feeding or bottle-feeding?" All eyes turned to me (and they were, creepily, just eyes, as everyone was wearing sterile hospital masks), eagerly awaiting my response.

"Um, uh, um," I stammered, trying to buy myself some time to think about it. Now, I realize that most people know in advance how they intend to feed their baby. I realize that most people take a breast-feeding class, and/or read books about breast-feeding, and that most people have a very definite opinion as to whether it is something they want to do or not (and by "most people," I mean the kinds of people they used to refer to as "yuppies" back when *thirtysomething* was still on the air). But, in a very uncharacteristic move for someone who is as anal and as *thirtysome-thing*-ish as I am, I hadn't done any of these things, and thus I had absolutely no idea how to answer. I suppose that my thinking was that I'd just sort of wing it (even though I've never "just winged" anything before in my entire life), and see how I felt about it after the baby was born. Because before the baby was born, the thought of breast-feeding kind of repulsed me. But I wanted to be open-minded about it, just in case I were to undergo a major personality adjustment upon giving birth and suddenly become the maternal, baby-loving person that I wasn't when I was pregnant (and still do not appear to be).

But I didn't realize that I would have to decide *immediately,* and so the question caught me off guard. But before I had a chance to mull it over, a voice from the other side of the room—the side of the room where a half a dozen people were weighing and measuring and fingerprinting the baby, and, for all I know, interrogating her about possible war crimes— responded to the question for me.

"She'll be breast-feeding," said the voice, which had a distinct New York accent and seemed to come from the shortest of the masked people in the corner.

Wait a minute, I thought. *Who said that?*

But then, through the fog of the drugs, I suddenly realized that it was Dr. Newman, the vertically challenged man from Brooklyn whom I selected as my pediatrician for one reason and one reason only: In the event of an emergency, I wanted a doctor who could make quick decisions and not be afraid to boss people around, and I figured that a New Yorker with a Napoleon complex would pretty much fit the bill.

And that was when it occurred to me that I really did need to be more careful about what I wished for.

I saw the nurse's eyebrows rise, and she glanced over at me to see if I was on board with this. But, again, before I could answer, Dr. Newman nodded at her.

"It's better for the baby," he announced to the room, and then he turned to Andrew for further reinforcements. "Much," he confided in him, nodding solemnly.

And so began my foray into the wonderful world of multipurpose boobs.

I should have known that it wasn't going to work out from the minute that I met the hospital lactation consultant. She appeared in my room about three hours after Parker was born, just in time to help me with my very first feeding session. On one lapel of her jacket was a white pin that read, BREAST IS BEST in bold red letters, and on the other lapel was a bronze-colored, hospital-issue name tag. One look, and I knew that I was in trouble. Her name, I saw, was Marge. She was, as is requisite for such a name, large, and she was a gruff, no-nonsense kind of gal who had definitely been traumatized by people like me in high school, and was now exacting her revenge one voluntary C-section patient at a time.

Marge's first requirement was that I sit up, which was totally ridiculous considering that I was lying flat on my back and that my stomach muscles had just been cut in half three hours earlier. But Marge would not compromise. I tried explaining to her that even shifting my weight was painful, let alone trying to hoist my entire upper body, but she just glared at me as if to say, *Well, you should have thought about that before you asked for a C-section, you big pussy.*

And so I had no choice. I glared back at her, put on my game face, and heaved myself up into a sitting position without so much as a wince. (If you're not impressed, you should be—major abdominal surgery, people.) Once I accomplished this, Marge got right down to business. She shoved my hospital gown off to the side and started squeezing my nipple, *hard,* allegedly "to see if anything will come out of it." And just when I was starting to think that Marge was being unusually cruel toward me and I was considering filing a class-action lawsuit against the hospital on behalf of all voluntary C-section patients, something did come out of it. It was a thick, buttercup-yellow liquid that Marge called colostrum, and apparently this was a good thing, because when she saw it, Marge actually smiled. I, however, was horrified—on several levels. First, there was nasty yellow stuff coming out of my nipple, and second, an unattractive woman badly in need of an upper-lip wax was fondling my left breast.

Anyway, once she saw my "liquid gold" (her term, not mine, and at first I thought she was talking about some kind of a sexual lubricant or something and I wondered if she was coming on to me), Large Marge grabbed Parker around the waist and practically threw her under my right arm. She then grabbed the back of Parker's head with one hand, manhandled my boob with her other hand, and before I could even figure out what was happening, Parker and I were attached.

And that's when I screamed.

I swear to God, it felt like a crab had my nipple by the pincers, or like a thirteen-year-old boy was giving me a purple nurple. I mean, it *hurt.* But Marge assured me that Parker was properly latched on.

She said, and I quote, "It'll take a few days for you—I mean your nipples—to toughen up."

And toughen up they did. They cracked, they bled, they scabbed, they even suffered the indignation of *hickeys*—and please, I haven't had a hickey since winter vacation of tenth grade, when I hooked up with some Canadian guy I'd met on the beach in Boca Raton—until they got so tough that they could go through a meat grinder and come out intact.

And every time I whined about how much it hurt, and every time I yelped in pain when my shirt would rub, ever so slightly, against my raw, chafed chest, Andrew was right there, running out at all hours of the night to buy me nipple shields and lanolin cream, and whispering words of encouragement in my ear.

It's better for the baby. It's better for the baby.

And then, once I realized that this breast-feeding thing was no joke—that it meant that I was at Parker's beck and call all day and all night; that it meant that I was the one who always had to go to her at two A.M., at four A.M., at six A.M., day in and day out; that it meant that I could never, ever leave the house unless I was willing to show the world my huge, swollen breasts—Andrew was right there again, but now the whispers of encouragement had turned to rumblings of guilt.

It's better for the baby. It's better for the baby.

The first time that I tried to quit was when we brought Parker in for her two-week checkup with Dr. Newman. I announced, through tears, that I wanted to start giving her formula, but Andrew and Dr. Newman just shook their heads at me. But when I didn't shut up about it, Dr. Newman whipped out a one-page piece of propaganda from one of his files and handed it to me across his desk.

Breast Milk: Nature's Perfect Food.
Statistics show that breast-fed babies:

- Have higher IQs
- Get sick less often
- Have fewer allergies

- Have straighter teeth
- Are less likely to become obese as adults, and
- Are more likely to win the Pulitzer prize

Okay, it didn't really say that last one, but it might as well have.

"Ideally," Dr. Newman announced, "you should do it exclusively for at least three months." At which point I started to cry even harder.

Three months? I thought. Three *months*? I couldn't believe him. I mean, three months is a really long time. It's, like, an entire fiscal quarter, or a college trimester. Please, convicted felons get shorter sentences than three months.

Anyway, once it became clear to me that Dr. Newman had an overly ambitious sense of my dedication as a mother, I decided to try to persuade Andrew, who has a much more thorough understanding of my character flaws. But so far, I haven't made much progress. Every time that I announce that I hate breast-feeding and that I'm ready to be done with it, which is pretty much every day, he makes a pouty face and shakes his head.

"But our baby should have every advantage," he says. "Don't you want our baby to have every advantage?"

And, not wanting to admit that, actually, I could care less if he took our baby and dropped her in a Dumpster, I cave. However, in a pathetic attempt to prove that I don't need his permission to quit (although I do, simply because I don't want to hear it fifteen years from now if she's obese, or if she can't master long division, or if she has an overbite), I inform him that I am only going to do it for one more week, and then I am done. D-O-N-E, done.

But seeing as how I've been saying that now for four straight weeks, and seeing as how I'm sitting here now, about to nurse Parker for the fifth time today, it doesn't seem that I've done a very good job of wearing him down.

"Well," I say, looking Deloris in the eye. "I haven't decided if I'm quitting for sure yet. I'll see."

Deloris grimaces back at me and nods her head, then disappears down the hall.

"I'll be in my room, unpacking my things if you need me," she hollers.

"Okay," I say, pretending to be cheerful. "Thanks!"

When Deloris is finally gone, I exhale. Parker is making crazy snarky noises as she frantically attempts to eat my boob through my shirt.

"Okay, okay," I tell her, as I lift up my top and unhook the right side of my nursing bra. As she latches on and starts to eat, I look down at her.

"And what's with you, anyway?" I ask her. "You like a big Jamaican lady more than you like me?"

I sigh, and try to sort out my feelings about this. Let's see . . . I'm always saying how miserable Parker makes me, yet I'm upset that she prefers Deloris to me. I want Deloris to be good with Parker, yet I don't want Parker to like her. I want Deloris to be like Mary Poppins and to take control of things, but I don't want her telling me what to do. I shake my head and roll my eyes at myself.

When did everything become so confusing?

So, in case you were wondering, as I was, Deloris stops working at seven P.M. Exactly. I've really never seen anything quite like it, to be honest. At six fifty-nine she was sitting with Parker on the rocking chair in Parker's room, singing "The Itsy Bitsy Spider" to her and just having a grand ol' time. But at seven o'clock on the nose, just as I am settling in on the couch to watch *Access Hollywood*, I hear the singing stop, midsong (really, the spider hadn't even been washed out yet), and suddenly Deloris appears in the den, holding Parker out to me.

"Here you go," she says. "Time for Deloris to call it a day." *Well*, I think. Perhaps I should install a time clock in the kitchen and give her a punch card.

"Okay," I say, flashing her a big smile and trying not to show my annoyance at the fact that I'm now going to miss the latest scoop on Ashton and Demi. I reach out to take Parker from her, but as soon as I gather her up in my arms she starts to scream. Deloris looks at me and shakes her head.

"Oh, now, Miss Parker, it's okay. Deloris just has to go to bed. You go on and spend some time with your mama. You'll see Deloris again in the morning; don't worry."

For the record, I find it really annoying that Deloris refers to herself only in the third person, and I'm starting to get a little insulted by how positive she is that Parker would rather be with her than with me, even if it's true. But I don't say anything, because I don't want to be the kind of woman who reprimands her nanny and who acts threatened by every little thing, even if I am. So instead I smile.

"Yeah, Parker, I'm not so bad, am I?" I ask her. At this, Parker starts crying even harder, so I change the subject. "Deloris, there's some frozen pizza in the freezer if you want it, or you can order takeout with me and Andrew when he gets home."

Deloris cocks that eyebrow again. "What kind of pizza?" she asks.

"Oh," I say. "Just plain."

She shakes her head at me. "No, what brand is it?"

I squint at her. Is she kidding? "I don't know," I say. I haven't been to the market in almost two months, and I can't even remember when I bought that pizza. It could easily be two years old. I walk over to the kitchen and open the freezer door to look.

"It's Tombstone," I say, trying to make myself heard above Parker's cries. Deloris makes a face.

"No, thank you. I only like Wolfgang Puck." Oh, well, excuse me. "What are you bringing in for dinner?" she asks.

"Chinese," I answer. "I can show you the menu." She makes the face again and shakes her head.

"No, that's okay. Too much MSG. The only Asian food Deloris eats is sushi." Oh, my God. My nanny, the diva. "It's all right," she says. "I brought some food for this evening. But maybe tomorrow you can go to the market. I'll give you a list of what I need for the week."

Oh, sure, I think. *And I'll be happy to pick up your dry cleaning and buy your nephew a birthday gift, since I am, obviously, your personal assistant.* I beam at her.

"No problem," I say. "I have a bunch of things to do tomorrow, so I'll go first thing in the morning, before I leave for the day."

"Thank you," she says brusquely. "Good night." And then, just like that, she walks down the hall, goes into her room, and shuts the door behind her.

* * *

An hour later, Andrew walks in with our subpar Asian meal, and Parker is crying louder than she ever has before. God. You'd think that Deloris would hear it and come out to help me, but it's like she's left the country. I guess I won't need to worry about her hanging out and watching television with us.

"Where's the nanny?" Andrew asks, looking around.

"She went to *bed*," I say. "At seven o'clock." I hand Parker to him, and as he paces around the room, she continues to scream over his shoulder.

"Oh," he says, sounding disappointed. "So, do you like her?" he whispers. "Is she hot?" Ah, hence the disappointment. Andrew seems to think that, because we used an agency and did not hire someone who got into this country by hiding in a barrel of flour on a shipping boat, we are going to have a nineteen-year-old Swedish girl living with us. In fact, when I told him that they were sending someone over today, he said that she had better be nineteen years old and Swedish for the agency fee that we're paying them.

"Hot? No. I don't think you'll find her to be hot. But I guess she's okay. She's no Mary Poppins, but she's good with the baby, that's for sure. Parker stops crying whenever she holds her. It's kind of irritating, actually." Andrew shakes his head at me and looks irritated himself.

"You're impossible, do you know that?" he asks.

"Why?"

"Because. You wanted someone to help you, and you wanted her to be good with babies, but now that you have someone, you're upset because she's too good."

I stick my tongue in my cheek and ponder when it was that he became so intuitive. "That's not true," I lie. "And even if it is true, it isn't just that she's too good. It's that she rubs it in my face. You weren't here. You didn't see the way she looked at me, or hear the way she talked to me. She kept implying that Parker would rather be with her than with me."

Andrew is quiet when I say this, and his silence says it all.

"Oh, thanks, Andrew," I say. "You didn't even meet her but you already know that Parker likes her better than me. That's great. That's very supportive." I start to cry. I can't help it. I've been holding it in all day because I didn't want Deloris to see it, but I just can't keep it inside any longer.

Andrew sighs. "Look, honey, I'm sure that she wasn't trying to rub it in your face. But if you're not happy with the way she talks to you, then you should say something to her. You're paying this woman, remember? She works for you."

I roll my eyes at him. "Oh, okay," I say sarcastically. "I'll just tell her that I noticed that she was being judgmental with her eyes, and that I didn't like how she made me feel that I was in a competition with her, even though all she said was that Parker didn't cry when I wasn't there." I snort at him. "I'm sure that will go over really well."

Andrew rolls his eyes back at me. "Okay," he says, giving up. "You do what you want to do. But you might want to consider that Parker can tell that you're unhappy, and that she's just reacting to that. Maybe if you were happier to be with her, she'd be happier to be with you."

I pretend to be awed by his genius. "Wow, Andrew," I say. "I never thought of that. You're right. I should just be happier. What a fantastic idea. You know, you should go public with that. I'm sure that depressed people everywhere would love to hear about your breakthrough."

He fake-smiles at me. "You're so funny, Lara. Maybe you should go on tour. Or wait—I have an idea. Maybe you should call your doctor and tell him that you're depressed, instead of just hoping that it will go away all by itself."

"Don't try to change the subject," I say, pointing at him. "This isn't about my depression. It's about you taking the side of a woman you've never even met over your own wife. That's what it's about."

Andrew shifts Parker to his other shoulder and shrugs in defeat. "Fine," he says. "If that's what you want it to be about, then fine. I'm going to give her a bath." He turns around and walks out of the kitchen, with Parker still crying over his shoulder. But when he reaches the hallway, he turns back around. "You know I'm right, though. I won't make you admit it, but you know I'm right."

He walks out, and I sneer at him behind his back.

Smarty-pants, I think. *Mr. Know-it-all.*

I sigh, and sit down on a stool in front of the kitchen counter. I have to admit, his timing is pretty good. I actually do have my six-week checkup with Dr. Lowenstein tomorrow. Maybe it is time to talk to him about how I feel. But deep inside of my stomach, I feel a pit of anxiety. Like I said before, I'm just not sure I want to hear what he has to say back.

four

I was up the whole night last night thinking about what Andrew said. Well, I was up the whole night anyway nursing Parker every ten minutes, but in between I was thinking about what Andrew said. About how I just need to be happier. And I decided that, actually, he is right. Of course, I would never tell him that, but I do think he's on to something here. And so, I have decided that I am going to force myself to get a grip. I mean, it's been six weeks, I have a nanny now, and I need to stop mourning the loss of my old life and just get on with my new one. And yeah, I'll still ask my doctor what he thinks about it, because if there is a pill to take for something, I'm the first one in line for a glass of water; but depression or not, it's time to stop the crying, it's time to get my act together, and it's time for me to get back out into the world. Oh, and it's time for a manicure. Definitely time for a manicure.

It's exhilarating, by the way, this sense of resolve. I feel like myself again, somehow—like I've cleared the cobwebs and taken control of my life. And isn't that what it's always about for me? Control? Yes. Of course it is. And thus, the first step in the Get a Grip Plan is to stop with this breast-feeding nonsense. I must stop. I must. *I must, I must, I must decrease my bust.* Sorry. I just had a little Judy Blume moment there for a second. Anyway, I know that I've said this before, but this time I really mean it. This time I am gathering ammunition.

I pick up the phone and dial my friend Stacey.

"Stacey Horowitz's office."

"Hi, is she in?" I ask. *Please, please, please be in.*

"May I tell her who is calling?"

"It's Lara Stone. Tell her that it's *very* important."

Ever since a few months ago, when Stacey found out that she would be up for partner at her law firm this year, I am not allowed to call her at work anymore. She said that unless she can bill for my time, she doesn't want to talk to me. And, apparently, if she can't bill for a visit to the hospital or even for just a quick, ten-minute hello to see her best friend's new baby, she won't do that either. Honestly, six weeks, and she still hasn't even seen the baby yet. If it were anyone else I would disown them. But with Stacey, it's par for the course. And besides, I know what it's like to work at a law firm, and I understand her obsessiveness, so I forgive her. I've even complied with her stupid no-calls policy until now, but this just can't wait.

The line clicks as Stacey picks up.

"This had better be good," she announces.

"I'm sorry, I just have to ask you a very quick question, and I need to know the answer now."

"What?" she says, sounding annoyed. God, I am so glad that I am not a lawyer anymore. Stacey is so stressed out about this partner thing. If she doesn't make it, I really don't know what she's going to do. I just know that I don't want to be around when it happens.

"Okay. Were you breast-fed?"

"What?"

"As a baby. Did your mother breast-feed you, or did you get formula?"

She exhales loudly. "This is what was so important? Lara, do you understand my life right now? If I don't bill twenty-five hundred hours by the end of August, I am screwed. Screwed. And right now I am only on pace for twenty-one hundred this year, which means that I need to find another four hundred hours of work to do in the next three months, and you asking me irrelevant questions about what I ate as an infant is not really helping my cause."

"Actually," I say indignantly, "if you had just answered me with a simple yes or no instead of giving me a lecture just now, you could have saved yourself one-twentieth of an hour. Jeez, Stacey. Now were you or weren't you?"

She exhales again. "I don't know. Wait. No, I don't think I was. Okay? Is that all?"

I smile. "Yes. That's perfect. Thanks." I am about to say good-bye, but she interrupts me.

"Why do want to know, anyway?"

"It doesn't matter. I don't want to waste any more of your time. I'll talk to you in three months."

"No," she says. "Just tell me."

"Okay," I say, in a you-asked-for-it kind of tone. "I'm taking a survey of all of the smart people I know to see who, if anyone, was breast-fed. Because I want to quit but Andrew is making me feel guilty about it, and if I know people who are smart and relatively normal who weren't breast-fed, I'll have an argument to make against him. Okay?"

She lets out yet another stressful-sounding exhale. "You've lost your fucking mind; I hope you know that."

"I'm well aware of it, thanks."

My survey is turning out better than I thought, actually. I've been on the phone all morning, and so far only two people have said that they were breast-fed. The first is Julie's husband, Jon, who, while smart, is not exactly one whom I would necessarily want my kid to grow up to be like. I mean, the guy's favorite band is the Miami Sound Machine, for God's sake; he can't be that smart. The second, unfortunately, is me. Yes, me. Leave it to my mother to be one of, like, three women during the seventies who actually breast-fed. For almost eighteen months.

It's maddening, actually. If I hadn't been breast-fed, I don't think that the guilt would weigh nearly so heavily on me. But I was, and I could be a poster child for those damn La Leche League pamphlets that Andrew leaves lying around the house for me to see. Everything that they say is a benefit of breast-feeding came true for me. I never got ear infections as a kid, I've never had a real weight problem, I attended an Ivy League university, hell, I didn't even need a retainer, let alone braces. So can you see why I'm concerned? I mean, it's totally possible that all of these things would still have been true if I hadn't been breast-fed, but the fact that I can't rule it out as a primary factor makes me incredibly anxious. Although adding Stacey to the "no" column makes me rest a bit easier. She's definitely one of the more intelligent people I know, and the girl has never had an ounce of body fat on her in her entire life.

Okay. There's only one more person I need to call. I pick up the phone and start dialing.

"Hello?"

"Hi, Mom, it's Lara." No, not my mom. Andrew's.

"Oh, hi, sweetie. How's my little granddaughter today?"

"She's a terrorist. But my new nanny started yesterday, so hopefully things will get better."

"Oh, thank God. I can't believe you've done it yourself for this long. I swear, Lara, I never heard of anyone who didn't have full-time help."

I roll my eyes to myself and lower my voice to a whisper. "You know, Arlene, I have heard rumors about a remote tribe in Zimbabwe that forces the women to raise the children all by themselves. But they say that they're dying out faster than they can repopulate. Childhood is just too much for them to survive."

"Ha, ha," she says. "You'll see, Lara. You won't believe how you ever managed without her." Ah, Arlene, Arlene. You have to understand, when Andrew was a kid, she had not one but two live-in nannies—actually, they were a live-in *couple,* a husband-and-wife team who lived in the back house—plus a housekeeper and a driver. Yes, you heard me. A driver. In Los Angeles, land of abundant free parking and valet service at the grocery store. Hilarious, I know.

Anyway, Andrew insists that he was breast-fed, but I just can't see it. Somehow Arlene does not strike me as the type to have been chained to a baby for months on end when there was perfectly good shopping to be done on Rodeo Drive, so I've decided to do a little fact-checking.

"Actually," I say, changing the subject, "I need to ask you a question. Andrew seems to think that you breast-fed him until he was a year old. Is that right?" On the other end of the phone, she is laughing so hard that I can almost feel myself being spit on.

"Is he serious? I gave him formula from the minute he was born. I never breast-fed; it's disgusting."

Thaaank you. That is exactly what I thought she'd say.

Okay, I think, smiling. *My work here is done.*

The rest of my day is jam-packed. My appointment with Dr. Lowenstein is at eleven thirty; then I'm meeting Julie for lunch, and then I have to go to the supermarket for Deloris. Again. I went for her first thing this morning at, like, seven A.M., but the Ralph's market down the street doesn't carry the kind of cheese that she likes, so now I have to make a special trip to Whole Foods for it this afternoon, because obviously I have nothing better to do on my first full day with help than drive across town to Brentwood in rush-hour traffic.

I look at my watch: ten A.M. Okay. I need to get moving. I have to pump so that Parker has something to eat while I'm out, and then I need to get dressed. I put on my S and M bra, sit down on the floor next to my bed, and hook myself up to the pump. I don't cry when I do it anymore— I've gotten past that by now—but man, I can't wait until I can return this thing to the hospital and throw away this nasty old bra. Oh, yeah, I can assure you I won't be shedding any tears when that happens. When I have produced two full bottles, I detach myself from the suction cups, put them away in the refrigerator, and then head back to my bedroom. Okay. Now all I have to do is find something to wear.

Oh, God. What am I going to wear?

On a positive note, let me say that, since my initial venture onto the scale the day that I got home from the hospital, I have dropped a total of twenty-one pounds. Twenty-one pounds lost without dieting, exercising, or sleeping. If you've ever wondered where they get the models for those cheesy weight-loss ads that are always in the back of magazines—*lose fifteen pounds and six inches in only three weeks!*—wonder no more. They must stand outside of hospitals and offer cash to all of the women who are wheeled out holding babies.

On a not-so-positive note, however, let me also say that I still have another twenty pounds to lose. Twenty pounds that have settled God knows where, because, until now, I have been too afraid to look. Seriously, I'm like a vampire from the neck down. I go to great lengths to avoid mirrors, and I try not to expose my body in daylight whenever possible. I even shower with my eyes closed. But now I have no choice. I am going out in public—in the middle of Beverly Hills—this afternoon, and I do not want to look sloppy. I mean, what if I see someone from work, or one of my former students? What if I see someone from my old law firm? No. I don't want people gossiping about what a mess I am now that I've had a baby. I have an image to protect, and I will protect it at all costs. Even if it means looking at myself in the mirror. Naked.

Which brings me to step two in the Get a Grip Plan: a no-holds-barred, take-no-prisoners, full-body assessment.

Needless to say, I am terrified.

Bracing myself, I enter my closet, shut the door, and, keeping my eyes closed, I drop my robe and stand in front of the full-length mirror that is hanging on the wall. I open one eye, then the other.

Whoa. I scan my chest, my stomach, my arms, my hips, my thighs, and then I turn around and look at my butt. Quickly, I turn back around. I take a few deep breaths. Okay. It's bad. Not as bad as I was imagining— I was imagining roll after roll of hanging, cottage-cheese flesh—but it's still pretty bad. I take a few steps back and look at myself again, piece by piece. All right. Here's the (not so) skinny:

Boobs: As you already know, my boobs are obscenely large. We're talking porn-star large. And not in a good way. But those, I am hoping, will shrink back to normal once they cease being used as milk jugs. Which is going to happen. Very soon.

Arms: My arms, while larger than usual, would probably not cause dogs and other carnivorous animals that pass me on the street to go after them on the assumption that they are stuffed sausages and not, in fact, arms, as was the case during the last few weeks of my pregnancy. However, when I hold them straight out and tap on my triceps, I am very disturbed to discover that they flap. Like wings.

Hips: My hips have definitely spread, but Julie has assured me that they go back to normal after a few months, so I'm just not going to stress about it.

Thighs: These have some padding that they didn't used to have, but at least they don't overlap anymore when I stand with my legs together, which is a huge development. Huge.

Butt: Also huge. We're talking *junk* in the *trunk*. Oh, yeah. I've definitely got some work to do there, no question about it.

And finally, what you've all been wondering about, I'm sure. What every woman wants to know. Ladies and gentlemen, the main attraction of this postpartum circus, the Scariest Show on Earth: Put your hands to-gether and give a warm welcome to . . . my stomach.

All right. I'm not going to mince words. There ain't no six-pack; that's for sure. But, to be fair, it's not *that* horrible either. It's sort of flat, if you're willing to define *flat* as not blocking the view to the floor, and I didn't get stretch marks, thank God, so at least it's a normal color and not all red and stripey-looking. It's a bit flabby, I guess, but really, what is most dis-turbing is the skin. The skin has this crepey texture, and it just kind of hangs. Especially right above my scar. There's a little pouch right there that looks like it needs to be pulled tight and snipped off—what they call a "tummy tuck," I guess. *Hmmm*. Perhaps it's time to rethink my views on plastic surgery.

Okay. You know what? I revise my prior statement. It's not *that* bad. Hell, compared to the pregnant me, I'm practically a supermodel. In fact, I would even go so far as to say that there are probably some people in the world who would be happy to have this body. Well, no one in Los Ange-les, of course, but perhaps someone in Minnesota, or maybe Nebraska. The point is, it could be worse.

I smile, and begin to try on my clothes.

I slip my right leg, then my left, through my size-twenty-seven Blue Cult jeans, and I start to pull them up. But the pulling-up comes to an abrupt halt just as the jeans reach the tops of my kneecaps, and I quickly stop smiling as I realize something horrible: This whole time, I've been comparing myself to the fat, pregnant me because I don't even remember the old, skinny me anymore.

Oh, my God, I think, as the reality of the situation begins to sink in. *Who am I kidding here? Of course I look good compared to pregnant me. Pregnant me was a beast.*

Jeans still pulled up to my kneecaps, I do a penguinish sort of half turn, and take another look at my butt in the mirror. Oh, yeah. I'm fat. Fat with a capital F. Hell, fat with a capital F, A, and T, for that matter.

I begin to frantically tear through my closet, looking for something, anything, that might fit.

Okay. Don't I have a pair of cords that used to be kind of big on me? Yeah. The brown ones that I got in New York. Perfect.

I dig through the back of my closet, where I keep the stuff that I haven't worn in years. Here they are. I quickly put them on, but I can't even get them past my hips.

Shit. Wait! What about those Banana Republic fat pants that I bought when I was taking the bar exam and I gained fifteen pounds? I unearth them from under a pile of clothes that needed to be dry-cleaned two years ago but that I never bothered to take once I got pregnant, and I put them on. They go up. All the way up.

Yesss, I think. *Here we go.* But when I try to close them, I can't get the button within three inches of the buttonhole. I practice some deep breathing. *Maybe I should try some shirts.*

I try on five in a row, but none of them fit me either. They're all too tight and three inches too short because my boobs are so damn big. I look at my maternity clothes, neatly piled in bags at the bottom of my closet, just waiting to be given away to the first friend, relative, or coworker to announce that she's knocked up.

No. No way. I will go naked before I will wear those things again. There must be something here. There must be.

By the time that I'm finished, I have tried on every single thing in my closet. And I do mean every single thing. I was so desperate for an outfit that I even tried on a pair of beige, iridescent, faux-snakeskin elastic-waistband pants that I had bought for a costume party five years ago— Andrew and I went as Dennis Rodman and Carmen Electra—and if they hadn't made my ass look like a giant boa constrictor that had just swallowed a two-humped camel, I swear I would have worn them.

All I can say is, thank God for skirts. You see, I discovered that if a skirt won't zip up when it is resting on your hips, you can get it to close if you pull it up to the narrowest part of the torso (which, in my case, just happens to be the top of my rib cage). And if you then wear a shirt long enough to hide the fact that your skirt is pulled up to just underneath your boobs, you can actually get away with the entire outfit. Therefore, despite the fact that it is summer and about ninety degrees outside, I am wearing a long brown turtleneck sweater and a cream-colored wool skirt that is supposed to be calf-length but is currently hitting me about midthigh.

Good thing that miniskirts are back in again.

* * *

When I have finally recovered from my shock and have retouched the makeup that I sweated off during my clothes-trying-on frenzy, I realize that I am now going to be late for my doctor's appointment, so I rush down to Deloris's room to tell her that I'm leaving. But when I get to her doorway, I stop dead in my tracks. I'm not trying to spy or anything, but the door is about a quarter of the way open, and Deloris is standing in the middle of the room with her eyes closed, turning in circles and waving a stick with one hand. With her other hand she is tossing out handfuls of some kind of powder every time that she turns. I clear my throat.

"Um, Deloris?" Deloris does not seem to hear me, and frankly, I'm kind of scared to interrupt her. I knock very softly on the door, and this time Deloris stops twirling and opens her eyes.

"Sorry," she says. "I didn't hear you. I go into a trance sometimes when I'm doing my spells." Her *spells*? She opens the door and waves me inside.

"Oh," I say, trying to be polite and nonjudgmental. "That's okay." Out of the corner of my eye I notice that the room looks different, and I glance around while Deloris has her back turned to me. Yesterday the room had nothing in it but some old sheets and a matched set of white wicker furniture that Andrew's mom pawned off on me a few months ago, and today it's a cross between a voodoo altar room, the set of a bad home decor show, and a head shop.

On the bed is a thick, bloodred quilt, on top of which is a collection of black teddy bears dressed in dashiki tops and matching hats. There is a red, shiny-looking valance made of what I think is chintz draped across the window, and on the far wall is a print of three scary white ghoulish creatures standing underneath a red sun. The bookshelf is littered with candles, bottles of oil, a miniature alligator head, a stack of colored incense sticks, a tiny black cauldron that I think (I hope) is meant to be an incense burner, and a collection of little straw people that I am almost positive are voodoo dolls. All right, then. In case there were any lingering questions, Deloris is officially *not* Mary Poppins.

I clear my throat again, as I wonder what the hell I have gotten myself into here.

"I just wanted to let you know that I'm leaving," I say. I look around, and suddenly I realize that she is alone. As in, without Parker. "Where's

Parker?" I ask suspiciously, wondering if ear of baby might have been an ingredient for the spell she was doing. Deloris puts down her stick—or maybe it's a wand?—and dusts the powder off of her shirt.

"Oh, she's taking a nap," she says.

I stare at her with disbelief. "In her *crib*?" I ask. Parker never takes naps in her crib. I must have tried a thousand times to put her in her crib after she's fallen asleep on my shoulder, but every time, she wakes up the second that her head hits the mattress.

"Yes," says Deloris. "It took a few tries, but Deloris has a magic touch." She winks at me as she says the word *magic*.

No way, I think. Did she put a spell on my baby? Is that why Parker never cries with her? I pause as I consider whether a) this is something that I believe in, and b) if it is acceptable, regardless of my answer to a). I decide that the answers to these questions are *no* and *hell, no*, but I'm too late to start a discussion right now.

"Great," I say instead with a big smile. "Well, I should be back in about two hours or so. There are two bottles of milk in the fridge, and I left my cell phone number on the counter. Oh, and I left the number at the doctor's office, since you're not supposed to use cell phones inside. And just in case, I also left my husband's work number—his name is Andrew—you were already, um, in your room last night when he got home—and the number for the pediatrician. And if there's an emergency, you know, just call nine-one-one."

Deloris looks at me like I'm completely out of my mind. "Don't worry, Mrs. Lara. We'll be okay."

I take a deep breath. "I know," I say. "I'm just not used to being able to leave like this." *And,* I want to add, *it is totally possible that I might not ever come back.*

Deloris nods. "Is it all right with you if I take her for a walk around the neighborhood while you're out?"

"Oh, yeah," I say. "Go ahead. The stroller's in the garage." I turn to go, giving her a little half wave good-bye. "Okay, see you soon!"

I grab my purse and my keys and make a run for it, and when the house disappears in my rearview mirror, I let out a long sigh. For the first time in six weeks, I am babyless. And, despite my weight, I feel as light as a feather. I feel unburdened. I feel un–tied down. I feel like an idiot for not hiring someone sooner.

I pull down the visor and smile at myself in the mirror. Today is the first day that I've actually had the time to put on makeup since Parker was born.

Baby, I think, *you are back.*

five

I arrive at Dr. Lowenstein's office ten minutes late, and I am ushered into one of the examining rooms almost right away. I lie down on the table and close my eyes, and I instantly doze off. When the door opens and Dr. Lowenstein bursts in, I literally fall off of the table, I am so startled.

"Well," he says, laughing, "I guess I don't have to ask if the baby's sleeping through the night yet."

I roll my eyes at this suggestion and shake my head. "Not exactly," I say. I climb back up and sit down and Dr. Lowenstein opens up my chart.

"So," he says. "How's everything going?"

"It's okay, I guess," I answer, though my tone suggests otherwise.

Dr. Lowenstein picks up on this and gives me a concerned glance. "Are you sure?" he asks. "Because you don't sound so convincing."

As Luthor emerges, I remind myself that I am supposed to be getting a grip today, not losing it in the gynecologist's office. I take a deep breath to steady myself, and swallow back the tears.

"No, it's fine," I say, hesitating. "It's just . . . I've been feeling a little . . . I don't know, a little off."

He narrows his gaze. "Off? What does that mean?"

I shrug. "Just, you know, depressed, I guess."

Dr. Lowenstein sits down and looks at me seriously. "Are you having suicidal thoughts? Or thoughts about hurting the baby?"

I am slightly taken aback by this line of questioning. I mean, I said I was depressed, not insane.

"No," I say. "Nothing like that." But Dr. Lowenstein doesn't relent.

"Are you sure? Because it's okay if you do. But you have to tell me."

I shake my head. "No, I swear. It's nothing violent. I just cry a lot. And I don't really feel that happy. I mean, I find myself wishing that I never had her a lot of the time."

Dr. Lowenstein looks relieved. "Oh," he says, nodding his head. "That's not postpartum depression."

"Well, then what is it?" I ask. My heart begins to pound as I wait for him to inform me that it's nothing medical; I just suck at motherhood.

"Some people call it the baby blues," he says. "It's mostly hormones, but it usually goes away after the first two or three weeks."

I raise my eyebrows. "But I still have it, and it's been six weeks."

He shrugs, as if he's trying to say, *Well, what did you expect?*

"Some women just take longer to adjust to motherhood. You'll figure it out. Everybody does, eventually."

Okay, so basically he just told me that I suck at motherhood, did he not? You see, I knew this was going to happen. I never should have asked. I blink three or four times, hard, to hold back my tears.

Then, without any warning, Dr. Lowenstein walks over and lifts up my sweater. As he gropes for the top of my skirt, he seems confused. Oh, no. How embarrassing.

"It's up here," I say, sheepishly, unzipping the skirt and pulling it back down to where it belongs. "It didn't fit the other way."

Dr. Lowenstein nods, as if he's seen it all before, and he pulls down the top of the thong underwear that I squeezed my fat ass into this morning, on the theory that it would be a cold day in hell before I would let any man—doctors included—see the giant cotton granny underwear that I've been wearing since I was seven months pregnant and I got a hemmorhoid.

"Your scar is healing nicely," he says, running his finger over it. "Are you still having any pain?"

"Not really," I say. "I feel it sometimes when I stand up or when I cough, but it's not pain."

He smiles at his handiwork. "Good. That's a good sign." He goes over to his chair and sits back down again, and starts to scribble something in my file. When he's finished, he looks up at me. "You should be able to handle any kind of physical activity now. There's really no danger of the incision tearing anymore."

I stare at him, and suddenly the tears give way to excitement. "You mean I can go back to the gym already?"

He nods. "Absolutely. I'd take it easy with sit-ups for another few weeks, but otherwise you should be fine."

"Tae-bo? Hiking? That's okay?"

"Fine," he says. But then he gives me a stern look. "Just don't overdo it right away. Your body goes through a lot with pregnancy. And you won't be able to lose all of the weight until you stop breast-feeding, anyway, so don't kill yourself at the gym. Your body holds on to at least five to ten pounds of fat during lactation."

What? Breast-feeding makes you fat, too? Oh, that is *so* it.

Dr. Lowenstein smiles at me, and then stands up as if he is about to go.

"Wait," I say meekly. He turns around and sits back down again, looking at me expectantly. I give him an earnest stare. "What if I wanted to stop breast-feeding now? What should I do?"

He frowns at me. "You're stopping after only six weeks?" he asks. "You know, ideally you should do it for at least three months." Again with the three months. Is there no one in this world who understands how long three months is?

"So I've heard," I say. "But just theoretically, if I wanted to stop now, how would I go about it?"

He sighs. "Well, you have two choices. You could just let it dry up naturally. If you don't nurse, your body will eventually get the message that it's time to stop. But that could take several weeks and it's quite painful because of the engorgement. The other option is to take a pill. I can prescribe it for you now, and when you're ready to stop, you take it twice a day for eight days. By ten days, it should be all dried up."

Bingo. "I think I'll take the pill, thanks."

"Okay," he says, pulling out a prescription pad. "And what about birth control? If you're not going to nurse anymore, I can put you back on the pill." *Birth control?* Is he kidding? Andrew and I can barely have a civil conversation these days. And besides, even if I wanted to, when? When are we supposed to have sex? During the four hours at night that she actually sleeps? I don't think so.

"Thanks," I say. "But I don't think I'll be needing that anytime soon."

He shakes his head at me. "You should make time for sex. If you don't get back in the saddle right away, it becomes very easy to forget about it altogether, and trust me, you don't want that."

"All right, fine," I concede. "Write me a prescription. I suppose I'll like my husband again at some point." Dr. Lowenstein rips off the two prescriptions from his pad and hands them to me, and then helps me off of the table.

"Okay," he says, kissing me on the cheek. "I'll see you in six months. Good luck with the baby." He starts to walk out the door, and then he turns around and sticks his head back in. "And try to hang in there with the breast-feeding. It really is the best thing for her."

Yeah, yeah, yeah. Like I haven't heard that before.

When I arrive at the restaurant, I see that Julie is already sitting at a table. With Lily. She tried to convince me to bring Parker—to have a girls' day out, she said—but I didn't think it was such a good idea. The Get a Grip Plan does not include the entire world bearing witness to how much my own baby loathes me.

"Hi," I say, kissing Julie on the cheek.

"Hi," she says. "You look fantastic!" I give her a please-do-not-lie-to-me look. "You do," she says.

"Whatever. You haven't seen me naked." I glance over at the chair next to her. "Oh, my God, look at Lily—she's huge!" Lily, if I'm calculating correctly, is just about eight months old now. Julie has managed to gather her hair into a tiny little ponytail on top of her head, and she's sitting in a high chair, chewing on a teether and not making a sound. When she sees me looking at her, she breaks into a huge grin.

"Is she always this quiet?" I ask.

"Always," Julie says. "Ever since she was born."

I close my eyes, feeling defeated. It's like the chicken and the egg. Does Parker cry because she can tell that I'm miserable, or am I miserable because she cries?

"Well," I say, changing the subject. "What's new?"

"Oh," Julie says, sighing. "Nothing much. Just this nursery school stuff is stressing me out. Have you decided where you want to send Parker?" What is she talking about? What nursery school stuff?

"Julie," I say, opening my menu, "she's six weeks old. I think I have some time."

Julie's eyes get wide and she starts shaking her head. "No, you don't," she says. "You need to start thinking about it now. I was on waiting lists when I was still pregnant. It's extremely competitive." Is she serious?

"Please," I say. "I do this for a living, remember? I help kids get into *college*. It can't be more competitive than that."

Julie shakes her head again. "It is, Lar. I'm telling you. Think about it: There are thousands of colleges out there, but there are only, like, four good nursery schools in all of LA, and the good kindergartens only take kids from those preschools. Trust me, you need to start calling places *now*." She sighs again. "We're trying to get into the Institute. I'm applying to the Toddler Program for next year. It's only one day a week, but if you get into that, then you're automatically in for nursery school for the next year. Anyway, you have no idea what they're putting me through."

The Institute? I think. Is that a preschool or an insane asylum?

"What's the Institute?" I ask. Julie looks at me like I'm from another planet.

"The Institute for Early Child Development? It's only the best preschool in the city. Everyone wants to go there. They have the best facility, the best credentials, the best program, the best teachers . . . once you've toured the Institute, you will not even want to look anywhere else. Trust me."

I can feel the hypercompetitive, type-A part of me shifting into gear as I listen to her, so I take a deep breath and try to tune her out.

I am not going to get sucked into this. I have no reason to get sucked into this.

You see, it doesn't matter where I send Parker to nursery school, because children of faculty automatically get into Bel Air Prep, which is K–12. Please. It's one of the reasons why I took the job.

"I want to send Parker somewhere low-key," I say to her. "We're in at Bel Air, remember?"

Julie sighs wistfully at this and nods. "You are so lucky," she says. "You wouldn't believe what I have to do just to get an interview. You can't even get an application if you don't take a tour, but they only have five tours a year and they fill up in twenty minutes. And then, even if you do get to apply, only a few families actually get interviews, and they're very secretive about how they decide who gets one. They're starting to make those decisions now, and I feel like I'm running a lobby in Washington. I've got people all over the city calling them on my behalf." She shrugs her shoulders. "Anyway, we'll see. Even if we do get an interview, we still won't know if we're in until September."

I shake my head at her. "It sounds awful," I say. "I'm not that well connected, but if there's anything I can do to help, just let me know."

Julie's eyes light up. "Actually, I was hoping that maybe you could help me with the application essays. You know, since you do this for a living."

My eyes go wide. "There are essays? For preschool?"

Julie nods. "Four of them." Four of them? Harvard doesn't even have four essays.

"Sure," I say, shrugging my shoulders at her. "Show me the questions and I'll take a look."

"Great. Thanks so much." She unfolds her napkin. "So, how are you doing? You seem better than the last time I saw you."

"I am," I say. "I'm much better. Deloris has only been here a day, and already I feel like I have a life again. And she's so good with the baby." I pick up my fork and tap the tines on the table. "But I don't know. I just feel like she hates me."

Julie looks at me, confused. "Who? Deloris?"

"No. Parker. She cries every time I go near her, and if I pick her up she screams. But when Deloris is around she's calm and she never cries. I mean, I want her to like her nanny, but not more than she likes me." I sigh, trying not to cry. "And I just feel so clueless with her. Do you know I spent the last six weeks carrying her around all day like a wet rag, and it never even occurred to me to try to play with her or anything. But then yesterday, Deloris put her on the Gymini, and she was playing music and singing to her, and Parker was so happy. Which of course made me feel like the worst mother in the whole world, like I've been depriving her of stimulation this whole time."

Julie's eyes are wide, and she is giving me the pity look that she always gives me. "Oh, Lara, you're not the worst mother. You're just new at it. It takes time."

"No," I say. "I am. I really am. I don't know what's wrong with me. My doctor brushed it off as nothing—he said that some women just take longer to adjust to motherhood. But it's been six weeks and I still don't feel like I love her yet. And sometimes I wonder if I ever will."

There is a long, awkward silence as Julie looks down at the table and begins to chew on her thumbnail. I look over at Lily, but instead of another smile, she gives me a scowl. Like she understands that I just said something rude about one of her homegirls. Finally, Julie looks up.

"Hey," she exclaims, trying to sound cheery. "Didn't you sign up for Susan Greenspan's class? Shouldn't it be starting soon?"

Oh, yeah. I forgot about that. I called back in September, when I was in my first trimester. Julie made me do it. Apparently, it's *the* Mommy and Me class in Los Angeles.

"Yeah," I say. "I did. I think she said that it starts in July."

Julie looks relieved. "Oh, good. You'll see—once you start Susan's class you'll feel so much better. She'll tell you exactly what you should be doing with the baby and she'll be able to answer all of your questions. You won't believe how good she is. She could turn Joan Crawford into Mother of the Year." I look at her sideways, unsure whether this is an insult or not. "Not that you're like Joan Crawford," she says quickly. "I just meant that she'll be able to help you, that's all."

"Yeah, I know what you meant," I say, deciding not to be insulted.

"Anyway," Julie says, "it will be good for you. And you might even make some new friends. It's nice to know people with babies the same age. I love the girls in my class. We all have lunch together every week."

Yeah, I think. It would be nice to know someone else with a baby. God, I would love to meet somebody who feels the same way I do about this motherhood thing. You know: Incompetent. Incapable. Totally Miserable. Oh, and don't forget about Completely Positive That She'll Fuck Her Kid Up For Life If She Hasn't Already.

At a table behind us, a baby starts to wail.

"Ugh," I say, "I am so tired of hearing that noise. How old are they when they start talking?"

Julie looks up from her salad and bites her lower lip. "Um, Lar," she says, glancing at my shirt.

"What?" I ask. "What's wrong?" But she doesn't have to answer. I look down and I see that two large, wet circles have formed on my shirt, directly on top of my nipples. "Oh, my God," I moan. "You've got to be kidding me. I just pumped an hour ago."

Julie makes an apologetic face. "Sometimes a crying baby can make your milk let down," she informs me.

"But it's not my baby!" I say, trying to wipe at myself with my napkin.

"Well," she says, "your body doesn't know that."

Oh, that's just great. It's not bad enough that my brain has no idea how to handle a baby, but now my body is stupid, too.

When I get home, the house is empty except for Zoey, who is sleeping next to the front door and doesn't even open her eyes when I walk in. Poor dog. I swore that I wouldn't be one of those people who ignore their dog once the baby is born, but I just don't have the energy for her. It's really sad, actually. She's given up on even hoping for me to pet her. Oh, well. She had a good run as an only child. She'll get over it.

Deloris and Parker must still be out on their walk, which is fine with me. It gives me some time to relax without feeling guilty about the fact that I'm leaving her with a nanny even when I'm home.

I put Deloris's new cheese in the fridge, and then I pick up the phone and dial Andrew at work. While I'm waiting for him to answer, I pull out the prescription bottle with my milk-drying-up pills in it.

TAKE ONE TABLET BY MOUTH TWICE A DAY UNTIL COMPLETED. DO NOT USE THIS PRODUCT IF PREGNANT OR BREAST-FEEDING.

Well, duh.

The phone stops ringing as Andrew answers.

"This is Andrew Stone."

"Hi," I say coyly.

"Hi," he says curtly.

"So, I found out some interesting things today."

"Yeah? About what?" he asks.

I answer him slowly, savoring the moment. "I have asked every person we know who obtained a higher degree from a top institution of learning, and all but two of them were formula-fed. And of those, nobody is seriously overweight, and only three people have minor pollen or dust allergies. So there. Hard proof that breast milk is not all that it's cracked up to be."

He sighs. "Yes, but Lara, the question is not how smart are they now. The question is how much smarter would they be if they *had* been breast-fed, and there's no way to know the answer to that." Oh, he is so exasperating sometimes. "Plus, you and I were both breast-fed, and I just don't see why Parker shouldn't have the same head start that her parents got. Really, we've talked about this a million times."

I smile to myself. *I know a secret, nah-nah-nah-nah-nah-nah.*

"Actually, babe, I hate to break it to you, but I talked to your mom this morning, and you, my friend, were never breast-fed. Not for one day."

There is silence on the other end of the phone.

"Andrew?"

Still nothing.

"Andrew, it's okay. It's not that big a deal."

Finally he speaks. And he sounds pissed. "Well," he says. "That explains a few things, doesn't it?"

"What?" I ask. "What could that possibly explain?"

"It explains my SAT scores, for one thing. You know, if I had scored just fifty points higher, I would never have been wait-listed at Penn. Do you have any idea how excruciating it was to have to wait all summer to know where I was going to college? If I had been breast-fed, I'll bet I would have gotten in regular like everyone else. You see? *This* is why you need to stick with it. This is *exactly* why. I can't believe my mother."

Okay. This is sooooo weird, even for him.

"You're absurd," I tell him. "I thought it would make you feel better to know that you are—or at least, I thought you were—totally normal despite not having been breast-fed, but obviously I was wrong. And besides, I *am* going to quit. I saw Dr. Lowenstein today and he gave me pills that will make my milk dry up, and I'm staring at them right now."

"Lara," he warns, "do not take them. If you're any kind of a mother, you will not take those pills." Oh, that is so low. I swear to God, if he doesn't stop with this guilt, I will use every ounce of my superior, breast-fed IQ to divorce him and leave him with nothing to his name except for a lifetime supply of infant formula. I will, too.

"Honestly, Andrew, I am so tired of your dictatorship. It's not like I want to stop when everything is going great. It would be different if she ate every three hours, like a normal baby. It would be different if she didn't fall asleep two minutes into every feeding during the day, or if she would just stay asleep at night after she ate. But she doesn't do those things. She's impossible, and the free-for-all eating fest is driving me crazy. I can't go anywhere, I can't do anything, I can't make any plans. It's making me resent her. And do you know that today my nipples started leaking in the middle of a restaurant?"

Andrew chuckles at this. "They did?"

"Yes, Andrew, they did. And I'm glad you think that it's so funny." I pause, and he says nothing. "You know how you said last night that I should try to be happy? Well, not breast-feeding would make me happy." On the other end of the phone, I hear him sigh.

"That's not exactly what I meant," he says. "But that's fine. If you want to be selfish and deprive our daughter of health benefits just so that you can go places and do things, then go right ahead. But you could at least have a little sympathy for the fact that I just found out that my entire life is based on a lie."

Oh, my God, he cannot be serious. You'd think he just learned that he was raised by wolves and adopted by the nice farm people who found him wandering the countryside in nothing but a fig leaf, howling at cars and chickens.

"Good-bye, Andrew."

"I hope you're happy now that I've been completely disillusioned."

"I am," I say. "Extremely."

I hang up on him and walk into my bathroom, still holding the pill bottle in my hand. Out of nowhere I start to cry. Why am I letting everyone make me feel so guilty about this? I mean, you should have seen me at the pharmacy counter. I felt like Hester Prynne. Like I had a big, scarlet can of formula pinned to my chest. I swear, I half expected the pharmacist to loudly accuse me of being a non-breast-feeder and to call for the villagers to throw rocks at my head.

Well, fuck it. I'm sick of everyone.

I remove the cap from the bottle and place one of the pills in my hand. I stare at it for a second, but just as I am about to toss it into my mouth, I feel a faint tap on my left shoulder. I turn my head: It's Andrew. Well, not really Andrew. It's a two-inch version of Andrew, wearing angel wings and one of those cheap headbands that people use for angel costumes at Halloween—the kind with a wire attached to the back that holds up a fake tinsel halo over your head. Anyway, the mini-Andrew is whispering in my ear, and he sounds like Yoda from *Star Wars*.

Do not the pill take. A good mother you should be. Better for the baby it is.

I hesitate, and then I feel a tap on my other shoulder. I turn my head again: It's me. Well, not really me, obviously. It's a two-inch version of me, and I'm wearing my skinniest, size-four Frankie B. jeans and the pink baby-doll T-shirt with the giant tongue on it that I got at a Rolling Stones concert a few years ago.

Take it, I'm saying. *Get your life back. Get your body back. It'll make you feeeeel good.* Oh, great. The mini-me is the drug pusher from that old Just Say No commercial that they aired back when I was in high school. Wonderful.

I feel my chest constrict with anxiety, and I put the pill back in the bottle. I sigh. I need to think about this some more. I place the bottle in the medicine cabinet and glance at my watch: ten after three. I walk out of my room and wander around the house, thinking that maybe Deloris and Parker came back and I didn't hear them. But they're not here.

Where are they?

I've been home since two thirty; the neighborhood is not that big. And besides, Parker is going to be hungry again soon, and she must have used both bottles by now.

Okay, Lara, don't freak out. She'll be fine.

While I'm waiting, I pick up the phone and call Andrew again.

"This is Andrew Stone."

"I didn't take it," I admit grudgingly. "Not yet, anyway."

"Look, did you just call to pick another fight with me?" he asks. "Because I don't have time right now."

"No," I say. "I'm not trying to fight with you. I'm sorry, okay? I'm sorry that your SATs were low, and I'm sorry that you got into college off of a wait list. It's just hard for me, okay? I want to be a good mother, but this is really hard." I take a deep breath and change the subject before I start crying again. "Anyway, what did you think of Deloris this morning?"

"She's fine," he says. "Not hot at all. But she seems nice."

"I don't know. She's kind of weird. I think she's into voodoo. She put up all of these dolls and potions and stuff in her room, and I walked in on her doing a spell this morning. I think she put a spell on Parker, too. I think that's why Parker never cries around her."

"That's ridiculous," he says. "You're just jealous because Parker always cries around you."

"No," I say. "I'm telling you, she told me that she works magic and then she winked at me. It was *weird.*" I can hear Andrew typing in the background, which means that he has completely stopped listening to me. "And she told me that she was going to make a voodoo doll of you and stick needles in its eyes. So you'd better watch out."

"Mm-hmm," he says. See?

"Anyway, they went for a walk. I'm just waiting for them to get home."

"That's nice," he says, still typing. Okay. I've had enough of him.

"Yes, and then I'm heading over to the bordello, where I'll be seeing a few of my old clients. Dr. Lowenstein said that I should get back in the saddle right away."

"Okay, have fun," he says. "I'll see you when I get home." He pauses. "Oh, I'm going to be late. I have a conference call with a client in London at seven."

I let out an annoyed sigh. "Andrew, you've been late almost every night this month," I protest. "If I didn't know better, I'd think that you were avoiding me." Actually, I wonder if I really do know better.

"Sorry," he says. "You know I have that big deal closing soon."

"Fine," I huff. "I'll see you later."

I wander into the den and sit down on the couch to watch the news. About halfway through it, I look at my watch again: four fourteen. Okay. Now I'm starting to get nervous. Even assuming that they left right before I got home, it's now been two hours, minimum.

Suddenly I have a nagging thought that I accidentally threw away the paper that the agency sent me with all of Deloris's information on it. I run into the kitchen and rifle through the stack of papers that I keep on the kitchen counter, but it's not there.

Oh, my God.

I threw it away. I'm sure of it. I don't have her phone number or the copy of her driver's license; I don't even know her last name. I close my eyes and try to picture what it said on the paper—it started with an S, I think. Or maybe it was an R. *Shit.* I can't remember anything anymore. All I know is, I gave her my *child,* and I couldn't tell the police one single thing about her if I had to.

Oh, my God.

I am paralyzed with panic as I think about all of the scenarios that could be taking place right now. For all I know, Deloris could have taken Parker and gotten on a bus bound for Mexico three hours ago.

I really am not fit to be a mother. I'm just not. I frantically dial Andrew again.

"This is Andrew Stone."

"It's me," I say.

"What *now*?" he asks.

"I just realized that they've been gone for at least two hours. I think Deloris might have kidnapped her. Or maybe someone shot Deloris and took Parker. Someone could have stopped and asked for directions, and then shot Deloris in the head and grabbed the baby." I am in tears. "I can't believe how stupid I am. I don't even know Deloris's last name. I don't know anything about her. All I could think about was getting some time to myself. I wasn't even careful enough to file the paper with all of her information on it, and now my baby is *gone*."

I am starting to feel extremely guilty for all of the horrible things that I've said about Parker. Like that I hate her. And that she's the spawn of the devil. Did it never occur to me that I might be jinxing myself? How stupid am I? I start to hyperventilate, but Andrew just sighs.

"Okay, calm down. I'm sure they're fine. Some people like to take long walks. And I'm sure that the agency can send you another copy of her information." That's a good point. But I still don't feel better.

"No. Something is wrong." I think that I am feeling some kind of a maternal sixth sense coming on. "I just have a bad feeling about this. Mothers know these things."

Andrew laughs at me. "Lara, you haven't had one maternal instinct since Parker was born, and suddenly you're a psychic? Look, if it will make you feel better, why don't you drive around the neighborhood and see if you can find them. Okay?" That's a great idea, actually.

"Okay. I'll call you in ten minutes."

I jump in my car and screech out of the driveway. My heart is pounding and I'm sweating and crying and all sorts of horrible images are racing through my mind, not to mention the report that will be on the local news about the West Los Angeles woman whose baby was kidnapped by her new nanny, and how there are still no details about what the mother was thinking when she left the baby alone with a perfect stranger whose last name is still unknown, but whom authorities believe is a voodoo high priestess on the FBI's ten-most-wanted list, and who may be responsible for a series of ritual sacrifices that involved the deaths of several infants in nine different states. And just as I am starting to picture myself at Parker's memorial service, sobbing over the tiny casket with no body inside because it still has not been found, I see Deloris walking toward me, pushing Parker's stroller and whistling one of the songs from the classical music CD.

I stop the car in the middle of the street and run over to the sidewalk. When Deloris sees me, she smiles.

"Hi, Mrs. Lara. How was your day out?" I lift Parker out of the stroller and clutch her to my chest.

"I thought something happened to you," I say, fighting back tears. "I thought she was kidnapped, or that you got shot and someone took her." I shake my head. "Do you know how long you've been gone?"

Deloris's eyes narrow, and she puts her hand over her heart as if she has been deeply wounded. "Mrs. Lara, Deloris is not a bad person. I would never hurt a poor little baby. We walked to the park and she fell asleep in her stroller, so I sat down and let her take a nice, long nap in the shade. I *told* you we were going for a walk." She shakes her head and starts walking ahead of me, muttering something under her breath about neurotic ladies and how she should have known better than to take another job on the west side.

"I'm sorry," I say, trying to catch up to her. "I didn't think that *you* hurt her; I just thought that maybe something happened to *both* of you. I got worried. You have to understand, this is the first time I've ever left her alone with anyone before." She keeps walking.

Oh, please don't quit. Please don't quit.

Suddenly she stops in her tracks and turns around to face me.

"I understand that you love this child," she says.

When I hear this, I am startled. *Wait a minute,* I think. *She thinks that I love her? Wait. Do I love her? Is that what this is? Okay, hold on, Lara. Don't get distracted. You're about to get fired by your nanny.*

"But I am a highly qualified, highly experienced child-care provider, and I do not appreciate being insulted like that to my face. Now, Deloris will consider this to be a misunderstanding between us, but there is only one misunderstanding per customer. Do you get what I'm saying?" I vigorously nod my head to show that I do, and her face relaxes into a big, toothy smile, as if the exchange that we just had never even took place.

"Well, then," she says. "Let's get this child home before she starves herself to death. It's been hours since the last time she ate." She reaches over and takes Parker from me, leaving me to push the empty stroller behind them.

Well. So much for the Get a Grip Plan.

six

Five days, four tae-bo classes, three lunches with friends, two hair appointments, and one pair of Jimmy Choos later, I am sitting on the couch with Parker, watching a show on the Disney Channel called *The Wiggles*. It's a ludicrous show—four Australian guys singing and dancing to songs that have terrible, yet oddly catchy lyrics (*Fruit salad, yummy yummy. Fruit salad, yummy yummy. Yummy yummy yummy yummy fruit sal-ahahad*)—but I'm suffering through it because it positively captivates Parker and keeps her quiet for record amounts of time. And yes, I know about the study that said that babies who watch television before the age of two are more likely to have ADD, but I'm sorry, after Deloris goes to bed at night I need to do *something* to make her stop crying, and besides, that's what we have Ritalin for.

To my great annoyance, Andrew is going to be home late yet *again*, so I'm just sitting here on the couch, killing time until I can put Parker to bed. I TiVoed this episode and this is the third time we've watched it tonight, but Parker doesn't seem to notice. It's almost over, though, because Captain Feathersword, the friendly pirate, is doing grand jetés across the hull of a ship while the Wiggles sing on the shore, and the only thing left after this number is a skit in which Dorothy the Dinosaur eats a cake made out of rose petals. I tap my foot to the music and tilt my head back and forth.

Go, Captain, go. Go, Captain, go. Go, Captain Feathersword, ahoy.

I let out a big yawn. Parker was up last night at eleven, three, and five thirty, and I'm exhausted. This getting-up thing is really starting to get old.

I close my eyes, thinking that maybe I can rest for a few minutes before the show is over and I have to actually pay attention to her again. I start to relax, and then . . .

I'm wearing a torn white dress, and I'm standing on the plank of a ship with my hands tied behind my back, à la Kristy McNichol in *The Pirate Movie*.

Ahoy there, me hardy, growls Captain Feathersword, ogling me with the eye that doesn't have a patch over it. *Now, let me have my way with ye or you'll walk the plank*, he commands.

Oh, Captain, I murmur, *come over here and tickle me with that big, red feather sword of yours*.

My eyes fly open. Okay. That's it. Andrew and I have *got* to start having sex again. I don't care how tired I am. Or how much I hate him.

Just then the doorbell rings, and Zoey begins to furiously bark, which of course startles Parker out of her *Wiggles*-induced trance and causes her to start screaming at the top of her lungs. Great. I stand up and put Parker over my shoulder, and I look at my watch. Who is ringing my doorbell at eight fifteen on a Thursday night? As I walk toward the front door, I start yelling at Zoey to quit the barking.

"Zoey, shut up! Enough! Zoey, stop!" But she's completely ignoring me, and my yelling is only making Parker cry louder. "Who is it?" I yell through the door, but I can't hear a damn thing with this racket in my ear, so I try to look through the peephole, but all I can see is black. *Shit*. I take a deep breath. Okay. I'm just going to throw caution to the wind and assume that it's a Jehovah's Witness, or an overly ambitious tree hugger trying to get me to join the Sierra Club, and not a serial rapist or an ax murderer who's been staking me out for the last few weeks and who knows that my husband doesn't get home until nine o'clock every night.

I fling open the door. A balding man with a gray beard, mid-fifties, is standing in front of me, his arms outstretched. He's wearing jeans, a bright blue, short-sleeved silk shirt buttoned all the way up to the top button, a pair of black suede driving shoes, and a huge gold-and-diamond pinkie ring on his left hand. I squint at him for a second or two, trying to place him, and when I realize who it is, my entire body freezes.

Oh, my God. I would *definitely* have preferred the ax murderer.

"Buhbie!" he yells. "When did you have a baby?"

Ohmigod, ohmigod, ohmigod. My father is standing on my doorstep.

My father, whom I have not seen or heard from in eight years, is standing on my doorstep.

"Dad?" I say, bewildered. "What are you doing here?"

He gives me a big grin and opens his arms even wider. "You are looking at Los Angeles's newest resident." He waits for me to smile, and when I don't he announces, as if I didn't get his initial reference, "I've moved!"

I stare at him blankly. I have no idea what to say. Just then the phone rings.

"Um, could you excuse me for a minute?" I ask. Without waiting for an answer I shut the door, leaving him standing on the front porch, and run upstairs, getting more hysterical with every step. I burst into the bedroom and pick up the phone.

"Hello?" I ask, praying that it is Andrew.

"Oh, um, is this BMW?" Ahhh. We have the same phone number as BMW in the Valley, and people are always forgetting to dial the area code.

"Eight-one-eight, lady!" I yell, trying to choke back my tears. "Dial eight-one-eight!" I hang up on her and speed-dial Andrew's office. No answer. He's probably on another call with London or something.

Okay, Lara. Stay calm. Try to stay calm.

I pick up the phone again and instinctively dial Stacey at work. Stacey was the one who was there with me in law school when my dad disconnected his phone one day and decided that he "no longer wanted to have ties to anyone," and she was the one who helped me track him down through a casino in Atlantic City two years later, just to make sure that he was still alive. She was also the one who nicknamed him @#*!, the Fuckup Formerly Known as My Father. Yeah, Stacey will know what to do. She's definitely still at the office; I just hope that she'll take my call.

As luck would have it, she picks up the phone herself.

"This is Stacey," she says, sounding rushed.

"Stace, its me."

"Lara, if you're calling to ask whether my mom used cloth diapers or disposable, I'm sorry, but I have work—"

"Stacey, my father is here. My doorbell rang, and I thought it was somebody selling something, but when I answered it he was standing there, and he says he's moved to the city." I am pacing my bedroom like a wild animal, and Parker has fallen asleep on my shoulder.

"Shut up," she says. "Are you serious?"

"Would I make this up?" I ask. "What do I do?"

"Well, where is he now?"

"He's still on the doorstep, I think. Unless he left. Hold on." I pull back the curtain on the French doors in my bedroom that look out over the street, and I see him standing there, illuminated by the porch light. He's picking at his cuticles, and suddenly I have a flashback to my childhood:

I was about six years old, maybe seven—no, I had to be six, because I remember that I had just gotten home from school and I was crying to my mom because Mindy Rosenfeld had said that my favorite sweater, the one that had Kermit the Frog and Miss Piggy posing like *American Gothic* on it, was stupid, and Mindy moved to New Jersey the summer that I turned seven, so I must have been six—and my father walked into the kitchen holding his hands up the in air like he was waiting for a manicure to dry, except that there was blood dripping from every fingertip. And then my mother screamed and told him that if he couldn't get his anxiety under control by himself, then he'd better start seeing a shrink. I knew better than to ask, but I remember that I spent the next several days wondering how in the world a Shrinky Dink could possibly make my dad's fingers better.

I drop the curtain.

"He's still there," I tell Stacey.

"Lara, you have to let him in. This is your opportunity for closure. Even if you never see him again after today, you have to talk to him and ask him why he did what he did." I hesitate. "Lara, if you don't find out for yourself, then find out for me, okay? I want to know what he was thinking almost as much as you do."

She's right. Of course she's right. I do want an explanation. I do. But I also want to slam the door in his face and tell him to go fuck himself. I want to make him suffer for all of the years that he's made me suffer.

"I don't know, Stacey. If I let him in and talk to him, he'll think that I'm forgiving him and he'll get to feel good about us, and he does not deserve to feel good about us."

"Of course he doesn't. I'm not saying that you should invite him in and pour him a cup of tea and break out the old family photos. I'm saying that you should take this opportunity to tell him how you feel. Get it all off your chest and ask him the hard questions. Then kick him out if you want and tell him never to contact you again. It's your choice. You're the one with the power here."

Wow. You can really tell how long Stacey has been in therapy sometimes. The Shrinky Dink has definitely worked for her.

In an attempt to summon my inner strength, I breathe in through my nose and out through my mouth, and I begin to walk back downstairs.

"Okay," I say. "I'll call you later. Thanks."

When I open the front door again, @#*! tears himself away from his cuticles and looks up at me expectantly.

"Sorry," I say coldly. "I had to get the phone; it was the pediatrician calling me back."

"No problem," he says, and then he takes a deep breath, perhaps to summon his own inner strength. "Listen, Lara, I know you're probably really mad at me for what I did, and I don't blame you, but I was in a bad place then, and I swear, everything is different now. *I'm* different now."

I square my jaw and stare at his beard, which was not gray the last time that I saw him. "Yeah, well, I'm different now, too. I'm not interested in getting you back in my life anymore." Ooh, that was a good one. I look at him, waiting for a response, and I see the hurt register on his face.

Good, I think. *Now you'll see how it feels.*

"Lara," he pleads. "I know I screwed up. I know that I did. But you have to believe me that I never stopped loving you and I never forgot about you. I think about you every single day." He reaches out and brushes my cheek with his hand. "You're still my little girl, you know."

Oh, he did *not* just pull the little-girl card. He used to do that to me every time I was upset with him, and I always fell for it. I feel the lump rising in my throat, and I have a sudden urge to hug him and never let go.

Why? I think. *Why do I always let myself get manipulated by this man?* I burst into tears.

"I love you, too, daddy," I cry.

Oh, God, did I just call him Daddy? I did. I just called him Daddy. I am such an idiot.

He smiles. He totally knows that he got to me. And then, just as quickly, the look in his eyes turns from one of love to one that is all business.

Oh, here we go, I think. *Here comes the real reason why he's here. Of course there's a catch. There's always a catch with him.*

"So," he says, smoothing out his shirt with his hands. "Can I come in now?"

Oops. I forgot that we were still standing on the porch.

"Yeah," I say, shrugging my shoulders, trying to compose myself. "Come on in." I turn and lead him into the den, and I can feel him appraising my net worth.

"Nice house," he says. "It must have cost you a fortune, with what houses are going for on the west side."

"Yeah, well, we bought it right before the market went up," I say quickly. I don't need him thinking that we're loaded. First of all, we're not, and second of all, I don't want him to view me as a potential source of revenue for his gambling habit.

I slowly sit down on the couch, being careful not to jostle Parker, and I cross my legs. @#*! gives me a sly look.

"I was thinking about buying a place myself," he says. "Something near the beach, maybe. It's been a while since I've been near an ocean."

I look at him skeptically. You can't get anything within ten miles of the beach for under a million, and for a million all you can get is a piece-of-shit teardown. And the last time I spoke to my father, he was up to his ears in debt and barely had a penny to his name.

"Really?" I ask. "With what money?"

He smiles. "Oh, I've got money now. Money is not really an object for me anymore." I raise my eyebrows at him and a slow smile spreads over his face. "I won a four-million-dollar slot payoff at Bally's in Vegas about seven months ago. I thought I might have heard from you, actually. It was in the *LA Times.*"

I shake my head. Unbelievable. It just goes to show you that it's better to be lucky than smart. Or a good person. Or a good parent, for that matter.

"I didn't see it," I say. "I don't read the *LA Times.*"

He laughs. "I figured as much. Do you still do the *New York Times* crossword?"

"I do."

"Do you finish it? The Sunday one?"

"As a matter of fact, I do." I look down at Parker. "Although not lately."
I look back up at him and I think I see a tear in the corner of his eye.

"How old is . . . she? He?"

I look down at her again. She kind of does look like a boy, doesn't she?
Wow. I hope that it's not a permanent thing. That would suck.

"She," I say. "She's almost seven weeks." This is starting to feel a bit too
intimate for me, so I abruptly change the subject. "So," I say, putting on
my legal interrogation voice. "Vegas. That's where you've been this whole
time?"

He closes his eyes and sinks back into the couch. "Not the whole time.
I spent a few years in AC; then I traveled a bit—Arizona, New Mexico,
Guadalajara for a few months. But yeah, the majority of it was in Vegas."

"And you couldn't talk to anyone during that time because . . . ?" I
open my hands to indicate that the concept is lost on me, and he sighs.

"Because I just needed to be alone. Because I spent my whole life taking care of other people and doing things for other people and being responsible for other people, and I never bothered to ask myself what *I*
wanted out of life."

I stick my tongue in my cheek. "So that's why you disappeared? Because you needed to *find* yourself? Don't you think that you're a little old
for that, Dad?" I am trying as hard as I can to control myself, but I can't
stop my voice from breaking.

"Parenthood is hard, Lara. You probably don't realize it yet because
she . . . What's her name, anyway?"

"Parker," I say impatiently.

"Because Parker . . ." He cocks his head for a second as it sinks in.
"Parker?" he asks. I give him a look to say that he is in no position to be
questioning my choice of names, and he moves on.

"Because Parker isn't old enough, but you'll see."

"No," I say. "She's plenty old enough for me to know that it's hard. But
this isn't about me. It's about you. And I don't recall you making that
many sacrifices for me, anyway. It's not like you had to take a second job
to put food on the table, or like you had to sell the house to pay for my
clothes."

"You have no idea how much I did for you," he snaps. "You went to your summer camps and took your dance lessons and your piano lessons and had your math tutors, all so that you could have every advantage in life, so that you could get into the best college and the best law school and have the best opportunities. And who do you think paid for all of that? Who do you think worked sixty hours a week, and put aside his own wants and needs for that?"

I stare at him, saying nothing, as tears drip down my cheeks. He takes a deep breath, and then leans in toward me, resting his elbows on his knees.

"Look, I know that cutting myself off was selfish, and I know that it's hard for you to understand. But I needed some time where there was no guilt about whether I was with you kids enough, and no voice in the back of my head always telling me not to do something or not to buy something because it was that much less that I could give to you." He smiles at me—a wistful smile. "I was young when you were born—too young—and I never had that time in my life to explore who I am. So after your mother and I got divorced, and you and your brother were both in college and old enough to take care of yourselves, I took it. And I'm sorry if I hurt you, but I'm not sorry that I did it. I have a much clearer understanding of life now, and of what's important, and that's the reason I'm here."

I wipe my nose with the back of my hand. "And that is what, exactly?"

He smiles. "To tell you that I am ready to have a family again. You and your brother—"

I cut him off. "He's in Malaysia," I inform him coldly. "He's teaching ESL there for a year."

He rolls his eyes. "Why am I not surprised?" he asks. "He always was an off-the-beaten-path kind of a kid, wasn't he?" He looks thoughtful for a second, then shrugs and continues where he left off. "Well, then just you, and your husband—"

I cut him off again. "His name is Andrew," I say snidely, but this time he ignores me.

"And now there's your beautiful new baby. . . ." He takes a deep breath before going on. "And there's someone else, too," he says.

I stare at him. "Who?" I ask, praying that he is not about to inform me that I have a five-year-old half brother or sister who's being raised in a clothing-optional commune somewhere in New Mexico.

"Well," he answers. "There's Nadine. My fiancée."

My heart stops. His *what*? "Your *what*?"

"My fiancée." He beams at me. "I'm engaged!"

Engaged? I think. *What kind of woman could possibly want to marry my father?* But then I remember the four million dollars, and I know exactly the kind of woman who would want to marry my father.

"What is she," I say sarcastically, "twenty-two? Twenty-three?"

He laughs. "She's forty-nine," he says. "I met her in Vegas. We were playing at the same craps table and we were having the most amazing run—the kid throwing the dice was there for his twenty-first birthday—I always look for those kids; they have the best luck, especially the girls—and afterward we got a drink and we've been together ever since."

"And she lives in LA?" I ask. "Is that why you moved here?"

"Yeah," he says. "She used to work in Vegas. She was, um, a dancer"—by the way, in case you're not familiar with Vegas lingo, *dancer* means stripper—"and then when she got tired of doing that"—and *tired of doing that* means that she got too old or too fat, or both—"she moved to LA, where she, um, did some other stuff for a while"—*other stuff*, in this case, could have several meanings. It could mean that she did porno movies, or that she was an escort, or even a hooker maybe—"but she's retired now"—and, of course, *retired* means that she found a rich guy to support the lifestyle to which she would very much like to become accustomed—"and now we're getting married." And so you see, children, the gambling addict/deadbeat dad/lucky, nouveau-riche son of a bitch and the former stripper/adult entertainer/ho-bag lived happily ever after, just like in *Pretty Woman*. What a lovely story.

"When?" I ask him.

"In September. Labor Day weekend. And I'd like for you to meet her." He grins at me like a schoolboy in love. I do not grin back.

"No," I say flatly. "Absolutely not."

His grin disappears. "Why not?" he asks.

"Because. *You* may have decided that you suddenly want this big, wonderful family, but it's not your decision to make." I'm sobbing, and there is snot pouring down my face. "I have my own family now, and you don't get to just walk in here and claim it for yourself. I'm not meeting her." I choke back a sob as I remember Stacey's advice. "I don't even know if I want to see *you* again."

He purses his lips. "Okay," he says, holding out his hands. "I can see that you're upset."

Wow, I think. *How intuitive.*

"If you don't want to meet her, that's okay. But don't shut me out, sweetie. Please. We can take it slow. I'm sure you still have a lot of questions for me, and I'll tell you anything you want to know. We need to work on our relationship. I get that."

"Oh, I'm so glad that you get it. And do you get that you're the one who wrecked it in the first place?"

He nods at me. "Yes. I do. Listen, I think that I should leave and let you process this for a little while. But I'd really like it if we could have lunch next week, just the two of us. Here's the number where I'm staying."

He pulls out a card from the Beverly Hills Hotel and puts it down on the coffee table. I can't believe that he's staying there. The Beverly Hills Hotel is, like, five hundred dollars a night. If I were a betting woman (which I'm not), I'd take the under on Nadine tearing through that four million in a year or less and then leaving him for the next big slot winner she finds.

He stands up and walks back toward the front door, and I follow him with Parker still asleep on my shoulder. He opens the door and turns around to face me, then leans in to give me a hug. I back away.

"Okay," he says with a touch of sadness. "Think about lunch, will you?"

I shrug my shoulders at him, and as he walks out, I close the door behind him with a slam.

Not twenty minutes later, Andrew arrives home to find me in Parker's bathroom, sniffling the tail end of my tears as I bathe her.

"Hey." He sighs, sounding weary at the sight of me crying yet again. "What's wrong with you today?"

Oh, he's going to feel so bad about that comment when I tell him. I close my eyes and inhale dramatically.

"My father was here," I announce, glaring at him.

"What? He was here, in our house?" I nod. "I don't understand," he says. "He just showed up out of the blue?"

"On the doorstep," I say. "Apparently he's moved to LA and he wants to have a family again. Oh, and he's engaged. To a stripper." Andrew raises his eyebrows, and I can see that he's trying to suppress his excitement. I know exactly what he's thinking—*a hot stripper in the family!*—so I roll my eyes at him. "Forget it," I say. "She's old." The eyebrows drop. He's such a *guy*.

"Well, what did he say? Did you ask him why he disappeared?"

"Yeah. He basically said that he resented me because he had to make sacrifices so that I could have advantages in life." I lift Parker out of the baby tub and wrap a towel around her as I sniffle. "Can you believe that? What kind of a parent feels that way?"

Andrew is silent, and I can tell that there's something he wants to say.

"What?" I ask. "What are you thinking?"

He shakes his head. "Nothing."

"I know you're thinking something. Just say it."

"It's nothing. Forget it."

But I'm angry now. "No. Tell me. You obviously have something that you want to say."

Andrew takes a deep breath. "Well, I just think that that's the pot calling the kettle black." He closes his mouth and makes a surprised face, like he can't really believe that he let the words come out.

"What's that supposed to mean?" I ask.

He smiles at me, as if somehow smiling is going to make him sound less mean. "Oh, I don't know. A certain person not wanting to breast-feed because it interferes with her life too much? Sound familiar?"

Oh, he did *not* just say that.

"That's the worst analogy I ever heard, Andrew. I don't want to breast-feed because Parker eats all day and I can't ever leave the house for more than two hours at a time. He disappeared for eight years because he didn't want to have to spend his gambling money on my college tuition. I don't really think that that qualifies me as the pot, here."

He shrugs. "I'm just saying, it's all relative." He pauses for a second.

"And I never understood that expression, anyway. Why does the pot care if the kettle's black? Why is the pot jealous?"

Oh, my God. How is it possible that I am married to this man? I am a former English major. I wrote an honors thesis on Chaucer, for God's sake.

"The pot isn't jealous, Andrew," I snap at him. "The pot is black, too."

He squints, like he's thinking really hard, and then a wave of understanding washes over his face.

"Ohhhh," he says. "Then why don't they just get new ones?"

I look up at the sky and storm out of the bathroom, leaving him to question the wisdom of the pot and kettle owners by himself. Still fuming, I lay Parker down on her changing table and pull out her towel just as she starts to poop all over the changing pad.

Wonderful. What else can go wrong tonight?

As I clean up the mess, I remember the first time that Andrew changed a poop diaper, when we were in the hospital. The nurse told him that he had to make sure that he really opened up the labial folds and got in there with the gauze pads, because otherwise Parker could get a bacterial infection. Andrew went pale when he heard the words *labial folds.* It was as if it had never before occurred to him that his daughter would actually have an anatomically correct vagina, and not a little plastic mound like the doll that we had practiced on in the stupid infant-care class that we took.

He does have a point, though. No, not about the labial folds. About me. And my dad. You know, maybe I am like him. They say that children of addicts are more likely to be addicts themselves; that it's a genetic thing. But I'm not a gambler. I hate gambling. Nothing upsets me more than losing money that could have been spent on a great pair of shoes. *Nothing.* But what about a selfish gene? Could I have inherited that instead?

My thoughts are interrupted as Parker begins to cry again, and my first instinct is to yell for Andrew and make him deal with her. I start to walk toward our bedroom to go get him, but then I remember what Deloris said, about how babies can sense when you're stressed. So I take a deep breath.

Try to be calm and loving. Try to be calm and loving.

"Shhh," I say to her. "What's the matter, sweetie? Shhhh. Don't cry." But she doesn't stop. Somehow I don't think she's buying my calm-and-loving act.

My God, why can't I be calm and loving? Why does it always have to be an act? Suddenly I can hear my mother's voice in my head, yelling at my father.

Ronny, get off the couch and help Lara with her homework.

No, Ronny, you cannot go to Atlantic City this weekend; you promised Lara that you would go to her softball game.

Ronny, stop watching the football game and read Lara a story.

And he did. He did all of those things. God, when he first took off, I remember crying to Stacey about how I didn't understand it, because he wasn't a bad father. I remember defending him, and saying that he did stuff with me all the time when I was kid.

He used to help me with my homework, I told her. *He used to cheer for me at my softball games.*

But now I get it. I finally get it. He didn't do those things because he wanted to. He did them because he had to. Because my mom made him. Or because, like he said, he felt guilty about not doing them. Suddenly it all makes sense. The leaving, the cutting off ties. He was able to do it because none of the time that he spent with me was real. There was always somewhere else he wanted to be.

Oh, my God.

My mind begins to flash through the last few days, since Deloris got here, and I realize that I've been spending every possible minute away from the house. The gym, lunch, the bookstore, hair appointments, nail appointments, bikini waxing, shopping; I just come home to feed Parker, or to pump so that Deloris can give her a bottle, and then I go right back out again. And when I'm with her after Deloris goes to bed, it's because I have to be. Never because I want to be. I feel my eyes well up with tears. *Just like him.*

Oh, my God. I am my father.

seven

Stacey has agreed to go hiking with me this morning. I called her yesterday, hysterical, to tell her about my revelation—about how I'm just like my dad—but she had to go into a meeting and then she had to be on a set all afternoon with one of her clients, so she didn't have time to talk to me. But I guess she could tell that I'm not joking around, because she offered to take a break from work today—just this one day, and only because it's a Sunday—to spend a few hours with me so that I can vent.

I haven't seen her in months—she still hasn't come by to see the baby—and when she arrives, ten minutes late, she looks pallid and, if it's possible, even thinner than usual.

"Hi," I say, giving her a kiss on the cheek. "You look awful."

"Thanks," she says, eyeing my flabby arms. "So do you."

We start out toward the trail, and I feel obligated to begin with some small talk.

"So, how's it going at work? Do you think you're going to make partner?"

She sighs. "I have no fucking idea. They're so secretive about it. They all know that I work my ass off, but there's that one partner, Liz, who has it in for me, and she's got a lot of power. If she can convince two other partners to vote against me, I'm out."

"Wow," I say. "So, have you thought about what you'd do if you didn't make it?"

She gives me a look of disdain, as if she doesn't want to even entertain the idea.

"Sorry," I say. "I just meant on the off-off chance that it doesn't happen, is there anything you'd *want* to do?"

"Like become a college counselor?" she quips. "No, thank you. And now that you've put all of this negativity out into the universe, do you think we can talk about something else? Like your dad, maybe? Isn't that why we're here?"

I sigh. "Fine. What do you want to know?"

She glares at me. "I want to know why you called me yesterday, hysterical. What did he say?"

"He didn't really say anything. He needed to find himself and he's ready to work on our relationship and some crap like that."

Stacey looks at me impatiently. "So then if he didn't say anything, what were you so upset about?"

I bite the inside of my cheek. "Well, after he left I started remembering some stuff about when I was a kid, and I realized a few things about him. Like how my mom used to always *make* him spend time with me. And that made me realize that he never *wanted* to spend time with me."

Stacey is looking at me like I am the stupidest person on the planet. "You just realized that? The guy disappears for eight years and it just occurs to you now that he didn't want to spend time with you?"

"No," I say. "I knew that. It's not that, exactly."

"Then what is it, Lara?" She sounds angry. Like I've wasted her time.

"Look, I don't expect you to understand. It's just that I realized that I'm more like him than I thought I was, and it upset me." Stacey's breathing has started to get heavy, and we're only about a quarter of the way into the uphill part of the hike. I have a sneaking suspicion that she hasn't been outside since the last time we went hiking, and that was almost four months ago, when I was eight months pregnant.

"How?" she pants. "How are you like him?"

I think about whether I should say what I want to say, because everyone knows that saying something out loud makes it true. But I decide to say it. After all, it is true.

"I'm a shitty parent," I exclaim. "I think that my baby is boring, and I have no desire to spend time with her, so unless I absolutely have to, I don't, and that's just how my father was. There, I said it."

Stacey starts to laugh. "Are you kidding me?" she says. "Your baby *is* boring. All babies are boring. Why do you think I haven't come by to see her yet?" She doesn't wait for me to venture a guess. "Because I don't have to. Because I already know that she's going to just sit there and do nothing except bore me, and if I'm going to be bored I'd rather do it at work, where I can at least bill for my time."

"That's nice," I say. "You know, if you don't make partner, you should think about getting a job at Hallmark."

Stacey grins at me. "Yeah," she says. "I can write the sympathy cards." I laugh. "Anyway," she says, "my point is, it doesn't make you a shitty parent just because you think your baby is boring. Only liars and people who are on heavy medication are enthralled by newborns."

"I don't know," I say. "Julie loves babies. You should have seen her with Parker. Parker screamed the whole time she was over and all she could say was how sweet she is and how much she misses that stage."

Stacey gives me a look. "Like I said . . ."

I make a face at her and take a swig of water. "Look, I hear what you're saying, but you don't want to be a parent. It's different for me. I want to love her, but I just don't feel it." I shake my head. "I'm telling you, it's a gene. It's a shitty-parent gene. The only time I've ever felt anything remotely like love for her was when I thought that she got kidnapped the other day. But as soon as I knew she was fine, I went right back to wanting to hand her off to Deloris again. That's pretty shitty."

Stacey looks confused. "Okay, I don't know what the kidnapping thing is about, but you're kind of overreacting. Try to remember back to when you had a real job—I know it's hard—and see if your brain cells are still capable of rational thought."

"That's exactly the problem," I say. "I can't think about this rationally. I have no idea how to approach it. All my life I've always been good at everything. I was good at school, I was good at being a lawyer, I'm great at college counseling. Things usually come naturally to me. But this is the one thing that's supposed to come naturally, and it doesn't. Not at all. It's like when I was in high school, and I took calculus. I always did fine in honors-level math classes, but then calc came along and I had no idea what I was doing. Everybody got it except for me, and no matter how hard I worked, I just felt lost. Lost and completely overwhelmed." I can feel myself starting to choke up. "Do you see what I mean?" I ask her.

"Not really," she says. "I got an A in calc."

I roll my eyes at her. "Well, believe me," I tell her, "you wouldn't get an A in this."

She nods. "I know," she says. "And that's exactly why I don't want kids."

Her smugness is starting to piss me off, and she can tell. She stops walking, takes a swig of her water, and then screws the cap back on. She's breathing like she's on the verge of a heart attack.

"Listen, Lara," she says, trying to catch her breath in between words, "you're being really hard on yourself. Just because it's not easy doesn't mean you can't be good at it." She bends over and rests her hands on the tops of her knees, as if she's trying to snatch up the rising air before anyone else can. "And even if there is such a thing as a shitty-parent gene, which I really don't think there is, people overcome bad genes all the time." She stands back up again, and her face is bright purple. "Please, half of my clients grew up with celebrity drug addicts for parents, and I can think of at least three who turned out okay."

I stare at her for a second. "You are the most out-of-shape skinny person I have ever seen," I announce.

She nods, and motions that she is ready to start walking again.

"So what are you saying?" I ask. "That even if I am genetically inclined to be a bad parent, I can learn to be different?" I put my hands on my hips as we start up a steep incline, and Stacey nods.

"Yeah," she says. "Just like how, if you had really tried, instead of pussing out and complaining about how hard it was, you probably could have learned calculus."

I give her a bitchy fake smile. "Okay," I say, ready to challenge her argument. "Then tell me this: How do you *learn* how to love someone?"

She shakes her head at me, as if I have disappointed her. "You don't," Stacey says, as if I am an idiot. "You *learn* how to parent. So even if you hate your kid, you can at least raise her well." She shrugs. "I'm telling you, though, it's not all that shocking that you don't love her yet. She doesn't *do* anything. What is there to love? People fall in love when there's a relationship, and there's no relationship with a newborn. Everyone is just full of shit, and they say that they love their babies so much because they're afraid of what people will think of them if they tell the truth."

I have to admit, she kind of makes sense. It's a harsh, mean kind of sense, but it's sense nonetheless. I shake my head.

"So basically what you're telling me is that I'm not a shitty mother; I've just got a shitty relationship with my daughter." I scoff at myself. "God, this is what it must be like to have a teenager. You know, all of those crazy parents I have at Bel Air are suddenly a lot more relatable."

Stacey laughs. "Yeah. I'll bet you we'll be having the exact same conversation in fifteen years." She pretends to imitate me, mock crying as she talks. " 'Stace, Parker is so moody and miserable. I can't stand being around her. Do you think that means that I'm a shitty mother?' "

I sigh. "Okay," I say. "So, then, it's just one more shitty relationship to add to the list. I now officially have a trifecta of shitty relationships."

Stacey looks at me, confused. "Parker," she says, lifting up her index finger. "Your dad," she says, lifting her middle finger. "Who else?"

I raise three fingers on my right hand and grimace. "Andrew," I say. "We haven't stopped fighting since Parker was born."

Stacey makes a face as if she suddenly understands, and then she smiles. "That one's easy," she announces. "You two just need to have some kick-ass make-up sex, that's all."

I nod at her. *Honey,* I think, *you're preachin' to the choir.*

That night, I decide to put Operation Kick-ass Make-up Sex into action. Andrew went into the office all day today to catch up with work and he's coming home late again, but for once I don't mind because, in this case, it actually helps my objective by giving me some extra time to prepare. Its ten o'clock, and I've already put Parker to bed, taken a shower, and gussied myself up for the festivities. And by *gussied,* I mean that I've tousled my hair, put on some lip gloss, and decked myself out in a black-and-white silk robe, underneath which I am wearing a two-piece Cosabella set that my assistant at work gave me as a happy-you're-not-pregnant-anymore gift. It's just a camisole and a matching boy-shorts/thong kind of bottom, but it is by far the sexiest thing that I've had on in months. And even though the camisole doesn't quite cover my entire stomach and therefore does nothing to hide the spare tire that has settled around my waist, it's definitely more flattering than any of the other lingerie that I own, all of which was bought around the time of my wedding, when I was superskinny and at my lowest weight since high school.

I sigh. I've had to pee for the last half hour, but with my luck he'll come walking in the door the second that I get up, and I'll lose the element of surprise. Of course, I could have peed fifty-seven times by now, but that's beside the point.

Ah. I just heard the garage door open. Perfect.

I run my hand through my hair and lie back on the pillows, striking the classic, I'm-so-sexy-because-I-have-one-knee-bent pose. I hear him stop in the kitchen to look through the mail; then I hear footsteps on the stairs, and finally he opens the door to our bedroom.

As soon as he sees me, he shoots me a confused look.

"Hi," I say, trying to sound seductive.

"Hi," he says, sounding just as confounded as he looks. "What's going on?"

Ugh. How does he not know what is going on? Normally when he gets home late I'm in an old T-shirt, sweatpants, and glasses and I have zit cream on my chin. I sit up and drop the pose.

"Nothing. I've just been waiting for you."

"Sorry," he mumbles, turning his back to me as he unbuttons his shirt. "I got caught up."

"It's fine," I say in my sweetest voice possible. "I just missed you." He looks at me again like he has absolutely no idea who I am, so I decide to get a bit more aggressive. I stand up and walk over to him, and I begin to rub his shoulders. "I was just thinking that, you know, it's been a while since we've really spent time together."

At this, he turns around to face me. "That's because you hate me," he proclaims.

I make a hurt face, and stick out my lower lip. "I don't hate you. I *resented* you because you got to go out all day and I had to stay home with the baby. But Deloris is here now, so I'm over it."

"Oh, I'm so thrilled," he says. "My wife has stopped resenting me now that she doesn't have to take care of our child."

I close my eyes and try not to get hostile. *Make-up sex. Make-up sex.*

He pulls off his undershirt and tosses it across the room, into the hamper, and I quickly change the subject.

"You look hot," I say.

"I'm fat," he declares, pinching the skin at his waist. "I've definitely gained at least three pounds since Parker was born." Oh, he's such a guy, yet sometimes such a woman.

"You're not fat," I murmur. "You look great." *And speaking of fat . . .* I stand up again and untie my robe, letting it fall away to the sides of me. "Look at this," I say, lowering my eyes. "What do you think?"

He stares at me. "Is that a trick question?" he asks, looking at me with suspicion in his eyes.

"No," I say, frowning. "Why? Do I look that bad?"

"No," he says quickly. "Not *that* bad."

Okay. That's enough. I put my hands on my hips. My ample hips. "Not *that* bad?"

He winces. "I didn't mean it like that. I just mean that, you know, you don't look like yourself."

I can't believe he just said that. How is it possible that he can still have the capacity to say something like that after being with me for almost ten years? Has he learned nothing? I am furious.

"I just had a baby seven weeks ago, Andrew," I shout. "I'm sorry that I don't look like *myself*." I tie up my robe again and walk away from him. "God, I'm trying to make an effort here and you're being so"—I pause as I search for the word—"so *rude*." His eyes open wide and I can tell that he has just figured out what's been going on.

"Ohhh," he says, his voice softening. "I'm sorry. I didn't realize that that's what . . . Wait, are we even allowed to have sex yet?"

I roll my eyes at him. "Yes, we are. I told you that last week, after I saw Dr. Lowenstein. I'm back on the pill and everything." I pout at him, trying not to cry. "I just want us to be us again. I miss us. I hate fighting with you all of the time."

He walks over to me and puts his hands around my spare tire, a sly grin spreading across his face.

"Me, too," he says. "And I'm so glad that you're willing to admit that it was all your fault."

Ahh, there's the Andrew that I know and love. I fake-hit him on the shoulder, but before I can say anything back, he's kissing me. *Finally*. I breathe a sigh of relief, and I lean into him.

Oh, yeah. That feels good. I forgot what a great kisser he is. He pushes me back onto the bed and kisses my ears, and then my neck, but I stop him when he gets to my boobs.

"Don't," I whisper. I'm thinking about what happened at the restaurant with Julie the other day. If my boobs aren't smart enough to distinguish between Parker's cries and some random stranger's baby's cries, then I certainly don't trust them to distinguish between Parker's mouth and Andrew's.

"Why not?" he whispers back.

"Just trust me," I say. Andrew seems puzzled, but he doesn't push it, moving back up to my neck instead. After a few more minutes of this, the two of us are going at it, and I am beginning to remember why I decided to spend the rest of my life with this man. Oh, and also why I'm so glad that I asked for a C-section. No stretched-out vagina or postepisiotomy pain for me, thank you.

God, this feels good. I really, really miss this.

After a few minutes more, my back is arched, my heart is pounding, and I'm in the zone. My eyes are closed, my nails are digging into Andrew's shoulder, and I'm concentrating really hard. I start to moan, but before I can even get out my first *Oh, yeah,* I am interrupted by Andrew, who is screaming like a girl.

"Uck . . . ick . . . uck," he yells.

My eyes fly open and I am confronted with the image of my husband, completely naked and on top of me, shielding his face with his hands while breast milk sprays straight up out of my nipples. And when I say *spray,* I mean *spray*. Like a blowhole, or a geyser. *Hi, nice to meet you, I'm Lara, but please, call me Old Faithful; all of my friends do.*

I want to *die*. As quickly as I can, I sit up and cover my boobs with both hands, pushing Andrew off of me. I jump out of bed and run to the bathroom, locking the door behind me. *I can't believe that nobody told me this could happen. I'm going to* kill *Julie.* About a minute later, Andrew is knocking on the door.

"Dolly? Lar? Are you okay?"

"No, I'm not okay," I yell, trying not to cry as I wipe myself off with a towel. "My boobs just went off like a sprinkler system. Would you be okay?" Silence. Then he knocks again.

"You know something, honey? I think that maybe you should just stop breast-feeding."

I am stunned to hear him say this. That's it? That's all it took? One squirt in the eye and he's sold our kid down the river?

"But what about the baby?" I ask, still not opening the door. "I thought that you wanted her to have every advantage."

He pauses. "Yeah, well, she'll live. I did."

I open the door. "Are you sure?" I ask. "Because I don't want a guilt trip from you eighteen years from now if she doesn't get into a good college."

He thinks this over for a minute. "Will it really make you that happy?" he asks. I nod at him. Vigorously. He sighs. "Then I'm sure. No more guilt, I promise."

I lower my eyes. "Do you think this makes me like my dad?" I ask meekly.

Andrew shakes his head at me. "No. I'm sorry I said that. It's not the same."

"Really?"

He nods. "I swear."

I purse my lips and give him a fake smile. "Okay, then," I say. "I'll stop. Tomorrow is it." I give him a big hug.

This is exactly what I wanted, I think. *So how come I don't feel happy about it?*

At nine o'clock the next morning, Parker still isn't up yet. By eight fifteen I was starting to think that maybe she had stopped breathing, or that she had died of SIDS, and I stared at the monitor for a good ten minutes, growing more panic-stricken by the second, until, finally, I saw her move her left hand, at which point I stopped worrying and just got annoyed again.

Annoyed because I have been lying in bed since six o'clock, my eyes wide open, my boobs chock-full of milk, anticipating the start of the banshee noise. But I just don't know if I can wait any longer. I mean, at six my boobs were full, but fine. At seven they were starting to get a little bit itchy. By eight, they had turned into two giant, hot, painful rocks, and a few minutes ago they started dripping like leaky faucets.

Shit. I don't want to wake her up—this is the longest stretch of sleep that she's ever had, and if this is going to become a habit I certainly don't want to interfere with it—but I really don't want to pump, either. I know it's hard to believe, but I was actually looking forward to our final nursing session this morning. I was up half the night planning for it. I was going to be sweet and gentle with her, and I was going to sing her songs and cuddle her, and do all of the things that the books say you should do while you're nursing your baby, because if, by chance, some buried memory of infancy happens to surface later in her life, I was hoping that she would remember that and not all of the times that I got impatient with her, or stripped her down naked to try to wake her up when she fell asleep midfeeding.

I can't wait another day to stop, either. Parker was born exactly seven weeks ago, and I'm entirely too anal to breast-feed for seven weeks and one day. No, if I want to end on a round number, I'm going to have to let go of my nursing fantasy and just pump.

Oh, well.

I assemble my breast pump and put on my S and M pumping bra, and as I sit on the floor, waiting for the bottles to fill, I am surprised to realize that I'm feeling nostalgic. I pat the pump gently a few times with my hand.

"We've had some good times, you and I," I say to it, feeling Luthor trying to form in my throat. "Good times."

When the ten minutes are up and I have two full, four-ounce bottles sitting in the refrigerator, I go into the bathroom, open the medicine cabinet, and take out the bottle of milk-drying-up pills, trying not to notice how heavy my heart feels.

You're doing the right thing, I tell myself. *You have nothing to feel guilty about.* And even though I'm not convinced that I believe any of this, I quickly swallow the pill that will begin the end of my lactation.

All right, then. Time for plan B.

By the time that I am showered and dressed, Parker has finally woken up, and Deloris has fed her one of the bottles, gotten her changed out of her pajamas, and is playing with her on the floor of her bedroom. I stand in the threshold of her doorway and watch them for a minute, and then I clear my throat.

"Hi, Deloris. She slept really late today, huh?"

"She sure did," Deloris says, poking her in the stomach. "My baby finally caught up on some sleep."

God, I hate that. She's been calling her *my baby* all week. But only to me. She never does it when Andrew's around. Deloris tickles Parker under her chin and makes little baby noises to her. "She should start smiling any day now," she says to me, not taking her eyes off of the baby. "Any day now, Miss Parker," she sings.

Great, I think. I can't wait for her to smile at Deloris and not at me. Just one more thing for me to be upset about.

"Um, Deloris," I say, "I'm meeting a friend of mine at the park, and I'm going to take Parker with me. I just need to pack up the diaper bag and then I'll be right back to get her."

"Okay, Mrs. Lara," she says, sounding shocked to hear that I'm not going out by myself, as I usually do. "Do you need me to come with you?" she asks.

No, I don't need *you to come with me.* God, I can't imagine what this woman must think of me. I'll bet she tells her voodoo friends that she works for an ice lady. I can just hear her *tsk-tsk*-ing me to them. *Not one minute with that child. I'm telling you, she's got a stone where her heart should be. Deloris knows these things.*

"No, thanks," I say with a big smile. "I'll be fine."

I walk back down to the kitchen, where I put the bottle of breast milk in a cooler, and I stick it inside the diaper bag so that Deloris won't see it. I'll tell her that I've stopped breast-feeding later. I don't need her giving me a guilt trip right now.

"Okay," I say, returning to the bedroom. "All set." Deloris picks Parker up off of the floor and proceeds to kiss her all over her face.

"Bye-bye, my baby," she says, waving her hand up and down, and then she lowers her voice to a whisper. "Don't you worry, Miss Parker, Deloris will be right here waiting for you when you get back. Don't you be scared."

I look at her like she's insane. Does she think I couldn't hear that? How rude is that? Ugh. Whatever. I don't have the energy for this right now.

Ignorning Deloris, I reach over and take Parker out of her arms, bracing myself for the screaming to commence, as it always does whenever I take her away from Deloris. But, miraculously enough, she doesn't scream. *Huh.* I wonder what that's about. I wonder if she's catching on to the fact that Deloris is a little loony. Well, in any event, I'll take it.

I walk down the stairs with Deloris behind me—she's holding on to Parker's foot and dabbing at her own eyes with a tissue—and then I strap Parker into her car seat. After a ridiculous, tearful good-bye, I finally get Deloris to shut the car door, and then the two of us head off for the park.

We need to have a talk, Parker and me.

When we get to the park—a quiet little place in Beverly Hills—I unload her from the car and find a bench under a nice, shady tree. I take her out of the car seat and sit down with her in my arms—she's still not crying, by the way—and after a few minutes I pull out the bottle and begin to feed her her very last four ounces of IQ-boosting, metabolism-increasing, teeth-straightening, allergy-fighting, might-as-well-be-magic breast milk. Luthor has made an encore appearance, and I look around to see if anyone is watching me. No. The place is empty.

Okay, I think. *I can let it go now.* And, just like that, I start to sob.

"I'm sorry," I say to Parker through my tears. "I'm sorry that I'm selfish"—*sob*—"and I'm sorry that I'm impatient." *Sob, sob, sob.* "And I'm sorry that I want to go out during the day and not be tied to you like a pair of handcuffs." *Biiiiiig sob.* "And I'm really, really, really sorry that I don't feel like waiting anymore to get skinny again."

She's staring up at me, sucking on the bottle and looking me right in the eye.

"I just don't have strong maternal instincts," I confess, "and I really have no idea how to be a good mommy." I take a deep breath and try to get my crying under control. "But here's the thing," I tell her. "My friend Stacey—you don't know her yet, but you will; she'll be the one who gives you your first cigarette and teaches you to say *fuck off* to me when you're two—anyway, she said something that made a lot of sense." I try to hold the bottle in her mouth with my left elbow so that I can wipe the tears out of my eyes, but it falls out and Parker starts to cry. "Sorry," I say, putting it back in. "Anyway, what she said—well, not in these exact words, really, but the gist of what she said—is that we have to build a relationship, and she's right." I sniffle.

"But I can't do that if I'm breast-feeding, because it makes me frustrated with you, and it makes me resent you." I take a deep breath, waiting to drop the bomb. "And so I've decided to stop. Because even though it probably doesn't seem like it right now, our relationship is important to me. More important than your IQ." I pause, afraid to tell her how else I may be ruining her life. "And more important than your weight. But if you need it, I'll get you a personal trainer, I promise. And if you need braces . . . well, braces aren't all that bad anymore. They make clear ones now; you can hardly even tell that they're there. And if you develop a peanut allergy . . . well, I'm sorry, okay? I acknowledge that that would totally suck, and I'm really, really sorry." I pause again, trying to think of something positive that I can say about this. Oh, I know. "The good news is, both of your parents went to Penn, so even if you're not that smart, you still have a really good chance of getting in. Of course, you'd have to apply early decision, but we can discuss the logistics of it later."

Parker still hasn't stopped staring at me. It's like she understands every word that I'm saying. Then, suddenly, from behind the nipple of the bottle, I see the corners of her mouth turn up. She must have gas. I take the bottle out of her mouth and I try to shake out some of the bubbles, but when I look down at her again, the smile is still there. It's big and toothless and the cutest thing I've ever seen.

Oh, my God, I think. *She's smiling at me. It's her first smile and she's giving it to* me.

Without thinking, I smile back at her, and I feel my eyes welling up again. Within seconds tears begin to spill down my cheeks, but these tears feel different from the ones that I've been crying since she was born.

That's it, I think. *From now on I am going to spend as much time as I can with her, whether I like it or not. Because I am not going to be like my father. She deserves better than that. We both do.*

As Parker finishes her bottle, we sit there like that: me crying away my guilt, and her smiling up at me, forgiving me for all of my flaws. And for the very first time in her short little life, I am overcome with love for my baby.

eight

"Well, good morning! Welcome to Mommy and Me."

A shockingly happy woman in her early fifties is standing by the front door of a large, empty room in the far corner of the Beverly Hills Recreational Center. She's about five-foot-three, her brown, shoulder-length hair is streaked with blond, and she's wearing pink Tods loafers with jeans and a V-neck T-shirt. When she reaches out to shake my hand, I notice that she's wearing a ginormous pear-shaped engagement ring, and that she's got Ballet Slippers on her short, freshly manicured nails. So this is the famous Susan Greenspan. *Huh.* Nothing like what I expected. But then again, I was expecting Miss Sally from *Romper Room,* so it's not that surprising.

"And who is this little love?" she asks, pinching Parker's cheeks, which have, I am convinced, become abnormally pinchable ever since we started her on formula. My mother (who hasn't even been out to see Parker yet since her sciatica prevents her from sitting on a plane for four hours, yet who miraculously can sit in a chair at the hair salon for three and half hours while she gets her highlights done), calls them "puhpee cheeks," and every time she sees Parker (via the webcam that I, in a ludicrous burst of optimism, assumed could be viewed by a person who calls e-mail "the e-mail" *without* my having to first spend forty minutes explaining how one logs on to the internet every time), she swears that they're considered adorable, but I don't think so. I think they make her look like somebody's using her to smuggle a wad of cash into Mexico.

"This is Parker," I say. "Parker Stone."

"Ahh, yes," Susan says. "So that must make you"—she consults a ledger that is sitting on a chair behind her—"Lara!" I nod. "Well, we're glad to have you here, Lara." I glance around, trying to determine who the "we" might be, but no one else is in the room. "It looks like you two are the first to arrive, so leave your stroller outside and have a seat on the floor. I'm sure the other mommies will be here soon."

"Okay," I say. I lift Parker out of her Snap-N-Go and walk toward the back of the room, where I sit down Indian-style. The floor is hardwood and it looks like it's just been cleaned, but I don't want to put Parker down on a wood floor, so I hold her on my lap.

"You can lay the baby down on a blanket in front of you," Susan calls from her post at the door. *A blanket?* I rifle through the new Burberry diaper bag that I bought last week, hoping that I tossed a blanket in there and just forgot about it. Nope. No blanket.

"Um, I don't think I have a blanket with me," I say.

Susan looks at me, surprised. "You don't have a blanket?" She gasps.

"Well, no," I say. "It's summer."

She purses her lips. "Babies can't regulate their body temperatures the way we can. You should always carry a blanket with you."

Shamed, I again glance into my bag. "I will," I say. "I have a changing pad, is that okay?"

She gives me a weak smile. "It's better than a dirty floor, I suppose."

I hang my head and pull out the waterproof nylon plaid Burberry changing pad that came with my bag and lay it on the floor in front of me, placing Parker on top of it, faceup.

After about two minutes of awkward silence, the other moms start to trickle in, and one after the next they whip out giant, beautiful Petunia Pickle Bottom blankets and carefully lay their babies down on top of them. I sigh. I have three of them at home that I've never used. Well, next week, I guess. Assuming that I decide to come back.

When Susan closes the door, there is a circle comprised of one brunette, eleven fake blondes, and thirteen babies (one poor girl has *twins,* if you can imagine), and, to my surprise, they all look pretty normal. Well, no, let me rephrase that. Not normal, rest-of-the-country normal, but normal for LA. Meaning that, on a Wednesday morning at ten A.M., to sit on a dusty floor and sing stupid baby songs, they have all chosen to wear jeans or cropped black pants, beaded and/or rhinestoned thongs, and some version of a lightweight summer poncho over a James Perse tank top. Six of them have Gucci diaper bags, four have Prada diaper bags, and one fancy girl has a Louis Vuitton.

I, of course, not being a native of Los Angeles and therefore not privy to *The West Side Girl's Dress Code Manual for All Events (Even the Most Insignificant)*, have shown up in black velour sweatpants, my old, beat-up black velvet platform thongs, and a blue C & C California T-shirt. I sigh again. I can't believe that I have underdressed for Mommy and Me. I didn't even get the diaper bag right.

At the front of the circle, Susan has settled into a folding chair with a green toile cushion on it, and she claps her hands together to get our attention.

"Ladies, welcome to Mommy and Me," she says with a huge, knowing smile on her face. "The goal of this class is to help you to become the best mommy you can be to your new baby, and to provide you with information and a safe place to discuss any problems or issues that you might be having. All of the babies here were born in April, so each week we'll cover a different topic that is relevant to the developmental stage that your children are in. Then, during the last fifteen minutes, we'll do some singing and dancing"—*dancing?*—"and at the end of each class we'll save a few minutes for questions." She flashes the smile again.

"Okay. Why don't we start by introducing ourselves. Please tell us your name, your baby's name, and when your baby was born." As each woman takes her turn, I take this opportunity to make quick judgments about the other moms and to compare Parker to the other babies. Oh, like you wouldn't.

Hmmm, I think, glancing around. *She's really skinny already—I don't like her; that baby has really big ears; mom near the door thinks her poncho is hiding her big stomach but it's not; whoa, that baby has a serious schnoz on him.* . . . The woman next to me, a short fake blonde whose poncho is made of a sheer green fabric with light pink flowers on it, taps me on the arm.

"Your baby is so big," she whispers. "What percentile is she?"

I glance down at Parker, and then again at all of the other babies. God, she is big. I never realized it before. She looks like she could eat some of these kids.

"Um, at her last checkup she was eighty-third in height and ninety-seventh in weight," I whisper back.

The woman's eyes go wide. "Ninety-seventh," she says. "Wow."

I squint at her, not sure what to make of this *wow*. *Is Parker that fat?* I'm starting to get panicky about it, but just then a baby across the room starts to cry. The mom, a tall, pretty fake blonde with rock-star bangs, bright blue eyes, and four diamond eternity bands on her finger, picks up the baby, lifts up her black, crocheted poncho, and starts to nurse him, right there in front of everyone. I am stunned, but nobody else so much as bats an eye.

She's breast-feeding? I think. *But she looks so cool.*

A minute later another mom starts to nurse, and then another, and then another. I have a sinking feeling that I am the only selfish, non-breast-feeding mom in the room, and I am so unsettled by this that I don't even realize that it's my turn to introduce myself. The *wow* girl nudges me.

"Oh, sorry," I say. "I'm Lara Stone, and this is my daughter, Parker. She was born April second." The rock-star-mom's face lights up.

"My best friend just named her baby Parker!" she says.

The really skinny mom, also a fake blonde, nods her head in agreement. "My sister-in-law is naming her baby Parker," she says. "But she's having a boy."

I fake-smile, pretending that I am thrilled to learn that the name I thought was so unique is actually the new Madison.

As the next mom takes her turn, I notice out of the corner of my eye that Parker is starting to get squirmy, and that she's making little grunty noises.

Oh, no, I think. *Please don't get hungry.* I look at my watch and see that it's now ten fifteen. She ate at seven o'clock this morning, and I was hoping that she'd make it until class was over at eleven, but I don't think I'm going to get that lucky. *Shit.*

Just then, with absolutely no buildup whatsoever, Parker lets out the banshee noise, and everyone turns to stare at me. I instantly reach for my diaper bag, and my heart starts to pound as I realize that Lara and the Bottle Production is about become the focal point of the room. *Great.*

As if in slow motion, I pull out a bottle from my diaper bag, take off the nipple, and set it down on the floor. But when I hear the collective gasp at this display of unsanitariness, I quickly pick it back up and balance it on top of my right knee. I then take out a bottle of water and, spilling everywhere, pour in four ounces. Parker, meanwhile, is screaming so loud that she's about to break the sound barrier, and when I glance down at her, I see that her arms and legs are flailing about like she's having a grand mal seizure. I make a pathetic attempt to calm her down by saying, "Shhh, shh," as I take the lid off of the travel-size can of formula that I am carrying with me. I measure one level scoop, dump it in the bottle, then another level scoop, and dump that in the bottle. By now Parker's face is turning purple and she's coughing like she's about to vomit, and everyone in the room has stopped talking because they can't hear anything over my obviously abused daughter's cries.

"Almost ready," I whisper to her, "just two more seconds."

As I screw the nipple back onto the bottle and start to shake it, I realize that I am sweating profusely, and when I look up to see if anyone has noticed, I see that every person in the room, babies included, is staring at me in horror. Their eyes keep going from me, to the formula can, to my purple baby lying on a dirty changing pad, and then back to me again.

Okay, I think, looking at the bottle, which is still clumpy with formula. *Clumps or not, I'm giving it to you right now.*

I scoop Parker up off of the floor and shove the bottle into her mouth, and she begins to furiously suck as if I haven't fed her for a year. Oh, God. I don't know if I can ever recover from this. I glance up again, and across the room, Skinny Mom's eyeballs are bulging out of their sockets. No. I definitely can never recover from this. I'll have to ask Julie if there are any other classes she knows about that I could go to. That is, if Child Services doesn't come to my house this afternoon and take Parker away from me.

"Sorry," I say to everyone. "I'm so sorry."

"Well," says Susan, trying to recover gracefully. "Where were we?"

* * *

When class is over, everyone lingers to play the requisite round of Jewish geography—as usual, I know no one, since my maps are all oriented toward the East Coast—and when Susan is practically kicking us out the door, we all shuffle out of the room and head toward the spot where we left our strollers. When we get there, I am mortified. Lined up against the side of the building are eleven identical $799 Bugaboo Frog strollers, and one lone $49.99 Snap-N-Go.

God damn that Andrew, I think, sighing to myself. I told him that I wanted a Bugaboo, but he balked at the very idea of it.

Eight hundred dollars for a stroller? he yelled.

I tried to convince him why I absolutely needed it: *It glides like water,* I said. *You only need one hand to steer it,* I explained. *Madonna uses it!*

I almost had him at Madonna, but once he got his hands on the *Consumer Reports Guide to the Best Baby Products,* she was just another sucker who spent $750 more than she needed to.

The Snap-N-Go got four and a half stars and it's only fifty bucks! Why do you need an eight-hundred-dollar stroller when you can have this?

Of course, he would never understand that moments like this— moments when I'm the frumpy girl in sweats who's using formula and doesn't have a decent blanket to lay her baby down on—are *exactly* why I need an eight-hundred-dollar stroller, but it's okay. Parker was the only baby who smiled during the dancing part at the end of class, and that makes up for everything. Susan even made a comment about how cute she was.

As we stroll along toward the parking garage, the lone brunette in the class suggests that we all go and have lunch together at the salad place down the street. I look at my watch: it's three minutes after eleven. Puzzled, I tilt my head to the side.

"It's only eleven o'clock," I say. "Isn't that kind of early for lunch?"

The brunette gives me a head tilt of her own.

"No," she says. "I always eat at eleven. That way you miss the work crowd."

Ah, I think, a wave of understanding washing over me. *I should have known.* None of them work. No wonder Julie loves this class so much.

"Yeah," says the one whose baby has the big ears. "And then you never have to wait for a table."

The other moms nod in agreement, as if this were the most basic principle of nonworkingdom. Then, all at once, they click on their car keys, and there is a chorus of beeps that are all the exactly the same tone. I look toward the source of the noise: Range Rovers. Seven black and four silver. Strangely, I feel a sense of kinship toward the two girls who have the older models, from before Range Rover switched to the new body.

"Oh, well, thanks," I say, loading Parker into my non–Range Rover, "but I already have lunch plans for this afternoon."

I know you think that I'm lying, but I'm not. I'm meeting my father for lunch at one, in the Polo Lounge at the Beverly Hills Hotel. I'll have to tell him that next time we should make it for eleven.

"Oh, bummer," says the brunette, sounding genuinely bummed. "But I'm sure we'll go again next week. I mean, what else do we have to do, right?"

I put my arms out in front of me, palms up.

"Right!" I say, trying to sound as cheery as possible.

Yeah, right.

nine

So, yes, I called him. I called @#*!. After several hours of spirited debate with everyone I know, I decided that it was the right thing to do. Of course, everyone had a different reason why I should make the call. Here, see if you can match them up with the people who offered them (answers will *not* be listed at the end, because if you can't figure it out, you clearly are not paying attention):

1. It will be nice for Parker to know her grandfather.   A) Andrew
2. Maybe he'll give us some of the four million.   B) Julie
3. Maybe you'll stop obsessing about the fact that
   he showed up on your doorstep wanting to have
   a relationship with you, and maybe instead you
   can actually have a relationship with him.   C) Stacey

I suppose that all of these reasons are, in fact, reasonable, but to be honest, none of them is why I called him. No, I called him because I believe that he can teach me something about parenting. He can teach me how *not* to be. Because if I am serious about developing a relationship with my daughter, which I am, then I think that how not to be is the best place to start. And, really, what resource could possibly be better than a man whom I refer to as @#*!?

Still, I'm feeling a little nervous about meeting him, and I think that I could use a pep talk right about now. I dial Stacey's office on the new, hands-free speakerphone that Andrew just had installed in my car ("I don't want you driving our baby with one hand"), and after two rings, her secretary answers the phone.

"Stacey Horowitz's office."

"Hi, Janine, it's Lara." Ever since my dad showed up, Stacey's no-calls-at-work rule has gone out the window. I think I've talked to her more in the last six weeks than I have in the last six years. I'm screwed if she doesn't make partner, though. From now until eternity, I will be the bitch who forever ruined her career.

"Hey, what's up?" she says, clicking onto the line. She sounds distracted.

"Sorry," I say. "But I'm meeting my dad in an hour. Tell me it's going to be fine."

"It's going to be fine," she drones. Poor Stacey. This is the forty-third time in three days that I've made her tell me it's going to be fine. Now that's a good friend. "Just stick to the rules, and don't let him fuck with your head."

Last week, before I called him, Stacey helped me make up rules for myself, so that I wouldn't allow him to talk me into something I don't want to do. She said that her therapist taught her this technique to use on her clients, for when they call her at three in the morning with random food requests because their personal assistants are on vacation, or running some other errand for them, and so they figure that their lawyer would be the next most logical option. We came up with five of them:

1. I will not meet his fiancée.
2. I will have nothing to do with his wedding.
3. He does not get to meet Andrew or spend time with Parker.
4. I will not be warm and loving toward him, ever.
5. While unlikely, it is possible that I might someday forgive him for what he did, but I will never, ever forget.

I suck in my stomach, trying to calm my butterflies. "Okay," I say, exhaling. "I feel better now, thanks."

"You're welcome," she says. "Are you on your way there now?"

"No. I'm on my way home. I just had my first Mommy and Me class, and I need to change and drop off Parker before I meet him."

"Oh," she says. "And how *did* the quest to become the perfect mother go?"

I sigh. "It was okay. I think I'll get some good information from it, but I don't know if I'll be making any new friends. I mean, I was hoping to find another mom who's as miserable and clueless as I am, but they were all superhappy and, like, born for motherhood. Or at least, they're pretending to be. Whatever. You would hate them. They were all wearing the same thing, and they all had the same stroller and the same car, and they all talk about the same stuff. It's like they're communists or something."

"They're mommunists," Stacey says, correcting me.

I smile to myself. I love Stacey sometimes. "Exactly."

"Well, be careful," she says. "Don't let them try to convert you to their evil ways."

"I won't," I promise her. "I am an American."

When I get home ten minutes later, I give Parker to Deloris and retreat to my closet. I've lost nine pounds since the last time I had to go anywhere that required an actual outfit, and I now fit into two pairs of pants, both of which are really starting to bore me. But I refuse to go out and buy new ones, because that would mean that I've accepted this eleven-pounds-heavier-than-normal fate, which I absolutely, positively have not.

As I reach for my black fat pants yet again, I wistfully run my finger across the dozens of beautiful, tailored, size-four skinny pants that have been hanging, unworn, for months. But when I reach the black Theory ass pants, I stop.

I miss you, I think. *I miss you so much.*

I just tried them on yesterday, and they were so tight on me that they looked like leggings, but I am, nonetheless, feeling an overwhelming urge to try them again.

Just in case, I tell myself. Just in case my hips have decided that today is the day for them to narrow back to where they belong, or just in case I've miraculously lost eleven pounds since yesterday afternoon. I take them off of the hanger and put them on. Nope. Still leggings.

I pull them off and put on the fat pants and the olive-green tank top that I wear every day because it is fashionably body skimming, yet loose enough to hide the roll of fat that hangs over the top of my pants, and I walk out without even glancing in the mirror. I sigh. Maybe they'll fit tomorrow.

* * *

When I arrive at the Polo Lounge, the maître d' informs me that my father has already been seated, and he leads me back to our table, where my dad is picking at his cuticles as he waits for me. When he sees me making my way through the dining room, however, he immediately stands up.

"Buhbie," he says, opening his arms for a hug.

I will not be warm and loving toward him, ever.

I fake-hug him back, barely touching him.

"Hi, Dad," I say. He looks me up and down before I have a chance to sit.

"You lost weight," he says. "Have you been hanging out in the closet?"

For a second, I wonder if he thinks that I am a secret homosexual, but then I get the reference. My father always hated fat kids, and when I was growing up he used to tell me that if I ever got fat, he would lock me in the closet and give me only bread and water until I thinned out. I had forgotten all about it until right now, but it certainly lends some perspective to why I'm so neurotic about my weight, don't you think?

Note to self: When you get home, tell Parker that you'll love her no matter what she weighs.

See? I knew this was a good idea. I've been here ten seconds and I've already learned one way not to be.

"You know," I say, "that's a really horrible thing to say to a child."

He shrugs. "Well, it worked, didn't it?"

I love that he attributes the fact that I am (was?) thin to his borderline child-abuse parenting techniques. I want to tell him that it could just as easily be due to the fact that I was breast-fed.

"Whatever," I say. "Let's change the subject."

"Okay. How's the baby?"

You do not get to spend time with Parker.

"She's fine, I guess. She's sleeping better, and she's stopped crying so much. And I just started a Mommy and Me class with her, so it's something for us to do together."

He pauses. "Wait a minute," he says, sounding alarmed. "*Where* is the baby?"

"Oh," I deadpan, "I left her in the car." His eyes widen, and I wonder if he really thinks that I am that much of an idiot. "Don't worry," I say, "I left the windows up, so nobody will be able to kidnap her."

He realizes that I am joking and his face relaxes. "Very funny," he says. "So where is she really?"

"I hired a nanny. Deloris. She practices voodoo and she only eats fine foods, but she's keeping me sane." I spread my napkin on my lap and open my menu. "I really have a whole new appreciation for Mom lately. I just don't understand how she stayed at home with me and Evan when we were little. Did you guys have any help?"

@#*! smiles and shakes his head no, and I shake my head back at him, unable to fathom the idea of eight entire years of nothing but motherhood.

"I told you," he says, smugly. "It's hard."

Is he kidding me? From now on I'm not saying anything personal to him. He just twists everything around to help make a case for himself. It's so narcissistic.

"Please," I say, getting hostile. "Don't think that we can bond over the fact that we both find parenthood to be a challenge. Just because I think it's hard does not mean that I suddenly understand your little disappearing act. Or that I have sympathy for you."

He bites his lower lip. "Okay. What can I say that will make you understand where I was coming from?"

While unlikely, it is possible that I might someday forgive him for what he did, but I will never, ever forget.

"Nothing," I counter. "Nothing you can say will ever make me understand. And it's totally different, anyway. I'm frustrated with an infant who has no personality yet. You walked away from a grown, fully developed person. It gets one thinking that maybe you just didn't like me very much."

"Oh, Lara, that's ridiculous. I don't know how many times I have to tell you, it had nothing to do with you. It was just something that I needed to do for—" Suddenly his face distorts and he begins to look panicked. "Oh, no," he whispers. "This was not my idea, I swear. I told her to stay away."

I look over toward the direction in which he is staring, and I see a tall, thin woman with enormous boobs and an even more enormous head of back-combed red hair walking in our direction. She's wearing a white jacket with a red low-cut camisole underneath and a short white pencil skirt, and she's teetering on red stiletto heels. Nadine. It's got to be Nadine. My head starts to spin as I recite rule number one to myself.

I will not meet his fiancée. I will not meet his fiancée. I will not meet his fiancée.

I can't believe this. I'm meeting his fiancée. As she approaches the table, she sticks out her hand. She has long acrylic nails that are painted the same color as her shoes.

"Hi, there," she says. "I'm Nadine, your dad's fiancée. You must be Lara. I have heard so much about you, but you're even prettier than he said." She has some kind of a Southern accent that I can't quite place, but then I realize that, like everything else about her, it's probably not real.

"I'm sorry," I say to her, trying to take control of the situation, "but we were supposed to be having lunch. Alone."

She smiles at me, completely unfazed by my rudeness. "I know that," she says. "And I'm sorry for interrupting, but I just *had* to meet you."

She waves her left hand in front of her face and I am almost blinded by the sparkle from her diamond. It's got to be at least five carats. Wow. She must be really good in bed, because my father is notoriously cheap. He used to do all of the grocery shopping for our family when I was a kid, and he would buy stuff that we didn't even eat, like four bags of pork rinds, just because he had enough coupons to get three of the bags for free. Oh, wait a minute . . . of course she's good in bed. She's a friggin' stripper. It's probably all she's good at.

Then, suddenly, the seriousness of the situation hits me. My father is about to marry a stripper. I am going to be the stepdaughter of a stripper. A stripper who wears cheesy red stilettos and has acrylic nails. No. I can't let this happen. I mean, I can't have this woman at family events. I can't have her at my house for Hanukkah. Or at Parker's first birthday party. Oh, my God, could you imagine the look on Julie's face?

I'm just going to have to break them up, that's all. I'm just going to have to talk some sense into my father and make him see that he cannot possibly marry this woman. Not if he wants to have anything to do with me, anyway.

As if she knows exactly what I'm thinking, Nadine rests the hand with the giant diamond right on top of my dad's crotch, and, still smiling, looks me straight in the eye, as if to tell me that I should watch myself, because she's the one who has him by the balls.

Well, we'll see about that.

"So," I say condescendingly, "my father tells me that you used to be a *dancer.*" But Nadine just smiles at me. Huh. She's either really tough or really stupid.

"Yes, well, that was a lifetime ago. I've been in LA for the last twelve years, and I ran a consulting company up until a few years ago."

"Oh?" I say. "What kind of consulting did you do? I have some friends from Penn who work at McKinsey. Maybe you'd know them?"

She lets out a little laugh, as if I am a child who has said something too adorable. "Oh, I don't think so, honey. My kind of consulting isn't the kind that you learn about in college." This catches me off guard. What is she talking about, exactly? What has my father gotten himself into here? But before I can ask, Nadine changes the subject. "So, Lara, I don't know if your father has told you anything about our wedding plans." She turns to my dad. "Have you, Ronny?"

He gazes at her. "Not yet, baby doll. Why don't you tell her. You're the one in charge of it all, anyway."

I start to shake my head. *I will have nothing to do with his wedding.* No. This time, I am not going to let my rule get away from me.

"I really don't want to hear abo—" But before I can finish, Nadine clasps her hands together and squeals like a little girl.

"Okay. Well, it's going to be huge. *Huge.* It's here, at the Beverly Hills Hotel, and I've got the caterer who did Brad and Jen's wedding, and Colin Cowie has agreed to be my coordinator, which is so incredible. Did you see him on *Oprah* last week? I still have to find a dress, but I've got my eye on that Vera Wang number—the one that they did that special-edition Barbie doll with, with the black trim. Have you seen it?"

I can't even answer her. She's a forty-nine-year-old former stripper and she's having a huge wedding at the Beverly Hills Hotel and wearing *white?* Is she kidding? I'm speechless, so I just nod and make is-she-crazy eyes at my dad.

"Nadine always wanted a big, traditional wedding," he explains. "And so I told her to plan the biggest, most traditional one she could think of." Nadine is nodding and gripping his arm with both of her hands.

"That's right. I am just so excited!" She stops smiling and, suddenly, her tone gets serious. "But, you know, Lara, a wedding wouldn't be a wedding without a matron of honor." She is looking at me, waiting for an answer, and I am not sure what she is getting at.

"Yeah," I say, trying to sound bored. "Who are you going to ask?"

She laughs. "*You*, honey, that was my way of asking you."

I put on the fakest smile I can come up with. No. No way. Obviously Nadine is not familiar with rule number two: I will have nothing to do with his wedding. I begin to protest.

"But, Nadine, you don't even know me. We just met. I mean, how could I . . . What would I . . . I don't even know you."

She starts to stutter, making fun of me. "I-I-I. Come on, Lara. So what? I don't have any sisters, and I've always wanted a daughter. We'll *get* to know each other. Please, honey. Who else could I ask?"

I don't know, I think. *Don't you have any stripper friends left from the old days?* I look to my dad for help, but he just shrugs at me.

"Um, Nadine, could you excuse us for a minute?" I ask. She stands up and pulls down her skirt.

"Sure. You two talk it over, and I'll just go powder my nose."

Powder her nose. Who says that? My father and I watch her as she sashays away from the table, each of us thinking very different things, I can assure you, and when she's out of earshot, I give him an earful.

"You ambushed me," I hiss. "I told you I didn't want to meet her."

He puts up his hands to defend himself. "I didn't," he says. "I told her not to come. But you don't understand. You can't say no to Nadine. That woman has a mind of her own."

"Dad, I am not going to be in your wedding. I don't even want to be *at* your wedding. It's absurd."

Oh, I know exactly how to put an end to this. I'll bet you I can get him to call it off right here. Nadine's been with him, what, a year? Please. She's an amateur. I lived with the man my entire life. I know how his mind works. Big ring or not, he's a cheap bastard. When I was in high school, he gave me seven dollars a week for my allowance. And when I told him that I couldn't even cover my lunch at school with that amount, he upped it to seven dollars and ten cents. Honestly. Good sex will only go so far with Ronny Levitt. I purse my lips, savoring the moment before I declare my victory.

"And by the way," I say, "do you have any idea what a wedding like that will cost? Colin Cowie and Brad and Jen's caterer? I don't know what she's telling you, but it'll be at *least* a million dollars, and that's on a budget." I sit back and cross my arms, waiting for the steam to come out of his ears, but he just shrugs.

"It's not my money," he says. "She's paying for it all by herself. I told her that I would take care of the honeymoon."

What? I do nothing to conceal my surprise.

"She has her own money?" I ask.

He laughs. "What, did you think she was after me for mine? Please. I'm small potatoes for a woman like Nadine, Lar. She's a smart lady. Smarter than she lets on."

Hmmm. Interesting. My whole image of her is completely turned up-side down now. If she has her own money and she looks the way the does, what is she doing with my father? Is it possible that she really loves him?

I try to look at him with an objective eye. He's almost bald, and he has a brown, thinning comb-over that is *this close* to being worse than Don-ald Trump's. He's still wearing the same clothes that he wore during the Reagan years, and he's got man boobs. No. Not possible.

"Does she know what you did?" I ask. "How you walked out on everybody?"

He nods solemnly. "She does. She thinks that it was a shitty thing for me to do, and she's told me a thousand times that she feels sorry for you and your brother. In fact, it was her idea for me to go to your house." He pauses, smiling, as he thinks about her. "She's the real deal, Lara. Believe it." But before I can respond to this, Nadine is back, and her hand has re-sumed its place on top of my father's penis.

"So, is it settled? You'll do it?"

I clear my throat. "Nadine, it's very nice of you to want to include me, but my father and I are sort of on shaky terms right now, so I don't think that it's the most appropriate thing for me to do. I'm sure you can understand."

Nadine sits straight up and beams at me. "That's great! I'm so happy you said yes!" She stands up and puts her purse over her shoulder.

I'm sorry, I think. *Did anyone hear me say yes?* But she's still talking.

"I'll give you a call next week and we can start planning the shower,

and the bachelorette party, of course. We have to do something *wild*. Oh!"
she squeals. "I am so thrilled about this, Lara!" She leans over and gives
me a hug, and I'm so bewildered by the Jedi mind trick she just pulled on
me that I actually hug her back. And then she's gone. Poof.

They're not broken up. I'm going to be in his wedding.

My father gives me a weak smile.

"I told you," he says. "You can't say no to Nadine."

ten

The next Saturday morning, Julie and I are sitting at my dining room table, reviewing the nursery school application for the Institute. I swear, in five years of college admissions counseling, I have never seen such a complicated, demanding application. Aside from the four essay questions (*What are your child's strengths and weaknesses? What can your family bring to our school's community? Why do you want your child to attend our school? What goals would you like to see your child accomplish during his/her early educational years?*), there are also six pages of what they call "Personal and Family Information," which are about as thorough as an FBI background check for someone requesting top-secret security clearance at the State Department.

"Okay," I say to Julie, after I've finished reading it all. "I think that the first thing to do is to break down these essay questions and try to figure out what it is they're looking for. I mean, I don't know what strengths and weaknesses a nine-month-old can have, but I think that, with the second question, they definitely want to know how much you're planning to donate. The third one is easy—colleges ask that question all the time—just tell them that you're seeking out a diverse environment and praise them up and down for their commitment to diversity. The last one . . . I'm not sure. My gut tells me that they're trying to weed out the psychos who think their kids are smart enough to be reading *War and Peace* by age three, but on the other hand, maybe they want to see if you're willing to push your kid to excel. I think we should hedge on that one; try to play it right down the middle."

As I am saying this, it occurs to me that I sorely miss my job. I mean,

I can't remember the last time that I felt this confident about anything. I'm so used to being such a puddle of self-doubt: I don't spend enough time with the baby, she's not getting enough stimulation, I let her watch too much television, I'm feeding her too much, she's not sleeping enough, and on and on and on and on . . . it's exhausting just thinking about it. But this . . . I could get used to feeling like this again. I take a deep breath. God, the sense of control is intoxicating. I know that I was bitching and moaning a few months ago about how tired I was getting of my job, but I've gotta tell you, I can't wait to go back to work.

Suddenly my thoughts are interrupted by peals of deep laughter coming from the den.

"What's going on in there?" Julie asks me. I roll my eyes.

"Oh, nothing. Just Andrew and Deloris are, like, BFFs now. It's sickening how much they love each other. They're always hanging out and laughing like that, and I have no idea what the hell is so funny. I'm starting to feel like a third wheel in my own house." Julie looks at me skeptically.

"Andrew and your nanny hang out together? For real?"

"Yeah," I say, nodding. "For real. And you should see what he got her for her bedroom. She asked if we would mind if she hooked up a VCR in her room so that she could watch movies, and Andrew said no way could she have a VCR, nobody uses VCRs anymore, and he went out and got her a DVD player, a new TV with surround sound, and a TiVo."

Julie's jaw drops. "He got her a TiVo?" she asks.

I nod. "Yeah. I swear, Deloris could have her own episode of *Cribs* with the setup Andrew has going on in there."

"I just can't believe that he hangs out with her. That's so weird. Have you said anything to him about it?"

I look at her like she's crazy. "What can I say?" I ask. "Should I tell him *not* to hang out with her? That makes me look like such a bitch. And plus, she'll know it was me if all of a sudden he stops talking to her, and I can't afford that."

"Why? What do you mean?"

I lean in toward Julie and lower my voice. "Well, you know how I told you she has all of that voodoo stuff in her room?" Julie nods, her eyes wide, and I lean in a little closer.

"I think she's been putting spells on me," I whisper.

Julie sits up and smacks her hand on the side of the table. "Lara, that's ridiculous," she yells. "Deloris is not putting spells on you."

"Shhh!" I say, motioning toward the other room. "I'm telling you, she is." Julie shakes her head and looks at me sideways, like she can't tell if I'm being serious or not. When I realize what she is thinking, I give her an are-you-kidding-me look.

"I don't think they *work*," I exclaim. Julie exhales and looks relieved.

"Okay," she says. "I wasn't sure what you were getting at. But if you don't think they work, then who cares?"

"*I* care. I don't want her running around my house casting spells on me and thinking that they're actually doing something." I tap my temple with my index finger. "These things are mind games. And they're all about interpretation."

"Fine," she says, indulging me. "So what kind of spells do you think she thinks she's putting on you?"

I nod at her, and make a serious face. "Well, ever since I told her that Parker smiled at me first, she's been really pissy with me, and she avoids me whenever I'm around. And in her market list last week, she asked for all of these fresh herbs, like sage, and frankincense, and something called devil's claw. So I went online and did a search for different kinds of voodoo spells, and there's one that's called Go Away Woman. They use it when a woman is interfering in someone's relationship, and I think she's trying to use it to get between me and Parker." Julie looks confused.

"But you're her mother," she says. "Why would she want to get between you?"

I sigh. "It's complicated," I say, trying to figure out how to explain the fact that Deloris calls Parker *my baby*, and that, up until my revelation that day in the park, she pretty much *was* Deloris's baby, since I was never around. "Let's just say that Deloris got used to being Parker's primary caregiver, and now that I'm starting to spend more time with her, Deloris is having a hard time relinquishing the role."

"So, you're saying that your nanny wants the baby all to herself?"

I nod. "Yes. That's exactly what I'm saying." I pause. "And she's vindictive, too. This morning I found blue powder on top of my scale."

"So what?" Julie asks.

"So, I think she put a spell on it to keep me from losing my last ten pounds."

Julie laughs. "You can't be serious," she says.

"Oh, believe me, I am dead serious."

Just then Andrew walks into the dining room and knocks on the wall.

"Hey, Jul," he says. "Sorry to interrupt, but I wanted to say good-bye. Agility starts in twenty minutes."

"You're still taking Zoey to that agility class?" Julie asks.

"Of course," Andrew says. "She loves it."

I roll my eyes at him. "What he means to say is that *he* loves it," I say. "He thinks it's fun to run around an obstacle course and make the poor dog jump over poles and sprint up and down a seesaw. Oh, and to hang out with lesbians who have dogs instead of kids." Andrew gives me the finger and Julie laughs.

"Okay," I say, dismissing him. "Have fun." He yells for Zoey, who is already waiting by the front door and who has been whimpering ever since she heard Andrew open the drawer where he keeps her portable water bowl, and then he disappears. Julie looks at her watch.

"Actually, I have to go, too," she says. "Jon and I are taking Lily to the beach this afternoon. She loves to play in the sand."

"Okay. Then why don't you start working on the essays," I suggest, "and we'll go over them again when you have a draft."

"Great," she says. "Thanks for the help. You're so good at this." I grin at her.

"Yes, I know."

When Julie leaves I walk out into the den, where I find Deloris holding Parker in her arms and smothering her with kisses.

"Are you my baby?" she asks her. "Who is Deloris's baby?"

All right, I've got to put a stop to this.

On an impulse, I decide that I'm going to take Parker and surprise Andrew at agility. Not because I want to go to agility, mind you, but because I just want an excuse to get Parker away from Deloris for a little while.

"Hey, Deloris," I say. "I'm going to take Parker with me to go watch Andrew and Zoey at the park."

Deloris looks up at me and narrows her eyes. "But I just took her for a walk," she says, sounding annoyed. "She shouldn't spend any more time in the sun."

I smile at her, trying not to lose my patience. "Well, there are lots of trees there; I'll be sure to keep her where it's shady." I walk over to them and wait for Deloris to hand the baby to me, but Deloris doesn't move. Instead, she starts talking to Parker in a baby voice.

"Your mommy wants to take you out in the hot sun where you don't belong," she says.

Ignoring this, I brazenly reach over and attempt to take Parker out of her arms, but Deloris holds firm, and for a minute or so we end up in a game of tug-of-war with my baby. Or, as Deloris would say, with *her* baby. Not a real game of tug-of-war, mind you—we're not breaking her in half or anything like that—but it's definitely some kind of war. I finally give Deloris a dirty look and pull on Parker just a little bit harder, and Deloris relents. I fake-smile at her, then put Parker over my shoulder and talk in my own baby voice.

"Okay, sweetie, let's go to the park. It'll be so much fun; Mommy and Daddy and Zoey. Everyone in your whole family will be there." I lower my voice back to normal, hoping that I've made my point. "Bye, Deloris," I say, as I walk out.

When we get to the park, I still have a few minutes before class starts, so I take my time loading the diaper bag, the cooler with Parker's bottle · in it, my purse, and a giant, folding spectator chair into the bottom of the Snap-N-Go. Ha. I'd like to see a Bugaboo carry all of that.

As I push the stroller across the grass to the back of the park, where the agility course is set up, I shield my eyes from the sun and scan the perimeter of the field, looking for Andrew and Zoey.

"Your daddy is going to be so happy that we're here," I tell Parker. "Mommy hasn't been to agility in ages." I look back and forth a few times, and finally I spot Zoey, whose leash is tied to the trunk of a small, skinny tree.

Where is Andrew? I wonder to myself. I scan the area again, and this time I see him. His back is to me, and he's standing in the far corner of the field, leaning against the shed where they store all of the agility equipment during the week. He looks like he's talking to someone, but I can't see who it is because his body is blocking my view. It's probably the instructor. Andrew is always asking her questions, and besides, it's not like there's anyone normal in the class with whom he could actually be having a real conversation.

When I get to where Zoey is camped out, I set up my chair and take Parker out of her stroller. I was thinking that maybe she'd like looking at all of the dogs, but she doesn't even notice the dogs. The only thing that she's interested in is trying to get her mouth around the side of the chair so that she can gum the fabric. Oh, well. So much for a fun-filled family outing.

The other dogs and their owners have begun to congregate near our tree, waiting for class to begin, and I notice that, while every single one of them says hello to Zoey and pats her on the head, not one person even comments on the fact that I have a brand-new baby sitting on my lap. Oh, except for the one woman dressed in head-to-toe border-collie paraphernalia, who lectured me about how I have to spend special alone time with Zoey now so that she doesn't feel like she's been replaced. Really, it just proves my theory that these dog people are all lunatics.

When the teacher walks over and takes her place in the middle of the field, I turn around to look for Andrew, and I see that he still hasn't moved from his position by the shed.

Who is he talking to?

I stand up to get a better look, but just as I do he turns around and starts walking back toward us. Next to him is a dark gray standard poodle, who is being pulled along by a tall, thin, very pretty, very tan woman who appears to be in her mid-twenties, and who also appears to be a natural blonde, which is practically unheard-of in Los Angeles, at least if you're anywhere east of Malibu.

Who the hell is that?

Andrew never mentioned that anyone attractive had joined the class. From a deep, primitive place inside of me, I am feeling an urge to mark my territory. I stand up and put Parker over my shoulder, and I start walking toward them. As I get closer, I see that Poodle Girl is not just thin, but that she's actually got a sick, hard body and perfect, perky boobs, all of which is on display, since she is wearing nothing but a pair of track shorts and a scoop-neck tank top. I keep thinking that she reminds me of someone I know, but I can't quite put my finger on it. And then it hits me: Except for the natural-blonde part, she reminds me of me. Me five years ago.

Oh, my God, I think, sucking in my stomach and sticking out my chest. When did I go from being her to being me?

When Andrew finally tears himself away from Perky Poodle Bitch— hey, I like that; PPB, that's what I'm going to call her from now on—he is startled to see me standing two feet in front of him.

"Hey," he says, his face turning red. "Um, this is Courtney." He points to the poodle. "And that's Zak. They're, um, they're in the class with us."

I fake-smile, trying not to show how acutely aware I am of every last crow's-foot on my face, not to mention the extra nine pounds that I'm carrying and the fact that my boobs are two saggy, flat pancakes, courtesy of seven weeks of breast-feeding.

"Hi," I say. "I'm Lara. His wife. And this is Parker. Our daughter."

PPB turns to Andrew and gives him a look of happy surprise. "You never told me you had a daughter!" she exclaims. I raise my eyebrows at him as PPB starts gushing over Parker, and Andrew avoids looking me in the eye. "She is soooo cute," she says.

As she tickles Parker's stomach, I notice the definition in her triceps, and I try not to think about how my own ultrapale, flabby arms must look in my olive tank top right now.

"Um, I think class is starting; we should probably go get in line," says Andrew, who has started walking back to where he left Zoey tied to the tree.

"Okay," says PPB. With her right hand she smacks her very tan thigh, which doesn't jiggle or quiver or even form an indentation from the pressure, and she calls to her dog: "Come on, Zak, let's go!" Upon hearing this command, Zak's ears perk up, and as he races to the agility course he looks like a curly, big-boned greyhound.

Fuming, I walk over to my spectator chair and put Parker back in her stroller, and as I begin to consider the implications of what I just saw, I start to feel sick to my stomach.

Is he having an affair, or is he just flirting with her? And if he's just flirting with her, is he planning on having an affair? And what about all of those late nights at the office lately? Was he really working? How can he even like her, anyway? She owns a standard poodle, for God's sake. What kind of a person owns a standard poodle?

I can't decide if I should stay and watch the two of them, or if I should just leave now, so that Andrew knows exactly how angry I am. I decide to stay. If I leave, I'll just be giving them an opportunity to talk about me. Or worse, to plan their next rendezvous. Of course, they ignore each other for the rest of the class, but the tension level is palpable. They've been busted, and they both know it.

When class is over I wait for PPB to get in her car and drive away, and then I storm off, pushing the stroller as fast as I can go.

"Lara!" Andrew yells, running to catch up to me. "Lara, wait!"

I ignore him and keep pushing, but I have to stop and redirect the stroller every few seconds as it catches on the grass or bumps into a rock. *Piece of shit Snap-N-Go.* See, this is why I need a Bugaboo; so that I can effortlessly run away from my husband after I discover that he's got the hots for a twenty-five-year-old. Now there's something that they might want to mention in the *Consumer Reports* guide.

Andrew has passed me now, and he stops directly in front of me, blocking my path.

"Lara, come on. Let's talk about this," he says, panting and out of breath.

"Talk about what, Andrew? About the fact that we've had a baby for ten minutes and you've already decided to move on? Or about the fact that you never even told her that you had a baby?"

"Lara, don't be ridiculous. I love you, and I don't even know how you can think that I would move on. Courtney's just the only other normal person in the class, so we've become friends. But we're just friends, I swear."

I stick my tongue in my cheek and put my hands on my hips. "Well, if you're just friends, how come you never told me about her? And how come she didn't know that you had a baby? That's a pretty big deal, Andrew. Most people tell their friends that kind of news."

Andrew purses his lips as he thinks about how to answer me. "Look," he says. "What was I going to tell you? That there's a hot girl in agility now? You had just had the baby, and you were feeling terrible about yourself, and I didn't want to bring her up."

Oh, that is perfect. He didn't tell me about her because he didn't want to make me feel bad about the fact that I am a hideous beast.

"So you think she's hot?" I ask him.

He looks up at the sky. "No. I mean, yeah, she's pretty, but I'm not interested in her that way."

"Then why didn't you tell her about the baby?"

"I don't know," he says. "It just never came up."

"It never came up because you never wanted it to come up." I point my finger at him. "I know what you're doing. You don't want her to think that you're tied down, so you didn't tell her about Parker. That is how affairs begin, Andrew. Little lies, little omissions here and there. Don't forget, I was cheating on my ex-boyfriend when I started dating you. I know how these things work."

"Honey," he says. "I am not cheating on you, nor do I plan to start. Please don't turn this into a thing."

"Well, it's too late," I say, pushing the stroller away from him and over to my car. "You made it into a thing all by yourself."

eleven

I'm standing in the lobby of the Peninsula Hotel, pushing the Snap-N-Go back and forth and praying that Parker doesn't wake up. My father called me yesterday, and despite my protests I somehow got roped into meeting Nadine here to go over the details of her bridal shower. The bridal shower, FYI, that she has been planning all by herself, and that she is paying for in its entirety, but that, according to the invitation that I received a few days ago, is being given, *with love,* by yours truly. I almost threw up when I saw it.

Out of nowhere, one of the bellmen drops a suitcase that he's bringing in for a guest, and the metal handle makes a loud *clanking* noise against the marble floor. I cringe and hold my breath as I glance at Parker: Her body jumps slightly, she turns her head from side to side, and then she settles down again, still asleep. *Whew.* That was close.

After about three more minutes I see Nadine stride through the door. She's wearing tight black capri pants, a short black jacket that is nipped at the waist, and a silk black-and-red polka-dot top underneath. On her feet are the red stilettos again, and I wonder if they're supposed to be her signature, like the way some women always wear the same perfume. Oh, I hope she wears with her wedding dress. That would be classic.

"Hi, honey," she says, in that drawl-of-inexplicable-origin that she has. To my shock, she leans in to kiss me on the cheek, and then she catches me off guard again when she goes to kiss the other cheek, as well. Like I'm supposed to think she's spent so much time in Europe that it's just an old habit by now.

"Hi," I say begrudgingly, half whispering and motioning to the stroller.

"Oh!" she exclaims, lowering her voice and peering inside to take a look. Parker and I are headed straight to Mommy and Me after this, and in an attempt to redeem myself after last time, I've dressed Parker in her cutest outfit—an orange T-shirt with rhinestones around the edges and matching pants with ruffles at the hems—and for the pièce de résistance, I have placed an orange satin barrette in her hair, which, inexplicably, has grown itself into a mullet. She looks cute, but still, even with the couture, it doesn't change the fact that, with her rolls of fat and three chins, she's a dead ringer for the Michelin man. If the Michelin man went deer hunting and listened to Slayer.

"How darling," whispers Nadine. "She's absolutely beautiful."

Liar, I think.

"Yeah, well, she's not nearly as cute when she's awake, believe me."

Nadine laughs, and just then a beautiful blond woman in a black pantsuit approaches us, smiling.

"Nadiiiine," she says, opening her arms.

"Marleeeeey," says Nadine. The two of them kiss each other on both cheeks, and I roll my eyes to myself. Nadine holds her hand out in my direction and makes an introduction. "Lara, this is Marley. She's the catering director here, and one of my best former employees from my consulting days." Marley smiles and blushes a bit, and Nadine puts her hand on my shoulder. "Marley, this is my daughter, Lara." *Her daughter?* I start to choke, and I quickly correct her.

"I'm not her daught—"

Marley interrupts me, taking my hand. "How nice to meet you," she says. "You are so lucky to have Nadine." She smiles at me warmly. "There was a time when I felt like she was my mother, too."

"No," I say, "I'm not her daught—"

"Well," Nadine says, clasping her hands together. "Let's talk about the menu, shall we?" Marley nods, and before I can say another word, she and Nadine are two feet ahead of me, walking toward the room where the shower is going to be held. The two of them are chatting about some people they both used to know, and I am walking behind them, pushing the Snap-N-Go and trying to keep up.

For the next half hour, Marley and Nadine debate the merits of sesame-crusted-salmon salad versus Chinese chicken salad, white-chocolate-covered strawberries versus mixed berries drizzled with dark chocolate, and Bellinis with fresh peach slices versus mimosas with mandarin oranges. They go back and forth between cream-colored linens with gold chairs or ivory-colored linens with white chairs, and get into a long discussion about whether to go with centerpieces of Colombian roses at each table, or bud vases of mini calla lilies at each place setting. They've completely forgotten about me, and I sit and half listen to them as I continue to push the stroller back and forth, wondering why the hell Marley couldn't have been her matron of honor.

When they have finally made their decisions (salmon salad, strawberries, Bellinis; cream with gold, mini callas), Marley walks us out, hugging us both good-bye, and Nadine and I each hand our parking tickets to the valet. Unbelievably, Parker is still asleep in her stroller, but I just know that she's going to wake up screaming the second that we get in the car.

"Well," says Nadine, turning to me. "That was fun. Thanks so much for coming."

I raise my eyebrows at her, making no attempt to hide my irritation.

"I'm not really sure why I was there," I say. I've decided that I'm just going to be blatantly obnoxious to her in the hopes that a) she'll kick me out of the wedding party, b) she'll decide that she can't be married to someone who has such a horrible person for a daughter, or c) all of the above.

Nadine gives me a fake smile, and we both look straight ahead, an awkward silence setting in between us. After a few moments, I clear my throat.

"You know, Nadine, it made me extremely uncomfortable that you introduced me as your daughter."

Nadine takes a compact and some lipstick out of her purse and begins to reapply as she answers me. "I call everyone my daughter," she says nonchalantly, rubbing her lips together. "And everybody knows that about me." She pushes on the compact with her thumb and forefinger, and it closes with a loud snap.

"Well, I don't know that about you. I don't know anything about you, actually."

Nadine purses her lips, and I detect the slightest hint of annoyance in her face before the fake smile reappears. As if somehow I am spoiling what is supposed to be a special morning for her as a bride. Good. It's working.

"Well, Lara, what is it that you would like to know?" she asks, using a cool, detached tone that I haven't heard from her before.

"Okay," I say, using a cool and detached tone myself. "How about, what did you really do before you met my dad? Because I'm not buying that you had a consulting company. Not with former employees like Marley. I mean, what kind of a consultant looks like her, and then goes on to become a catering director at a hotel?" I feel like I'm Velma in an episode of *Scooby-Doo.* "The Case of the Mysterious, Soon-to-be Stepmonster."

Just then the valet pulls up with a long black Mercedes sedan, and Nadine takes a step forward.

"If you must know, I ran an escort company," she says matter-of-factly, opening the driver's-side door. "You're looking at the original Hollywood Madam." She hands the valet a ten-dollar bill, and I stare at her in disbelief.

"You mean, like Heidi Fleiss?" I ask. Nadine steps into the car and the valet closes the door behind her. The window is open, and I hear her chuckle.

"Honey," she says, back to using the drawl again, "I taught Heidi everything she knows." She turns the ignition key and puts the car into drive. "Well, except for the part about getting caught." She puts her index finger in front of her mouth and pushes her lips out into a silent *shhhhh.* Then she rolls up the window and drives off, leaving me standing there with one hand on the stroller, mouth agape.

No fucking way. I'm disgusted by her, but even more disgusted by my father.

Lucy! I think. *You've got some 'splaining to do.*

When I arrive at Susan's class, I'm still reeling from my discovery about Nadine (here's a movie title: *My Stepmother Is a Pimp*), but I'm smiling and talking to people in an effort to force myself to put it out of my head.

"Good morning, ladies!" Susan yells over the chatter, and, right on cue, my classmates and I take our places in a circle on the floor. The mommunists are in full matching regalia again today—this time it's long, straight cotton skirts, rhinestone-studded thongs, and Hard Tail T-shirts—but since I am dressed from my meeting at the Peninsula this morning—black fat pants, Dolce & Gabbana thongs, and a pink Marc Jacobs tank top—I'm feeling much less out of place. Plus, I've got Parker spread out on a beautiful lilac-and-cream Barefoot Dreams receiving blanket, and when several people comment on how adorable her outfit is and how lucky I am that she already has enough hair to hold a barrette, I feel as if my heart is going to burst with pride. Pride that I have produced a child whose hair naturally grows into a style worn by hockey players and monster-truck-rally fans, but pride nonetheless.

Susan claps her hands, and we all quiet down and turn our attention to her.

"This morning we are going to be talking about sex after childbirth," she announces. There is snickering all around, and we sound like a bunch of sixth-grade boys whose health teacher just started the unit on menstruation. Susan nods at us, as if she has seen this before. "All right, settle down. Let's start by taking a poll. How many of you have tried having sex since your baby was born?" There are audible gasps throughout the room, and I, too, am somewhat taken aback by this question. I mean, our babies are all three and a half months old at this point. How could anyone not have tried having sex yet? And even if they haven't, who would admit it? Nobody moves.

"Come on," Susan chides. "Don't be shy. Raise your hand if you've had sex since your baby was born." We all look around at one another, and slowly, each of us raises our hand. "Great!" Susan exclaims. "So how was it?" Immediately everyone looks at the floor. Now I really feel like I'm in school. I'm afraid to look up for fear that Susan will catch my eye and call on me. Finally, one brave fake blonde speaks.

"It hurt," she says. "I was really sore afterward."

Susan beams. Obviously this is the answer she was looking for.

"That's right!" she exclaims. "Sex can be very painful after childbirth sometimes."

The minute hand on the wall clock has just jumped to ten fifteen, and I start counting in my head. *Ten, nine, eight, seven, six, fi—* And there goes the banshee noise. Right on time. I swear, the kid is a machine. Everyone turns to stare at me, anticipating another spectacle like last week's, but I just smile at them and reach into my diaper bag. Being unprepared with food is not a mistake that I will make twice, believe me. I pull out a small cooler in which I have packed an already-made bottle of formula, and in less than five seconds Parker is in my arms, happily sucking away. Susan smiles at me appreciatively and resumes her lecture.

"As I was saying, sex can be quite painful after having a baby, but what you must know is that there is something you can do to minimize the discomfort." She leans forward, as if she is about to reveal one of life's greatest secrets to us, and then she lowers her voice to a whisper. "You can use a lubricant."

No shit, I think. That's the big secret? Who doesn't use a lubricant? But then one mom raises her hand.

"What do you mean?" she asks, a quizzical look on her face. Susan nods at her sympathetically.

"Well, after you have a baby your estrogen levels drop, which is what causes the vaginal dryness that leads to painful intercourse. So, some people use a lubricant before they have sex, in order to moisten things up down there."

Astounded, the same woman raises her hand again. "Where do you buy this stuff?" she asks.

I look at her with disbelief. Is she kidding? Has she never been in the feminine hygiene aisle at Rite Aid? But Susan doesn't bat an eye.

"Any drugstore," she responds casually, as if this degree of cluelessness in a grown woman with a child is totally normal. I look around the room to see if anyone else is having the same reaction to this as I am, but they all seem genuinely interested. *Hmmmm.* I start to wonder if perhaps I am a dirty girl and I just don't know it. I mean, I've been using K-Y since I was sixteen years old. And I just came from a meeting with a former madam! Oh, if the mommunists ever met Nadine, I think they would die on the spot.

Just then one of the other moms raises her hand. She's a short fake blonde with huge, round Bambi eyes, and her hair is about three inches too long for her face.

Oh, God. Not her.

She was the one person whom I absolutely could not tolerate from last week. She talks reeeeallllyyyy slowly, and her questions are inane. For example, last week she asked Susan if she thought it was dangerous that her son sometimes gets his blanket wrapped around his neck in the middle of the night. I mean, *hello?* Even I know the answer to that one.

Susan points at her to speak, and, to my surprise, she proceeds to present an infomercial for K-Y jelly.

"She's right, you guys," she gushes. "Everyone told me that sex was going to hurt after having a baby, and I was soooooo scared to try it, but then my friend told me about K-Y, and I didn't even believe her." For some reason, I am picturing her and her friend having this discussion at a slumber party, and then I realize that it is because she reminds me of Sandy from *Grease.* I try not to smile as I imagine all of the moms crowding around her, spontaneously breaking into a rendition of "Tell Me More," right here in the middle of class.

"But I decided to try it, and it really worked! Sex didn't hurt at all! Now it's like a private joke between me and my husband—whenever we're about to have sex, I'll say, 'Honey, go get the K-Y,' and we both crack up."

Ooh, bad girl. I'll bet she shows up next week in black spandex and a perm.

Okay, I think. *I've had just about enough of this.* On the off chance that anyone else is as troubled by this discussion as I am, I don't want them lumping me into the story when they recount it later for all of their friends, who, undoubtedly, will be doubled over with laughter. I raise my hand as high as I can, impatiently waiting to be called on. Finally Susan nods at me.

"Actually," I say, "I prefer Astroglide. It's much smoother than K-Y." From the looks that this comment has garnered, I think that my concern was probably unfounded. But I can't resist going on. Emboldened by my newfound status as a sexual deviant, I continue. "But of course, if you're doing it in a pool or in the shower, then you have to use something with a silicone base, like Eros Bodyglide. The water-based stuff will just wash right off." Everyone is staring at me like I have just whipped out a gigantic spiked dildo and threatened to make them touch it.

"Thanks," Susan says, blinking. "I didn't know about that last one; I'll have to look into it."

I humbly nod a "you're welcome" to her, and then I look around the room, smiling. All of the mommunists are fake-smiling back, but it's clear that they're a little bit afraid of me and my arsenal of scary sex knowledge.

Uh-oh, I think. Looks like I've just earned myself a reputation.

The second that class is over and I am in my car, I start dialing my cell phone. I've got two important calls to make, and they can't wait until I get home. Julie answers on the first ring.

"Hello?"

"Please tell me that you know what K-Y is," I say.

"Lara," she says in a slightly reprimanding tone, as if I have just said a bad word in front of young children, and then she lowers her voice. "Of course I know what K-Y is. Why?"

"Because I just left Susan's class and nobody knew what K-Y was, and I was starting to feel like a slut. But as long as you know what it is, I'm okay. You're my barometer for normalcy."

"I am?" she says, sounding genuinely shocked.

"Jul, I hate to break it to you, but it doesn't get more normal than you. I, however, am steadily creeping toward the lower end of the scale, and as such, I must go."

Yeah, I need to call my father to ask him why he's decided to marry a pimp. "Hey," I muse. "Do you know if there's a female word for *pimp?* Pimpess, maybe?"

"Wait," Julie says. "What are you talking about?"

"Nothing," I say. "Just a thought. Love you!"

I hit the end button on her, and then I call 411 for the Beverly Hills Hotel. When I reach my father, it is apparent that he has been sitting by the phone all morning, just dying for either me or Nadine to call and tell him how things went with us at the Peninsula. It seems that I'm the first to check in.

"So how did it go?" he asks, excitement in his voice.

"How did it go?" I repeat back to him sarcastically. "Well, let's see. I met one of her former *consultants,* she referred to me as her daughter, and then she pretty much ignored me for half an hour. Oh, and I almost forgot. When we were leaving, she told me that she's the original Hollywood

Madam." I make my voice as cheery as I can. "So it was great!" There is silence for a moment on the other end of the phone.

"She told you that?" he asks.

"Mm-hmm. She sure did." Long, long pause.

"Lara, it's not a big deal. She closed the business four years ago, long before I met her. She's completely legitimate now."

"Okay," I say, "first of all, let's stop referring to it as a 'business,' shall we? And second of all, what is legitimate? The fact that she's running around town spending the millions that she made illegally during her years as a prostitute?"

"Hold on, there," he says, sounding angry. "Nadine was *never* a prostitute. She handled the bookings and managed the clients, but she was never out in the field."

I snort. "Out in the field? Is that what they call it? What is she, a CIA agent?"

"I'm serious, Lara," he says. "Nadine didn't do anything that a million other corporations don't do every day. She's no worse than Enron, or Tyco, or any of those guys. They were all doing illegal stuff."

"Dad," I say, baffled by this argument, "just because other people do illegal things doesn't make it right, and we're not talking about a corrupt CEO in an otherwise legitimate company. Her entire business was illegal. How do you not see that?"

"I do see it, Lara," he says with a sigh. "But I just don't care. Look, I've spent a lot of time out in the world, and believe me, there are plenty of people who make an honest living who are still terrible people. But Nadine is a quality person. She treated those girls like her own daughters, and they have all gone on to have successful, legitimate careers. Like the girl you met today. If it weren't for Nadine, she'd be dancing at some strip club in the Valley." He lowers his voice, as if he thinks that someone might be eavesdropping on him. "And Nadine is very well connected, Lar. You'd be amazed at some of the people she knows. She can call in a favor for just about anything."

I exhale loudly to make sure that he understands my disgust with him. "The only favor that I need is for her to leave me alone. You may be happy consorting with criminals, but Andrew and I haven't worked our asses off for the last ten years so that our child can be exposed to the underworld of Los Angeles. Believe me, she'll have plenty of opportunities for that in high school."

"She's not going to expose Parker to anything. She's retired. Just give her a chance, Lara. She's harmless."

"No. I don't want to give her a chance. I don't want to have anything to do with her. I don't want to see her socially, I don't want her popping up whenever you and I meet, nothing. If you want to be in my life, you're going to have to do it without her."

He lets out a long sigh. "Fine," he says. "I'll do my best." Oh, well, that's encouraging. His best has always been so thorough in the past. "Just, one thing, Lar," he says, hesitating.

"What?" I ask.

"Don't tell anyone, okay? The statute of limitations isn't up for another few months, so if the government finds out, they can still prosecute her."

Yeah, because I'm just dying for everyone to know that my father is engaged to a former pimpess. I really like that word, by the way. If it's not real, it definitely should be.

I exhale loudly.

"Of course, Dad. I'll be happy to obstruct justice for you and your lovely fiancée. Just do me a favor: Don't tell me anything else, okay? If you're really a fugitive, or if Nadine killed somebody, I'd rather just not know."

"I swear, Lara, there's nothing else," he says.

"Great," I say. "Glad to hear it. Look, I've gotta go, Dad. I've got my own problems to worry about."

I hit the end button, wondering how this happened to me. I mean, I used to be just a regular old girl who grew up in the suburbs. My biggest trauma in life was that I was a latchkey kid. And now I've got a fucked-up dad who's driving me crazy, my husband is inches away from having an affair with a twenty-five-year-old, I've got a baby whom I have absolutely no idea how to raise, a nanny who thinks she's putting voodoo spells on me, and I'm the soon-to-be stepdaughter of Heidi Fleiss's mentor.

My God. I'm not creeping toward the low end of the normalcy scale. I've jumped off of it.

twelve

The Wiggles are singing "Hevenu Shalom Aleichem." Or, as the banner at the bottom of the screen says, "Havenu Shalom Alachem." I swear, I am not making this up. Each Wiggle is standing on a raised white platform, and on the floor below them are five preteen girls wearing Bavarian-looking costumes, dancing around in circles with ribbons attached to sticks. It's like the Wiggles thought that it would be some grand lesson in multiculturalism to show a bunch of kids dressed like German beer wenches celebrating May Day in Israel.

I laugh out loud, and glance down at Parker to see if she finds this as amusing as I do. But she's just staring straight ahead, mesmerized. Doesn't see the humor, I guess. Well, diversity training or not, I'm only letting her watch for half an hour tonight. Actually, let me rephrase that. I'm only going to let myself be a lazy, piece-of-shit mother for half an hour tonight, even though I would like nothing more than to stick her in front of *The Wiggles* for the rest of the evening so that I can sit and close my eyes, like I used to do when Deloris went to bed, back when I didn't care about what kind of mother I was turning out to be. Ah, the good old days.

But now that I do care, the two hours after Deloris goes to bed are crucial for me if I have any chance of maintaining my place at the top of the Mommy/Deloris/Daddy totem pole. Assuming that I am at the top of the Mommy/Deloris/Daddy totem pole. You see, the totem pole is a fluid concept, and just being the mommy does not automatically guarantee the top spot. It has to be earned with cold, hard face time—singing, playing, engaging—and given that Deloris would like nothing more than to achieve a Deloris/Mommy/Daddy totem pole (or, likelier, a Deloris/Daddy/Mommy totem pole), I have to take full advantage of any alone time that I get with this kid.

Andrew, by the way, thinks that I'm delusional about Deloris. I complain to him about her all the time, but he just thinks that I'm being hypersensitive. Of course, he's not here during the day. He doesn't see the constant hovering, the blatant attempts to keep Parker away from me, and the overall attitude that she can take care of Parker better than I can. She doesn't even try to be subtle about it, either. If she knows that I'm coming home at noon, she'll take Parker out for a walk at eleven forty-five. If I come home unexpectedly, she'll immediately announce that Parker's tired and she'll put her down for a nap. And if I try to hold Parker or play with her, she practically stands on top of me and then acts all impatient until I give Parker back. I'm convinced that Deloris thinks I'm not worthy of having a baby. I'm not worthy because I spend my time with Parker in spurts, and because I don't have the patience to spend all day, every day doing nothing but sitting on the floor, cheering for her to roll over. I'm not worthy because I can't tolerate pacing back and forth for hours whenever Parker cries. Oh, and I'm definitely not worthy because I stopped breast-feeding. That just about devastated Deloris. You'd have thought I decided to feed Parker nuclear waste, the way that she carried on about it. For a week, she got teary every time that she walked by a can of formula.

Anyway, because I'm not worthy, Deloris has decided that Parker should be *her* baby, and she's doing everything she can to make sure that Parker knows it. She's not fooling around, either. Deloris is in this to *win*. Believe me, it's no coincidence that she's sidled up to Andrew. She's always making him cookies, and TiVoing daytime shows on Animal Planet for him, and whenever he's around she's all, *oh, yes, Mrs. Lara, ha, ha, ha,* pretending that she just loves me to pieces, all so that he'll believe her when it comes down to her word against mine. Which it would, if I weren't so afraid of upsetting her.

Oh, come on, what am I supposed to do? I can't reprimand Deloris. I can't even reprimand my twenty-six-year-old assistant at the office, let alone a woman who's twice my age and half a foot taller. No, no. It's much better for me to walk around with my stomach in knots all day than for her to have to hear that I think that she's a manipulative, overbearing baby hog. I just don't do conflict well with people I'm not related to. It's *soooooo* much easier to be passive-aggressive. Plus, let's not kid ourselves here. As much as I can't stand living with Deloris, I'm smart enough to know that living without her would be infinitely worse. And I'm going back to work soon. I *need* her. I mean, yeah, I could fire her and start looking for someone new, but you know what they say: The devil you know is better than the devil that you don't. And she is good with Parker. She's fantastic with Parker. She just happens to be bitchy and judgmental with me, that's all.

Well, whatever. It's a moot point, because Deloris isn't going anywhere. I'll just have to be vigilant about using my alone time with Parker to reinforce the concept that *I'm* the one whom she should be calling Mommy.

When *The Wiggles* are over, I turn off the television and take Parker into her room, where I lay her down on the Gymini and pull out a few toys for her to play with. But she's not interested in the toys. She's just fixated on trying to get her toes into her mouth, and when she realizes that she can't do it, she starts to cry.

"Here," I say. "Try this." I hand her a little stuffed dog that plays "B-I-N-G-O" when you pull its tail, and I help her guide it into her mouth. She chews it for a second or two, and then starts crying again. Oh, God. I am soooo tempted to stick her back in front of the television right now. But the thought of Parker's first word being *Deloris* is enough to keep me going. I close my eyes and take a few deep breaths, then open them again. Okay. Let's try something else. She likes that stupid motorboat song that we do at the end of Susan's class. I'll try that. I pick up her feet and start moving them back and forth in a bicycle motion.

"Motorboat, motorboat, goes so slow, motorboat, motorboat, goes so fast, motorboat, motorboat, step on the gas. Wheeeeeeeeee!" I tickle her on her stomach and under her chin, and she starts crying harder.

"All right," I say wearily. "I'll pick you up. Just a second; let me get a burp cloth." I stand up and open the top drawer of the changing table to look for a burp cloth, but there aren't any in there. Great. I'm wearing my favorite vintage *Coke Is It* T-shirt—today is the first day that I could actually fit into it without having visible rolls of back fat—and I can't have her spitting up all over it, because I'm afraid that if I wash it, it'll shrink and I won't be able to get back into it again. I look around the room for something else to use, but then I remember that, the last time I went to Target, I put a few extra packages of burp cloths, wipes, and diapers at the top of her closet. I wonder if they're still there or if Deloris has already discovered them.

Parker is about T minus ten seconds to full-fledged screaming, so I quickly reach my hand up to feel whether anything is up there. *Shit.* I can't reach. I stand on my tiptoes and sweep my hand across the top of the shelf, and I feel something plastic hit the tips of my fingers. Parker's cry is starting to escalate. *Shit.* Okay. I'm going to have to jump up and try to bat it down. I bend my knees like I'm about to shoot a free throw, and then I jump as high as I can, swiping the top of the shelf with the palm of my hand. *Ow.*

From behind me I hear a cackle, and I twirl around. Parker has stopped crying, and she's smiling up at me.

"Did you just laugh?" I ask her. "Did you think that was funny?" Her bottom lip juts out and she makes the pouty face that she always makes before she's about to start screaming. "No, no," I plead, "don't cry. Here, watch this." I jump up as high as I can, and she lets out the cackle again. "Oh, my God," I say. "You're laughing. I didn't know that you could laugh."

I wonder if she's been laughing for Deloris and Deloris didn't tell me, or if this is a new development. No, it's got to be new. Deloris would have rubbed it in my face if she laughed for her. Just like I'm going to rub this in Deloris's face first thing tomorrow morning.

"You like that, huh? Okay," I say, getting excited. "Watch this." I put my legs together and place my hands against my sides. "Ready?" I sing, slapping my right thigh, "O-kay."

I jump into the air, spreading my legs wide and clapping my hands above my head, and then do it again two more times.

"V-I-C-T-O-R-Y!" I yell, in time with each jump. On Y I land with one knee bent and one knee on the floor, with my arms spread into a wide vee. Okay, yes, I was a cheerleader in high school. Captain, if you must know. And I wore my hair in a side ponytail with a big red scrunchie in it for every game, and I had big, hair-sprayed mall bangs, and sometimes I even used a crimping iron. But my squad never went to cheerleading camp or used spirit sticks or did anything ambitious like that. We were like the anticheerleader cheerleaders: a bunch of Jewish princesses who couldn't do flips or pyramids because we all had bad backs and trick knees, and who missed the entire week of city basketball play-offs because we had AP exams to study for. I've always kind of regretted having been part of such a cheesy, universally mocked, antifeminist "sport"—by the way, thank God I didn't know Stacey in high school, because she would have terrorized me—but that was before I knew that it would make Parker crack up like this. Now, if for no other reason, I am thrilled to have been a high school cheese ball.

"Okay, okay," I say to her, "I'll do it again. Ready? O-kay." I jump. "V-I-C-T-O-R-Y!"

She cackles again, this time louder, and I start laughing at her laughing. I do the victory jump again and again and again, until both of us are hysterical and I am sweating and out of breath.

"V-I-C-T-O-R-Y!"

"What are you doing?" From my kneeling-with-vee-shaped-arms position on the floor, I spin my head around. Andrew is standing in the doorway, and behind him is Courtney, the Perky Poodle Bitch, as thin and tan and perfect as ever. Quickly I stand up and wipe the sweat off my forehead with my hand.

"I was doing cheers for her," I say. "It was making her laugh." I glance at PPB, and then glare at Andrew. "What are *you* doing?"

"Oh," says PPB, answering for him. "I left Zak's collar on the ground near Zoey's stuff the other day, and Andrew took it by accident, so I just stopped by to pick it up. I hate leaving him home all day without a collar, you know, in case he gets out."

"Courtney has really long hours," Andrew says, chiming in. "She works in a commercial real estate office."

"It's just temporary," she says, blushing. "My degree is in hospitality; I just haven't found anything in that industry yet." I bite the insides of my cheeks and say nothing, which seems to make PPB uncomfortable. "You have a really nice house," she offers, her smile faltering.

"Thanks," I say curtly, but all I can think about is how bad my ass must have looked, jiggling all over the place while I was jumping up and down, doing my old high school cheerleading routine. Oh, God. How pathetic am I?

"Well," she says, holding up the collar to show me. "I'd better get going. I'm sure you guys are busy with the baby and everything, so . . ." She lets her sentence trail off.

"Here," Andrew says, moving in front of her. "I'll walk you out."

"No," I say, picking Parker up off of the floor and handing her to Andrew. "I'll do it." PPB and Andrew exchange nervous glances, and PPB follows me down the stairs.

"The baby's really cute," she says. "You guys are, like, the perfect family. Beautiful mom, beautiful kid, beautiful house, beautiful dog." I notice that she failed to mention the beautiful dad. Or else she doesn't think that Andrew is all that good-looking. I'll have to remember to mention that to him when we're fighting about her later on.

It does takes me a second to figure out how to respond to her, though. I so wish that I were the kind of person who could just tell her that, damn right I have a perfect family, and she'd better stay the fuck away from it, but, like I said, I don't do conflict with nonrelatives. So, I'll just smile and pretend that I don't at all mind that a gorgeous blond woman in her mid-twenties is hanging out with my husband, and then I'll make perfectly-pleasant-yet-still-somehow-nasty comments to her in an attempt to show that, in fact, I do mind. I mind very much.

"Yeah, well, I'm sure they said the same thing about the Manson family," I say. I see her tilt her head ever so slightly as she tries to figure out if I meant that to be a threat or not. But before she can say anything, I unlock the door and swing it open, flashing her a way-too-big smile. "Okay," I say. "This is the end of the line."

She smiles back and walks past me onto the porch. "Good night," she says, turning around to look at me. "Nice to see you again."

"Yeah, you too," I say, and I close the door in her face.

Just in case Andrew isn't sure if I'm pissed about this or not, I stomp back up the stairs and down the hallway to Parker's room as loud as I can.

When I get there he is walking around the room with her, and she's screaming.

"You didn't start her bath yet?" I half ask, half accuse, looking at my watch. "It's almost nine o'clock." I reach over and snatch her away from him. "Go fill up the tub," I command.

His head hanging, he mopes off into the bathroom and turns on the water. I undress Parker and get her pajamas ready for bed, and then I take her into the bathroom and ease her into the baby tub that is sitting on top of the counter. Andrew just watches me, not saying a word. Chicken. If I weren't holding the baby, I would flap my arms and squawk at him. But instead I think I'll prolong his agony.

"Okay, Parker," I say, placing a washcloth over her stomach to keep her warm and rinsing the rest of her with water. "Look at the duckie; here's your duckie." I squeak the rubber duckie that is floating in the tub, and she reaches out and sticks it in her mouth. Andrew has been standing behind me, shuffling his feet back and forth, just waiting for me to bite his head off, and when he can't take me ignoring him any longer, he speaks up.

"What did you say to her?" he asks timidly.

"Nothing. I just walked her out."

He looks at me like he doesn't quite believe this. "Are you mad?"

I turn my head around and shoot him a look of death. "Mad?" I ask. "Why would I be mad? Just because you brought her over to our house when you know that I think that something is going on between the two of you? Why should that make me mad?" I rub some shampoo onto Parker's head and he catches my eye in the mirror.

"Lara, I swear to you, there is nothing going on. Why would I let her come over if I was sleeping with her? Do you think I'm that stupid?"

I grab from off of the toilet seat the pink towel with the hood that has yellow flower petals attached to it, and stick it against my neck, clutching one of the petals with my chin. Then I lift Parker out of the tub, position her head into the center of the hood, and wrap the towel around her in one swift motion. She looks like an Anne Geddes picture.

"Andrew, do you think that *I'm* that stupid? I believe you that you're not sleeping with her. But whether you're sleeping with her is not the point. The point is that you're attracted to her and you *want* to sleep with her, but since you're not mature enough to admit that to yourself, you keep pretending that she's just some new friend you made so that you can continue to hang out with her and not feel guilty about it."

I walk out of the bathroom and turn off the light while he is still standing in there, and he quickly follows me out.

"That is not true," he insists. I give him a yeah-right look and place Parker down on the changing table, patting her dry with the towel. "What am I supposed to do?" he whines. "She just moved here, she doesn't have any friends, and so she latched on to me because I'm the only other normal person in the class. I can't just tell her that we can't talk anymore. That's so mean."

"Oh, so her feelings are more important than mine. That's just great." I slather some Desitin on Parker's butt and put a diaper on her, and then snap her up into her pink terry-cloth footie pajamas.

"No," he says. "You're being ridiculous."

I stop snapping and throw my hands up in the air. "God," I say, frustrated as I realize that I am stuck with an extra snap and nowhere to put it. "Whose idea was it to put nine thousand little snaps on these things?"

I start checking the pajamas again, trying to get Parker to stop kicking by holding her feet down with one hand, and I finally find the culprit. I undo the snaps along her right leg and start over.

"Are you listening to me?" Andrew asks.

"Yes, I'm listening to every word. You just called me ridiculous for saying that you have a crush on a hot blond twenty-five-year-old with a huge rack and a permatan."

When I finally get the snaps right, I pick Parker up and take the bottle out of the bottle warmer, place it on the nightstand next to the glider, and then dim the lights and sit down to feed her.

"No," Andrew says. "I called you ridiculous for saying that her feelings are more important than yours." Parker turns to look at him, and her head tips back off of the side of my arm.

"Shhhh," I whisper. "You're distracting her."

"Fine," he whispers. "But your feelings are more important to me. You know that."

"Okay," I whisper back. "Then stop talking to her."

"Lara, we're in the same agility class."

"Then switch classes," I hiss.

He throws his hands up in the air. "I can't do that," he says. "That's the only class at Zoey's skill level. The other ones are too easy for her."

"So now the dog's more important than me, too," I snap. "You know what?" I ask. "Just get out of here. I need to put our daughter to sleep." Andrew looks at me like he's not sure what just happened, and then he turns around and shuffles out of the room.

"And that, Parker," I whisper to her, "is called 'wearing the pants in the family.' Watch and learn, young grasshopper. Watch and learn."

The next morning I'm exhausted. I was up most of the night, yelling at PPB in my head and thinking about all of the bitchy things that I wish I weren't too much of a pussy to actually say to her, and now I feel like I'm getting a sore throat. I lie in bed, pretending to be asleep until I hear Andrew leave to take Zoey for her morning walk around the block. I gave him the silent treatment the whole night last night, and I really don't feel like dealing with him this morning.

When he's gone, I open my eyes and glance at the clock: eight twenty-two. The boxing class that I go to every day is at nine, and I just can't imagine motivating enough to get up and out the door in the next fifteen minutes. Oh, fuck it. I'll just skip the gym today. It's not like that stupid class has even made a dent in those last ten pounds anyway. Besides, it'll give me a chance to spend some time with Parker. She's been sleeping for almost ten hours straight lately, and most days I'm usually out the door before she even wakes up. I really can't believe I'm saying this, but I almost miss her waking up at night. It was good, quality, Deloris-free bonding time for us.

I peer at the video monitor and see that she has somehow managed to completely turn herself around in her crib, and her head is lying right next to the camera lens that I stuck in the corner, between the crib rail and the mattress.

Okay, I think. *Let me get dressed before she wakes up.*

I head for the bathroom to pee and brush my teeth, and then I put on a pair of sweatpants and a tank top. By the time that I emerge from my closet and check the monitor again, she's awake. She's squirming around and trying to get her toes in her mouth, but she hasn't started crying yet, so I decide to watch her for a minute or two, just because it's funny to see what she does when she thinks that nobody is looking. After three failed attempts to roll herself over onto her stomach, she gives up and just lies there on her side, completely still. Her face is now directly in front of the camera, and she's so close to it that I can only see about three-quarters of her head. She's staring right into the lens, and then, suddenly, she notices it. She reaches out her arm and begins to jostle the camera; I can hear her breathing and the noise of the camera being moved around, and between the sounds and the extreme close-up on her face, I feel like I'm watching *The Blair Witch Project*. She pulls the camera toward her until all I can see is her mouth, and then the camera goes black.

Oh, shit. She's trying to eat the camera.

I jump up and run out the door to her room, slightly panicking as I wonder whether she can electrocute herself this way. I arrive at the doorway of Parker's room within seconds, but it seems that I have been preempted. Deloris is already there, lifting Parker out of her crib.

"You need to take that camera out of the crib," Deloris says without looking at me. "She could get the cord wrapped around her neck."

"I know," I say. "I saw it on the monitor. I was coming in to get her." Deloris carries Parker over to the changing table, still not looking at me.

"Oh," she says, "I didn't realize you were still here." That is such bullshit. I never leave without telling her first.

"Yeah, well, I've decided to stay home today. So I'll take her now. It's fine."

Deloris glances at me sideways. "No, no," she says. "Deloris doesn't mind a bit. You go on and do what you have to do."

"I don't have anything to do," I say. "Really, I'll take her." I walk over to the changing table and stand behind Parker's head. She looks up at me and gives me an upside-down smile. "Hi, sweetie," I say. "Mommy's here." Deloris finishes changing her diaper and snaps her pajamas back up again. As she lifts Parker up, I reach out and grab her under her arms. "Thanks," I say.

Deloris reluctantly lets go and then follows me out of the bedroom and downstairs to the kitchen, where she makes a bottle while I stand beside her, waiting for her to finish.

"Are you hungry?" I ask Parker, in a voice about six octaves higher than usual. "You must be starving. You haven't eaten since last night, and I'm sure you worked up an appetite with all of that laughing we were doing together." At this, I see Deloris's eyebrows go up ever so slightly.

That's right, girlfriend. Mommy/Deloris/Daddy.

Parker grins at me again.

"I know," I say, in my falsetto. "Mommy's so funny, isn't she?"

Deloris finishes shaking the bottle. "Okay," she says. "All ready. I'll take her now."

"No," I say, trying to be polite, "I'll feed her."

Deloris glares at me and hands me the bottle. "Fine," she say, abruptly. "I'll go start the laundry."

I smile to myself and carry Parker away toward the den, where I sit down on the couch and flip on the *Today* show while I feed her.

Not ten minutes later, Deloris is back.

"All done?" she asks, reaching her arms out to take Parker. I pick up the empty bottle and hand it to her.

"Yes, thanks so much." Deloris scowls, but I ignore her. "Come on, Parker, let's go play."

I stand up and walk over to the empty space behind the couch, where Andrew has set up a makeshift playroom. There's a rubber play mat covering the hardwood floor with a bunch of toys strewn on top of it, and a fluorescent green nylon tunnel sitting alongside it. I gently place Parker down on the mat and get down on my knees, but before I can even pick up a toy, Deloris has plopped herself down next to me.

Oh, that is so annoying. She picks up a rattle and starts shaking it in front of Parker's face, and Parker turns her head toward the noise.

"Here, Parker," she says. "Look what Deloris has!"

Oh. My. God. I can't believe her. She's trying to distract Parker to keep her from looking at me.

Well. Two can play at that game. I pick up a bigger toy that plays "Yankee Doodle Dandy" when you roll the handle, and I wave it next to Parker's ear.

"Par-ker," I say, starting to sing along. She turns her head and looks over at me, and I clap my hands together to the beat. "And with the girls be randy!" I sing. It occurs to me that those are the words to the dirty version of "Yankee Doodle" that we used to sing at my overnight camp, but whatever. It got her attention. She stares up at me and I smile at her and tickle her chin, trying to ignore Deloris, who is still shaking the rattle and calling Parker's name. Finally Deloris stands up.

It's about time, I think. But then, out of the corner of my eye, I notice that she is pulling the tunnel onto the mat. *What the hell is she doing?* She positions it so that one end is right next to Parker's head, and then she kneels down in front of the other end.

"Yoo-hoo, Parker," she calls. Intrigued by the tunnel, Parker turns her head, and Deloris quickly sticks her face into the opening. "Peekaboo!" she shouts, then pulls her head out again. Parker smiles. "Peekaboo!" This time Parker lets out a cackle, and I have to restrain myself from jumping on Deloris's back and putting her into a headlock. I sit up on my heels, fuming, and I glare at Deloris.

That was my cackle, bitch.

Just then Zoey races into the den, paws muddy from her walk, and Andrew appears a few seconds behind her.

"Hey," he says, sounding pleasantly surprised to see the three of us together. "What are you guys doing?"

Deloris turns around and beams at him. "Oh, we're just playing, Mr. Andrew. We're having a great time."

Andrew smiles back at Deloris and then glances over at me to gauge my mood toward him. I give him an icy stare and his smile fades.

"Can I speak to you for a second?" I ask him. He gets a nervous look on his face.

"Sure." I stand up and walk over to him, and then I grab his arm and pull him out into the kitchen. "What's up?" he asks me, trying to sound upbeat.

"Don't think that I've forgiven you just because I'm talking to you right now," I snarl. His face drops back into a frown. "That woman is crazy," I whisper. " 'Oh, we're just playing, Mr. Andrew,' " I say, imitating Deloris. "*We* were not playing. *I* was playing, and she was infringing on me."

Andrew looks flummoxed. "What are you talking about?" he asks.

"Andrew, I'm telling you, she hates me! She thinks that I'm a bad mother, so she's trying to do everything she can to keep me from spending time alone with Parker. I feel like I've got a court-ordered chaperone in there."

He shakes his head. "That's ridiculous."

"No, it's not ridiculous. It's true. She's competing with me for Parker's love. She wants Parker to think that she's her mommy!" My eyes are welling up with tears.

"She's a big, black Jamaican woman," Andrew says, smiling. "Unless she's color-blind or really, really stupid, I don't think that Parker will be confused." I give him an I-don't-find-you-to-be-even-one-bit-funny look, and his face turns serious. "Lara, she's just doing her job."

"Yeah, if it were her job to edge me out."

"No," he says sternly. "You're just projecting your type-A, East Coast, aggressive personality onto her. She's not the competitive one here. You are."

I roll my eyes at him. "Oh, spare me the Psych One-oh-one crap, Andrew, okay?"

"Hey," he says defensively. "I got an A in that class." He straightens his back, rising a few proud inches taller. "The professor suggested that I look into graduate programs."

I snap my fingers with both hands. "Clicks for Andrew," I say.

He ignores me. "Look," he says. "You hired her to take care of the baby, so that's what she's going to do. I'm sure she'd feel awkward just sitting in her room doing nothing, while you do what's supposed to be her job."

I shake my head no. As usual, he has it all wrong.

"So you're taking her side. That's great. First Courtney, and now Deloris. Are there any other women in your life who are more important than I am whom I should know about?"

He closes his eyes and looks up at the sky. "Lara," he says. "Whether you believe it or not, you are the most important woman in my life. Sometimes I'm not exactly sure why, but you are. However, just because you're the most important does not mean that I always think that you're right. And in this case, I don't think that you're right. Deloris is a wonderful person who treats Parker like she's her own. She's trustworthy, she's reliable, and she isn't capable of hurting a fly."

My mouth drops open. "Andrew," I yell, "the woman has voodoo dolls in her room!"

"They're *decorative*," he says. "Now, try to see things from her perspective and stop this before you scare her off and we're left with nobody to take care of Parker. Because I don't think you want that, do you?" I pout at him, saying nothing. "That's what I thought," he says. He looks at his watch. "Now, I have to go to work. Can we finish talking about this later?"

"I don't know," I hiss. "I haven't decided if I'm talking to you or not."

"Fine," he says, sounding completely fed up with me. "When you've decided, let me know." He picks his keys up off of the counter, stuffs his wallet into his back pocket, and walks out.

Great. He's probably going to call Courtney on his way to work to tell her what a bitch his wife is, and how much he wishes I could be more like her.

Well, Andrew, I think. *I used to be more like her, before you knocked me up.*

I sigh. How is it possible that he's the one who's practically having an affair, but I'm the one who's the bad guy?

thirteen

Later that afternoon, while Parker is taking her nap, I sit down at the computer to check my e-mail. I haven't checked it in almost a week, and I've got about forty messages. A third are advertisements for porn (*Hot!!!! teens w/strangers. Sexxxxy girl w/dog*), a third are e-mails from alleged dignitaries in countries I've never heard of who are willing to give me a handsome reward if I will just use my status as an American to help them with a multimillion-dollar bank transaction, and a third are actual e-mails from people I know.

Let's see . . . two from teachers at work who want to know how the baby is; three from former students—oh, Marc just got back from a prefreshman program at BU, and he loved it. Thank God. I was worried about him. There's one from my mom, begging for me to e-mail more pictures of Parker, even though she can never figure out how to view them so that they're not gigantic and so that the whole screen isn't taken up by an arm or an ear; one is from an e-mail address that I don't recognize, and one is from Nadine. I click on the one from Nadine.

Hi, Lara,

Only six more weeks to the wedding . . . we need to start planning the bachelorette. Let's meet for lunch?

xoxo
Nadine

That's interesting, I think. This is the first time I've heard from her or my dad since I told him that I don't want to have anything to do with her. Of course he didn't tell her. Or, if he did, of course she didn't care. Miss You-can't-say-no-to-me. What did I do to deserve having these people in my life? I sigh. Like I'm going to know where to have a bachelorette party, anyway. I haven't been out since I got pregnant, and that was over a year ago. I couldn't even tell you the first initial of a good club.

I'll just have to find a way to get out of this. Maybe if I don't answer her, she'll go away. That's a good strategy. I close Nadine's message and go back to my in-box. The e-mail from the address that I don't recognize says, *Don't Think I'm Crazy* in the subject line.

Intrigued, I click on it. Oh, it's from Melissa, the lone brunette girl in Susan's class. I wonder what she wants.

Dear Fellow Moms,

I hope you don't mind that I'm e-mailing you, but I've been thinking about the "discussion" that we had in Susan's class last week, and I had an idea for a girls' night out that could be a really fun bonding experience for all of us. A friend of mine was telling me about a party that she went to recently—girls only—where a "sexpert" showed them how to improve their oral techniques, if you know what I mean. She said that it was hilarious and such a blast, and I thought that maybe we should do it as an unofficial class "field trip." We are going to be together every week for the next eighteen months, so we might as well get to know one another and have some fun, right? If anyone is interested, please e-mail me back, and if we can get a group of six or more, I'm willing to kick my husband out for the night and have it at my house. I look forward to hearing from you!

Melissa (Hannah's mom)

A blow-job party? She wants to have a blow-job party with the virgins from Susan's class? Is she kidding? I reread the e-mail. I can't decide if I am more disturbed by the content or by the fact that I am receiving correspondence from a woman whose main source of self-identification is as somebody else's mother.

The phone rings, and I grab it before it has a chance to ring again because I don't want Parker to get woken up. I swear, that kid sleeps lighter than the ex-cops who are always in action movies; you know, the ones who've had some kind of traumatic, in-the-line-of-duty experience, and who wake up from a dead sleep whenever the wind blows, whipping guns out from under their pillows.

"Hello?" I half whisper.

"Hey, is something wrong?" It's Stacey.

"No, I'm just talking softly so that I don't wake Parker up."

"She wakes up from you talking? Aren't babies supposed to sleep like babies? I thought they could sleep through anything."

"Not mine," I say. "Leave it to my child to be the exception to an age-old simile. She doesn't have a smooth bottom, either. It's actually got little zits all over it from sitting in pee, and I think she's got some eczema right near her butt crack."

"Thank you for the imagery," she says.

"No thanks necessary. What's up?"

"Nothing," she says, lowering her voice. "But I just heard a rumor that the partnership vote is going to happen at the end of this week, and now I'm too nervous to concentrate on anything real, so I thought I'd call you."

"Okay," I say, switching to a serious tone. "Putting aside for the moment your implication that I'm not real, I don't understand. It's only the middle of July. I thought they weren't going to decide on partners until the end of the summer."

"So did I, but then a very reliable source told me that they were meeting this week. I don't know what happened."

"Oh, my God. Are you freaking out? When will they tell you?"

"I don't know," she says, her pitch rising just slightly, which, for Stacey, is borderline hysterical. "I don't know anything. It's like a fucking fraternity around here. The partners are the brothers and the associates are the pledges, and everything's a secret. I'm not allowed to ask any questions."

I sigh sympathetically. "Well, look, it will be over soon. And you'll either make it or you won't, and if you don't, then at least you can stop working so damn hard a few weeks earlier than you were supposed to."

"Yeah, whatever," she says. "I don't want to talk about it. Tell me things about you. What's up with your dad?"

"Oh, God, when was the last time I talked to you? Do you even know about Nadine?"

I spend the next twenty minutes filling her in on the wedding *(Think they'll have a pole on the dance floor? Maybe Colin Cowie will cover it with roses)*, on how I got snookered into being the matron of honor *(You're such a pussy. What happened to the rules?)*, and on the bridal shower at the Peninsula *(It really said "with love"? I take it back. You're not a pussy. You're a double pussy)*. I give her the scoop about Courtney *(So Andrew finally cracked. Interesting. Although I had my money on you driving him to drink, not cheat)*, about Deloris *(You're pathetic. I yell at my secretary if she breathes the wrong way)*, and about the e-mail that I just received from Melissa (Hannah's mom) (Silence. Too disturbed, apparently, to think of a put-down for this one).

The only thing I don't tell her about is Nadine's business. I want to so badly, and I know that Stacey wouldn't care, but I'm just too mortified to talk about it with anyone. I mean, my father has embarrassed me plenty of times in my life; please, he got me kicked out of my elementary school carpool because he always used to listen to Howard Stern in the mornings, and one day Maggie Feurstein went home and asked her mom what *anal* was. And when I was in the seventh grade, he came to visiting day at my overnight camp and insisted on examining my boyfriend's lips to see if they were swollen from sucking on anything of mine. But this one takes the cake. Marrying a Hollywood Madam. I'm not even sure that I can say it out loud. I haven't even told Andrew.

"Wow," Stacey says when I've finished recounting the last three weeks. "You're a regular soap opera. I had no idea that the life of a stay-at-home mom could get so complicated."

"Yeah, well, there're only six more weeks until the wedding, and then I start work, so hopefully things will calm down and I can go back to being boring old me again. Although this thing with Andrew . . . I don't know."

"Listen, Lar. I really don't think that Andrew will physically cheat on you, but you've got to give him a reason to stop hanging out with this Courtney chick. You know, going to that blow-job party might not be such a bad idea. It might be just what you need to get him to stop thinking about her and to start thinking about you again."

"Stacey," I protest, "I don't give blow jobs. Blow jobs are for girls who are trying to get a ring, not for girls who've been married for five years."

"I bet Courtney gives blow jobs."

I close my eyes and exhale. "Okay," I say. "I'm e-mailing her back right now." I click back on the e-mail and hit the reply button, reading aloud to Stacey while I type. " 'Dear Melissa,' " I recite. " 'This sounds great. You can count me in. Thanks, Lara.' "

"That's it?" Stacey asks snidely.

"*Fine*," I retort. " 'Lara, parentheses, Parker's mom.' "

Stacey laughs out loud. "I never thought that it would come to this," she says.

"Yeah, well, join the club."

Parker wakes up from her nap just in time for me to get her to Dr. Newman's office by three thirty. She's almost sixteen weeks old, which in my book is four months, but we've got her three-month checkup today because Dr. Newman has been on vacation for the last week and a half, and his office said that actually she won't be four months until August second, which is still two weeks away. I swear, this whole baby thing is so confusing sometimes. I just found out the other day that I've been strapping her into her car seat wrong this whole time. I was trying to stick her legs through the straps instead of just buckling the straps over her legs, and I was practically breaking the poor kid in half to make it work. I'm such an idiot. I couldn't figure out why people kept saying this car seat was so great when it was such a pain in the ass for me to get her in and out of it every time we had to go somewhere.

Anyway, Andrew's supposed to be meeting us at the doctor's office, but he's late. I've already signed in and I'm sitting in the waiting room, feeding Parker the bottle that she was supposed to eat at three fifteen but that I had to put off giving her so that we could get here on time—which made for a fun car ride, let me tell you—when Andrew bursts through the door.

"Hi," he says to me. "Sorry. I was on the phone."

"With Courtney?" I snort.

He gives me a dirty look. "With my accountant." He lowers his voice and sounds annoyed. "I don't know what kind of scenarios you've got playing out in your head, but can you just let the Courtney thing go? We don't talk on the phone. I only talk to her at agility. That's it. She's just a friend from agility."

"Fine," I say, dropping it. Not because it is fine, of course, but because the other mom in the waiting room is pretending that she's not eavesdropping on us, but I know that she is, and I don't want to provide her with fodder for her dinner conversation tonight.

By now Parker has finished the bottle, so I sit her up on my lap to try to burp her. Just then the nurse opens the door to the waiting room and calls our name.

"Parker Stone," she says, looking at me. "We're ready for you. The yellow room." I gather Parker up and leave the car seat and the diaper bag sitting on the chair next to me for Andrew to take, and I follow the nurse down the hall to the examining room with the yellow floor. "Take off everything but her diaper," she says. "I'll be right back to weigh her." She walks out and closes the door behind her, and Andrew sits down on the chair in the corner while I begin to undress Parker in silence.

"How is she, anyway?" Andrew asks me, as I slip off the pink-and-white-striped diaper cover that she's wearing under her pink sundress.

"She's fine," I say. "She laughs now. Did you know that? And she tries to roll over."

"I know," he says. "Deloris told me." He stands up and walks over to her, stroking her head with his hand. "Hi," he says to her. He lifts her up and puts his face in front of hers. "Who's your daddy?" he asks, in a voice that sounds kind of like Cookie Monster's, if Cookie Monster were in a porno. "Who. Is. Your. Daddy?"

Parker's lips start to quiver, and she lets out a wail. I reach out and take her from him, and she puts her head on my shoulder and whimpers.

Hmmm. Perhaps the totem pole is shorter than I thought. Daddy might not be on it at all.

"She has no idea who her daddy is," I say accusingly. "You're hardly ever home anymore."

Wow, I think. The times, they are a changin', if I'm the one lecturing about never being home. But Andrew looks positively crushed.

"She hates me," he moans.

"She doesn't hate you. She just doesn't know you." I give him a look. "Now you know how I feel with Deloris."

Andrew starts to open his mouth, but the door swings open before he can get any words out, which is probably for the best.

"Okay," the nurse says. "Take the diaper off and let's put her on the scale." I do as instructed, and we wait while the numbers on the digital scale adjust. When it stops, the nurse takes out her pen and talks out loud while she writes it down.

"Seventeen pounds, four and half ounces." She looks at me. "She's four months?" she asks.

"Three months," I say. The nurse's eyes widen. "But she's sixteen weeks," I add quickly. The nurse makes a *whatever* face.

"Big girl," she says, in a completely judgmental tone of voice. She grabs her chart and walks out, looking back at me over her shoulder. "Doctor will be right in."

I put Parker's diaper back on, trying not to be upset. "She's F-A-T," I say to Andrew.

"Why are you spelling it?" he asks.

"Because," I say, "F-A-T is not a word that I want her to learn from me." I lower my voice and turn my head away from her. "And neither is *diet,* or *calorie,*" I say. "So watch yourself."

Now, in case you're wondering why I would need to issue such a warning to my husband, please recall that I am married to Andrew Stone, King of Strange Habits and Laughable Eccentricities. You see, Andrew, metrosexual that he is, is notorious for knowing the exact calorie content of various foods. It's scary, actually. The whole thing started when he turned thirty and had a bit of a life crisis, and he decided that he wanted to look and weigh what he did his senior year of high school. Mind you, the guy is five-eight (five-eight and a quarter, according to him) and his waist is almost as small as mine was *before* I got pregnant. But just being thin wasn't good enough for him. He insisted that he was going to regain both his six-pack and the smooth, hairless, prepubescent appearance of his youth. So, he shaved his chest (which resulted in months of itchy stubble and ingrown hairs the size of small tumors), did three hundred crunches before bed every night, and went on a crash diet to lose six pounds.

For three months he was obsessed with not eating more than fifteen hundred calories a day, and he practically memorized *The Dieter's Calorie Counter*. He was *insane*. If we were going to the movies, he'd pack snacks in plastic Baggies—one cup of light microwave popcorn (twenty-five calories) and five Red Vines (thirty-five calories each)—and then make me smuggle them into the theater in my purse. If we were at someone's house and they had a dish of M&M's out on the table, he'd sit there and try to figure out how many he could eat without going over his limit for the day *(ten M&M's are thirty-four calories, which means that each M&M is three-point-four calories, which means that if I eat thirty-three of them— hey, does anyone have a calculator?)*. And if we were at a party and there were cookies, or cake, or some other dessert food of unknown caloric content, he would just stand there and sniff them, in full view, while everyone else wondered what was wrong with me for having to marry such an odd little man. And then, of course, he felt compelled to tell me the caloric value of everything that I ate, too.

Honey, he'd say, raising his eyebrows as I reached for the grated Parmesan cheese to sprinkle on my steamed spinach at dinner. *That's an extra twenty-three calories. One tablespoon of that a day is an extra pound a year.*

Can you imagine? One of my friends is a therapist, and she once cornered me at a birthday party after Andrew pulled one of his sniffing routines, and proceeded to give me a twenty-minute lecture about how men can have eating disorders, too. So you'll have to forgive me for being just slightly concerned that Andrew might give Parker an even bigger food complex than I will.

The door opens again, and this time Dr. Newman walks in. He's all business.

"Hi," he says, not waiting for us to say "hi" back. "So, congratulations. You made it through the first three months. Is she sleeping yet?"

I nod. "Eleven hours."

Dr. Newman nods back and motions for me to put Parker down on the table, which I do. "Rolling over?" he asks.

I shake my head. "No, but she tries."

He nods again and places his stethoscope on her chest, and she grins at him. He smiles back and takes out a tongue depressor, placing it in her mouth.

"Okay. You're going to see her start to drool all of the time and she'll try to put everything in her mouth."

Yeah, I think, *thanks for the heads-up.*

"It's preteething," he continues. "Teeth will start to come in anytime between five months and a year." He's talking really slowly and enunciating every word, as if he thinks that this is too much information for me to handle all at once.

I nod at him to show that I get it, and then I clear my throat. "Is she too heavy?" I ask bluntly. He looks at her chart, then looks at her. Yeah, yeah, I know that she's just a baby and that I shouldn't fixate on her weight, but I can't help it. It just doesn't seem normal for a sixteen-week-old to have fat rolls thick enough to lose things in. I swear, sometimes I think I might find Jimmy Hoffa hiding in her neck.

"Seventeen-four," Dr. Newman muses, bobbing his head from side to side as he thinks about it. "She's on the big side, but she's all right." He looks me in the eye and gives me an I-told-you-so look. "It's the formula," he says, shrugging. "It makes 'em fat."

Thanks, I think, waiting for him to inform me that, ideally, I should have breast-fed her for three months. But he doesn't. Instead, he turns to look at both of us.

"Have you noticed that the back of her head is getting a little flat?" he asks, sounding mildly concerned. I instantly feel my eyes begin to bulge, and I wonder if it is possible for them to actually pop out of their sockets. Andrew drops his car keys on the floor.

"What?" we both yell in unison.

Dr. Newman puts his palms out as if to tell us to relax. "It's very common," he says. "Their skull bones don't harden right away, and the pressure of the mattress on the back of the head can cause it to flatten."

I stand back a little and scrutinize her from the side. He's right. She looks like someone hit her in the back of the head with a frying pan.

Oh, my God, I am so awful. Here I am all worried about her weight, and I didn't even notice that her head is shaped like the letter D.

"So what can we do?" I ask frantically. "Will it ever be normal?" I'm beside myself. I'm having visions of her walking down the aisle on her wedding day, her veil looking like it's stuck to a piece of cardboard. But Dr. Newman doesn't seem upset.

"It's very correctable," he says. "Just start putting her to sleep on her side at night, and it will develop normally."

I start to exhale, but then I remember that I am now a neurotic Jewish mother, and as such, I am required to be as annoying as possible. "But what if it doesn't?" I ask him in a panicky voice.

He shoots me a look and picks up her chart. "It will," he replies, in a tone telling me that this is the end of the conversation. "Trust me."

fourteen

Two days later, I'm sitting on the floor in Susan's class, surveying the room to see if any of the other babies have freakish physical deformities, or if mine is the only one. I think that mine is the only one. Some of the babies are completely bald, but that doesn't really count. One has a colossal nose—we're talking a *serious* beak—and one poor little girl is just downright ugly, but that's not what I'm looking for, either.

No, I think, trying not to cry as I realize that all of the other babies are perfectly normal. *There's nobody else.* Eleven perfectly normal, skinny little beanpoles with perfectly normal round bowling balls for heads, and one gigantic round bowling ball topped with the head of a tennis racket. God, I wonder if formula causes flathead syndrome, too.

I sigh. Ever since the appointment with Dr. Newman, I've been obsessed with fixing Parker's head. I went out and bought a little pillow with a hole in the middle of it—it looks like the part of a massage table that you stick your face in, except that it's for the back of her head, for when she's lying on the floor—and I've instructed Deloris to try to keep her on her stomach as much as possible, even though she hates being on her stomach and screams bloody murder whenever I make her do "tummy time."

But her sleeping is turning out to be a real problem. I've been putting her down on her side, like Dr. Newman said, but she always rolls onto her back within twenty seconds. The first night I kept running into her room every five minutes to push her back onto her side, but that's obviously not a long-term solution. So I called Dr. Newman yesterday to tell him that it wasn't working, and he recommended using crib wedges to keep her in

place. So I ran out and bought two different kinds, but they don't work either. She slides right over the damn things.

I swear, you have no idea how much this is stressing me out. I mean,
how am I supposed to trust him that her head is going to get better if the
solutions he's giving me don't work? Trust him, my ass. I wonder if Susan
has any ideas. I think I'll ask her at the end of class, during the Q & A time.

The lecture today is about language development, and Susan has pro-
vided us with a long list of books that we should be reading them at this
age. I'm not really paying attention because I'm so consumed with comparing Parker's head to everyone else's, but I'm pretty sure I just heard her
say that we should be reading to them for an hour a day. Which is absurd,
by the way. I mean, I don't know when the last time was that she tried
reading a book to a three-month-old, but it's pointless. I tried to read *Pat
the Bunny* to Parker just last week, but all she wanted to do was gum the
pages. It was gross, really. She drooled all over the bunny, so the bunny
fur got all wet and slimy, and then Parker ended up with stray pieces of
bunny fur in her throat, which she kept hocking up all afternoon. Really,
it was not a pleasant experience for me. Not at all. But I must be doing
something wrong, because all of the other moms are nodding as Susan is
talking, like they read to their babies all the time and have no problem
with it whatsoever. I roll my eyes at myself.

Wow, so I'm doing something wrong. What else is new?

Across the room, a baby wearing a pink Juicy sweat suit flips over onto
her stomach, and her mom claps and gasps with delight, interrupting Susan midsentence.

"Oh, my God, you did it!" the mom says. "You rolled over!" She leans
down to kiss her baby, whose name is Ava, I think, and everyone in the
room freezes as they watch her. Out of nowhere, a palpable tension forms
in the air.

I know this tension, I think. It's the same tension that always forms
during the yes-it-matters-if-your-kid-didn't-take-any-honors-or-AP-
classes part of the Eleventh-grade Parents College Night that I run
every year. It's the tension of neurotic, hypercompetitive mothers who
have just discovered that someone else's child is more advanced than
their own.

Suddenly there is whispering. The fake-blond mommunist sitting next to me leans over.

"Is she rolling over yet?" she asks, pointing to Parker. I shake my head no.

"Okay, good," says the mommunist, sounding relieved. "Mine isn't either, but if yours was, I would really be worried." I give her a funny look. What is that supposed to mean? Has Parker been anointed the class moron or something? She sees that I'm insulted and leans over again to explain. "Just because she's so big," she whispers. "I'd think that it would be harder for her to roll over because she's so heavy, that's all."

Okay. I just realized something. When they all go to lunch and the talk turns to me, I'm not called Parker's mom. I'm called the fat baby's mom. That's how I should have signed my e-mail reply to Melissa: *Thanks, Lara (the fat baby's mom)*.

I sit back, fuming, and try to listen to Susan, who is pretending not to notice that ten mothers are pretending not to care that someone else's baby was the first one to roll over.

"It is your responsibility to build your child's vocabulary," she says, "and the best way to do that is through repetition. I suggest that you pick one object a week—a light, for example—and every time you walk by the light with your baby, you point to the light and say, 'Light.' Eventually, when you ask your baby where the light is, she'll point to it."

That makes sense, I think. *I'll try that.* But maybe I'll start with *girdle*, since that's obviously going to be a crucial part of Parker's repertoire.

The mommunist bitch next to me raises her hand.

"Yes," Susan says, nodding to her.

"What about Baby Einstein videos?" she asks. "I've been putting them on for Emma and she seems to really like them."

Susan frowns with disapproval. "Absolutely not," she says. "No television before the age of two. Just because it has *Einstein* in the title doesn't mean that it's good for your baby."

Unsatisfied with this answer, the mommunist bitch pushes on. "But they have language labs on them. And they say the word and write it out whenever they show a picture of something."

Susan leans in and points her finger. "Do you want to give your child a learning disability? Because that's where you're headed if you're letting her watch television at three months old."

The mommunist bitch slinks down and looks like she's about to cry. If she hadn't just insulted me the way she did, I would lean over and tell her that she shouldn't feel bad, as Parker surely already has brain damage from the amount of television that I let her watch. But she did insult me, so instead I purse my lips and give her a wow-that's-too-bad-that-you've-already-fucked-up-your-baby-for-life, better-luck-with-the-next-one look.

"Okay," Susan says. "That's all I have for today. Does anyone have any questions?"

I do. I have a question. I really, really, really have a question, but now I can't ask it. Because if I ask it, I won't just be Lara (the fat baby's mom) anymore. I'll be Lara (the fat baby with the flat head's mom), and I do not want to be that mom. I sigh. I guess I'll just wait until everyone leaves, and then I'll try to corner Susan when class is over, in private.

After the questions are all answered, we spend ten minutes doing the motorboat song, "The Itsy Bitsy Spider," and "Twinkle, Twinkle, Little Star." Then we all stand up and, holding our babies, we form yet another circle and do what feels like a square dance to the tune of "Kookaburra," with Susan calling out instructions after every verse. A kookaburra, in case you didn't know, is actually an Australian bird that eats the babies of other birds; I'm having a hard time deciding whether the song is obscenely inappropriate or just exquisitely fitting for this particular Mommy and Me class.

Kookaburra sits on the old gum tree—"Sway back and forth."
Merry, merry king of the bush is he—"Now walk to your right."
Laugh, Kookaburra, laugh—"Now to the left."
Kookaburra gay your life must be—"And dosie-do." (Just kidding.)

When we finally finish, my back is killing me from holding Porker—I mean Parker—in front of me for so long, so I put her back down on the floor while I wait for everyone else to clear out. But as the other moms are gathering their things and packing up their Prada diaper bags, Melissa (Hannah's mom) stands in the middle of the room to make an announcement.

"You guys," she yells, trying to get everyone to quiet down. When she has our attention, she continues. "It seems that everyone responded yes to my e-mail," she says, giving us all a sly look. "So, I wanted to pick a night when everyone can do it. I was thinking about next Friday. Does anyone object?" We all look at one another, and nobody speaks up. "Great," she says. "I'll order some salads and we'll start at seven. Let our husbands put the babies to bed for a change." Everyone laughs at this and she says good-bye, adding that she'll e-mail directions to her house.

Fantastic. Looks like the blow-job party is on.

I shuffle around for a few minutes, pretending to be looking for something in my diaper bag, and when the last person has gone, I pick Parker back up and walk over to Susan, who is sitting at her desk.

"Um, Susan," I say, trying to get her attention. Susan spins around.

"Yes," she says. "What can I do for you?"

"I actually have a question, but I felt more comfortable asking you in private. I hope you don't mind."

She smiles at me. "No, no, not at all. Tell me your name and your baby's name again. I'm terrible with these things." *Oh, of course*, I think. *I'm Lara, and this is my daughter, SpongeBob SquarePants.*

"I'm Lara, and this is Parker."

"Right," she says. "Okay, Lara, what's your question?"

"Well, at her checkup last week, my doctor said that she's starting to get a flat head. He told me to put her to sleep on her side, but I can't get her to stay that way. Do you have any ideas? I tried using the crib wedges but they don't work."

Susan frowns. "Hold her over your shoulder and let me see it," she commands. I hoist Parker over my shoulder, and then, like a judge at a dog show, Susan walks around us in a circle, carefully examining Parker's head. She tilts it from side to side, then circles around us three more times. When she's finished, she is still frowning.

"It's definitely not the worst I've ever seen, but it's pretty bad." I gulp as she continues talking. "I want you to set up a consult with a specialist immediately. She may be a good candidate for a helmet, and you want to deal with this now before it gets any worse. The pediatricians always wait too long. Sometimes it can take months to get in to see a specialist and by then it's too late."

I feel like I'm hearing her in slow motion, and I think I lost her at the helmet part.

"I'm sorry," I say. "A helmet?"

Susan nods. "Yes. When babies have flat heads, sometimes they'll put them in a helmet for six months or so. It takes the pressure off and then the head usually pops back out again." I think I'm going to be sick. And I must look like I'm going to be sick, too, because Susan smiles at me and puts her hand on my arm.

"Oh, don't worry, they make really cute helmets now." I picture a Swarovski crystal–studded helmet in a leopard-print design, kind of like a Judith Leiber bag, but it doesn't make me feel any better. Susan reaches over onto her desk and picks up a pad of paper and a pen. "Here," she says, as she writes on the pad. "This is the name of a fabulous pediatric neurologist. He's wonderful, and his partner is a craniofacial plastic surgeon, so once she's diagnosed you can stay in the office for treatment." She hands me the slip of paper, and my hand shakes when I take it from her. Neurologist? Plastic surgeon? I look at Parker, whose head is now resting against my chest, and my eyes fill with tears. This can't be happening. It can't be.

"Okay," I say, almost whispering. "Thanks."

By the time I get outside and get Parker strapped into her stroller, I am totally hysterical and on the verge of having a nervous breakdown. I grab my cell phone out of my diaper bag and frantically dial Andrew's number at work.

"This is Andrew Stone," he says.

I heave loudly into the phone, unable to speak.

"Hello?" he asks. I take a deep breath, and start talking as I exhale.

"I just left Mommy and Me and I asked Susan about Parker's head and she said that we need to call a neurologist right away and that our baby is going to have to wear a helmet for six months." I start to sob. "I don't want our baby to have to wear a helmet. That's the saddest thing I ever heard."

"Is it that bad?" he asks. I can tell from his tone that he's upset.

I sniffle. "Susan said that it's not the worst she's ever seen, but that it's definitely bad. She said it can take months to get in to a specialist and that we need to call now before it's too late. I want to tell Dr. Newman what she said. Will you call him right now?"

"I'm calling. I'll call you back as soon as I talk to him."

"Okay." I sniffle again. I am feeling so much love for him right now that I can't even stand it. I mean, there is no one else in the world who could ever understand how upsetting this is except for him. For the first time since Parker was born, I really do feel like we're partners in this parenthood thing. "Andrew?" I say.

"Yes?"

"I don't care about anything else. I don't care about Courtney, I don't care about Deloris, I don't care about anything. I just want her to be okay." I sniffle again. "I don't want her to be a helmet head."

"I don't either," he says. "Let's just see what the doctor has to say."

As befits my shitty luck, I made plans to have lunch with Julie after class so that we could go over the essays that she wrote for the Institute, which is just about the last thing that I feel like doing right now. Right now, all I want to do is go home and spend the rest of the day scouring the Internet for information about flat heads and helmet treatments, but it's too late for me to cancel on her. She's probably already at the restaurant by now. And by the way, her essays sucked. They're the most pathetic, kiss-ass essays I've ever read, and believe me, I have dealt with a lot of pathetic, ass-kissing essay writers in my time.

Ugh. The thought of Julie right now is making me ill. I really can't think of anyone with whom I would want to discuss Parker's condition less. I mean, I love Julie, but I do not want my baby's head becoming fodder for the LA-mommy rumor mill. I can just imagine her calling people up and whispering to them about how awful it is that Lara's baby has to wear a helmet. Not that I can blame her, of course. I would do the same thing if her baby needed a helmet, but still, I think that the wise move here is to keep the whole helmet thing on the down-low. I'll just pretend that nothing is wrong and make sure that I keep Parker facing forward during lunch.

* * *

Ten minutes later I am pushing the Snap-N-Go through the restaurant, over to the table where Julie and Lily are sitting, waiting for us. Lily
is in a high chair, and she's eating minuscule bits of turkey off of a plastic
place mat that Julie has attached to the table in front of her. Immediately,
I check out her head. I have to. And, of course, it's perfect. Round as a full
moon. I feel Luthor rising in my throat—it's been a while since he's vis-
ited, actually. I almost didn't recognize him—and before I can get hold of
myself, I start to cry.

God damn it. Julie looks at me, alarmed.

"Lara," she says, sounding concerned. "What's wrong? Are you okay?"

I shake my head no, and I break down and tell her the whole story.
When I'm finished. Julie looks shaken.

"Can I see it?" she asks, sounding unsure whether this is an appropriate thing to ask. But I nod and lift Parker out of her stroller, hoping that
Julie will say that Susan is overreacting. I turn her around so that her back
is to Julie's face, and Julie bites her lower lip.

"I mean, it might be a *little* flat," she says.

I close my eyes. *Great.*

"This is terrible," I cry. "I can't put her in a helmet for six months. I'm
not doing it. What's the big deal if she has a flat head, anyway? She'll grow
hair. Nobody will even notice."

Julie looks troubled by this idea. "Susan said the helmets are cute?"

"Yeah, I'm sure they're just adorable." I tell her about my Judith Leiber
image. "There's a business you could start. Designer baby helmets. Go out
and get yourself a Bedazzler and you'll be all set." I am just about to burst
into tears again when my phone rings. I grab it.

"Hello?" It's Andrew.

"I talked to the doctor."

"And what did he say?" I ask anxiously.

"He said to get a new Mommy and Me class."

I exhale. Julie looks at me and mouths the words, *What did he say?*

I put up one finger for her to wait until Andrew is finished.

"He said that helmets are an absolute last resort and that Parker's head
looks like a soccer ball compared to the kids who get helmets. She's fine.
He said that if the wedges aren't working, you can try facing her in the

other direction when she sleeps, and maybe she'll just naturally turn her head to the other side and take the pressure off of the flat spot."

"But what if she doesn't?" I ask, panicking again.

"I knew you would ask that," Andrew says. "He said that if she doesn't, then eventually, once she starts rolling over, she won't spend as much time on her back and it won't be a problem anymore. But he assured me that she is absolutely *not* a candidate for a helmet. He said that he refers dozens of kids to specialists every year, and that it didn't even cross his mind when he saw Parker the other day. He said to tell Susan that she's an idiot."

"Okay," I say, feeling better, but not completely reassured. I hug Parker close to me. "Thanks for calling him. I'll talk to you later, okay?"

"Wait," he says, and then pauses for a second. "Did you really mean what you said before?" he asks. "About not caring about Courtney?"

I let out a long exhale, buying myself a few seconds to reconsider. "Yeah," I say, finally. "I did." Oh, come on. Andrew's not cheating on me. And he knew to ask the doctor my "what if she doesn't?" question. That kind of training is priceless in a husband. Besides, I've just been told that my baby needs to see a neurologist and a craniofacial plastic surgeon. I mean, on the let's-get-some-perspective scale, that's about a ten.

"That's great," Andrew says, sounding happier than he has in weeks. "She is just a friend, Lar. You have to know that I would never cheat on you. I love you too much."

"I know," I tell him. *But do you really need a friend who looks like that?* "I love you, too, dolly," I say, and then click on the end button. Julie is staring at me expectantly.

"So?" she asks.

"So, the doctor said that it's fine. He said that Susan's an idiot."

Julie looks terribly upset by this statement. As if I just told her that Lamaze toys contain carcinogens.

"Susan is *not* an idiot," she huffs. "Susan gives invaluable advice to mothers every day. My sisters swore by Susan when their kids were babies. They said that they never could have gotten through the first year without her. And I love her. Just last week she gave a great lecture about traveling that I will totally use the next time we go away." She shakes her head. "I just find it hard to believe that Susan would be wrong about something like this."

I stare at Julie, unsure of how to respond to her. It occurs to me that this is what it must be like to have to tell a kid that Santa Claus is really a pagan myth. Well. There's one good thing about being Jewish, I guess.

"Jul," I say, trying to not to be patronizing. "Everyone is wrong sometimes. Even Susan."

She shrugs. "Look, you can listen to your doctor if you want to. But I would trust Susan over my pediatrician any day of the week."

I decide that this is not a fight worth continuing. If Julie wants to believe that Susan is an all-knowing deity who can diagnose illnesses better than a trained professional with a medical degree, then let her. Far be it from me to ruin the magic.

"Well, whatever," I say, trying to act nonchalant about her weird hero worship of Susan. "Do you want to talk about your essays?"

"Yes," she says, seeming relieved that I have changed the subject. She reaches down into her diaper bag and whips out a red laminated folder that is filled with papers. "My Institute file," she says, flipping her chin in its direction. "I have one for every school that we're applying to. They're color-coded."

I roll my eyes when she's not looking. I know exactly who Julie was in high school. I have dozens of girls just like her at Bel Air Prep. They're not that smart, so they try to compensate by being super-psycho-organized. I swear, if they spent half as much time studying as they do making intricately divided binders with alphabetized tabs and highlighting their notes in sixteen different colors, they'd actually have a shot at getting into some of the colleges whose materials they lug around in three-ring binders that are organized by geographic region and cross-referenced with the student-to-faculty ratio.

"Okay," I say, getting into counselor mode. "So, I read your essays, and I'm not sure that you're really on the right track."

Her face falls. She thought her essays were amazing, I'm sure. "Really?" she asks. "But I did exactly what you said."

"Yeah," I say, "you did, but it kind of got lost in the execution. They make you sound like you're sucking up. And there's nothing unique about them."

Julie appears to be insulted by this. "I'm not trying to suck up," she insists.

"I know that wasn't your intention, but that's how it comes off. Here," I say, pulling out a copy of one of the essays from my purse. "Listen to this." I hold up the paper and begin to read from it, trying as hard as I can to keep myself from using a mocking tone of voice.

" 'I believe that the Institute is the right match for my family because the Institute is one of the most esteemed preschools in the country. Your outstanding credentials, accomplished teachers, and commitment to diversity are exactly what we are seeking for our daughter.' "

I put the paper down and look up at her. "Jul, you sound like you're Miss America. All that's missing is a line about how you want world peace."

"You're not funny," she says.

"I'm not trying to be."

Julie looks like she's going to cry. "Well, I don't know what I'm supposed to do. You said to tell them why I want to go there, and to talk about diversity, and that's what I did."

I sigh. God, I really feel like I'm dealing with a seventeen-year-old right now. I had no idea that Julie was so bad at taking criticism.

"You need to tell a story," I explain. "You need to weave your reasons into a narrative, so that they learn something about you and your family and so that it's interesting. All you've done here is tell them things about their school that they already know."

"You know what, Lara?" she says, regaining her composure. "Maybe this wasn't such a good idea. I don't really think that the essays are that important, anyway. I mean, it's preschool. It's all about who you know." She gathers up the papers and puts them back inside the red folder. "I think I'd be better off spending my time just trying to work connections."

God, I think. *Talk about lazy.* This is a whole side of Julie I've never seen before. No wonder she doesn't have a job. She isn't willing to do any work.

"Whatever you say," I tell her. "I'm just trying to help."

"Thanks," she says. "I appreciate it, really. But maybe you could see if anybody at Bel Air Prep knows anyone at the Institute. That would help."

I shrug. "I'll see what I can do," I say, having absolutely no intention of seeing what I can do. I'm not going to pull any strings for her. Not with an attitude like that.

I can tell she knows that I'm full of shit, but Julie just smiles.

"Great," she says, opening her menu. "So, what should we have for lunch?"

fifteen

I keep forgetting about the goddamned light. I must walk past it while I'm holding Parker a hundred times a day, and every time I forget. To point to it and say, "Light," remember? Yeah. Me neither. Of course, I always remember when I'm in the car, or when I'm in the shower, or when I'm kicking the shit out of a heavy bag at the gym, and I'm like, *Damn, I have to remember to say, "Light" the next time I walk by it with her,* but by the time I'm actually walking by it, I'm thinking about a hundred thousand other things, like how I'm going to get out of planning Nadine's bachelorette party, or what I'm going to wear to this blow-job thing tonight, or why Stacey hasn't called me back even though I've left her at least seventy-three messages since the alleged partnership vote last week. It's freaking me out, too, because I can just imagine all of the mommunists in my class walking around their houses, pointing to their lights all day long, and I just know that Parker is going to end up at least three grade levels behind in reading.

Of course, I could just tell Deloris to do it—I'm sure that she would remember—but I don't want to. There's something about the idea of putting Deloris in charge of my daughter's vocabulary that rubs me the wrong way. I mean, yeah, maybe she'll learn what a light is, but God knows what else she'll pick up. And besides, I'm keeping my child-care techniques close to the vest. I need every advantage that I can get over Deloris right now, because she's worse than ever. Listen to this: Yesterday, while she was out for a walk with Parker, I went into her room to put a few new tissue boxes in there, and I found a voodoo doll that looks suspiciously like me. It has blond hair, and it's wearing a black sweat suit, which is what I always wear around the house. And it wasn't there when she started with us, either. There were no blond dolls when she started. Plus, it wasn't out in the open, like the other ones are. I just happened to notice it sticking out from behind some stuff on one of her shelves . . . well, actually, it was in the top drawer of her dresser. At the back. Under some T-shirts.

I know, I know, I'm a horrible person and I shouldn't have gone through her things, but I *knew* that she was doing spells on me and this confirms it. I'm starting to think that they might be working, too, because I haven't lost a single fucking pound since that blue powder started showing up on my scale, and I've been dieting and working out like a maniac for weeks.

Wait a minute. What was I talking about again?

Oh, right. The light. The bottom line is, I keep forgetting to point out the stupid light, and I'm such a bad mother that I'd rather have my kid be three grade levels behind in reading than let my nanny have the satisfaction of pointing it out instead.

I swear, sometimes I'm not sure who is crazier: me or Deloris.

The phone starts to ring.

Maybe it's Stacey. I grab the receiver and look at the caller ID. It's not Stacey. It's my dad. Or, I should say, it's @#*!. I need to keep reminding myself that that's who he is—the Fuckup Formerly Known as My Father. I can't allow myself to think of him as anything else, because the second that I do he'll up and leave, and then I'll have to go through all of that hurt all over again. And believe me, I do not want to go through that again.

Another ring resounds through the house. *Ugh.* @#*! has been calling me every day, sometimes twice a day lately, but I never call him back. Frankly, I'm just disgusted with him. I mean, it's one thing to get remarried, but to remarry someone like Nadine . . . I just can't get past it. The more I think about it, the angrier I get, but there's no way to talk him out of it. And believe me, I've tried. But he just doesn't seem to care that it brings down our whole family. Nor does he care that I will never be able to show my face in public again if anyone ever finds out about this. Or worse, if she gets arrested. *Ugh.* It just confirms for me that he hasn't changed at all and that he still hasn't learned that his decisions have consequences that go beyond himself.

The phone is still ringing, and I glance at the baby monitor on my nightstand. I'm going to have to pick it up. Parker just fell asleep, and if I let it keep ringing and the machine picks up, it's definitely going to wake her. *Shit.* I press the talk button.

"Hi, Dad," I say flatly.

"Hi, buhbie," he says, sounding cheery and nervous at the same time. "How's my girl?"

Oh, please. "I'm not your girl, Dad," I say, annoyed.

"It's just an expression, Lara. Don't be so senstive."

"Well, next time don't disappear for eight years and maybe I won't be."

He sighs. "Am I going to hear about this for the rest of my life?" he asks, sounding weary. I swear, what is it with men? Why do they think that they can completely fuck up and then never have to be reminded of it?

"Barring removal of my larynx, yes. Yes, you are."

"Okay, fine. I didn't call to fight with you, anyway."

"So then why did you call?" I ask.

He takes a deep breath and slowly lets it out. "I called—I've *been* calling—to ask you to please stop avoiding Nadine. She's very upset that you haven't responded to her e-mail about the bachelorette party, and she said that she's called you three times and you haven't called her back."

I bite my lip. *Busted.*

"Look, Dad," I say. "I already told you, I just do not want her in my life. She bullied me into being her matron of honor, and to be honest, I don't feel all that honored. I feel imposed upon. I have a new baby and I'm really busy, and I just don't have time to be planning parties for a har- lot. So you can tell her that I said thanks, but no thanks."

"You know what, Lara?" he asks, sounding pissed. "You haven't changed at all. Even when you were a kid, you were always judgmental, and you always wanted things your way. As long as you got what you wanted, you didn't care who got hurt."

I don't say anything for a minute as I absorb this accusation. Wasn't I just saying the same thing about him? For some reason the conversation reminds me of something that happened during my sophomore year of high school.

It was October, I think, maybe the beginning of November, and my

Spanish teacher assigned me to be partners on a monthlong project with Gretchen Flickert, who was the nerdiest kid in my grade. The girl had two *Little House on the Prairie* dresses that she alternated wearing every other day, and all she talked about was this horse that she used to ride after school. I think his name was Dandelion. Anyway, I wanted to be partners with my friend Allison, so I went to the señora and told her that I was allergic to horse hair, and that I couldn't be partners with Gretchen because she smelled like horse. The señora didn't buy it, but poor Gretchen became known as Horsepits for the rest of high school. I felt terrible about it. I still do, actually. If I ever go to any of my high school reunions, I am definitely going to apologize to her. Assuming that she shows up. I mean, I probably wouldn't, if everyone who was going to be there had called me Horsepits for three years.

"Well, Dad," I say bitingly, "I learned it from the master."

"Maybe," he snaps back. "But at least *I'm* trying to change." Then, as if saying this just reminded him that he's supposed to be changed, he softens his tone. "I guess if I had tried sooner you might not be this way. Just like how, if you don't change, Parker will learn it from you."

Okay. That one got me where it hurts. I didn't realize that he knows that I'm petrified of screwing up Parker. But then, it occurs to me that maybe he was once afraid of screwing me up, too. *Hmm.* For a moment I feel strangely empathic toward him—as if we're not father and daughter, but rather just two parents, trying their best to do right by their kids. I drop the edge from my voice.

"Look, I'll think about it, okay?"

"Okay," he says. "But either way, you need to decide soon. The wedding is in five weeks."

"I know, I know," I say. I close my eyes and sigh to myself. "I have a thing tonight that I need to get ready for, but I'll call her tomorrow morning."

"That's great," he says, sounding relieved. "I'll tell her. She'll be thrilled."

"All right," I say, sounding less than thrilled. "I've gotta go."

"Go, good-bye. I'll talk to you later. And Lara?"

"Yeah?"

"Thanks, honey." *Don't thank me,* I think. *I'm doing this for Parker. Not for you.*

"Yeah," I say. "Bye."

I told Andrew that he had to be home early tonight, and, for once he's actually on time. He has no idea where I'm going, by the way. He thinks that I have a special nighttime Susan class tonight. I didn't want to tell him that it's really a blow-job party, because a) I don't want him to have any expectations just in case I change my mind, and b) if I don't change my mind, I want it to be a total surprise. He'll think it's much hotter if he believes that I was spontaneously inspired to go down on him out of the blue. He doesn't need to know that I sat around with a bunch of girls and practiced first.

But, to be honest, Andrew really doesn't care where I'm going. He's just excited to have a night alone with Parker. I think that, because he's at work so much, he totally romanticizes what time alone with Parker is actually like. I mean, I know how Andrew's mind works. All of his ideas about everything come from television, so I'm sure that he envisions it as one big montage of sappy commercials. You know: Long afternoon naps together on the couch. Reading her a book while she sits quietly in his lap. Rocking her in his arms as she looks up at him in wonder. I'll admit that there are moments of fun, but those moments are still few and far between. The rest of the time she's just a squirmy, orally-fixated predator. Please, there is no such thing as a long afternoon nap on the couch with this child. Every nap that she takes is preceded by twenty minutes of screaming in her crib. And I already told you about the reading. Oh, I've tried again—on multiple occasions—and now all of her books are either shredded or have huge chunks missing from them where she gummed off the cardboard. And rocking her never happens anymore. She practically catapults herself out of my arms the second that I sit down, and if she ever does happen to look up at me, it's not with wonder. It's with the intention of trying to gnaw on my nose, or to scratch out my eyeballs.

But he'll see. Three hours is *plenty* of time for his little fantasy to be shattered. I'm looking forward to it, actually. Maybe he'll finally understand what I've been complaining about for three and a half months.

"Honey!" I am in Parker's room, changing her diaper before I go, and

Andrew is yelling to me from downstairs. I look at my watch: it's almost six forty-five. I needed to leave five minutes ago. Of course, when I actually need Deloris, she's nowhere to be found.

"What?" I yell back.

"Don't you have a CD with 'Just the Two of Us' on it?"

Oh, my God. I knew it. Full-fledged fantasyland.

"Bill Withers," I yell back. I look down at Parker. "Your daddy is cra-a-azy," I whisper to her. Ten seconds later the sound of a saxophone is blasting through the house, full volume. I pick Parker up and walk downstairs, trying to cover her ears, and I find Andrew standing in the den, arranging Parker's toys on the alphabet mat and humming along to the song.

"She's small," I yell, "not deaf."

He smiles and bounces his head from side to side in tune with the music, ignoring me.

"Here you go," I say, handing her over to him. "She's all yours."

Andrew reaches out to take her from me as Bill Withers begins to sing the chorus.

Just the two of us. We can make it if we try-y, just the two of us . . .

"You and I," Andrew sings to her. He places her against his chest and starts to dance in circles, and she grabs a fistful of his arm hair. "Ow!" he yells, pushing her away and trying to pry open her fingers. He looks at me. "That hurt."

Ah. The first crack. I smile at him, trying not to laugh, and I grab my purse off of the kitchen table.

"Have fun!" I say.

I go out into the garage and spend the next five minutes searching for my keys in my purse, and then I finally get into my car and drive halfway down the block before I realize that I forgot the bottle of wine that I was going to bring. *Damn.* I consider going empty-handed, but then I remember that I am dealing with mommunists here, and such a faux pas would be gossiped about for months, if not years. So, I turn the car around with a sigh and head back to my house, where I leave the keys in the ignition and run back inside to grab the wine, which I think I left on top of the coffee table in the den.

Oh, man, I am going to be so late.

The first thing that I notice when I walk inside is that the music is off. *Ha,* I think. I guess Just the Two of Them wasn't so great, after all. I slip my shoes off in the foyer because I can run through the house faster without heels, and I head straight for the den. When I get there, I see that Parker is lying on her back on the alphabet mat, and Andrew is standing in front of her, with his back to me. Well, not standing, exactly. He's actually doing high kicks and wildly waving his hands in the air.

"Be. Aggressive. B-E Aggressive. B-E. A-G-G. R-E-S-S. I-V-E. Aggressive. B-E Aggressive. Whoooo!" Parker is staring at him, not even cracking a smile. I, however, start to laugh. Hysterically.

Andrew spins around.

"What are you doing?" he asks me.

"I forgot this," I say, picking the bottle up off of the coffee table. "What are *you* doing?"

He pretends not to be embarrassed. "I'm trying to make her laugh," he says matter-of-factly. "The way that you did."

I shake my head at him, as if to say that he's doing it all wrong. "Try V-I-C-T-O-R-Y," I say. "She likes that." I start walking back out. "And jumps," I call out over my shoulder. "She likes jumps."

I laugh to myself as I run back out to my car. I don't care if I'm late anymore. Seeing that was well worth it.

At sixteen minutes after seven, I am standing on the doorstep of a home in Beverly Hills, bottle of wine in hand. I ring the doorbell, and a few seconds later the door swings open and I am greeted by Melissa (Hannah's mom).

"It's Lara!" she announces at the top of her lungs. Her cheeks are flushed and her eyes are kind of glassy, and I have a feeling that Melissa got started way before the party did.

I step inside and walk into the den, where all of the mommunists are congregated around a cheese platter and a bowl of vegetables with ranch dip. Of course, they're all wearing virtually the same thing: True Religion/Rock & Republic/Blue Cult jeans, silver or gold sandals, and a tank top. Even the accessories are the same: two or three necklaces of varying length, big diamond studs, lots of bling on the fingers, a fancy bag. It's like *The Stepford Wives* meets the Beverly Center.

Melissa hands me a glass of wine, which I down in about five seconds flat, and then refills my glass and pours another for herself. Over her shoulder I notice that there is an index card taped to the lamp shade that is in the corner of the room. Written on it in big, kindergarten-teacher handwriting is the word *light*.

"What's that?" I ask her, nodding my chin in the direction of the lamp. She turns around to see what I'm talking about, and her face gets serious.

"Oh, I just started that. You know how Susan told us to point to the light with them, to build their vocabulary?" I nod. "Well, I'm using index cards, too. It helps with early word recognition."

Okay. Make that five grade levels behind in reading.

"So," she says. "Who's with Parker tonight?"

"I left her with my husband," I say. "Well, and the nanny, technically, but she gets off at seven, so he'll be on his own for a while."

"Your husband is putting her to sleep?" she asks, sounding incredulous. I nod as I take a sip of my drink. "Wow," she says. "I was just kidding when I said that in class. You couldn't pay my husband to take care of the baby. He wouldn't even know how. I had to ship Hannah off to my mom's for the night, and Scott went to a poker game. He couldn't wait to get out of here." *Interesting,* I think.

"Yeah, well, Andrew's been working a lot lately, so he hasn't had a lot of time to spend with her. It was cute, actually. He was really excited to hang out with her by himself."

Lisa (Carter's mom) brushes past us, but before she can get by, Melissa grabs her arm and pulls her over so that she can hear of my miraculous tale.

"Listen to this," Melissa says. "Lara's husband is taking care of the baby tonight *by himself.* He *wanted* to. He's putting her to sleep and everything."

Lisa's mouth drops open. "Is he giving her a bath, too?" she asks.

I nod, and Lisa shakes her head, amazed. "Wow," she says. "Can he talk to my husband?"

The two of them laugh, and suddenly I am annoyed that Andrew is getting all of these props for being such a great dad. I mean, it's one friggin' night in three and a half months. Their husbands must really suck if they can't do better than that. Of course, I'm also buzzed already, which helps to explain what comes out of my mouth next. Sort of.

"Please," I say. "He's not all that fabulous. He's practically having an affair with a hot twenty-five-year-old. That's why I'm here tonight. To try to lure him back."

As I am saying it, I know that I shouldn't be saying it. I can't believe that I am saying it. But it's too late. I've said it. Their faces freeze as they struggle for something appropriate to say in response.

Oh, my God, I think. *What did I just do? I need to distract them. I need to make them focus on something else so that they forget what I just said.*

"And Parker has a flat head, too," I blurt out.

Oh, I am so awful. I just sacrificed my kid to save myself. I am an even worse mother than I thought. It looks like it worked, though. Their eyes just got huge and they're practically salivating for more.

"Really?" asks Lisa.

I grimace, and nod my head. "Susan said that she might need a helmet, but my pediatrician said that it's not that bad."

Melissa puts her hand in front of her mouth. "Oh, my God, I know someone whose baby needed a helmet. It was terrible. Are you sure she doesn't need one?"

"Not according to my doctor," I say.

Melissa and Lisa look disappointed to hear this, but before either of them has a chance to advise me to get a second opinion, the doorbell rings again. Melissa looks at her watch and then looks back up excitedly.

"This must be her! Hey, you guys, I think our sexpert is here!"

There is a chorus of nervous laughter, and then the room falls silent as Melissa goes to get the door. Thirty seconds later Melissa reappears, followed by the sexpert. I'm standing in the back of the room and I can't really get a glimpse of her face, but it doesn't matter. As soon as I see the red stilettos, I don't need to see any more.

I put my hand over my mouth, as if I'm trying to keep myself from throwing up, and I slowly move as far back as I can, hoping to avoid being seen.

This cannot be happening.

Oddly, my mind flashes to those *Worst-Case Scenario* books. *The Worst-Case Scenario Survival Handbook: My Stepmother Is the Blow-job Teacher.* Oh, God. I close my eyes.

Breathe, Lara. Just breathe.

My anger toward my father right now is almost unbearable. You see, this is *exactly* why he shouldn't be with her. Now I'm going to have to drop out of Susan's class, and I'm going to have to make sure that Parker doesn't go to the same preschool as anyone here tonight, because once this gets out, we're both finished. LA is a small city—everybody knows everybody. No matter where we are, Parker will always be the girl whose grandmother is a sexpert, and it makes no difference that it's not her real grandmother. Believe me, she'll be yearning for the days when she was just the fat baby with the flat head. And I can just hear them all talking about me. *It figures,* they'll say. *Remember how much she knew about lubrication?* Oh, man, I can't believe this. We're going to have to move to the fucking Valley.

I am pushed up against the table with all of the wine on it, thank God, and I slowly turn around and refill my glass to the very top. When I put the bottle back down, I notice an eight-by-ten photo of Melissa on her wedding day, posed with an older man in a tuxedo who must be her dad, because they have the exact same nose. I feel a pang of something in my heart as I stare at the picture—I would say that it's sorrow, but that sounds a little melodramatic, so I'll just say that it's a general, nonspecific pang of the sadness variety. Her dad looks so normal. So upstanding and responsible. I'll bet he never had a gambling problem. And I'll bet he never dated a stripper, either. I'll bet he never disappointed Melissa once in his entire life.

I sigh to myself, and then I down my drink, pour myself another one, and turn back around, still trying to keep myself hidden. I wonder if anyone would notice if I ducked down behind the couch? Yeah. They'd probably notice. I'll just make sure that my face is behind someone's hair, and pray that she doesn't see me.

"Hello, ladies!" Nadine shouts. "Welcome to what may be the most enlightening night of your lives." The mommunists giggle, and Nadine continues. "My name is Anna"—*Anna?*—"and if you'll all take a seat we can get started."

To my horror, the crowd in front of me begins to disperse, and within seconds I am fully exposed. *Oh, God.*

In a desperate attempt at camouflage, I lift my wineglass and try to stick my entire face inside of it, but it's too late. Nadine has already spotted me. Our eyes lock, and my heart begins to pound. I hold my breath as I wait for her to smile, or wave, or run over and hug me and tell everyone that I'm her daughter. But she quickly drops her gaze, and her face doesn't register even the faintest glimmer of recognition.

Well, I think, feeling surprised and relieved and confused all at the same time. *That was cool of her.* I take a few more sips of wine as I begin to breathe again, and then I move to the corner of the room and sit down in the most inconspicuous spot that I can find. I figure that there's no need to remind her that I'm here, just in case she changes her mind.

Nadine/Anna is dressed like a teacher straight out of a fifteen-year-old boy's wet dream—tight black pencil skirt, white blouse unbuttoned to show her lacy, red push-up bra, black-framed glasses, and a messy bun with a pencil sticking out of it. As she talks to us, she opens up her brief-case and begins to lay out twelve medium-sized plastic penises on top of Melissa's very expensive-looking, dark wood coffee table. I'm guessing that it's the first penis that coffee table has ever seen.

"Now, ladies," she says, looking us over one by one. "If you remember nothing else from this class tonight, I want you to remember that a blow job should *never* be called a blow job. Because it is *not* a job. When done properly, it can be relaxing, fun, and erotic for both you and your partner. So." She claps her hands together. "Instead of calling it a blow job, we are going to refer to it this evening as an *oral holiday.*" Everyone laughs at this, and Nadine/Anna smiles back at us.

"Okay," she says. "Let's get started." She pauses, daring us with her eyes. "Now, be honest. How many of you have gone on an oral holiday in the last year?" We all look at one another, and nobody raises her hand. Okay. At least I'm not the only one. Nadine nods, as if she expected this.

"Two years?" she asks. Still no hands. "Okay. Let me ask a different question. How many of you have gone on an oral holiday since you got married?" We all grin at one another, and still, no hands. "That's what I thought," she says. "How about before you were married? How many of you went on an oral holiday before you got married?" Every hand in the room shoots up, and we all get hysterical.

"Ah, the plight of the married man," laments Nadine, shaking her head. She reaches back into her bag, pulls out a plastic Baggie filled with condoms, and hands it to Melissa. "Everybody take one and pass it around," she says.

When we all have our condoms, she begins passing out the penises, and instructs us to place our condoms over them, which we all obediently do. Then, out of nowhere, Nadine sticks hers in her mouth and starts going to town on the thing. She's moaning and closing her eyes and moving her head in an exaggerated up-and-down motion, and I just keep picturing her doing this to my father, which is quite possibly the grossest picture I have ever conjured. It does, however, certainly clear up any remaining mystery as to why he would want to marry her.

After about ten agonizing minutes, Nadine slowly licks her lips, peels the condom off of the plastic penis, and places them both down on the table. She looks up at us, and the room breaks into rousing applause. Nadine curtsies.

"Now that, ladies, is what I call a vacation," she says.

Everyone cracks up at this, and several of the more drunken mommunists actually begin to whoop. I have to admit, they're being pretty good sports about it. I expected them to be much more uptight and giggly about the whole thing. Of course, it helps that Nadine has a sense of humor and that she's not taking it too seriously. You know, if I didn't already hate her, I'd probably think that she was pretty cool.

Anyway, after a brief lesson on where to find the most sensitive spots of the penis, an explanation of various tongue approaches, and a mortifying group demonstration of what we learned (picture twelve drunk women with about five grand worth of blond highlights between them, all trying not to gag on a condom-covered dildo), Nadine wraps it up. A few of the moms go over to her to thank her and take her card, and then she's finally out the door.

Oh, thank God. I am so drunk that I can barely see straight, but I need to get out of here. I don't want to tempt fate by hanging around and giving myself an opportunity to say something stupid and blow my cover. I walk over to Melissa.

"I think I'm going to go," I say. "But thanks so much. This was a lot of fun."

Melissa fake-pouts and puts her arm around me. "You're going already?" she says. "But the salads just got here. And I wanted for us all to stay and bond."

I give her a wistful smile and pretend that I am sad to have to miss out on the bonding. "I know," I say. "But I'm kind of anxious about the baby. I've never left my husband alone with her before, and I just want to make sure she got to sleep okay." This is such a lie, but it's the perfect mommunist excuse. Who can argue with motherly concern?

"Okay," Melissa says, sounding disappointed. Then she leans in and lowers her voice to a whisper. "But I don't believe you." At this, my heart starts to pound. Did Nadine say something to her on her way out?

"You don't?" I ask nervously.

Melissa shakes her head and makes a teasing face. "You just want to go home and try out our new techniques. You need to lure your husband back, remember?"

Oh, man. I can't believe she remembered that through all of that alcohol. But I pretend to go along with her, on the theory that it will expedite my exit.

"Yeah," I say, as if I've been busted. "That's it."

Melissa squeals. "I'm going to do it tonight, too," she says. "I can't wait until Scott gets home." She runs her tongue over her teeth the way that Nadine did. "That Anna really turned me on." Okay, that's so gross. TMI, honey. Too Much Information.

I fake-smile at her and raise my eyebrows.

"You go, girl," I say, raising my fist in sisterly support. She starts to hug me, but then suddenly realizes that she can't remember where she put her drink, and she glances around the room, trying to locate it.

All right, I think. *Get out while she's distracted.* Without saying another word, I sneak away and let myself out through the front door, which I quickly close behind me, undetected.

sixteen

In through the nose, out through the mouth. In through the nose, out through the mouth. There's no way that I can drive yet, so I'm doing some deep breathing while I sit on the steps of Melissa's front porch, trying to absorb what just happened in there. What *did* just happen in there, anyway? I mean, I know what just happened: A bunch of drunk, bored, HBDW (Have Babies and Don't Work) girls (not to be confused with stay-at-home moms, who also have babies and don't work, but who do so in lowercase letters, as they actually take care of their babies without the aid of a household staff, and also cook and clean and do laundry, and sew Halloween costumes by hand), just got a lesson in how to orally pleasure their husbands from my very own father's fiancée, and now I feel like I'm going to cry.

But why I am so upset?

That's what I can't figure out. Nadine didn't rat me out. It's not like anyone knew that she's practically my stepmother.

Actually, I don't think it's Nadine that I'm upset about.

Then what? Why is Luthor back in my throat *again?*

I put my arms around my shoulders and hug myself to keep warm. I hate that LA is cold at night, even in the summer. That's one thing I do miss about summertime on the East Coast—those warm, humid nights. That and rain. It never rains here in the summer. The first summer that I came out here, after I graduated from college, I worked as a counselor at a day camp, and not once in a whole week of orientation did they mention what to do with the kids if it rained. So at the end of the week I raised my hand and asked, and everyone just looked at me funny.

It doesn't rain in LA in the summer, they said.

Ever? I asked.

Never, they assured me.

And it never did. Not once the whole summer. I couldn't believe it. I still can't, and I've lived here almost ten years. But I miss it. There's just something about a rainy Saturday in the summer; it's like an excuse to stay in bed and watch television all day without feeling bad that you're not outside. It must be some kind of East Coast sun guilt or something. You know, if it's sunny and warm, then you have to be outside because you never know when it's going to be sunny and warm again. I tried explaining this to Andrew once, but he didn't get it. He told me that it doesn't matter if I waste an entire sunny day lying in bed, because it'll just be sunny again the next day. But it's not the same. In my book, sunny days are just not squanderable, no matter how many of them there may be. Just the whole idea of it makes me anxious.

Okay. I think I'm ready to stand up now.

I hoist myself up off of the step, hold my arms straight out from my sides, and attempt to walk in a straight line. Well, I guess it's straight enough. I only live a mile or so away. I walk down the driveway to the sidewalk, and start walking the half a block to where I parked my car. I'm about halfway there when I hear a voice come out of the darkness. I try to find its source, but my eyes won't seem to focus.

"I don't think that you're in any condition to drive, honey." It's Nadine. I turn around to see if anyone else from the party has come outside, but the street is empty, so I walk over to her.

"You're probably right," I slur. As I approach her, I lose my balance and my right foot slips off of my shoe. Nadine catches me by the arm. "I'm a mom now," I say. "I should be responsible."

"Why don't you come with me," she suggests. "I know a place close by here where you can sober up. We'll get you some coffee."

"I don't drink coffee," I say. "It upsets my stomach."

"Then we'll get you some water. Come on. Get in the car."

She opens the door for me and I slide in, collapsing onto the black leather of the front seat. She walks around to the driver's side, gets in, and starts the car. For a few minutes neither of us says anything, but then I finally muster up the courage to break the silence.

"How come you didn't say anything in there?" I ask.

A wry smile crosses Nadine's face. "Honey, in my line of business, the cardinal rule is that you don't say hello to someone unless they're expecting to see you."

I nod, taking this in. Wise rule.

"Well, thanks," I say, lifting one shoulder. "It just would have been hard to explain."

She looks straight ahead, her eyes locked on the road. "It always is."

A few minutes later she pulls up to the curb, and when I look out the window I see a valet guy rushing up to my door and a line of five or six old guys by the front door.

Wait a minute, I think, suddenly remembering the "Anna" getup that she was wearing at the party. *I can't go out with her dressed in that school-teacher outfit.* I glance over at her again, ready to protest, but now she looks normal. Her shirt is buttoned up, she let her hair back down, and she took off the glasses. If it weren't for the red shoes, you'd think that she was just somebody going out for a drink after a long day at the office. *All right. Fine.*

I get out of the car and look for a sign above the door to the bar, but there's nothing there. Oh, how trendy. I wonder if you need a secret password to get in, too.

"What is this place?" I ask her.

"This Place," she says.

I tilt my head sideways. "I know. But what's it called?" I feel like Abbott. Or Costello. Whichever one is the one who's confused.

"It's called This Place," she explains, as we walk up to the front of the line. "It's been around forever. I used to go here when I was in high school. Jimmy, the owner, is like, two hundred years old, and he still tends the bar every night." She gives me a knowing look and raises her eyebrows. "Jimmy will hook us up. He's an old friend of mine," she says, putting verbal quotation marks around the phrase *old friend.* I gather that this is code for *former client,* and I find myself wondering if this is a universal term in her industry, or if it is something that she made up herself.

Nadine walks up to a guy wearing an earpiece and whispers something to him, and he opens the door for us immediately. We step inside;

it's a surprisingly large space, dimly lit, and there's a guy playing Frank Sinatra–esque songs on a black piano in the corner. The place is pretty crowded, actually, but, as foreshadowed by the line outside, it's an older crowd. Lots of skeevy guys in their fifties sporting suits and unhealthy-looking tans, and every single one of them is staring at Nadine. I haven't gotten a single once-over. Not even a glance.

Whatever, I think, trying not to be bothered by the fact that I've been relegated to the role of homely sidekick for a woman practically twice my age. *At least I won't run into anyone I know.*

The earpiece guy leads us to a booth covered in red vinyl, and seconds later a waitress appears. Nadine orders herself a vodka gimlet and I ask for a glass of water, and while we wait for her to come back with them, I lean my head back against the vinyl and close my eyes. But my head starts to spin when I do that, so I open them again. Maybe I should just try to talk so that I don't think about how awful I feel. I stare at Nadine for a second, watching her as she checks out the scene.

"So why do you do it?" I ask.

Nadine turns her attention back to me and taps her long red finger-nails on the top of the table. "Do what?"

"Those parties. I thought you were retired."

"I am retired, honey," she says, smiling. "But being retired gets boring. I need to do something to keep myself occupied."

I balk. "Haven't you ever heard of golf?" I ask.

At this, she roars with laughter. "Oh, that's a good one. I'll have to tell that to your father. He said you were funny. I didn't believe him, but he said it."

"He did?"

The waitress delivers our drinks and Nadine asks her to open a tab. When the waitress is gone, Nadine stirs her drink, squeezes some lemon into it, and then takes a small sip. She nods at me.

"He sure did." Picking up on my surprise, she continues. "He's real proud of you. Says all kinds of things. You were top of your class, cheer-leading captain, went to an Ivy League school. He brags about you to any-one who will listen."

"He *does?*"

Nadine nods again.

"He's your dad, honey. He loves you. He was stupid, sure, but that doesn't change how he feels."

"I don't know," I say, shaking my head. "I'm confused about love lately. I'm not sure I even know what it is anymore."

"Oh, come on," Nadine chides. "Like and love are like art and porn. Sometimes it's hard to describe the difference, but you know it when you see it."

"I've heard that before," I say, trying to concentrate. "Wait, that's from an old Supreme Court case I read in law school. Why are you quoting Supreme Court cases?" I close my eyes, my brain tired from the effort of recalling that factoid, but then I quickly open them again. Spinning red vinyl is definitely not a good thing.

Nadine laughs. "Let's just say that I am well versed in pornography law," she says with a snort. "But that's beside the point. What do you mean, you don't know what love is?"

I sigh. In the back of my head I can faintly hear the sober me trying to stop the drunk me from spilling my guts to Nadine, of all people, but drunk me is just too damn wasted to care.

"I just . . . okay. Andrew, my husband, he takes the dog to this agility class—have you ever seen agility on Animal Planet?" Nadine shakes her head no. "Oh. You should watch it. It's cute. Anyway, there's this new girl in the class, and she's twenty-five, and she's skinny and a natural blonde, and Andrew's been flirting with her, and he didn't tell her that he has a baby, and he didn't tell me that she's in the class, and I just feel like I'm this old ball and chain compared to her, you know? She's single, she doesn't have kids, she's not tied down, and I think that that appeals to Andrew."

Nadine is listening and nodding as I talk. "Do you think he's having an affair with her?" she asks.

I grimace. "Maybe I'm just naive, but no, I don't." I sigh. "I mean, look, I know he loves me, and he's always put up with my ridiculousness before, but I just feel like, ever since the baby was born, I've become this huge drag. I'm always tired, I'm always feeling fat, I'm stressed out about everything. I wouldn't blame him if he did have an affair. I wouldn't want to be with me if I were him. And we barely ever have sex anymore. I mean, we have, since the baby, and things were getting better, but ever since I found out about that Poodle Bitch . . . I don't know. I'm probably overreacting, but I just feel really insecure. So I went to that thing tonight, hoping to get inspired—you were very good, by the way—but I just didn't feel it. I don't feel like that's me anymore. I don't even feel like I'm capable of being that sexy. I just feel like a mom now. An overweight, overtired, overstressed, cliché of a mom."

Nadine nods again. "And that's it? That's why you're confused about love?"

I shake my head and finish off my water. "No," I say. "That's not it. I'm confused about Parker, too. Like, those girls tonight, they're all from my Mommy and Me class, and they all totally love spending time with their babies. They're obsessed with them. It's like their babies are the only things that matter to them. And I know I love her, but I just don't feel that way. I want to feel that way—I *wish* I felt that way—but I don't. I still get bored with her, and frustrated with her, and I don't want to be with her all the time. And do you know what's so sick? I can't wait to go back to work. And it's not even because I love my job so much. I mean, I do love my job, but that's not the only reason. It's because work is the perfect excuse for me to spend time away from Parker without having to feel guilty." A light-bulb goes on in my head, and I smile excitedly. "Actually," I say sticking up my right index finger, "work is like rain. Rain in the summertime." I am nodding to myself, extremely pleased with this analogy.

"I lost you," Nadine says. The waitress appears with another water for me and another vodka gimlet for Nadine, and then she vanishes back into the crowd. Damn. I really wanted to ask her for a Diet Coke. I think I need to get some caffeine in me.

"It doesn't matter," I say. "I was just thinking out loud. But sometimes I think that I don't really love her. Or that maybe I do love her, but not enough, or not the right way."

Out of nowhere, a wave of drunken understanding washes over me, and suddenly I know exactly why I was so upset before. Suddenly it all makes perfect, total sense.

"You know what?" I say, getting excited that I've figured myself out.

"I think I'm jealous of those mommunists. Those HBDW girls. Their lives are so simple, you know? They don't expect anything from their husbands, so they're never disappointed. They don't have jobs, so they're never stressed about trying to find a balance. They can spend all of their time talking about their babies, and taking them to classes, and buying them things, and putting index cards on lamp shades, and since they don't have anything else to do, it's okay if they leave the kid with the nanny for a few hours a day. But I'm not like them. I want Andrew to participate, because Andrew and I have always been partners in everything that we do, and I don't see why this should be any different, so it pisses me off when he acts like I should do everything. And you know what else?"

Nadine shakes her head at me. "No," she says. "What else?"

I stick my index finger back up in the air and begin to punctuate myself with it. "I know that I'm going back to work in a few weeks, so I feel like I have to squeeze in all of this quality time with her right now, before my maternity leave is over. I feel like all I have are these five months to make an impression on her, and to make her love me the most, because once I go back to work, I won't have time. And *that's* why I always feel so guilty about leaving her, and *that's* why I'm always so stressed out about where I am on the totem pole, and *that's* why I'm driving myself crazy calculating the ratio of Parker hours spent with me to Parker hours spent with Deloris. *That's* my problem." I am shaking my head, astounded by this revelation.

"Honey," Nadine says. "I've got to tell you, you're not making a whole lot of sense here."

"Sorry," I say. "But it makes sense in my head."

Nadine nods. "I've got you," she says. "It just sounds to me like you need to get your confidence back. You're not feeling sexy, and you're not feeling like you're doing a good job as a mom. Is that the gist of it?"

"Mmm-hmmm." I finish my water again and start chewing on a piece of ice. Where is that waitress?

"Look," she says. "First of all, your husband would be a fool to cheat on you. You are the prettiest girl that I have met in a long time. If this were ten years ago, I would be sitting here trying to recruit you to work for me.

And believe me, my clients did not go for anything less than stunning."

I snort at her. "Yeah, well, if I'm so pretty, how come every guy in here is looking at you?"

Nadine smiles. "Well, now, that's the secret. You don't have to be pretty to get men, honey. You just have to be confident, and you have to exude that confidence." She pushes both of her hands away from her breasts as she says the word *exude*. "You have to feel it, that's all. Come on, Lara. That girl that your husband is flirting with? She's *twenty-five*. A kid. Think about how intimidating you must be to her. You're a woman. A wife. A mother. So what if she's skinny? You're *experienced*. You're worldly." A wicked smile spreads across her face. "And now you know how to give a mean blow job."

"Actually, it's called an oral holiday," I say, correcting her.

"That's right," she says, patting me on the hand. "I was just checking to see if you paid attention." She takes another sip of her drink and shakes her head at me. "And your baby? Lara, there is no right way to be a mother. You're overthinking things. You love her however you know how, and she'll adore you just for trying."

I sigh. "But those other moms . . . I can't compete with them."

"It's not a competition."

"It feels like it is."

This time, Nadine is the one who sighs. "I don't have kids," she says. "And maybe I'm not the right one to be giving you advice. But you look like you're doing a pretty good job to me, and the fact that you even care this much has got to count for something."

I shrug, unconvinced, and Nadine leans in toward me. "Listen, honey, you have all of these forces working against you, and you just need to find a way to make them work for you. And if you can figure out how to do that, there will be no stopping you. Believe me, I've done it myself. It's how every success story gets its start. Every one of them."

I have no idea what she's talking about—forces working against me? What am I, Luke Skywalker? Well, I guess that's what I get for soliciting marital and parental advice from an unmarried, childless, retired madam who teaches people how to give blow jobs in her spare time, and who is engaged to my father, no less. I mean, her taste in men is not exactly lending her much credence in my eyes. Although, I think I'm actually starting to like her. Maybe it's just the alcohol, but she's kind of growing on me.

"Nadine, can I ask you a question?"

"Sure, honey."

"What is it that you see in my dad?"

Nadine smiles wistfully, and she thinks for a minute before she answers. "I see myself," she finally says. "Someone with a good heart, and good intentions, but who hasn't always made the right choices in life. You know, honey, all your dad needs is for someone to take care of him, and to nurture him." She chuckles to herself. "And to teach him how to be in a relationship. He's not so good at that, but we're working on it."

"It sounds like you're talking about a child."

"All men are children, Lara. That's the key to understanding them."

"Then I guess I'll never understand him then, because children aren't exactly my forte."

Nadine is stumped by that one. She gives me a sympathetic look, but says nothing in response, which is just as well, really, because I'm starting to sober up and I'm getting tired of listening to myself talk.

"I need a Coke," I say, standing up. "Do you want another drink?"

"No, thanks," she says. "But I'll come with you. I want to say hi to Jimmy, anyway. I haven't seen him in months."

We both slide out of the booth and make our way up to the bar, and we stand there for a few minutes while we wait to get Jimmy's attention. I'm looking around, checking out the scene, when, out of the corner of my eye, I spot a woman sitting a few seats down from me at the bar. She looks really, really familiar.

No. It can't be. There's no way it's her.

I stare at her, trying to get a look at her whole face, but I can manage to get only a side view. I have to see, so I walk a few feet over to where she's sitting, and I wedge myself into a spot next to her and lean in sideways. It *is* her. I tap her on the shoulder and she spins around.

"Stacey," I say. "What are you doing here? Why haven't you called me back?"

She looks positively horrified to see me. "What are *you* doing here?" she asks defensively.

I put my hands on my hips and glare at her. "You first," I order. She rolls her eyes at me and sighs.

"Fine. I didn't make it, okay? I was two votes short. They offered me an of-counsel position and I told them to fuck off, so now I'm unemployed, and I've been spending my days in this bar, drinking myself into oblivion as I try to figure out how to put back the pieces of my shattered life. Happy?"

I shake my head. "Oh, my God, I'm so sorry. I can't believe it." Stacey nods, and I notice that her eyelids are swollen. "They're idiots," I say. "They'll never find anyone as good as you."

"Whatever," she says, "you can spare me the pep talk. I'm over it. I was going to call you this weekend to tell you. I just wasn't ready to talk about it before."

"It's okay. Do you know what you're going to do?"

She shrugs. "I have some ideas I'm exploring. What are you doing here, anyway? I thought I was the only person under fifty who knew about this place."

"You were. I'm here with Nadine."

Stacey stares at me, confused. "Wait a minute," she says. "You're hanging out with Nadine? I thought you hated her."

I nod, kind of confused by this myself. "I do," I say. "I mean, I did. I don't know." I blush as I think about how to explain this. "It turns out that she was the instructor at the blow-job party tonight, and I got a little drunk, so she brought me here to dry out."

Stacey's eyes go wide. "She was the instructor at the blow-job party? Were you dying?"

I shake my head. "No. That's the thing. I mean, I was when she walked in, believe me. But she just pretended like she'd never seen me before. She was really cool about it."

Stacey makes a face like she's impressed. "Wow. You've gotta respect that."

"I know. Especially after I was such a bitch. Anyway, I've spent the last forty-five minutes baring my soul to her. She's over there." I point to her and Stacey scans the crowd.

"The redhead? That's Nadine?" I nod. "I pictured her being trashier."

"She cleans up well," I say. "Except for the shoes."

Stacey cranes her neck to see what I'm talking about. "Ooooh," she says, wincing. "Unfortunate."

I nod again. "We're sitting at that table over there," I say, pointing to it. "Why don't you come sit down with us?" Stacey hesitates for a few seconds. "Come *on*. You don't always have to be antisocial."

"Fine," she says. "But I don't want to talk about the firm."

I hold up two fingers in the scout's-honor position. "I promise," I say. "Besides, I'm entirely too self-absorbed tonight to talk about you."

Stacey laughs. "Perfect."

I order my Diet Coke, and Stacey and I carry our drinks over to the table and sit down. A minute later Nadine comes back, looking distracted.

"Nadine," I say, pointing to Stacey. "This is my friend Stacey. I just ran into her at the bar." Stacey and Nadine shake hands, and Nadine sits down. She seems pale. "Is everything okay?" I ask. She shakes her head no.

"I just spoke to Jimmy." She looks at Stacey. "He's the owner here," she explains. "He's got cancer. His doctor got him into a clinical trial for some experimental treatment, but it's in New York and it starts next week, so he has to just shut down the bar. He doesn't have time to try to sell it and there's nobody who can run it. He doesn't have any family or anything." Nadine has tears in her eyes. "Poor guy. Everything he has is in this bar." We're all quiet for a moment, and then Stacey looks from Nadine to me and back to Nadine again.

"I'll buy it," she announces. Nadine and I both stare at her.

"What?" we both say in unison.

"I'll buy it."

"Stacey," I say, "are you sure? That's kind of a big decision to make on just a whim."

"It's not a whim. I've been thinking that I'd like to open a restaurant or a bar, and I don't have anything else to do." She looks at Nadine and gives a quick explanation. "I'm a lawyer, and I just found out that I didn't make partner at my firm, so I've been sitting here all week trying to figure out what to do next." She looks back to me. "Look, I love this place. I've been coming here for years. I had my first legal drink here with my mom when I turned twenty-one. It's perfect. And it's not like I don't have the money. I've been making a fortune and it's all just sitting in mutual funds because I haven't had time to spend it." She starts looking around, making plans. "I can renovate it a little bit, hire some hot bartenders and waitresses, update the music, try to attract a younger crowd . . . I think it could be cool. It's an amazing location." She nods her head enthusiastically. "I want to do it."

Nadine looks at me excitedly. "We could have my bachelorette party here! It could be your grand opening."

Stacey frowns. "Well, I don't know if it could happen that fast. I mean, I'll need to get a liquor license, I'll need to hire a contractor and get permits from the city, and I'll need to find employees. It might take a few months."

Nadine waves her hand and winks at me. "Honey, I can get you up and running in two weeks. The director of the Alcoholic Beverage Commission is an old friend of mine, and so is the head of the Building and Safety Commission. And trust me, I can get you hot women."

"Really?" Stacey asks. "How can you get those kinds of favors?"

Nadine laughs, but before she can say anything, I cut her off. I don't know how she was going to answer, but I'd rather handle this flow of information myself.

"She just can," I say. "She knows a lot of people." Nadine nods, and Stacey shrugs her shoulders and smiles, as if it's a no-brainer.

"Then you've got a deal," she says.

Nadine puts out her hand, and I watch as my best friend, the former lawyer, and my future stepmother, the former Hollywood Madam, shake hands across the table.

seventeen

When I finally make it home, Andrew and Deloris are sitting on the couch, watching *Almost Famous* and sharing a bowl of kettle corn.

"Hi," I say, trying not to show how agitated I am at the sight of them there, together like this.

"Oh, hi," Andrew says, smiling. Deloris looks up at me, midchew.

"Hi, Mrs. Lara," she says. Then she turns to Andrew and slaps him on the knee. "This popcorn is so *good*," she exclaims.

Andrew beams at her. "Deloris has never had kettle corn before," he says. "Can you believe that?"

I lift my eyebrows. "A travesty," I say. This is so unbelievable. Deloris never stays up late when I'm around. I'll bet you she even helped him put Parker to bed and everything. After I went and told everyone how cute he was for wanting to spend alone time with the baby.

Oh, God, I think, cringing as I remember what else I told them. I'm going to have to do some serious damage control in class next week. I slip off my shoes and walk out of the den, leaving the two of them sitting there.

"Good night," I yell over my shoulder. "I'm going to bed."

A few minutes later Andrew walks into the bedroom.

"Why did you leave?" he asks me.

"Because," I say, "I didn't want to intrude on your date."

Andrew laughs. "So now you think that I'm dating Deloris, too?"

I'm about to toss off a bitchy, sarcastic reply when I notice that his lips are bright red. "Andrew, are you wearing strawberry lip balm again?" I ask him accusingly.

He sticks his tongue out and licks his lips, then smacks them together a few times, as if he just tasted something delicious. "Mmm-hmmm," he says enthusiastically.

"You have to stop. I've told you this a hundred times. It makes you look like your whole mouth is chapped. Please, just wear the clear kind."

He makes a sad face at me. "But I like the strawberry," he says. "It tastes good."

You know what? Nadine was right. He is a child. I roll my eyes at him and walk into the bathroom.

"So how was your night?" he asks.

"Fine," I lie. "How was yours? How was Parker?" I splash some water on my face and reach for my glycolic cleanser.

"She's so cute," he answers. "I just wish that I could spend more time with her."

I am about to tell him that he could, if he quit agility, but then I remember that I'm not supposed to care about Courtney anymore. At least, not out loud.

"You just need to *make* time," I say as I begin to scrub. "But if it makes you feel better, the other husbands don't spend time with their babies, either. They don't even want to."

I rinse my face and pat it dry, and Andrew sighs.

"Whatever," he says. "I just really can't believe how much I love her."

"That's because you're not with her every day," I say as I spread some Crest whitening toothpaste onto my toothbrush.

He shakes his head at me. "No, that's not true. I swear, I could spend every second with her. If I could retire right now and just be with her all the time, that's what I would do."

I stare at him for a second. "Andrew," I say. "Did you even spend time alone with her tonight? Because being by yourself is not the same as when Deloris is there to help you."

He looks severely offended by this suggestion. "I did *everything* by myself," he declares. "Deloris was only with me because I knocked on her door after I put Parker to bed and I asked her if she wanted to watch a movie."

"Then I don't understand," I say. "Don't you hate it when she cries? And don't you get bored just sitting there with her? She doesn't *do* anything."

He shakes his head.

"No. The crying doesn't bother me. And I don't see what you think is boring about her. She's taking in the whole world. Every time you show her something different, it's the first time that she's ever seen it. It's like you're literally teaching her about how the world works. How cool is that?"

I feel like I want to cry again. It's bad enough that the mommunists make me feel inadequate. Now I'm getting outmothered by Andrew. I should have sent *him* to the blow-job party, and I should have gone and played poker with the dads. It would have been much more appropriate.

Andrew pauses and gets a concerned look on his face.

"But have you noticed that weird thing she does with her left arm?"

"What?" I ask skeptically. I have no idea what he's talking about.

"She lifts it up and down over and over and over again." His brow is furrowed and he looks anxious. "Do you think she might be slow?"

Oh, here we go. I knew this was going to happen eventually. It was only a matter of time before Andrew started in with the slow thing again. And by "again," I mean that he has done this before. With the dog.

When Zoey was a puppy, Andrew tried to do this thing called clicker training with her—basically, you say a command, and when the dog does what she's supposed to do, you push this little metal thing that makes a clicking noise, and then you give the dog a treat. Zoey was fine when they were just doing "sit," but then Andrew tried to get fancy with "lie down," "speak," and "high five," and poor Zoey got so confused. Every time she saw the clicker, she would do this weird thing where she would lift her front paw, bark, and drop to the floor all at the same time, before Andrew even had a chance to tell her what he wanted her to do. Of course, he then became convinced that she was slow. Every night he would spend half an hour agonizing over the difficulties that a mentally challenged wheaten terrier would have to face in this cruel world, and he became so obsessed with it that he made an appointment with a dog psychologist to have her tested, at which point I stepped in and put the kibosh on things, as I was not about to let him spend two hundred and fifty dollars on a Weschler test for a three-month-old puppy.

"She's not slow, Andrew," I say through the foam of my toothpaste. I spit into the sink. "She might be a little bit behind, though."

"What?" Andrew's head spins around so fast that I am afraid it might keep going and break off. I can just picture it rolling across the floor, yelling at me for not breast-feeding longer. "What are you talking about?"

"I don't know," I say, "I just wonder if we're doing enough to educate her. I was at one of the other moms' house tonight, and she had flash cards attached to the furniture to promote early word recognition."

Andrew looks like he's going to start convulsing.

"Well, then we have to do that, too. We can't let Parker get behind. That's unacceptable."

Shit. I never should have said that. He's going to be like Rick Moranis in *Parenthood;* the dad who is constantly quizzing his three-year-old in four different languages and who walks around with stacks of flash cards in his pocket. I step out of the bathroom and climb up onto the bed.

"Actually, I think the flash cards are overkill at this age. But I just wonder if Deloris stimulates her enough when I'm not around." Yeah. Blame it on Deloris. He doesn't have to know that I deliberately didn't tell her to point out the light.

But he's not buying it. "Deloris stimulates her plenty," he says, following me back into the bedroom. "But you're her mother. It's *your* responsibility to teach her things."

Ugh. I am so tired of this you're-her-mother bullshit. When did mothers become the ones who have to do everything?

"Why is it *my* responsibility?" I ask. "Why can't it be *your* responsibility?"

"Fine," he says. "From this point forward, Daddy is in charge of Parker's education." He turns on his heel and starts to walk out of the room.

"Where are you going?" I call out after him.

"To do research," he says. "She's already behind. There's no time to waste." Oh, God. He's going to be up all night, I know it. I'm sure he'll have multiple spreadsheets waiting for me in the morning. As an afterthought, he comes back in and gives me a kiss on the forehead.

"Good night," he says, and then walks out and closes the bedroom door behind him. I roll over and hug my pillow, and I close my eyes.

Oh, well. I didn't really feel like giving him a blow job anyway.

* * *

When I wake up the next morning, my head feels like it's going to explode, and my mouth feels like I spent the night chewing on cotton. God, I can't remember the last time I had a hangover. And by the way, it sucks. I roll over and look at the clock: ten-oh-two. Suddenly my heart starts to race. Ten-oh-two? I slept until ten o'clock? I glance at the baby monitor, but it's been turned off. What happened? Where is Andrew? Who has Parker? I jump out of bed and throw on my robe.

"Andrew," I yell across the house. "Andrew!"

"What?" he yells back.

I run downstairs toward the sound of his voice, which seems to be coming from the den. When I get there, he's sitting on a few squares of the alphabet mat, the rest of which has been completely disassembled and is now strewn across the floor. Parker is on his lap.

"Good morning," he says, smiling.

"What happened?" I ask, pressing one hand to my temple in an attempt to keep my head from spontaneously combusting.

"You were out cold," he says. "Parker started crying and you didn't budge, so I turned off the monitor. I thought you could use the sleep."

"Thanks," I say. "That was nice of you. Where's Deloris?"

"I don't know," he says. "I think she's cleaning Parker's room." I shake my head. Unbelievable. How come she never cleans when *I'm* trying to play with Parker?

"So what have you been doing?" I ask suspiciously, as I glance over the flotsam and jetsam that was once the alphabet mat.

"Oh," he says, excitedly. "I've decided that I'm going to teach Parker the alphabet."

"I'm sorry. You're what?"

"I'm teaching her the alphabet. I read some fascinating stuff last night about early childhood education. One article in particular was great. It said that babies can learn to recognize different kinds of animals and different household objects at this age, so I figure that there's no reason why they can't learn to recognize letters. Think about it. If I teach her one letter a week, in five months she'll know the whole alphabet."

"That's the dumbest thing I ever heard," I say. "Babies learn animals and household objects because animals are fun, and because they use household objects every day. But letters are just a bunch of lines on a piece of paper. She's not going to be able to differentiate between them at barely four months."

"You're underestimating her," he says. "The brain of an infant is capable of much more than we realize."

I swear, there is nothing worse than Andrew with a little bit of information under his belt. He gets totally obsessive. When we were remodeling our house, he had to learn about every single kind of granite and limestone that existed, and then whenever we were in a house that had limestone or granite, he would study it like he was some kind of kitchen countertop archaeologist. *Is this a Jerusalem Gold or a Madura Gold? Mmm. The ogee bullnose edging is a really nice touch.*

"Here, just watch," he says. He picks up the rubber square with the letter A on it, and holds it up in front of Parker's face. He begins to talk in a deep, monotone voice, like the narrator of those wildlife observation movies that they used to make us watch in middle school.

"Parker, this is your father speaking. What I'm holding here is the letter A," he drones, pointing to it. "Aaaaay. A is a vowel. A can be pronounced in two different ways, aay or ah. For example, *apple* is a word that begins with A, but so is *apex.*"

"Are you kidding?" I ask.

He looks up at me. "What?" he asks with genuine puzzlement in his voice. "The article said to talk to her like she's an adult, and to expose her to lots of different words early on." He points his finger at me. "They quoted a study that showed a correlation between SAT scores and the number of words a child hears as a baby." Parker lunges for the letter, but Andrew holds it just out of her reach, and she begins to cry.

"But you're not talking to her like she's an adult. You're talking to her like she's an android."

"Well, it's better than baby talk," he says.

"Not really," I say. But my head hurts too much for me to argue with him. I start to walk out of the room.

"Where are you going?" he asks.

"To get dressed. I need to go to the drugstore. We don't have enough diapers to get through the day, and I want to get some Aleve for this headache." Parker is shrieking now. "Andrew, give her the letter. She wants to chew on it." He hands it to her and she instantly stops crying as she begins to gnaw on the A. I give him a look. "I hope you know that you're absurd," I tell him.

He looks down at Parker and puts on that voice again. "Parker, Mommy says that I'm absurd, which also starts with the letter A. *Absurd* means crazy. But I don't think so. I'm just trying to make you intelligent. In-tell-i-gent. That means smart." There's no point in trying to rationalize with him. If he thinks that he can teach a four-month-old baby the alphabet, let him go ahead and try.

"Okay, I'll see you later," I say.

"Wait," he says, "don't go now."

"Why?"

He pouts at me and answers in a pleading tone of voice. "I have agility in an hour. Hang out with us and go when I leave. We never spend time together as a family."

I bite the inside of my cheek. I'm not going to say it. It would not be at all productive to say that we could spend lots of time together if he didn't spend half of every Saturday hanging out with the dog and another woman. I sigh.

"All right," I say. "But only if you promise not to talk to her like that anymore." Andrew makes a pouty face. "Promise," I warn.

"Fine," he relents. "I'll talk to her like a baby and stunt her mental growth, if that will make you happy."

"It will," I say, sitting down on the floor. "It will make me very happy."

He takes Parker off of his lap and lays her down on the mat, and for the first time I am able to see his outfit. He's wearing a white Hanes undershirt and light blue jeans that are ripped at the knee.

"What are you wearing?" I ask him, staring at the hole in his pants.

"What?" he says. "I thought that ripped jeans are in again."

"*Distressed* jeans are in," I tell him. "You look like Bruce Springsteen on the cover of *Born to Run*. You just need a red bandanna."

Andrew looks confused. "But you like Bruce Springsteen," he says.

"Yes, and I like Snoop Dogg, too, but I don't walk around in big gold chains and my pants hanging around my waist."

He looks at me. "All right, all right," he concedes. "I'll change."

"Good," I say. "Now, show me what it is you do with her that you think is so much fun."

Andrew's face lights up. "Okay," he says. "Did you know that she loves 'Old MacDonald'?" he asks.

"Yes," I answer. "I did know that."

He nods. "It makes her crack up when I do it. Watch." He lays her down on her back, puts his hands around her ankles, and starts moving her legs back and forth while he sings. "Old MacDonald had a farm, ee-ah-ee-ah-oh."

I interrupt him. "What's 'ee-ah'?" I ask. "It's 'ee-eye.' 'Ee-eye-ee-eye-oh.' Ee-ah; you sound like a mental patient."

He gives me a dirty look and continues his song. "And on that farm he had a duck, ee-*eye*-ee-*eye*-oh."

"Much better," I say, nodding.

"With a quack here, a quack there, a quack everywh—"

Unbelievable.

"Andrew, how do you not know the words to 'Old MacDonald'?" I ask. "Did you not go to nursery school? There are two quacks. 'A quack quack here, a quack quack there.'"

He gives me another dirty look and then smiles down at Parker, who is screeching with delight.

"A quack quack everywhere," he sings.

I stare at him. "It's not that hard, Andrew. The quacks are here, there and everywhere. 'Here a quack, there a quack, everywhere a quack quack.'"

Andrew drops Parker's legs and glares at me.

"You take the fun out of everything," he says. His voice is trembling, and he sounds like he's about to cry. "Do you want to know the real reason why I love playing with Parker so much?" he asks. I'm guessing that this is a rhetorical question, so I just stare at him and say nothing. "It's because she doesn't care if I mess up the words. She doesn't care if I don't know how to spell, she doesn't care if I wear ripped jeans, or strawberry lip balm, and she doesn't care if I'm friends with the nanny. She loves me because I'm me. Which is more than I can say for you."

He stands up and storms out of the room, leaving me sitting there on the floor. I hear his footsteps pounding the stairs, and a few seconds later I hear our bedroom door slam shut. I look down at Parker, who has started whimpering.

"Hey, sweetie," I say, picking her up. My heart is racing. Andrew has never thrown a tantrum like that before. I hold her up to my chest and rock back and forth, and she grabs a fistful of my hair and puts it in her mouth. "It's okay," I whisper, trying to convince myself more than her. "It's okay."

But it's so not okay. My eyes have started to fill up with tears. I always knew this day would come. The day when Andrew would finally realize that he was married to a complete and total bitch, and that he didn't want to put up with it for one more minute.

I kiss Parker on top of the head and I close my eyes, burying my nose in her mullet.

Well. It looks like my dad isn't the only one who isn't so great at relationships.

eighteen

I t seems that in my drunken stupor on Friday night, I invited Nadine and my father over to our house for dinner this evening. I vaguely recall it happening on the drive back to my car—Nadine said something like, *Honey, I'd just love to meet Andrew,* and I said, not really meaning it, of course, *Oh, yeah, you guys should come over for dinner one night,* to which Nadine replied, *Great! Let's do it on Sunday.* I had completely forgotten about it, too, until Nadine called this morning to ask what she could bring.

I was on the other line with Julie—or at least, someone who sounded like Julie, though it was hard to tell for sure through the I-Didn't-Get-An-Interview-At-The-Institute-Oh-My-God-What-Am-I-Going-To-Do hysteria—and this person who may or may not have been Julie was somewhere between Low-Paying-Factory-Job-That-Could-Lead-to-Lung-Problems-Later-in-Life and String-of-Divorces-to-Men-Who-Wear-Wife-beaters-For-Real in the chain of events that will, undeniably, take place in Lily's life as a direct result of her not attending the Institute for preschool, when I clicked over to answer the other line.

Needless to say, Nadine completely caught me off guard. Being totally flustered by both Lily's tragic fate (which ends, by the way, with her Dying Alone in a Trailer Park Located Somewhere Near Pacoima) and by the sudden, jarring recollection that I had, in fact, extended such an idiotic invitation, I couldn't for the life of me come up with a good excuse for why I had to back out. I mean, I *had* a good excuse, but it's not like I could just tell her that Andrew almost walked out on me for good yesterday, and that, when he left for agility and didn't come home for six hours, I was going out of my mind imagining all of the ways that Courtney was "being his friend," and that the only reason why I didn't swallow the whole giant-sized bottle of Aleve that I bought was because I didn't want Parker to grow up hearing stories from him about what a horrible, mean person her mother was. And it's not like I could really explain to her that, after he got home and I learned that he didn't even go to agility—he took Zoey and went over to his mom's house for the afternoon, a fact that she confirmed when I called her to check—I had to spend two hours groveling on my hands and knees, until he finally believed that I don't actually think he's having an affair with Courtney, and that I would never, ever, ever make fun of him again. And then, you know, it's not like I could just blurt out that I've been tiptoeing around him for the last eighteen hours, trying my hardest to be extra-special, super-duper, whipped-cream-with-a-cherry-on-top nice to him, and that, as such, perhaps today would not be the best time for me to introduce him to my father and his new soon-to-be wife.

No, the only excuse that I could come up with was that Parker has had diarrhea since yesterday afternoon, and that the whole house smells like dirty diapers. To which Nadine replied, *No problem, honey, we can just eat outside.*

And so, in just under three hours, Andrew is going to meet my father and Nadine for the very first time, and I am a nervous fucking wreck. I keep thinking that it's like a ghetto version of *Meet the Fockers*; you know, instead of a sex therapist and a stay-at-home dad, I've got a pimp and a deadbeat.

But since they are, indeed, coming for dinner, I need to run to the market. I've decided that the best way to play this is to let my dad barbecue, because it will keep him occupied and therefore unable to spend much time talking Andrew's ear off, saying God knows what about me, and also because, frankly, I don't cook and I didn't think it would be appropriate to order in Chinese food. Nadine is easy—I'll keep her busy by working out the details of her bachelorette party with her, and Andrew can be responsible for dealing with Parker. Deloris isn't invited. I don't want her around, and I figure that she probably won't want to eat with us, anyway, seeing as how we're not cooking Kobe beef or anything.

* * *

I grab the diaper bag and strap Parker into her car seat—I'm bringing her with me because Susan said that there is no experience more stimulating for babies than the supermarket—and I lug her out past the den, where Andrew is lying on the couch watching golf and inhaling a bag of Pepperidge Farm Goldfish.

"Honey, I'm going to the market," I say in my most saccharine voice. "Is there anything that you need?" He gives me his I'm-still-hurt face.

"I need for you to apologize," he says.

"But I've apologized a hundred times," I whine. He gives me a look, and I remember that I am being super-duper nice, so I relent. "I'm really, really, really sorry," I say, bringing my hands together under my chin.

He lets out a long, dramatic sigh. "Okay," he says. "I forgive you." Then, as if he just realized that he's been eating, he quickly closes up the bag of Goldfish and looks down at himself, making a face.

"I just ate that whole bag," he says, bewilderment in his voice. "I'm disgusting. I'm F-A-T." He stands up and brushes the crumbs off of himself. "I have to work out. I'm going to the J-Y-M right now."

I bite my lower lip. I swear to God, I'm trying as hard as I can to not laugh, or even to crack a smile, but I just can't help it. I feel a snicker creeping out, so I try to cover it up with a cough, but Andrew is onto me.

"What?" he says. "What's so funny?"

"Nothing." He makes a face like he doesn't believe me, and I bite down on my lip so hard that I think I'm going to draw blood. "Nothing, I swear."

"Tell me," he demands. "What now?" I shake my head, refusing to say anything. "Tell me!" he yells.

I can't tell him. I want to tell him so badly—every fiber of my body is shouting at me to be insolent, and to inform him that he spelled the word *gym* wrong—but I can't do it. I'm on thin ice as it is, and if I tell him, it will be over between us. I have no doubt about that.

"I have to go to the market," I say, composing myself. "I don't have time to play games with you." I turn around and start to walk out, and Andrew calls out after me.

"Lara!" he says. I stop and turn around to look at him.

"What?"

"We need more peanut butter," he says.

I beam at him, the way that moms do in 1950s television shows when someone wants something from them and they're more than happy to oblige, since, after all, fulfilling the needs of others is their primary purpose in life.

"Of course. Do you want Skippy or Jif?" I don't even know why I just asked him that. Of course I'm buying Skippy. I might as well be Annette Funicello, the way that I'm acting this morning.

"I don't care," he answers, shrugging his shoulders. "It's six of one, a dozen of another."

I quickly turn back around so that he can't see me smile. "Okay," I say as I walk out. "I love you."

"Love you, too," he says.

I should have been finished at the market twenty minutes ago, but fucking Deloris is such a pain in the ass with her weird foods—I have to stare at every shelf for, like, ten minutes to try to find what she wants. You should see the market list that she gave me, by the way. It's *editorialized*, for God's sake. Here, look at this:

- orange juice (NOT from concentrate)
- turkey hot dogs—make sure no nitrates; they upset my stomach
- tofu (softest)—last time you got medium. Soft has picture of straw on package
- bulgur wheat (only if they have organic)
- whole-wheat English muffins—Thomas', not the generic brand you got before.
- enoki mushrooms (three bunches)

And on, and on, and on.

I'm about halfway down the rice aisle, looking for the bulgur wheat, when I smell something funky. I wrinkle my nose and turn around.

What is that? I glance at the other people near me in the aisle, and I see that their noses are wrinkled, too. *Oh, no.*

I look at Parker, who is sitting in her car seat, which is snapped into the front of my shopping cart, and I lean down and sniff her butt.

Eeeewwww.

Okay. I've got to change her diaper *right now*. I ask a guy who is straightening bags of pasta where the bathroom is, and he directs me to the back of the store, where I go immediately. When I reach the door to the bathroom, I realize that my cart is not going to fit inside, so I unbuckle Parker and lift her out of her seat, putting my right arm around her back, and putting my left arm under her butt, which feels very, very squishy.

I walk into the bathroom—oh, perfect, they have one of those Koala changing tables—and I pull it down from the wall and place my Burberry plaid changing pad on top of it. I smile to myself as I realize that I am really starting to feel like a pro at this. I lay Parker down on the changing pad and reach for my diaper bag, when I notice that there is something streaked across my sleeve. I look a little bit closer, and then I turn my arm so that I can see the underside of it.

Oh, no.

My whole arm is covered in poop. How did that happen? I lift Parker up and turn her around, and my heart starts to race. *Oh. Oh, my God.* Her entire back is covered with diarrhea. It must have oozed out over the top of her diaper. Her shirt and the top of her pants are wet and brown, and they *stink.* By the way, in case you ever wondered about the origin of the expression *oh, shit,* this has got to be how it happened.

I grab Parker under the arms, holding her away from my body, and I run out of the bathroom to look at her car seat: It's covered. I stand there for a minute, dazed.

I have absolutely no idea what to do.

Okay, I think to myself. *Calm down. Let's think about this.*

I go back into the bathroom and put Parker back down on the changing table, and I take a few seconds to gather my thoughts.

All right. Wipes. I need wipes. I reach into my diaper bag and take out the plastic Baggie that I keep wipes in, and I open it as fast as I can. Inside there are two wipes, and one of them is almost completely dried out.

Oh, God. I forgot to refill the wipes.

I take out the one good wipe and I begin to rub it across my sleeve, but the poop isn't coming off. *Okay, just forget it.* I roll my sleeve up as many times as I can, hoping that the extra layers will contain the smell, and then I pull off Parker's clothes. Of course I don't have a spare set with me. I know I'm supposed to always keep a clean shirt and pants in my diaper bag, just in case her diaper leaks or she spits up—or has a massive attack of diarrhea in the middle of the supermarket—but I'm just not that kind of person. The mommunists in my class all have wipes cases, and they keep pacifiers in little Baggies so that they don't get dirty, and they have compartments filled with Desitin and nail clippers and baby lotion and extra diapers and extra onesies, and enough medicine to handle an outbreak of leprosy. But I'm not an organized-diaper-bag kind of girl. I'm more of a used-bottles-growing-mold-because-I-forgot-to-take-them-out-and-clean-them-diaper-bag kind of girl, which is why I am completely panicking right now.

I rifle through the diaper bag, frantically looking for a diaper.

Please let there be a diaper. Please let there be a diaper. Finally I find one, crumpled up in the bottom of the bag. *Thank you, God.*

I take off Parker's clothes and put them in the bathroom sink, and I start washing her off with the brown paper towels that come out of the little roller thingy on the wall. I have no clue what I'm going to do with her when I'm done, by the way. I don't even have a blanket to wrap her in, because, of course, I didn't listen to Susan's advice, and I never bring a blanket with me anywhere except to Susan's class. But I'll cross that bridge when I get to it. Right now, I just need to focus on cleaning Parker's back.

About thirty-five paper towels later, Parker is finally poop-free, so I put the clean diaper on her, and then I take her dirty clothes and wrap them up in some more paper towels and shove them into the bottom of my diaper bag.

Aha, I think. *So that's why the mommunists always keep an empty plastic bag with them.* I always wondered about that.

I pick up Parker, who is naked now except for a diaper, and I grab another fistful of paper towels and walk out of the bathroom, back to where I left the cart with her stinky car seat.

"Oh, Parker," I whisper to her. "Why couldn't you have waited until we were home to do this, huh?" She looks at me and squeals.

Holding her around the waist with my left arm, I use my right hand to wipe at her car seat with the paper towels, hoping to absorb whatever I can. But it's no use—the poop was like water, and her seat is completely soaked. I try pushing the cart with one hand and holding her with the other hand, but I make it about three steps before I realize that this is not going to work, because she's squirming and grabbing onto my necklace and I can barely manage to hold on to her.

Oh, well. Fuck it.

I line her car seat with some dry paper towels, and then I put Parker, who is naked except for a crumpled diaper, down on top of them. Then I lay a few more paper towels across her chest to keep her warm, and I buckle her in, using the straps of her car seat to hold the paper towels in place. Talk about ghetto.

I take a deep breath and decide to forget about the extraneous stuff on my list. I'm only going to get what I need for dinner tonight and then I'm out of here. I look at the list—all that I still need to get is a bottle of wine, barbecue sauce, and something for dessert. All right. That's easy. I head for the liquor aisle, but before I can take three steps, Parker scrunches up her face and a really loud noise emanates from her butt.

No.

I close my eyes, and when I open them again she is smiling at me and laughing. By now, people in the market are passing by me, and they're all staring at my naked, paper towel–covered, stinky-assed baby.

"I'm glad you think this is funny," I whisper. "But Mommy doesn't have another diaper." She laughs again, and I feel like I'm going to cry. If this doesn't win me the Worst Mother of the Year award, I don't know what will.

As fast as I can, I get the things that I need, and then I head for the checkout aisle. I count the items in my cart—twelve.

Sorry, Deloris. You lose.

I take out the bulgur wheat and the turkey hot dogs and I put them down on the nearest shelf, next to a stack of M&M's bags that are on special, and I push my cart into the express line. As if on cue, Parker starts to scream, and everyone who wasn't already staring at me and making disapproving faces now turns their head in my direction to see what all of the racket is about. I smile apologetically, and I root through my diaper bag, desperately searching for a pacifier. I know there's one in here . . . I dropped it in before I walked out the door. Where is it? Where is it? I start digging through the bag, completely forgetting about the poopy clothes that I stuck in there until my hand hits a wet, mushy spot.

Oh, that is so gross.

And, of course, there's the pacifier, the nipple stuck right in the middle of the poop-stained elastic waistband of her pants. Perfect.

I take my hand out of the diaper bag, sans pacifier, and I notice that there is now a chunk of poop sitting on the edge of my thumb.

"Shhh," I say to Parker, "shhhhh, shhhhh."

I have to wipe the poop off of my thumb. My turn is next and I can't put the groceries onto the conveyor belt when I have shit on my hand. I glance around to see if anyone is looking: Yeah, they're looking. Everyone is looking. And some of them are holding their hands over their noses, and a few people downwind are even gagging, I think.

I really might die right now. In fact, I wish that I *would* die right now. Unfortunately, however, I don't see any potential armed robbers hanging around who might find it in their hearts to shoot me, and the chance of a freak avalanche of canned peas washing through the market seems unlikely at this time. So, I take a deep breath and, with everyone still staring at me, I pluck the paper towel that is covering Parker's nipples out from under the straps of her car seat, wipe my thumb with it, and then crumple it up and stick it inside my diaper bag. The woman in line behind me actually recoils in horror, and several people let out audible gasps. The old guy in front of me pays cash and walks away, and I breathe a sigh of relief that it is finally my turn.

I lean over my cart and reach down to remove the carton of eggs, but the checker stops me.

"Um, why don't I do that?" she suggests. I'm sure she's thinking that my child is already abused enough; she doesn't need for me to be passing on a bacterial infection to her in addition to the beatings that I surely dole out on a regular basis.

I nod at her and smile weakly, and she pulls the things out of my cart and rings me up while I try, in vain, to calm Parker down by pushing the shopping cart back and forth and telling her to *shhhh*. Then, as if this isn't already my own personal version of hell, the lady behind me taps me on the shoulder. I whirl around to look at her.

"Maybe you should pick her up," she says to me condescendingly.

Thank you, lady. Like it hadn't occurred to me to pick her up. I mean, yes, I may not have the strongest of maternal instincts, but I'm not a total idiot. I stare at her for a second. She's older, maybe in her early fifties, and she either doesn't have kids or had them so long ago that she clearly doesn't remember how much it sucks. Well, I think I'll just have to remind her. Being careful not to touch anything with my fecal thumb, I use my forearm to brush a strand of hair away from my face.

"Well," I say matter-of-factly, "her back is covered with diarrhea and I don't have any more diapers. And, as you can see, I've devised an intricate and, if I may say so myself, quite resourceful paper-towel barrier between her and her car seat, which, for your information, is also covered in poop. So picking her up isn't really an option for me right now, but if you'd like to do it, you're more than welcome to. Actually, if you'd like to adopt her, you're more than welcome to."

I smile a big, fuck-you smile at her, and then I turn around, take my credit card back from the checker, and, holding my contaminated thumb away from the cart, proceed to push my paper towel–clad, poop-diapered, inconsolably screaming baby out of the market with my head held high.

By the time that I have decompressed with a glass of wine, debriefed with Andrew—*Lara, they sell diapers at the market. Why didn't you just grab a package?* (a good point, actually, but nothing that I ever would have thought of in a million, bazillion years)—and gotten the house straightened up, Nadine and my father have arrived.

I want to die the second that I answer the door. Not only is my father wearing one of those eighties abstract sweaters with the puffy neon-colored squiggly lines on them, but he is also wearing a toupee. A bad toupee. It's about three shades darker than the rest of his hair, the front of it is poofy and sort of curly in spots, and it looks like it's been hair sprayed. With Aqua Net. Honestly, it looks like a small animal built a nest on top of his head and then settled in to die. Of course, given that it's my dad, I'm really not all that surprised that he's wearing it, but I'm down-right shocked that Nadine would allow him to walk out of the house in that thing. I was positive that she had better taste than that.

I lead them through the den and out though the French doors that open into the backyard, where Andrew is struggling to light the grill with a ten-foot-long butane lighter.

"Here," my father says, walking over to him. "I can take care of that for you." Without a word Andrew hands the lighter to my dad, who expertly gets the coals glowing to a dim red. When he's finished, he puts down the lighter and sticks out his hand.

"I'm Ronny," he says.

Andrew grips his hand and pumps it up and down. "Nice to meet you," he says. "I'm Andrew." Andrew glances at my dad's head and then shoots me a confused look. I nod back to confirm that, yes, I have seen it, and no, I don't think he's fooling anyone either. Then I hold my hand out toward Nadine.

"And this is Nadine," I say. Nadine gives a little wave.

"Hi," she says. "I've heard a lot about you." *No, no, let's not go there.*

"Okay," I say, quickly changing the subject. "Why don't we start dinner? Dad, I've designated you the barbecuer." It occurs to me that perhaps this was not the best idea after all, as his toupee, which looks highly flammable, could easily catch fire, but it's too late now.

"Sounds good to me," he says. He slips on the ridiculous apron that Andrew bought last year that says *Licensed to Grill* on it, and I quickly try to usher Andrew away from him. But before we can get back inside, he calls out to us.

"Andrew," he says. "Why don't you stay out here with me? We can hang out, mano a mano."

Oh, God. This is exactly what I was afraid of. I grimace. "Actually, Dad, Andrew needs to watch Parker."

My dad frowns. "Well, where's the nanny? Isn't that what she's here for?" I roll my eyes and sigh at him.

"Yeah, but I wanted this to just be family tonight. There are four of us here. We don't need Deloris." Just then Deloris walks outside, carrying Parker in her arms.

"That's crazy," my dad yells to me. He turns in the direction of Deloris and waves. "Hi, there!" he says to her. "I'm Lara's dad. Why don't you stay out here with Parker and have some dinner with us?" I cringe when he says this. Deloris was definitely not in my plans for this evening.

"What are you making?" Deloris asks cautiously. Oh, here we go. Miss Picky Palate rides again.

My dad looks over at the plate of food that I put out next to the grill. "Looks like some grilled veggies, chicken breast, and"—he looks over at me—"what is this Lara? Filet?" Reluctantly, I nod my head. "And filet mignon," he says. Deloris smiles.

"I'll have some filet," she answers. *Wow.* That's a shocker.

"Great," my dad answers, grinning. "Now, then, Andrew can stay with me. See? That was easy."

Andrew gives me an unsteady glance and trots back over to the grill. Well, there's no chance that I am leaving the two of them—no, make that the three of them—out here alone. I definitely need to monitor this situation. I turn to Nadine.

"Then why don't we just stay out here, too?" I suggest. "We can work on the party over there." I point in the direction of the wicker love seat that is a few feet away from the grill.

"Fine with me," Nadine says, smiling.

The two of us go over to the chair and sit down, and I take out the pad and paper that I've been carrying with me and put it down on the side table.

"So," I say to her. "I guess the first thing we need to do is to make a guest list. How many people were you thinking?"

Nadine pauses to think; then she shrugs. "Eight, maybe ten."

"Okay." I start to write this down, but just then, out of the corner of my eye, I see my father wipe his brow with his sleeve.

"Wow," he says, fanning himself with his hand. "This grill is so hot, it's making my head sweat." He reaches for a napkin and dabs at his forehead with it, blotting the beads of sweat that have originated underneath his toupee. Oh, man, that is so disgusting. I turn back to Nadine.

"And what were you thinking about food? Do you want to have dinner with everyone first, or should we just let people eat on their own and then meet up at the bar later?"

But before Nadine can answer me, Deloris lets out a shriek. We both turn to look at her. She has placed one hand over her mouth, and she's staring in the direction of Andrew and my dad, as if she's just seen something too horrible for words. Oh, God, I knew it, the fucking toupee is on fire. I spin around to look at my dad, but his head is not engulfed in flames. In fact, his head is bald, and he is wiping it with a napkin and holding the dead toupee animal in his left hand.

"Ahh," he says, smiling. "That's much better."

I rub my forehead with my hand and close my eyes. I'm so mortified right now. "Dad," I say, "what are you doing?"

"What?" he asks, sounding surprised. As if removing a toupee in public is something that everyone does. "I was hot, so I took it off."

I shake my head. "Well, why were you wearing it in the first place?"

He shrugs his shoulders. "I like having hair sometimes. I only wear it for special occasions."

Well, I think, *there go the wedding pictures.*

"But Dad, it's awful. It doesn't even look like hair."

He makes a hurt face. "It does, too. The best wig maker in Vegas did this for me. It was custom." The best wig maker in Vegas. It sounds like it could be the sequel to *The Best Little Whorehouse in Texas*.

I turn to Nadine, who hasn't said a word so far.

"Do *you* like it?" I ask her. She purses her lips, and I get the feeling that she's not happy with this conversation.

"It makes your father feel good about himself, Lara, and I like that." Oh. Well, isn't she just Miss Positive Self-esteem. Just then Andrew pipes up.

"Don't worry," he says to my dad. "She says stuff like that to me all the time, too."

I give him a look as if to say, *Thank you for helping me out, Andrew,* and I hear Deloris clucking her tongue behind me. Okay. That's it. I don't care if she quits. I've had enough of this woman. I turn around to look at her.

"Is there something you want to say, Deloris?" Deloris's eyes widen into a who-me look, and she shakes her head no.

"Not a thing, Mrs. Lara. Deloris is not getting involved in this discussion." She picks up Parker, who is ripping up fistfuls of grass and trying to shove them into her mouth, and starts to walk back inside. "Let's go, my baby," she says. "We can get the table set." She disappears back inside, and when I turn back around, everyone is staring at me.

"What?" I yell to them. Nadine puts her hand on my leg.

"Lara, honey, I need to powder my nose. Do you think you could show me where the little girls' room is?"

I point to a door off the back bedroom. "There's a bathroom right there," I say.

Nadine smiles and takes my arm. "Yes, but I'd love it if you could show me yourself."

Oh. I get it. She wants to talk to me. Fine. We both stand up, and as I walk toward the door she walks over to my dad and kisses him on the mouth. With tongue. *Ugh*. I hate being around couples who are still honeymooning. Let's see if she's still kissing him like that after ten years. Let's see if they're still *speaking* after ten years.

"We'll be back in a minute, boys," she says to them, as she heads back in my direction. "Don't hurt yourselves out here."

We walk back inside and she leads me into the kitchen, where Deloris is taking out plates and silverware. Nadine flashes her a big smile.

"Would you excuse us for a minute, Deloris?" Deloris nods.

"I was just leaving," she says to Nadine, as she shoots me a dirty look. She picks up the stack of dishes and carries them with one hand while she holds Parker with the other hand. I have no idea how she does that. I couldn't even push a shopping cart and hold Parker at the same time.

"Honey," Nadine says, trying to get my attention.

"Yeah," I say, refocusing on her. "Listen, I'm sorry, okay? I wasn't trying to be mean or anything out there, but he's my dad. I can say things to him that other people can't."

Nadine presses her lips together. "The same way that you can say things to Andrew that other people can't, because he's your husband?"

"Yeah. Exactly. I mean, he thinks that I'm being vicious, but if I don't tell him that he looks ridiculous sometimes, or that he sounds stupid, who will?" I shake my head. "We actually had a huge fight yesterday about it, too. He didn't know the words to 'Old MacDonald,' so I tried to correct him, and he was wearing ripped jeans from, like, fifteen years ago, and he *flipped out* when I told him to change."

Nadine nods. "Well, that's just it, honey. You can't change people. They are who they are, for better or for worse."

"No," I say, shaking my head as I try to clarify. "I didn't tell him to change who he *is*. I told him to change what he was *wearing*."

"But honey, don't you see, in his mind it's the same thing." Nadine takes my hand with both of her hands. "Do you remember when I told you that all men are children?" she asks.

I nod. "Vaguely," I say.

"Well, it's true. Now think about it: If you didn't like something that Parker was wearing, or if she said something the wrong way, would you talk to her the way that you talk to Andrew, or to your dad?"

"No," I say. "I'd never be that harsh with her. But they're adults. They should be able to take constructive criticism."

Nadine inhales, as if she just realized that this is going to take longer than she thought. "They *should*," she says. "But sometimes they can't. Especially not from the people they love." She exhales. "Listen, honey, I've been around a lot of men in my time, and the one thing that I've learned is that they just want somebody to cheer them on and tell them what a great job they're doing. It's as simple as that." She pauses and looks me straight in the eye. "And most of the men who I know, I know because they weren't getting that from their wives."

I take a second or two to let this sink in. Is she trying to tell me that Andrew is going to go see a hooker because I make fun of him sometimes? No. Andrew would never—Oooh, it's all coming back to me now. I told her about Courtney the other night. She's trying to tell me that Andrew is hanging out with Courtney because I'm not giving him what he needs.

"You're talking about Courtney, aren't you?" I ask her.

"I don't know," Nadine says. "Is she the bitch with the poodle?" she asks. I nod. "Then yes. That's who I'm talking about. They may be just friends for now, but you don't want to take any chances. You've got a good man, honey. Don't let somebody else steal him away from you." She leans in and lowers her voice to a whisper. "But what about Deloris?" she asks. "What's going on with the two of you?"

"We don't get along," I whisper back. "She hates me because she thinks that I don't spend enough time with Parker, and she probably thinks that I don't deserve Andrew, either. And she practices voodoo." I roll my eyes. "I found a voodoo doll that she made of me in her room. Can you believe that?"

Nadine bites her lower lip and thinks for a minute. Then she straightens back up and crosses her arms in front of her chest.

"Listen, honey. Let me ask you a question. How would you like to get rid of Courtney for good, get along with Deloris, and get your marriage back to how it used to be?"

"No," I say. "I wouldn't want that. That would suck. If that happened, I wouldn't have anything to complain about anymore, and then I'd actually have to be happy."

Nadine laughs. "Well, start working on that smile, honey, because I have a *plan*."

nineteen

O kay, mommies!"
Susan claps her hands three times to get everyone's attention, but we're all too absorbed with the post-blow-job-party wrap-up discussion to even notice. Basically, everyone had fun, a few girls slummed it and actually gave their husbands blow jobs that night, and *everyone* remembered that Parker has a flat head and that Andrew is potentially cheating on me with a twenty-five-year-old.

Susan is now standing on top of her folding chair, and she's banging on a Fisher-Price xylophone with the yellow plastic drumstick that is attached to it with a string.

"Ladies! Ladies! We're running late. We need to get started!"

Finally everyone stops talking and we all sit down in a circle with our babies, just as Lisa (Carter's mom) is informing me that her husband once defended a pediatric neurologist after he accidentally fitted the helmet too tight on a five-month-old little boy and slowly crushed part of his skull over the course of four months.

"Okay, everyone," Susan says breathlessly. "Today's topic is going back to work. I want everyone to go around and say what you used to do before you had your baby, and what your work plans are for now, or for the near future. Okay?"

I can see everyone's eyes glaze over, because, as we all know, mommunists don't work. Please, half of them didn't work even before they had babies, so they have nothing to go "back" to anyway. Except for me, of course. Why is it that I always feel like someone should be singing that *Sesame Street* song whenever I walk into this class? You know, "One of these things is not like the others; one of these things just doesn't belong."

I love *Sesame Street*, by the way. Parker's been waking up early the past few days, what with the diarrhea and all, so we've been watching it together every morning before Deloris goes on duty. Well, I watch it, and she just kind of lies in bed next to me, trying to eat the remote control. But that Cookie Monster is fucking hilarious. Today they had him dressed in a velvet smoking jacket and an ascot, and he was doing a bit called Monsterpiece Theater. He reviewed *One Flew Over the Cuckoo's Nest*, about the historic journey of the number one as it flew over a nest of cuckoos. It was genius. Way better than those stupid Wiggles.

The mommunist to Susan's right begins to talk.

"I was trying to get my hours for my MFT before Cooper was born, but I don't really see myself finishing. At least, not for a while." She looks down at Cooper, who has spit-up dribbling down his chin, and she smiles. "I just really can't imagine leaving him right now."

Susan smiles back, and nods for the next person to go; the mom with the rock-star bangs, who, by the way, is the skinniest mother of a four-month-old that I have ever seen. Bitch.

"I'm definitely not going back to work. I would die before I would leave Emma alone all day with someone else. Plus, I'm still breast-feeding, so I don't know how that would even work."

Actually, I know how it would work. It's called a pump screen. When I was pregnant, the head of building operations at school accosted me for two months about whether I was going to need one for my office when I got back from my maternity leave, because if I did, he would need to order it before he left for his summer vacation in August, and could I please let him know ASAP (which he pronounced *aysap*). And since I didn't have an answer for him before I left to have the baby, as I was, at that time, still blissfully unaware that five minutes of breast-feeding would be more than I could handle, let alone five *months*, he then sent me about six e-mails a week at home, until I finally responded to him a few days ago and informed him that no, I am not breast-feeding and, therefore, I will not be requiring a pump screen upon my return. To which he responded, *Okay. But did you at least breast-feed for three months?*

As the rest of the women take their turns, it's the same story over and over again.

"My husband said that I don't ever have to work again if I don't want to, and I definitely don't want to."

"I wasn't working before, because I knew I was going to have kids. And none of my friends work, so I have a million people to call for play-dates. Maybe in ten years, when I'm done having kids and they're all in school full-time. But I don't know."

"I liked my job, but I can always go back after he's in school. He's only going to be a baby once, you know?"

By the time they get to me, I'm almost in tears. I can't help thinking that there's something really, really wrong with me, if I'm the only person in a roomful of twelve women who actually *wants* to spend eight hours a day away from my child.

"Lara," Susan says, smiling. "What about you?"

Trying to hold back my tears, I take a deep breath and put on a brave smile. "I actually *am* going back to work." There's a collective gasp, and I feel the need to explain myself. "It's going to be so hard to leave her," I find myself saying, "but I really, really love my job."

Everyone is staring at me, as if this is something that they simply cannot comprehend.

"I work with teenagers," I say. Still staring. "It's extremely gratifying." Not so much as a blink. All right. I'm going to have to explain it in terms that they can understand.

"It's not full-time yet. It's just three days a week, from eight to four." Finally they all smile, and make *oooohhh* kinds of faces.

And then the bullshit starts. Lots of fake admiration, like, *Wow, that is so great that you're doing something for yourself,* or, *That is so amazing that you're going back to work. You must be so strong,* or my favorite, *Good for you! You'll be such a positive role model for Parker.* Blah, blah, blah, blah, blah. I know what they're really thinking. They're thinking, *Poor Lara. Her husband must not do very well if he's making her leave her baby to get a part-time job.*

At the end of class, Melissa and a bunch of the other moms make plans to go to lunch at the pizza place down the street, and I decide to join them, if for no other reason than to keep them from conjecturing about how far Andrew and I are from having to go on food stamps.

When I arrive at the restaurant, it is total chaos. Seven moms, seven babies, seven strollers—we've completely taken the place over, and I now totally understand the lunch-at-eleven-o'clock thing, because this would never fly if the place weren't totally empty right now. I wheel the Snap-N-Go around to an empty spot at the table and pull up a chair, and immediately Melissa starts in on me.

"So, Lara, I had no idea that you were going back to work. That's so crazy. You're going to be, like"—she makes quotation marks in the air with her fingers—" 'a working mom.' "

I nod and smile uncomfortably, not sure how to respond, when Lisa chimes in.

"Will you still be able to come to class?" she asks.

"Yeah," I say. "I'm working Mondays, Tuesdays, and Thursdays, so I can take her to this class on Wednesdays, and maybe pick up a music class or something on Fridays when she gets older."

"Oh," Melissa says, sounding as if she just understood the arrangement for the first time. "So then it will always be three days. I don't know why, I got the impression that it was just for this year."

I shake my head. "It is just for this year," I say. "After next summer I'll have to go back full-time. I mean, I'm the director of the college counseling department. They need me to be there." Amy (Cooper's mom), who is sitting to my left, looks concerned.

"But what about preschool?" she asks.

"What about it?" I shoot back, shrugging. "She'll start in the fall after she turns two."

Amy gives me an uncomfortable smile, as if she hates to be the one to burst my bubble. "But how will you do transition?"

Melissa and Lisa and the other moms at the table all nod.

"What's transition?" I ask.

Lisa frowns, as if she was afraid that I was going to say that, and leans in to explain.

"The first year of preschool, you have to go with them until they can handle being there without you. I've heard that some kids can take six months before they're ready."

I stare at her. I've never heard of this transition thing before.

"Well," I say, "what do other people do who work?"

Melissa and Lisa look down at the table, and Amy gives me the uncomfortable smile again.

"I mean, I guess some people send their nannies to do the transition, but there are a bunch of schools that have a no-nanny policy. They feel that the children are more secure if their parents are there with them."

I look at her like she has to be joking.

"So you're telling me that there are no working mothers in this city at all," I say flatly.

She shrugs. "No, I'm sure there are lots of working mothers in this city. They just don't send their kids to preschool until they're three."

My jaw drops. *Let me get this straight,* I think. *My daughter is going to have to miss an entire year of preschool just because I have a job? Parker is going to be penalized because I work?* This cannot be for real.

"I don't see how that's possible," I say. "It doesn't make any sense." I'm trying really hard not to get upset right now. *Consider the source,* I keep telling myself. They're not exactly the brightest crayons in the box, these girls. But Amy is insistent.

"I'm telling you," Amy says cockily. "If you want to put her in school at two, she's going to have to transition. But you have a nanny, right? Just don't apply to schools that have a no-nanny policy, that's all."

Okay, first of all, over my dead body is Deloris going to preschool with my kid, and second of all, how pretentious is it to have a "no-nanny" policy? And how do they convey that policy to the world, anyway? A thick red slash through an image of a Latino woman pushing a stroller? Honestly. It's so LA.

Melissa puts her hand on my arm.

"Lara, do you *have* to work?" she asks gently. I know that she isn't trying to be condescending right now, but I want to slap her across the face.

"No," I say, trying to keep my voice steady. "I don't have to. I mean, my salary is nice, but we could survive without it if we needed to." I pause for a second. "I know that you can't understand this, but I don't work for the money. I *like* working. I *miss* my job."

Amy puts her hands out, palms up, and then brings them together, as if she just closed the case. "Well, then that's your choice, that's all."

An uncomfortable silence falls over the table, and the words hang in the air, echoing over and over and over again in my head.

That's your choice. That's your choice. That's your choice.

At the other end of the table, Sabrina (Ashton's mom) smacks her hand on the table and tries to change the subject.

"Oh, my God, you guys," she says. "I have the funniest story." Everyone turns to look at her, and she starts talking a mile a minute.

"I was at Gelson's yesterday, and the checker was telling me about this mom who was in there over the weekend with her baby, and the baby had diarrhea and the mom didn't have any extra diapers or clothes or anything with her, so she left the baby sitting in the diarrhea diaper, took off all of her clothes, and covered her up with paper towels. The checker said the whole market reeked for, like, three hours afterward. Can you believe that?" Everyone is cracking up, and I am praying that nobody notices how red my cheeks are right now.

"Oh, my God," Melissa says. "That is so funny. Why didn't she just buy some diapers?"

"Why didn't she just leave?" Lisa asks. She turns around to look at me. "Who stays at the market when something like that happens?"

"I know," I say, rolling my eyes. "What an idiot."

When lunch is over I don't feel like going home, so I decide to drop in on Stacey at the bar. That Nadine is no joke, by the way. She set up a meeting for Jimmy and Stacey on Saturday morning, and by Monday afternoon Stacey had construction permits, a new liquor license, and a licensed, bonded contractor with references from sixteen other bars in the area. I mean, I can't even imagine the dirt that she must have on these people. But Stacey is thrilled. The idea of having to do nine thousand things in two weeks is right up her alley, and as impossible as it sounds, she's actually been working *more* hours since she left her law firm. I really have no idea what she's going to do when the bar is actually open and her biggest pressure is making sure that they don't run out of Grey Goose. She'll probably start suing people just to keep herself busy.

I walk in, trying to navigate the Snap-N-Go between pieces of plywood and crates of barware, and I find Stacey on her hands and knees underneath a table, ripping out the vinyl covering of the booth seat with a knife.

"Hi," I say, startling her. "Glad to see that you're using your education."

She almost hits her head when she looks up at me, but she catches herself and then glances at Parker, who is asleep in the Snap-N-Go. "You're one to talk, *Ms.* Stone," she says, referring to the name that my students call me. "What are you doing here, anyway?"

"I just stopped in to say hi. I didn't feel like going home and dealing with Deloris yet."

Stacey crawls out from under the table, stands up, and brushes herself off. She lifts her right arm and waves it around, à la one of the *Price Is Right* girls.

"So, what do you think?" she asks.

I take a look around. The bar counter has been completely removed, and the booths have all been uncovered, their yellow stuffing fully exposed. The carpet has been ripped up, there are rusty nails sticking out of the floorboards, and there is trash everywhere. I lift one side of my lip.

"I think it looks like Beirut. Are you sure that you can pull this off in a week and a half?"

Stacey looks insulted. "First of all, we have accomplished in three days what would take most people three months. Second of all, bars never look good during the day. You should know that. And third, of course I can pull it off. I've completed acquisitions of major movie studios in less than a week and a half. This is nothing."

"I hope so," I say. "Because Nadine sent the e-vite out yesterday, and you're going to have a dozen women here expecting a good time whether it's ready or not."

"Yeah, yeah," she says, looking at her watch. "Hey, it's almost one o'clock. Come get some lunch with me; I'm starving."

"Actually," I say, "I already ate, sorry. But I'll sit with you. Parker should sleep for at least another half an hour, I think."

Stacey shrugs. "Okay. Let's go. There's a pretty good deli next door."

We walk outside and I lower the sun visor on Parker's car seat, then follow Stacey a few storefronts down the street, where she stops and opens the door. She walks inside, letting go of the door behind her, and it almost slams shut on the stroller.

"Thanks," I call to her. "You're so thoughtful." She turns back around and watches me struggling to get the stroller through the door, and then she finally comes back and holds it open for me.

"God," she says. "What a pain in the ass you are."

I grab a table while she orders her lunch at the counter, and then she sits down and joins me while she waits for them to bring it to her.

"So, really," I say. "How's it going? Are you happy?"

Stacey pauses for a second to think, and then tilts her head from side to side. "For now," she says. "It's mindless, and it's keeping me busy, and I think that I can turn it into something cool. But I don't know if this is forever. I can see myself getting bored pretty quickly."

"I was thinking the same thing," I confess. "It's kind of like my maternity leave. You know, nice for a few months, but nothing I'd want to do permanently. Although . . . Well, it doesn't matter. I don't want to make you listen to mom stuff."

Stacey laughs through her nose. "Hey," she says, "I've got nothing but construction, so if you don't start talking you're going to have to hear about how shockingly complicated it is to remove vinyl from the underside of a booth seat."

"I'll pass," I tell her.

"Then bring it on, honey," she says, holding out her hands and curling her fingers inward, as if she's coaxing a dog out of a corner.

"Well," I say, hesitating. "Okay. I'm just feeling a little conflicted now about going back to work. I mean, I want to—I'm dying to—but I'm starting to think that maybe it's not the best thing for Parker."

Stacey stares at me like I just told her that I'm thinking of jumping from an airplane without a parachute.

"Are you serious?" she asks. "Would you really not go back to work?"

I sigh. "It's not what I want to do, no."

"Then why would you even utter such blasphemy?" She pauses. "Did something happen?"

I shake my head at her. "Nothing happened. Well, not nothing. I had lunch with the mommunists today, and I found out that if your kid goes to preschool at two, they have to do this transition thing where the parent goes with them, and if you can't do it because you work then you pretty much have to wait until they're three for them to go to school. But I don't know how I feel about that. I mean, Parker would be at a huge disadvantage. That's a whole year of school that she would miss that other kids would have."

Stacey is squinting at me, and I get the feeling that she's trying to find the old Lara underneath this person sitting in front of her.

"I knew it," she says, shaking her head.

Just then the waiter brings her food over: a bacon cheeseburger, cheese fries with a side of ranch dressing, and a chocolate milk shake. It looks like a heart attack on a plastic tray.

"What?" I ask when he leaves. "What did you know?"

She shovels a handful of cheese fries into her mouth, and answers me while she's still chewing. "I knew that they would try to convert you. I told you they would."

I roll my eyes at her and marvel at the smallness of her thighs, which look like two twigs resting on her chair. "They weren't trying to convert me, Stacey. They were just telling me the facts. And the fact is, if I go back to work full-time, Parker will miss out on an entire year of school, and God knows what else."

Stacey rolls her eyes back at me and takes a bite of her burger.

"First of all, they have no idea what they're talking about. Parker could transition in two days, for all you know."

I make a yeah-right face. "Sorry, Stace, but I think I'd trust them on something like this more than I'd trust you. I doubt that kids can transition in two days."

She gives me an openmouthed, cheeseburger smile. "Actually, kids transition in two days all the time. I had a client once who had a baby—she was a television writer—and her kid went to the preschool at Universal and transitioned in the first week. She said half the class was transitioned by the second week, and there were only two or three kids who took more than a month."

"Universal has its own preschool?" I ask.

She nods. "All the studios do. Right on the lot."

Amazing. Because working in film and TV doesn't have enough perks, so they need their own preschools, too.

"Okay," I say, "fine. But what if Parker is the one kid who takes more than a month? I can't take that chance."

She sucks on the straw of the milk shake. "No way," she says. "Do you know who the kids were who had the hardest time transitioning?" I shake my head, waiting for an answer. "The ones whose mothers didn't work. The kids who had working moms were used to being with a nanny, or being in day care all day, so they had no problem. But the ones who spent every day with their mothers, like, totally freaked out. One kid was so attached that she wouldn't even let her mom sit on the other side of the room. She would color with one hand and hold her mom's hand with the other hand for almost four months." Stacey shakes her head. "It's not healthy, that kind of attachment. I'd much rather spend less time but have my kid be well-adjusted."

I stare at her for a second. "Your client told you all of that?" I ask, incredulously.

Stacey nods and scrunches up her nose. "She was a talker."

I sit back and cross my arms, taking this in. "I'm just confused," I say.

Stacey wipes up the rest of the ranch dressing with her finger and then sticks it in her mouth. "About what?" she asks.

"About who to listen to. I feel like every time I turn around, someone is telling me something different. Like, I thought that I could trust my pediatrician, but he's turned out to be worthless. He tells me to watch out for things two months after they've already happened, and he always makes me feel guilty for not breast-feeding longer. And I thought that Deloris would teach me how to be good with her—I thought that Deloris would be like Mary Poppins—but I can't trust anything that she says, because she *wants* me to mess up. She's like the anti–Mary Poppins. So then I thought that Susan was the answer, but I find out that she's practicing medicine without a license. And I figured that the mommunists would at least know what they're talking about, but now you're telling me that they're full of shit, too." I throw my hands up in the air. "So who do I trust? Who's going to tell me what to do with this kid?"

Stacey loudly slurps the remaining few sips of her milk shake, then

pulls the straw out of the cup and licks it off. She's so disgusting sometimes. It's like eating with a ten-year-old boy. When there isn't a molecule
of milk shake left in the cup, on the straw, or on the plastic lid, she looks
up and makes a face at me. The face, in no uncertain terms, says that I am
a total moron.

"Nobody is, Lara," she says matter-of-factly. "You can't trust anyone
but yourself. That's why it's so hard to be a parent. Duh."

I sit back in my seat and ponder this for a minute.

Nobody is.

I can't believe this, but she's right. If you had asked me to guess who
would be the one person who would give me the best parenting advice, I
would have opened up the phone book and started reading out random
names before I would have said Stacey. But she's absolutely right. Miss
I-Hate-Kids came up with exactly the right answer.

I get up from my seat, walk over to her, and give her a kiss on the
cheek.

"I love you," I say. I take a twenty out of my wallet and put it down on
the table. "Lunch is on me."

Then I hurriedly grab my diaper bag, push Parker out of the restaurant, and wave good-bye to Stacey, who, by the way, is still looking at me
like I am a total moron.

twenty

I've decided that the situation with Deloris needs to improve. I mean, if I'm going to go back to work in a few weeks, I can't have her trying to undermine me all of the time while she pretends that she's just doing her job. I swear, sometimes I feel like Deloris and I are in the Cold War, around the time of the Cuban Missile Crisis. It's really a perfect analogy if you think about it: I'm Kennedy (obviously), and she's Khrushchev, quietly stockpiling missiles behind my back. Please, you know what she does to me. She's evil. And it's only getting worse. You should see what's been going on with naptimes lately.

It all started because I noticed one day that Parker is the most smiley right after she wakes up from a nap, and I made some comment to Deloris about how she acts like you've just rescued her from Alcatraz when you go in and get her out of the crib. It's the cutest thing, really. She stares through the bars, waiting for someone to come get her, and when she sees the door to her room open she gets this huge grin on her face—it's like one-half sheer joy, one-half total relief—and when you actually pick her up she's practically shaking with excitement, and she makes these happy baby gurgly noises, as if she's trying to convey just how thrilled she is that you're there. I'm telling you, it's priceless.

So anyway, I decided that I wanted to get a piece of this smile action on a regular basis, because a) it's delicious, and b) if she's that happy about being rescued from the crib, it's got to be good for the totem pole if I'm the one who rescues her. So, for the last week or so, I've been hanging around at home while Parker naps, and I've been trying to go get her when she wakes up. I say *trying*, however, because Deloris has turned it into a fucking

Olympic event. The Naptime Dash, I call it, because the woman literally races me to Parker's room every time that Parker wakes up. It's ridiculous. I want to beat her there, I have to sit in my room and stare at the monitor, and then *the second* that Parker stirs, I have to sprint out the door and into the hallway. But, if you look at Figure 1, below, you can see that once I get into the main hallway, things start to get tricky.

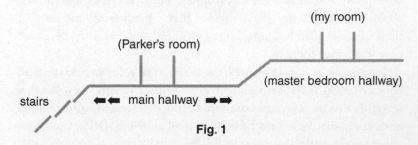

Fig. 1

You see, Deloris is usually running up the stairs at the other end of the hall just as I'm rounding the corner from the hallway outside my bedroom. As soon as we see each other, the starting gun gets fired. First, we both slow down to a brisk walk, so that the other one doesn't think that it's actually a race. Then I walk as fast as I can and she walks as fast as she can, and we both usually reach the doorway to Parker's room at exactly the same time. And this is where we come to the crucial part of the Naptime Dash, because whoever can get through that doorway first is clearly going to be the winner (unless, of course, someone were to cheat and stick her foot out, thus tripping the other contestant and causing her to lose; a strategy which I haven't yet used, but which I am by no means beneath trying). So, with giant, fake, I'm-not-trying-to-beat-you-are-you-trying-to-beat-me smiles plastered on our faces, Deloris and I let elbows fly and we push and shove each other out of the way until one of us emerges through the doorway, victorious, and the other one stands back, pushing her mussed hair out of her face and rubbing her bruised, sore arm.

So far, I'm two for six with one draw, which sounds horrible, but really isn't such a bad record when you consider that Deloris has around half a foot and a hundred pounds on me. But I'm working on it. I've taken up tai chi.

The Naptime Dash, however, is only a small part of the problem. I mean, just in case a blond voodoo doll stashed in her drawer isn't enough for you, there have been other incidents, too. For example, just yesterday Deloris was playing with Parker in her room while I was getting dressed, and on the baby monitor I heard her trying to teach Parker how to say *Dada, Delo,* and *Zoey,* but no mention of the words *Mommy* or even *Mama.* Needless to say, I was fuming, and after tossing and turning about it all night long, I have decided that, regardless of how stupid I think Nadine's plan is, I am going to go ahead and give it try, because I have finally had enough.

And so, today, if all goes well, the Berlin Wall is coming down. If all goes well, Deloris and I are going to unite as allies against a new threat, a threat that is much greater and more potentially devastating than either of us could ever be toward each other. If all goes well, Deloris and I are going to take on the Perky Poodle Bitch.

My God, I hope Nadine knows what she's doing.

Right after Parker goes down for her morning nap, I walk into my bathroom and stand in front of the mirror. As hard as I can, I rub my eyes with my fists, trying to make them as red as possible, and then I wipe off all of my under-eye concealer so that my dark circles are fully exposed. I take one last glance in the mirror—okay, I look sufficiently awful—and then I walk downstairs to the kitchen, where Deloris is peeling cloves of garlic. Normally, when I walk into the kitchen and Deloris is there, we just ignore each other and go about our business in silence. But, since to-day is Victory Deloris day (better known as V-D day; an unfortunate moniker, I know), I sit down at the counter, sigh loudly, and sniffle every few seconds while I flip through the mail. Out of the corner of my eye, I see Deloris turn around to look at me.

Okay, I think, *it's time to pounce.*

Trying to make my voice sound shaky, I start talking.

"Deloris?" I say, trying to get her attention. She turns around again and looks right at me.

"Yes, Mrs. Lara, what is it?"

I sigh again and pretend to hesitate before I speak. "Deloris, I hate to bring you into something personal, but I don't know who else to ask for help. . . ." I let my sentence trail off and I act as if I need to compose myself.

Deloris puts down her garlic and looks at me. "What's the matter, Mrs. Lara?" she asks. "Is it something with the baby?"

I shake my head. "No, no," I say. "It's not Parker. It's just . . . well, have you noticed Andrew acting any differently lately?"

Deloris's eyes narrow, and I can tell that she doesn't know what I'm getting at. "Different how?" she asks.

I sniffle and try to picture puppies being slaughtered in an attempt to conjure up some tears. "I don't know," I say. I inhale shakily, then exhale. "But I think . . ." I pause, and she stares at me. For dramatic effect, I lower my voice almost to a whisper. "I think that he's being seduced." As soon as I say the word *seduced*, I put my hand over my mouth, as if it's just too much for me to bear.

Deloris looks offended. She straightens herself up and shakes her head. "I don't think so," she says. "Mr. Andrew wouldn't do anything like that to his family."

I dab at the corners of my eyes with my index fingers. "I don't think he would, either, but I'm pretty sure that another woman is after him."

Deloris crosses her arms. "Why?" she asks. "What makes you think this?"

I have to be careful here. I don't want Deloris to get angry with Andrew or she'll blow my whole plan. I need for her to feel like he's a victim in all of this.

"Well," I begin, swallowing hard. "There's this woman who is in the class that he does with Zoey; she's really pretty, and she's just kind of latched onto him. She's always making excuses for why she has to see him or talk to him, and I just don't think that it's normal." Deloris still looks skeptical. I hate to do this, but I think I'm going to have to make up a little white lie. I cross my fingers behind my back. "Last week she baked him chocolate cupcakes because he told her that they're his favorite, and the other night I picked up the phone by accident and I overheard her telling him that she would do anything for him, and that all he has to do is say the word." Okay. Two little white lies. But it's for a good cause.

I sneak a glance at Deloris, who is seething.

"Do you think that Mr. Andrew would fall for this?" she asks.

"I don't know, Deloris. I just don't know. I mean, he's so naive sometimes. I've told him that I don't like her hanging around so much, but he
insists that they're just friends. He feels bad for her because she just
moved here and she doesn't know anybody. But I'm a woman. I know
what she's trying to do."

Suddenly, Deloris looks up as if she's had an epiphany.

"Does she have blond hair?" she asks. "And very dark skin?"

"You *know* her?" I ask, pretending to be angry. Deloris nods, and her
hands close into fists. Oh, this is too perfect. "How?" I ask. *Yeah, how?*
Maybe my little white lies aren't so far off, after all.

"She was here one night," she says, practically yelling. "Outside the
house. You were with the baby, and I heard someone outside, so I looked
out the window and I saw her. She stood outside the front door for almost
five minutes. I thought that maybe she was dropping something off for
you. But maybe she just wanted to see him and changed her mind when
she realized that you were home." She thinks about this, trying to play out
scenarios in her head. "Or maybe she was stalking him. Maybe she was
waiting for him to come home so that she could talk to him, and maybe
she got tired of waiting. Or maybe she knew that I saw her." She points her
finger at me. "Something like this happened on *All My Children* once. It
was almost the same thing."

Deloris is slowly nodding her head now, putting it all together in her
mind, and it occurs to me that she's talking about the night that Courtney
came over to pick up Zak's leash. Deloris must not have realized that Andrew brought her inside and that I spoke to her. She must have seen her
standing on the doorstep just after I walked her out.

I pretend to look horrified at this new piece of information, and I rest
my elbows on the counter and place my hands over my face. I watch Deloris through the cracks in my fingers, and I see her purse her lips and
shake her head.

"What are you going to do?" she asks me.

"I don't know," I say through my fingers. "I just don't know."

Deloris hesitates, and then she walks over to the counter, opposite from where I'm sitting. She's about two feet from me now, and she leans in closer and softens her voice.

"Tell me the truth, Mrs. Lara. Do you think that they are lovers?" she asks.

I shrug my shoulders and take my hands down so that I can look at her. "No," I say, shaking my head. "I don't know why, I just don't think that it's gotten that far."

Deloris lets out a sigh of relief and nods. "You should trust your instincts," she says, pointing her finger at me. "A woman can always tell."

I shrug again. "But just because it hasn't happened yet doesn't mean that it won't," I say quickly, before I lose her interest. "If she's really trying to seduce him, who knows what could happen in a few weeks?" I pause, drawing her in again. "But if he does that . . ." I stare off into the horizon, pretending to be imagining the worst. "If he does that, I don't think that I could ever forgive him. I love him, but I could not stay married to him."

Deloris looks like she's going to cry. She's dead silent for a good thirty seconds before she says anything.

"Mrs. Lara," she says. "Do you trust Deloris?"

Oh, sure, I think. I trust Deloris about as far as I can throw her. But I nod my head yes.

"Of course I do," I lie. "I mean, I know we don't always see eye-to-eye, but you take care of my baby. There's nobody I trust more." Well, actually, when I put it that way, it's not such a lie, after all.

Deloris nods at me and makes a grave face.

"Okay, then," she says. "Deloris is going to help you before this gets any worse." She looks up in the direction of Parker's room. "My baby must not grow up in a broken home. It's not good for the child."

Okay, Nadine either has ESP, or she's a genius. She *totally* predicted that Deloris would say that to me.

Deloris reaches over and pats my hand. "Don't worry," she says. "Deloris can make this right."

I look up at her. "What are you going to do?" I ask.

Deloris smiles and waves at me to get up. "Come with me," she says. "Deloris needs to show you something."

I follow her down the hallway and into her bedroom, and Deloris motions for me to sit down on the bed while she opens up her top drawer. She reaches out toward the back of the drawer, and a few seconds later she turns around, holding the blond voodoo doll in her hand.

"Do you know what this is?" she asks me. I stare at her for a second.

Yeah, I know what it is, I think. *It's a friggin' voodoo doll that you made of* me. But I play the naïf.

"It looks like . . . I mean, is that a voodoo doll or something?"

Deloris nods her head. "It is," she says. "It's a protection doll, to keep away evil influences and evil effects." *Yeah, like me.* She studies the doll for a minute, and turns it around in her hand. "But if I alter it just a bit, it can act as a destroyer doll, which will do just what the name says."

Okay, time out. I hold up my hands.

"Wait a minute, Deloris. I don't want you to kill her or anything."

Deloris chuckles. "It's a myth that voodoo can cause physical harm," she says. "The doll will not destroy the woman; it will only destroy her powers over the man. And to be extra safe, we can do a spell that will make her invisible to him."

"Really?" I ask, cocking one eyebrow.

Deloris nods at me. "It's called Go Away Woman," she says. "It's a most powerful antilove spell."

I *knew* it. I knew she was doing that spell on me so that Parker wouldn't love me. And Julie thought that I was crazy. Wait until I tell her.

I shrug my shoulders.

"Okay," I say. "Let's do it. What do you need me to do?"

Deloris spends the next hour or so spinning in circles and tossing different-colored powders and potions over the blond voodoo doll, and finally its metamorphosis from me into Courtney is complete. Well, perhaps *metamorphosis* is too strong a word. Actually, the doll looks exactly the same, except that now it's wearing a white shirt instead of a black one, and I made Deloris put a little bit of my Nars bronzing powder on its face so that it would look tan. But according to Deloris, we now have ourselves a bona fide, Haitian-priestess-made, love-destroyer doll that is going to use its powers to banish Courtney from Andrew's life and heart in a matter of days.

I'm telling you, this lady is off her rocker.

But crazy or not, her attitude toward me has done a complete one-eighty in the last ninety minutes. I mean, Parker woke up from her nap about twenty minutes ago, and Deloris actually *asked* me if I wanted to go get her. And when I said yes, she actually *smiled,* and then when I brought Parker back down to Deloris's room and held her in my arms while Deloris worked on the voodoo doll, she actually said *nice things* about me to Parker. In fact, if my memory serves me correctly, I believe her exact words were, *Now there, Parker, aren't you happy to be with your lovely mama?* It was shocking, I tell you. Just shocking. God, if I had known that all it would take was a little bit of fake indulgence in her voodoo nonsense, I would have asked her three months ago if she had any weight-loss spells up her sleeve. Hmmm. Come to think of it, maybe I should ask her that now. Oh, come on. It can't hurt.

"Mrs. Lara," Deloris says, holding up the doll. "It's time for your part. You must make your wish to the doll."

My wish? I have to make a wish? I shift Parker to my left shoulder, which she gums.

"Okay," I say. "But can you give me an example or something? I don't want to mess it up."

Deloris makes a solemn face and shakes her head. "Your wish must be of your own desires, and it can be anything, as long as you follow the rule of the universe." Oh, of course. Because everyone knows what the rule of the universe is.

"Okay, Deloris, I'll bite," I say, trying not to sound too sarcastic. "What is the rule of the universe?"

Deloris holds up her index finger and wags it at me. "The rule is that you cannot wish upon the woman any wrong greater than the one that she has caused to you. Do you understand? Because if you break this rule, Deloris will not be able to help you with the karma that the universe will bring to you." I have to close my eyes for a second in order to keep myself from rolling them at her.

"Okay," I say. "I get it." Deloris nods her head and holds the doll out to me, which I take with my right hand.

"Good," she says. "Now give me the baby so that you can do this properly."

I hand Parker over, and I look to Deloris for instructions. She walks

over to the white wicker bookshelf in the corner of the room and she re-
moves a small tray that looks like it was painted by a four-year-old. She
holds it out to me.

"Here. Take this and put it on the bed, and then place the doll on top
of it." I do this, and then she points at the floor. "Now, kneel down in front
of the bed, put your right index finger over the doll's heart, and when you
are ready, close your eyes and make your wish."

Oh, my God. If watching television causes ADD, I wonder what
watching one's mother kneel down before a straw doll in a blond wig
causes. I'll bet Susan's never gotten that question before.

"Do I have to say it out loud?" I ask as I start to kneel down.

Deloris shakes her head at me. "No. Say it in your mind, and the doll
will hear you."

Oh, man. I can't believe that I'm doing this. Reluctantly I get down on
my knees and put my finger on the doll's chest, and then I look up at Deloris for approval. She nods, and makes a face as if to tell me to go ahead.
Okay. My wish, my wish. What do I wish?

*Let's see . . . I wish that I had a normal nanny. I wish that I had Sarah
Jessica Parker's shoe collection. I wish that I had whiter teeth. I wish that—*

"The doll can only help you with your wish regarding the woman,"
Deloris says sternly. Startled, I turn my head and look up at her suspiciously, and she gives me a you're-so-busted face.

No way. She couldn't possibly have known what I was thinking. I'll
bet you everyone makes other wishes first.

"I'm just *thinking,*" I say. "I want to get it right." Deloris sticks her foot
out and starts to tap it, as if she's getting impatient with me. "Okay," I say.
"I'm ready. Jeez."

I take a deep breath and close my eyes.

This is so stupid.

"The wish!" Deloris demands.

I put my finger to my lips. "Shhhhh!" I say, my eyes still closed. *Ugh.*
I'll just make the stupid wish to get her off my back. I switch the tone of
voice that is in my head to one of fake contrition, like how Bart Simpson
sounds when he's saying that he's sorry for throwing spitballs in class, and
I make my wish.

Even though he's not cheating on me, I wish that Andrew would stop being friends with Courtney, and I wish that she would have to drop out of agility class.

There. I did it. I open my eyes again and take my finger off of the doll, and then I stand up.

"Well-done," Deloris says, picking up the doll. "And you'll see. Your wish *will* come true. Deloris's dolls always do a good job."

"I hope so," I say, reaching out to take Parker. To my surprise, Deloris lets her go immediately. Now *that's* what I call magic. All right, then. Let me see what else I can get away with. "I'm going to take her to the den to play," I say cautiously.

"Okay," Deloris answers. "I have some washing to do, so I'll be in the laundry room if you need me."

I stand there for a second, too stunned to speak. "Great," I finally say. "See you later."

I walk out and carry Parker to the den, where I proceed to play with her, unchecked and chaperone-free, for close to forty-five minutes.

Okay, people, it's official. This Cold War has finally thawed.

twenty-one

"Julie, you are coming with me to this bachelorette party. It's not a choice."

"But I don't know any of these people," she whines, "and I don't feel like going out and watching a bunch of strangers get drunk. Why do I have to go?"

"Because you're my friend," I tell her. "And friends don't let friends go to random bachelorette parties by themselves."

She lets out a protest sigh. "But you won't be by yourself," she says. "Stacey will be there, too."

"It's Stacey's bar," I inform her. "She'll be working, not hanging out. Look, do you want me to beg? Because I'll beg." There is silence on the other end of the phone. "Okay. Pleeeeease, pleeeeeease, pleeeeeease come with me. I need you there. Please." Another sigh, but this time it's one of resignation. I smile.

"Fine," she says. "I'll go with you. What are you wearing?"

"I have no idea," I say. "Whatever fits."

"How much do you still have to lose?" she asks, sounding surprised. "You look so thin."

"I still have four pounds, and it's all in my stomach. I swear, I can pinch about half a foot. Oh, that reminds me. Can you ask your sister if she has a flap of skin that hangs over her scar, too? Because mine is disgusting. I think I'm going to ask my doctor to cut some of it off next time."

"Next time?" Julie asks. "Are you going to have another baby?"

"Well, not anytime soon," I say, "but eventually, yeah."

"Really?" she asks. "Because you hated being pregnant so much, and you were so miserable when Parker was born, I can't believe you're going to do it again."

"I never said that I was looking forward to it, but I'm going to have another kid. I have to. I think that Andrew would die if he didn't have a son."

"But what if you have another girl?" she asks. "Would you have a third?"

"Hell, no. Andrew can die. Or maybe we'll sperm-sort. I've heard that it's around eighty-five percent if you're trying for a boy. But it doesn't matter. It's a long way off. Let me lose my baby weight before you have me impregnated again, okay?"

"Okay," she says. I can practically see her stupid smile through the phone. "But I'm so proud of you. If I had told you three months ago that you would ever even talk about doing this again, I think you would have come after me with a shotgun."

"Well, thanks, Mom," I say, "that means a lot to me. What's happening with the Institute, by the way? Have you heard anything new?"

Julie lets out a frustrated sigh. "Nothing. I've called them three times to see if they'll change their mind about giving us an interview, but I'm not getting anywhere. They keep saying that an interview isn't a requirement for admission, but if it's not such a big deal, then why do they even have them?"

"I don't know," I say. "Maybe they only use them for borderline cases. Did you ever think of that? Maybe you're so in that they didn't feel that they needed to interview you." I can almost hear her glass changing to half-full as she considers this possibility.

"Really?" Julie asks. "Do you think that's possible?"

"Anything is possible," I say. "Has anyone ever gotten in who didn't have an interview? Maybe you should ask them that."

"That's a great idea," she says. "I'm going to call them right now."

"You do that," I tell her. "So listen, I'll pick you up on Saturday night at eight thirty, okay?"

"Okay," she says begrudgingly, but much less so now that I've brightened her day.

"And no flaking," I warn her.

"I won't flake," she says.

"You're the best," I say. "Bye."

About half an hour later, my father rings the doorbell. He called me this morning and asked if he could come over to see Parker for a little while this afternoon, and I decided to be charitable and say yes. Of course, after I did that, it occurred to me that I have now broken three of the five rules that I made for myself with regard to him. A recap, if you will:

1. I will not meet his fiancée. *Uh, yeah, okay.*
2. I will have nothing to do with his wedding. *Let's see, matron of honor, hosting bridal shower two days before the ceremony, and planning bachelorette party at best friend's new bar, the sale of which fiancée, whom I am not going to meet, completely orchestrated.*
3. He does not get to meet Andrew or spend time with Parker. *Andrew: Please recall the BBQ toupee incident. Parker: See above.*

But I'm still holding firm on rules four and five, and those are the most important ones, anyway.

4. I will not be warm and loving toward him, ever.
5. While unlikely, it is possible that I might someday forgive him for what he did, but I will never, ever forget.

Now, if you're wondering why I decided to break rule number three and let him see Parker, I feel your pain. I mean, I would be wondering that if I were you. Of course, you probably think that it has something to do with the four million dollars, but it doesn't, I swear. I mean, yeah, it would be great if he set up a trust fund for her, but I'm not holding my breath. Ronny Levitt is not a man who parts with money easily, and I don't expect him to part with it for my kid any more than I expect him to part with it for me. Although he did tip Deloris after dinner on Saturday night. It was so weird. He walked over to her and handed her a fifty, then thanked her for cleaning up the dishes and watching Parker while we ate. I was like, *Dad, you don't need to tip my nanny,* but he insisted that it was the right thing to do. Andrew thought that maybe he's getting less thrifty in his old age, or that having millions has made him realize that he doesn't need to be cheap anymore, but I don't think so. I think he's just spent too much time in Vegas. Come on, gamblers are notorious for tipping big. It's part of their culture.

Anyway, the reason I'm letting him see Parker is because I'm starting to suspect that Nadine just might be right about him. I have decided to open myself to the possibility that he does actually mean well, but that he's just been a little bit misguided in his efforts. It's a huge step, I know, but the more time that I spend with him, the more I can kind of see where Nadine is coming from. For example, it does really seem like he wants to settle down and have a family again. He calls me all the time, and he's always trying to make plans with me. He even offered to babysit whenever Deloris takes a day off. Not that I would let him, but it's the thought that counts. . . .

Look, I still don't trust him one hundred percent—I really don't know if I ever will—but I figure that I might as well give him a chance. It's not like it's beyond the scope of possibility that I might massively fuck up with Parker one day, and if that ever were to happen, I guess I just hope that she would do the same thing for me. You know, it's the whole bad-karma, what-goes-around-comes-around theory. I don't really believe in it, but I'm afraid to flat-out not believe in it, just in case it turns out to be true. It's funny, though; my dad really picked the right time to come back into my life. I don't think that I would be nearly as generous with him if I hadn't just had a baby. In fact, I'm not sure he even would have made it through the front door that day that he showed up here. I guess becoming a mother really does change how you feel about certain things.

I answer the door and my dad walks in. He leans in to give me a hug, but I back away. Hey, I said that I was giving him a chance, not forgoing the rest of my rules.

"Hey, buhbie," he says, backing off.

"Hi, Dad." I lead him inside to the den, where I left Parker lying on her alphabet mat. (Andrew's letter-of-the-week plan never made it past A, by the way. After about the third day, Parker started crying as soon as he started in with that *a*sinine, *a*trocious voice.) When he sees Parker lying on the floor, he gets down on his hands and knees and then puts her on his lap.

"Oy, vey," he says, as he feels how heavy she is. "What do you put in her bottle, chocolate malteds?"

I put my hands on my hips. "That's not funny," I tell him. "Babies understand when people are saying mean things about them. She might not know exactly what it means, but she knows that you don't approve of something. So do me a favor and cool it with the F-A-T comments, okay?"

"Okay, okay. I didn't know you were so PC all of a sudden."

I roll my eyes at him. "It's all of a sudden to *you*," I answer. "But actually, I've been this way for a while."

He squeezes Parker's thigh and looks up at me. "Your legs were the same way," he says. "Chubby, chubby, chubby." I give him a what-did-I-just-say look, and he nods to show that he gets it. "Sorry. No more F-A-T comments, I promise." He turns Parker around to face him, and she flashes him a big smile.

"Is she not the cutest thing you ever saw?" I ask him, as I lower myself down onto the floor next to them.

He nods, and then sighs. "I just can't believe that you're a mother. I have such vivid memories of you as a baby. And now you're so different. You're all grown-up and I feel like I don't even know you."

"Dad," I say, trying extra hard not to sound hostile, "I mean this in the nicest way, but you *don't* know me. You were gone for my entire adult life."

"I know," he says, sadly. "I guess I just thought that you wouldn't be that different. I thought that I'd come back, and everything would be the same as it was. You know, you'd still be like you were in high school: captain of the cheerleading squad, stressed out about a test. I just didn't expect for you to be this whole different person."

"I'm not *that* different," I tell him.

But he nods his head. "Yes, you are," he insists. "You're tougher than you were, and you're less trusting. And you speak your mind. You never used to do that when you were a kid. You always used to keep quiet if you disagreed with something, because you didn't want to upset anyone. It used to worry me about you so much. I always used to tell your mother that you were going to get walked on once you got out in the real world." See, I told you that I'm a wuss. Always have been.

"I speak my mind with *you*," I tell him. "But not always with other people." *Just ask my nanny.* "Anyway, you're making me sound like such a bitch. Is that how I come off to you?"

"No," he says, shaking his head. "I'm not criticizing you. I think it's wonderful. I'm proud of how you turned out." He shrugs. "Maybe not having me around all of those years was good for you."

"Or maybe I'd be even better if you had been around."

He stares at me for a second and then drops his gaze. "You used to worship me," he says, still looking at the floor. "No matter what I did, you always forgave me. You didn't care if I wasn't there for every dance recital, or if I missed your birthday party. Your love was unconditional." He juggles Parker on his lap and kisses her on top of the head. "That's the best part of having kids, Lara. They love you no matter what." He pauses. "And then they become adults, and they learn better." He looks up at me, and I notice that his eyes are watery. "That's the part that I didn't expect, I guess. I took it for granted that you'd still love me even after what I did, because you always used to still love me before."

Parker starts to fuss, so I reach out and take her from him. I turn her around and put her over my shoulder, and instantly she calms down. I sigh. I really wasn't expecting a therapy session during this visit. I thought that maybe we could just hang out with Parker, ignore the giant elephant in the room and pretend that everything is fine, the way that WASPy people do. But it doesn't look like that's going to happen. Damn, why do Jews always have to talk so much? I bounce Parker over my shoulder for a few seconds as I gather my thoughts.

"You know, Dad, after you left, I used to refer to you as an unpronounceable symbol, and I called you the Fuckup Formerly Known as My Father."

He winces at this. "Okay," he says. "That's fair enough."

I nod. "But you know, I've been thinking about this a lot lately, and there's actually a lot of truth to that name." He looks like he's about to get angry, but I wave my hand to tell him to wait for a second. "I'm not trying to say that you're a fuckup. That's not what I'm talking about. But the part about how you were formerly my father—that's how I feel. I mean, I still love you, but I love the old you," I say, trying not to cry. "I love the guy who was my dad when I was a kid. Or at least, the guy who I thought you were when I was a kid. But you're not that guy anymore. And maybe you never were; I don't know." I shrug my shoulders, then go on.

"But just how you feel like I'm a different person now, I feel like you're a different person now. So, I guess what I'm trying to say is, I have to get to know you again before I can love you again. And, I don't know, maybe you have to get to know me before you can love me again, too." I remember what Stacey said to me about Parker that day that we went hiking, and I smile. "You know, you can't love someone until you have a relationship with them."

He looks sad, like what I said just broke his heart in half. But then he nods his head. "You're right," he says. "It just caught me off guard, that's all." He looks at his watch, and then, as if he didn't realize how late it had gotten, he quickly stands up.

"I have to go," he says, anxiously. "I'm late for my appointment to have my tux fitted." He reminds me of Cinderella at the ball, just as the clock strikes midnight, and I wonder if his big Mercedes outside is going to turn into a pumpkin. I put Parker down and hoist myself up off the floor, and he stands, awkwardly, in front of me.

"Lara," he says, "would it be okay if I hugged you?" It almost sounds like a plea, and it's so pathetic that it brings tears to my eyes. There's no way that I can say no. Even I'm not that heartless.

I sigh. "Of course you can hug me," I tell him, and I open up my arms. He moves closer and puts his arms around me, and we hug for a long time.

So much for rule number four.

"I love you more than anyone or anything in the world, Lara," he says, his voice so low that it is almost a whisper. He pulls away and there are tears in his eyes now, and he gives me a weak smile. "When you're a parent, that never changes, no matter how much time has passed, or how different you might be." I look down at Parker, and I have to bite my cheek to keep myself from breaking down.

"I know," I tell him. "I know."

When Andrew gets home, Deloris and I are both in the den with Parker, watching her as she struggles to roll over on the alphabet mat.

"She is so close," Deloris says.

"I know," I say. "I just wish that she would do it soon. Half of the babies in Mommy and Me are rolling over now. I really don't want her to be the last one."

"She'll do it," Deloris says. "She'll do it in her own time." Andrew clears his throat and puts his keys down on the end table next to the couch.

"Hi," he says, sounding surprised to see us together.

"Hi," we both say in unison. He smiles, though it is clear that he's not quite sure what is going on here. "You're home early," I say, standing up and walking over to him. I give him a quick kiss on the mouth. "What's going on?"

"Nothing," he says. "I just wanted to spend some time with you and Parker tonight and I wasn't that busy, so I decided to come home."

"That is so wonderful," Deloris says enthusiastically. She's beaming, and I look at her for a second, trying to figure out why she's acting so weird. She raises her eyebrows ever so slightly at me, with an I-told-you-so kind of look. *Oh, God.* She thinks her spell is working. I have to keep myself from laughing out loud. "Okay, then," she says. "Deloris is going to eat dinner, if that's all right with you. Let you all spend some family time together."

"Okay," I say. "Thanks, Deloris."

She turns to me and smiles again. "You are very, very welcome," she says, and then walks out into the kitchen. Andrew looks totally confused. Poor guy. He probably feels like he walked into a parallel universe or something.

"What was that about?" he asks.

"Nothing," I say. "Deloris and I just had a little talk today. She and I are sort of becoming friends, I think."

"Really?" he says, sounding excited. "What changed?"

"Nothing *changed*," I say. "I just filled her in on how I was feeling about certain things, and she responded positively. It's something that I should have done a long time ago." Parker is grinning at Andrew and flapping her hands around in front of her face.

"Do you see your daddy?" I ask her. "Do you love your daddy?"

"So why didn't you?" he asks.

I pick up Parker and hand her to him. "Why didn't I what?"

He takes Parker and squeezes her thigh. "Why didn't you fill her in on how you were feeling before?"

"Oh," I say. "Because I didn't think of it before. It was Nadine's idea. She said that you can't approach someone like Deloris in an accusatory way. Remember at the barbecue, when I kind of yelled at her, and she just walked away from me?" Andrew nods. "Well, Nadine said that it was the wrong way to deal with her. She said that if I want to get anywhere with her, I have to show her that I'm vulnerable. So that's what I did. And you know what? It worked. It's like she's a completely different person with me now."

Andrew cocks his head sideways and looks at me suspiciously. "You're acting weird," he says. "You're taking advice from Nadine, and you're being nice to Deloris. Is something going on that I don't know about?"

I look at him and let out a sardonic laugh. "Andrew, there's always something going on that you don't know about. Haven't you figured that out by now?"

He shrugs his shoulders and shakes his head. "I don't want to know, do I?" he asks.

I smile at him. "No," I say. "No, you don't."

twenty-two

I'm standing in my closet, staring at the ass pants. I went through a period where I tried them on every single day—remember?—then I finally cut it down to every week, and then, when it just got to be too depressing, I stopped trying them on altogether. I'd say it's been close to a month since the last time that I even contemplated them. But tonight is the bachelorette party, and, coincidentally, it is Parker's four-and-a-half-month birthday, so I'm feeling kind of lucky. I take the pants off the hanger and step out of the sweatpants that I've been wearing all day.

If they don't fit, I tell myself, *it's okay. But please fit. Please, please, please, please, please fit.*

Slowly I put my right leg in, then my left, and I pull them up. All the way up, and they don't fit like leggings. But wait, don't get excited yet. I've been here before. It's getting them closed that's the problem. They're low-waisted, so the sides need to reach each other across my last four pounds of fat, which, amazingly enough, has all settled in my lower abdomen, thus making the phrase *getting them closed* easier said than done. But I'll give it a try, I guess. Sucking in my gut as best as I can, I straighten myself up and attempt to get the button inside the buttonhole.

Oh, my God. It closed. It closed! My ass pants fit! My ass pants fit! I wish I lived in an apartment building in New York so that I could go and shout it from the rooftops. *Hey, everyone! My ass pants fit!* Of course, all of my grumpy neighbors would yell things like, *Shut up, people are trying to sleep in here,* but I wouldn't care. I would spread my arms open wide and break into song or something.

You can't get me down, I won't wear a frown!
I'll sing it and shout it and yell it, I won't quit,
'Cause my (beat) ass pants fiiiiiiiiiiiit!

That's it. *Ass Pants, the Musical.* If anyone knows Tim Rice, could you put him in touch with me? Thanks.

I turn around in front of the full-length mirror and admire my posterior from every angle. It just looks so . . . good. Really, everyone should have a pair of pants like this. It's like instant ego boost. Not to mention instant butt-lift. They're perfect. I try on a few different tops and heels, and I settle on a long, pale-pink, V-neck sleeveless top, silver Christian Louboutin stilettos, and a silver lamé clutch.

Perfect. Now I'm excited to go out tonight.

I get to Julie's house at eight thirty on the dot, but of course she's not ready, so I have to go in and chitchat with Jon while she finishes blowing out her hair.

"Hey, Jon," I say, giving him a kiss on the cheek.

"Hi, Lar. I feel like I haven't seen you in forever. You look good."

"Thanks," I say, doing a little hair toss. "How are things with you?"

"Pretty good. Just working hard." I nod. I don't really have that much to say to Jon. I usually have Andrew around to act as a buffer. "So, whose bachelorette party are you going to tonight?" he asks.

"Oh, it's my dad's fiancée. She's forty-nine, but she acts like she's twenty-one." He raises his eyebrows. "It should be interesting," I say.

There is an awkward silence as we both think of something else to say, but Jon comes up with an idea first.

"So," he says. "Have you thought about preschools yet?" I swear, he and Julie are so perfect for each other, it's sickening.

I shake my head. "Not really," I tell him. "We're in at Bel Air Prep for kindergarten, so I'm not that worried about it."

Jon nods again. "That's great," he says. "I guess Julie told you about the Institute, huh?"

"Yeah. But it's just an interview. It doesn't mean you're not in."

Jon shrugs. "Maybe," he says, lowering his voice. "But to be honest, I think that it was because of the essays."

Well, yeah, I could have told you that. Oh, wait, I did tell you that. Silly me. I am about to launch into a diatribe about how I told her that they sounded canned but she didn't listen, when Jon starts talking again.

"You know, I thought she did a great job writing them—all of that stuff about diversity and everything was so good—but she spelled *commitment* wrong in two different places. I couldn't believe it. Who in this day and age doesn't use spell-check? Ugh. I was so mad at her."

He's got to be kidding me. He thinks that they didn't get an interview because of a *spelling* mistake? How about, the whole essay was a mistake. Jeez. I seriously hope that Lily doesn't get into Bel Air Prep for kindergarten, because I do not want to deal with Julie and Jon seventeen years from now when she's applying to colleges. Talk about your nightmare parents.

Just then Julie comes bounding down the stairs. She's wearing white capri pants, a turquoise tank top, silver flat sandals with turquoise stones on them, and she has a matching turquoise cardigan tied around her neck. As usual, she looks like she's going yachting.

"Sorry," she says. "Lily got to bed late and I didn't even get in the shower until seven forty-five." She grabs her giant Louis Vuitton bucket bag and slings it over her shoulder. "Bye, honey," she says, as she kisses Jon on the cheek. Then she looks at me. "When will we be home? Midnight or so?"

She's out of her mind. There is no way we're going to be home before two. It's a *bachelorette* party. But I nod.

"Oh, yeah," I say. "Definitely."

Jon smiles and waves good-bye to me. "Okay," he says. "Have a good time."

"We will!" I call out, and then I grab Julie's arm and lead her out the door.

We get to the bar—Stacey has renamed it the California Bar, in honor of her former profession—with about half an hour to spare before the party is set to begin. When we walk in, I am dazzled. It's like a completely new place. The booths and the bar stools are covered in cobalt-blue suede and trimmed with silver studs. The tables and the bar have been stained a rich chocolate brown, and the nasty carpet is now a gorgeous dark wood floor. There are new light fixtures, a booth for a live deejay, and on either side of the bar is a huge raised platform edged in white crown molding.

I have to say, the place is *gorgeous*. I also have to say that I am *astonished*. Not only can I not believe that she pulled this off in two weeks, I also can't believe that Stacey's taste is this good. I mean, the girl has been living in an empty apartment for almost seven years. I had no idea that she could do anything besides IKEA and some stackable crates.

As Julie and I are taking everything in, Stacey appears out of nowhere in black leather pants and a light blue wrap shirt that is barely containing her boobs.

"So what do you think?" she asks, startling us.

"It's amazing," I tell her. "I'm just standing here with my mouth open. Did you have a decorator?"

She shakes her head. "Nope. I did it all by myself. I had a vision."

Julie's eyes go wide. "It's really good," she says. "I mean, you could be an interior designer. I would definitely hire you."

I bite my lip and try not to laugh at the idea of Stacey working as Julie's decorator.

"Yeah," Stacey says, looking at me with disdain. "Thanks, but no, thanks."

In case you didn't know, Stacey can't stand Julie. She's way too perky for Stacey's taste. Of course, Julie has no idea, because she's too nice for it to occur to her that someone might not like her for being too nice, but I think she can kind of tell that Stacey gets annoyed by her, which only causes Julie to overcompensate and act even nicer whenever Stacey's around, thus making Stacey want to punch her in the face. It's kind of funny to watch, actually.

"Well," I say, "you did a kick-ass job. I'm very impressed. Now, if you don't mind, can you help me get set up for the party?"

Stacey shakes her head. "Hello?" she says. "Opening night here. I have a few things to do that are more important than your party." She points to a hot guy wearing black leather pants and a tight black T-shirt who is standing in the corner, talking to a waitress who is also in black leather pants and a black T-shirt.

"That's my manager over there," she says. "His name is Tom. Tom Collins." She laughs. "Isn't that so perfect for a bar manager?" I nod my head yes. "Anyway," she says, "he can help you with whatever you need. I've got to finish setting up the bar. I'll see you later."

Stacey walks away, so I head over to Tom Collins, who is now standing by the front door with a headset attached to his ear. I clear my throat and give him the flirty, hi-I'm-a-cute-girl-so-please-let-me-in smile that I used to use with doormen back in the day, but I've got to tell you, using it now just feels wrong. It feels like a lie; like I'm trying to pretend that I'm young and carefree, and a regular on the club scene, and not the old ball and chain who hasn't seen the inside of a club since the Clinton years that I actually am. But Tom Collins doesn't seem to be onto me.

"Hi," he says, smiling back. "Can I help you with something?"

Ooooh, he's cute.

"Um, yeah," I say. "I'm throwing a bachelorette party here tonight, and I wanted to see if I could get a few tables reserved, and maybe have some bottles set out on them for when everybody gets here."

He nods his head and smiles again, then checks out my cleavage. I blush. God, it's been a really long time since anyone did that. I wonder what he would do if he were to find out that I'm almost thirty-one, and that hidden under this shirt is four pounds of flab, a six-inch C-section scar, and a gross flap of skin that hangs over it. Yeah. He'd probably tell me to go get in line outside.

"No problem," Tom Collins says with a sexy grin. "Let me get that set up for you. Can I have someone get you a drink while you wait for your party to arrive?"

"Sure," I say, giving him the flirty smile again. "I'll take a vodka tonic."

Normally I would also get a drink for Julie, but I'm just trying to savor his attention for a few more minutes, and if I point out that she's with me he'll totally know that I'm old. I mean, I know she can't help it, but she always looks like such a *mom*.

"Great," he says. "I'll take care of it right now."

I turn away from him, then look back over my shoulder and see that he is walking backward, staring intensely at my butt. I blush again and he smiles and then turns around. God, I love these pants.

Julie has settled herself into a booth, and I walk over to her and sit down.

"I just got flirted with," I announce. "By a hottie." I am grinning from ear to ear, but Julie looks shocked.

"Really?" she asks. "Did you flirt back?"

I nod at her, smiling. "I did," I say. "It felt so good."

Julie gives me a concerned look. "Is everything okay with you and Andrew?" she asks.

"Of course," I say. "I'm not going to have sex with him. I probably won't even see him again tonight. It's just nice to know that I've still got it, that's all."

"Well, I won't be doing any flirting," she says. "I'm just here to observe."

I roll my eyes at Jane Goodall, and a waitress walks over with my drink and sets it down in front of me. "It's on the house," she says, pointing toward the back, where my new boyfriend disappeared to a few minutes ago. "And I'll get your tables set up for you right now."

"Thanks," I say. She walks away and I give Julie a knowing look.

"Just be careful, Lara," she warns. "Don't do anything stupid."

"Oh, please, Julie, loosen up. You're such a buzz kill sometimes. Here," I say, holding out my drink to her. "You take this. You need it way more than I do."

Ten minutes later some people start to trickle in, and by the time Nadine arrives, the place is bordering on crowded. Nadine has decked herself out in tight black pants and a low-, low-, low-cut black top with gold sequins running down the front of it. To my amazement, the red stilettos have been replaced with black kitten heels. But just in case she was worried that she wouldn't draw enough attention to herself without them, she came with a gaggle of impossibly gorgeous, impossibly skinny women in impossibly skimpy outfits. They definitely look like they *could* be strippers, or maybe like they were strippers at one point, but somehow you get the sense that these women don't take their clothes off for dollar bills. For diamonds, maybe, but definitely not for dollar bills.

In any event, I feel like a moose next to them. So much for feeling good about myself tonight.

"Wow!" Nadine says, looking around. "I can't believe this place. Jimmy would not even recognize it!"

"I know," I yell. "Isn't it amazing?"

She nods, then steps back to introduce me to her posse. "Lara," she says, "these are my friends." She points to each one as she introduces them. "Leila, Tawny, Brandi, Gemma, Eden, and you know Marley, of course." They all wave at me, and I smile at them, trying not to stare at their boobs.

"Hi," I say. "I'm Lara. And this is my friend Julie." I look over at Julie, but she is frozen. Like she's never seen a boob job in real life before. I elbow her under the table, and she immediately breaks into her fake smile.

"Hi," she says. "It's so nice to meet you." Then she turns to Nadine. "And congratulations," she says. "You must be so excited."

Nadine smiles back and nods. "Oh, honey, you have no idea."

I wave my arm out and interrupt. "We have these three tables," I say, motioning to the two behind us. "And there are bottles already set out. You just have to find the waitress to come over and mix them for you."

Nadine, Marley, and Gemma, I think, slide into our booth, and the others decide to take a lap and check the place out. When they've left, Julie turns to me and smiles.

"I have to go to the bathroom," she says in the cheeriest voice I've ever heard, even for her. "Will you come with me?"

Oh, she's definitely going to yell at me. She's the only person I know whose voice actually gets higher and more polite when she's upset. I sigh and slide out of the booth behind her. When we get to the bathroom, she is almost in tears.

"Who are those women?" she asks. "Did you know that they would be here?"

I shake my head. "No," I say. "I mean, I knew Nadine was bringing her friends, but I've never met them before. Well, I met Marley, but she was at work. She looked totally different."

"Lara, I don't want to hang out with them all night," she says. "They're, like, porn stars or something. I've never been so embarrassed in my whole life."

"They're not porn stars," I tell her. "I think a few of them might have been strippers once, though." Julie blanches. "Listen," I say, "Nadine is a really good person. She wouldn't be friends with them if they were drug addicts or prostitutes or anything like that. You just have to trust me, okay? I know that they don't look like us, but I'm sure they're very nice."

Julie, however, doesn't look so sure. "I don't know, Lar, I think I should just go."

"Come on, Julie, just give them a chance. If you're still miserable in an hour, then I'll take you home. I promise. Just please? Please stay with me."

She frowns. "Okay," she says. "But just an hour."

I nod and give her a hug. "Thanks," I say. "Thank you so much."

We walk back out of the bathroom and return to our booth, where Marley and Gemma are holding court with about six different guys. Julie and I push our way through the fog of testosterone and sit back down.

"We're back," I say to Nadine, who is trying to keep clear of the activity going on at the table.

Nadine beams at me. "This is fabulous," she says. "That Stacey is a dynamo." I nod my agreement, and Nadine turns her attention to Julie. "So, Julie, what is it that you do?" she asks.

Julie turns a little bit red. "Oh, nothing," she says, sounding uncomfortable. "I'm a stay-at-home mom."

"Julie has a ten-month-old daughter," I inform Nadine. "She's the one who taught me everything I ever needed to know about babies." Nadine makes a *wow* face, and I keep going, trying to butter Julie up and make her feel better about staying. "I would be lost without Julie," I say. "She told me about my Mommy and Me class, she went with me to buy all of my baby stuff when I was pregnant, she's getting me started with preschool. She knows *everything*."

Nadine looks surprised by this. "You're already thinking about preschool?" she asks me. "But Parker is so little."

At this, Julie perks up. "You have no idea how competitive it is," she says. "You have to start worrying about it almost the day that you conceive."

As Julie is talking, I notice that Marley and Gemma's man-harem is starting to migrate to the table behind us, so I turn around to see what could possibly be more enticing than Marley, Gemma, me, Julie, and Nadine. Ah. Brandi, Tawny, Eden, and Leila have returned from their lap, and Brandi is showing Eden the new tattoo that she got on her hip bone. Oh, well. I guess there isn't too much that can compete with that. I turn back around and catch the last half of Julie's sentence.

". . . we really were trying for this place called the Institute, but we didn't get an interview, so I don't think we have any chance now."

Suddenly Nadine waves her hand in the air. "The Institute?" she yells. "Is Dan Gregoire still the headmaster there?" Looking completely shocked, Julie nods her head yes, and Nadine makes a *pshaw* kind of face. "Oh, honey. I can get you into the Institute. Dan is an old, old friend of mine."

Unbelievable. Is there no man in this city who isn't an "old friend" of Nadine's? I'm starting to think that I must be way more naive than I realize, because I had no idea that so many men see call girls on a regular basis.

"Are you serious?" Julie asks. She looks like she's about to throw herself at Nadine's feet.

"Absolutely," Nadine says. "I'll call him first thing on Monday morning. You'll have your acceptance letter on Tuesday."

"Oh, my God," Julie exclaims. "You have no idea how much that would mean to me." She pauses for a second, in what looks like an effort to get control of herself, and then she starts again, but slower. "I just can't believe what a coincidence this is. What a small world, that you're marrying Lara's dad, and you know Dan Gregoire. This is just so unbelievable, I can't—"

Suddenly Gemma tears herself away from her cosmo and interrupts. "Dan Gregoire," she yells drunkenly to Nadine. "Isn't he that guy who liked little kids? He used to make me dress up in a school uniform and then he'd hit me with a paddle. Wasn't that his name?"

Julie puts her hand up to her mouth and Nadine looks like she's about to shoot fire out of her eyes. "Excuse me, girls," she says to us with a big smile, and then just as quickly she grabs Gemma's arm, yanks her out of the booth, and pulls her over to a corner. I can't hear what she's saying, but she's pointing her finger right in Gemma's face and Gemma looks petrified. Julie, Marley, and I are all staring at them as this is happening, but after a minute or so Marley excuses herself and walks over to them. She puts her hand on Nadine's arm, like she's trying to get between the two of them to referee.

Julie turns to look at me.

"What was she talking about?" she asks. "What did she mean that he made her dress up in a school uniform?"

I close my eyes. *Oh, shit.* There are so many reasons why I do not want

Julie to know the truth about Nadine, not the least of which is that she is a huge gossip and could have the entire west side waking up to this news in the morning with just a few strategic phone calls.

"I have no idea," I say. "I don't know what she's talking about."

Julie stares at me for a second. "Yes, you do," she insists. "I can tell. You're a terrible liar. Now tell me what is going on here. Who are these women?"

"Jul," I say, trying to stall. "It's not my place to tell you anything. If you want to know, you're going to have to ask them yourself."

Julie crosses her arms in front of her and cocks one eyebrow. "Lara," she says, pulling her cell phone out of her purse. "If you don't tell me right now, I am going to call the police and tell them that there are seven prostitutes in here who need to be arrested."

I roll my eyes at her. "First of all," I say, "that's ridiculous. Even if they were prostitutes, which they're not, but even if they were, they're not soliciting anyone right now. It's not illegal to be at a bar in skimpy clothes. And second of all, your bluffing is horrendous. Way worse than my lying. Don't ever try to play poker, please."

Julie looks infuriated with me, and her voice is rising to a fever pitch. "Tell me right now!" she demands. "Tell me, or I will never speak to you again. I mean it, Lara. You brought me here; you owe me an explanation." This time I don't think she's lying. She's really angry. God, it's so weird. I don't think I've ever seen Julie get angry before. I didn't even know Julie *got* angry.

"Jul," I say, pleading. "Please understand, it's not my secret to tell."

She grabs her purse and stands up. "Right now, Lara. Tell me right now, or our friendship is over. Forever." I hesitate, and she shakes her head at me. "Fine," she says. "I'll see you around." She turns away from me, like she's going to start walking.

God damn it. I can't believe that I'm going to have to tell Julie about Nadine. I mean, I have kept this secret for so long, and I have to blow it by telling Julie, of all people?

"Wait," I say, grabbing her arm. "Sit down. I'll tell you, okay?"

Julie nods, then slides back into the booth. She turns her body to face me, her arms still crossed in front of her chest. "Talk," she orders.

Wow. Julie's, like, a dominatrix or something. I try to keep a straight face as I play this scenario out in my head: Julie in black leather, cracking a whip at poor Jon, who's tied up in the secret torture chamber that she had built behind the closet in their bedroom. I shake my head to try to clear the image from my brain.

"Okay," I say. "But you have to promise me that you will not tell anyone what I am about to tell you. Not *anyone*. Not Jon, not your mother, not your sisters, not anyone."

"Okay," she says. "I promise."

Suddenly I remember how she told people whom I didn't know that I was pregnant before I announced it, on the theory that if I didn't know them, it didn't matter if they knew my secret. My stomach churns at the thought of it, and I realize that I'm going to have to clarify further.

"And you can't tell people who don't know me, either," I say. "This is not like telling someone that someone else whom they don't know is pregnant. This is real. If this gets out, it could ruin people's lives. Nadine could get arrested. Do you understand?"

Julie nods solemnly. "I understand," she says. "I promise, I will not tell anyone."

"Good," I say. "Because I am trusting you with this. I haven't told anyone about it. Not even Andrew." Julie's eyes go wide when I say this, and I can tell that now she understands. I look around to see if anyone is listening to us, and then I take a deep breath. "Nadine used to run an escort service," I say, lowering my voice, "and the girls she's with tonight were some of the escorts. Everybody went to them. Movie stars, studio executives, government officials . . . and heads of private schools, apparently. She was, like, the original Hollywood Madam."

Julie's mouth has dropped open, and she's struggling to close it.

"Oh, my God," she whispers. "And your dad is marrying her?"

I nod. "I know," I say. "I tried to talk him out of it, but they're really in love." I shrug. "Although, now that I know her, I think that she's the one who's getting the raw deal in this relationship. She's actually really cool. And she's got a heart of gold. She'll help anybody, even people she doesn't know. Look at what she did for Stacey. And how she said she'd help you. Although I can't believe that about Dan Gregoire." I chuckle. "I'll bet you're not so upset that you didn't get an interview now, huh?"

Julie looks at me blankly. "It's the *Institute*," she says. "It's the best school in the city. Of course I'm still upset that I didn't get an interview." She puts her elbows on the table and leans in toward me. "Lara, do you have any idea who the parents are at the Institute?" I shake my head. "Movie stars. Studio executives. Government officials. They probably *gave* Dan Gregoire Nadine's number." She straightens up, looking supremely pleased with herself. "Please, his seeing a call girl is the best thing that ever happened to me. He *has* to let me in if Nadine tells him to. Promise me that you'll remind her to call him on Monday."

I am shocked. I don't even know what to say to her. "Julie, are you serious? The guy didn't just 'see a call girl.' You heard what she said. He likes little kids. There's a name for that. It's called pedophilia. Do you really want Lily walking around there, knowing that he could be getting turned on by the sight of her in a uniform?"

Julie shakes her head at me. "First of all, you're assuming that she's telling the truth. And second, even if she is, as long as he never touches a child, what turns Dan Gregoire on is none of my business. I've never heard one complaint about him from anyone. In fact, the parents adore him." She looks me straight in the eye. "Believe me, Lara, you don't have to worry about my telling anyone about Nadine. I have no interest in being the person who brings down the Institute. I just want her to get me in, and then we'll pretend that you and I never had this conversation. Okay?"

My stock in Julie has just plummeted to somewhere around the molten center of the Earth. I just can't believe her. I mean, what kind of a parent doesn't care about something like this? Huh. And I've always thought that Julie was the perfect mother. I've always wished that I could be more like her. My God. Is Stacey right? Is everyone just pretending? But before I have a chance to really think about this—or to accuse Julie of being a social climber who will put her own child in jeopardy in order to get invited to better parties—Marley comes running over.

"Lara," she says. "I need you for a second." I hesitate, unsure whether my conversation with Julie is over or not. "It's important," she implores. I look at Julie, who motions at me to go.

"I'll go talk to Nadine," she says. "Don't worry about me."

Wow. Talk about a change of heart.

"Okay," I say, turning back to Marley as Julie walks away. "What's up?"

She looks concerned, and she leans in close to me. "We have a problem."

twenty-three

Ten minutes later I am scouring the room looking for Nadine, but by the time I find her, things are already happening. From the other end of the bar I spot her on a bar stool, deep in conversation with Julie. I make my way over to them as fast as I can, but just as I reach them, a man in a police uniform is placing his hand on Nadine's shoulder. Marley, Gemma, Brandi, and the rest of the Scooby gang have crowded around her, but none of them is saying a word.

"Nadine Conlan?" the officer asks. Nadine looks startled, and her face goes pale. Julie stares at me, her eyes filled with horror.

"That's me," Nadine responds calmly. "Is there a problem, Officer?"

"Come with me, please," he instructs. Nadine stands up as the policeman pulls out a pair of handcuffs. Julie jumps off of her bar stool and grabs my arm.

"Oh, my God," she exclaims. "I swear, Lara, I didn't tell anyone."

Her eyes are filling with tears, but I'm pretty sure it's not because she's upset for Nadine. I'm pretty sure it's because she knows that Nadine will get only one phone call from jail, and it's not going to be to Dan Gregoire. But now is not the time to start a fight with her.

"I know," I tell her. "Don't worry." The officer turns Nadine around and places the handcuffs on her wrists, and then he spins her around to face him. She looks terrified.

"You have the right . . . to remain sexy," he announces, and just like that, he rips open his shirt to reveal a tanned, hairless chest and six-pack abs. The look of anxiety that was on Nadine's face morphs into a smile, and all of the girls start whooping and cheering as he places his hat on

Nadine's head and leads her up onto one of the raised platforms on the side of the bar. I can't decide who looks more relieved, Nadine or Julie.

"Did you know about this?" Julie asks me.

I shake my head. "No. I just found out about it when Marley came over. The guy was outside and the doorman wouldn't let him in, so she needed me to go find Stacey to straighten things out."

"And Stacey doesn't care that they're doing this on her opening night?"

A chair is being hoisted up to the platform, and as Nadine takes a seat on it, the stripper points to someone in the audience. I follow his finger with my eyes to the deejay booth, and I see Stacey standing inside of it with black leather headphones covering her ears. She gives the stripper a thumbs-up, and within seconds, "It's Raining Men" is blasting through the room.

"No, I don't think she cares," I say. "If anything, it will get people talking about this place."

I watch as the stripper, who is now in nothing but a pair of briefs, straddles Nadine and starts grinding on her. He leans over and slides his chest down over her body, and when his face reaches hers, she whispers something in his ear. The stripper nods and turns around, and before I even know what is happening, he has bounded down the stairs and is tugging on Julie's arm.

"No, no, really," Julie is saying to him, trying to wriggle her arm free of his grip. "I can't do this. I don't do things like this."

At this, the stripper laughs. "Well, she says you do," he replies, pointing to Nadine. "And she's the boss tonight."

Julie vehemently shakes her head. "No, you don't understand," she protests. "I'm not even really here with her. I've never even met her before tonight. I think she must have meant for you to get her."

Julie extends her arm and points her finger right at me. *Wow*, I think, marveling at her willingness to sell me down the river. Good thing Julie wasn't around during the McCarthy era. The whole town would have been blacklisted.

But the stripper shakes his head. "Nope," he says, glancing at me. "She was definitely talking about you. She said to get the prissy one." I laugh out loud, and the stripper gives her a look as if to say that the discussion is over. Then, just like that, he puts one sweaty, greasy arm around Julie's neck, the other sweaty, greasy arm behind her knees, and he scoops her up.

"No," Julie yells as he carries her up to the stage. "You can't do this! I'm a mother! I have a ten-month-old baby!"

Ooohhh, I think. *This is going to be good.*

Another chair has been hoisted up onto the platform, and the stripper deposits Julie—still protesting—onto it and straddles her to keep her from jumping up and running away. He grabs the police hat back from Nadine and places it, cockeyed, on top of Julie's head, and then he unties the sweater around her neck and tosses it to the floor. Then he leans over and takes a long, slow lick of Julie's neck.

As his tongue touches her skin, Julie instantly stops complaining; her entire body tenses and her face scrunches up, as if she is too creeped out to even breathe. But the stripper either doesn't notice or doesn't care, because he then lifts up her right arm and slides his tongue down the length of it, from just below her armpit to just past her elbow. Julie clenches her lips together so that they almost disappear entirely, and even I can't help wincing at that one. I mean, the guy isn't even that cute. Well, he looks kind of like Scott Baio, actually. Not the fourteen-year-old, *Happy Days* Scott Baio, and not the really-feathered-hair, *Joanie Loves Chachi* Scott Baio, either. Picture *Charles in Charge* Scott Baio, but slathered with oil and on steroids. Anyway, he's not cute enough to be licking her armpit, that's for sure. Although, come to think of it, even if the guy was a dead ringer for Brad Pitt, it would still be a pretty gross move. Even if the guy *was* Brad Pitt, it would still be a pretty gross move.

But just when I thought that things couldn't possibly get any skeevier, the stripper reaches down to his crotch, adjusts himself, and then rips off his briefs in one swift motion. The audience—which is formidable by this point—roars, and Julie opens her eyes, only to find that they are now level with an impossibly large package covered by nothing but a skintight, neon-orange G-string. For a second her eyes grow wide; it's as if, even in the midst of her revulsion, she still can't help but marvel at the size of this guy's penis. But as soon as he sees that she's looking, he does a pelvic thrust right into her nose, and any marveling that she was doing is over. Now she just looks like she's going to pass out.

All around me, women are hooting at the top of their lungs and toss-ing dollar bills up onto the stage, and Nadine, who has been standing off to the side this whole time, laughing and clapping with delight, begins to gather them up and stick them down Julie's shirt and pants.

Oh, man, I think. *This is about to get so much worse.*

I've got to be honest; I'm starting to feel bad for Julie. I mean, it's def-initely funny to see her up on a stage with a nasty, two-shakes-away-from-naked guy on her lap, but to have to be within smelling distance of his testicles . . . well, that's just wrong. But I guess there are no limits to what some people will do when they're trying to get their kid into an elite, private preschool. Didn't that Grubman guy in New York commit securities fraud in order to pull some strings at the Ninety-second Street Y? And please, if you think for one second that Julie would still be sitting up there on that stage if Nadine weren't the one responsible for it, well, then I need to call Missing Persons, because I heard that there's a turnip-truck driver who just filled out a report. Okay. Come to think of it, I guess I don't feel that bad for her, after all.

I open up my purse and pull three singles out of my wallet, and I hold them up in the air, just behind where Nadine is standing.

"Nadine!" I yell. "Nadine, here!"

Nadine turns around and plucks them out of my hand. She winks at me. "Thanks, honey. I'll be sure to put these somewhere special."

I look at Julie and laugh, and she catches my eye. She knows that I can't hear her from up there, so she mouths the words *I'm going to kill you.* I grin at her, then clap my hands.

"Wooooooo-hooooooo!" I yell, looking her right in the eye. She shakes her head at me and closes her eyes as Nadine stuffs a dollar bill into her shoe. Just then someone in the crowd places two full shot glasses on the edge of the stage, by Nadine's foot. Nadine picks them up and hands one to Julie.

"One, two, three," Nadine shouts.

For a split second, Julie looks like she's going to cry, but then, to my surprise, she tosses it back like she's a professional arm wrestler. She closes her eyes and makes an awful face, then motions to Nadine for the other one. Nadine raises her eyebrows and hands it to her, and Julie throws it down and hands the empty glass back to Nadine, who looks mightily impressed. As the music segues into Tom Jones's "Sex Bomb," Nadine pats Julie on the back, then returns to her chair on the side of the stage.

I spend the next five minutes or so watching, somewhat horrified, as the stripper fishes dollar bills from various places on Julie's body using nothing but his teeth, while Julie, who has loosened up *ever* so slightly from the shots, sits in her chair, politely waiting for him to finish. Finally, after a finale that ends with him doing a headstand and wrapping his waxed, Mystic Tanned thighs around Julie's neck, and with me wanting to run home to take a shower, the stripper/Scott Baio doppelgänger is finished with his act.

After taking a big bow, he puts his Velcro pants and shirt back on, gathers up his stripper accoutrements, and then takes Julie by the hand and leads her down off the stage to rousing applause. He plants a big kiss on her mouth before he walks away, and then Julie makes her way over to me, dazed and confused. Well, so much for her just observing tonight.

When she reaches me, I give her the once-over: Her cheeks are flushed, her hair is tousled, her pants are rolled up to her ankles, and her face is glistening with sweat. I swear, she's never looked sexier in her life.

"Hey," I say cautiously. I have a feeling that she's probably pretty pissed off at me right now.

But she just smiles. "Whoa," she says, closing her eyes and holding out both of her palms, as if she's trying to make a train stop. "That was an experience." Her voice has a drunken sound to it that I've never heard before. Of course, I've never seen Julie drunk before, which might have something to do with it.

I cock my head and squint at her. "A good experience or a bad experience?" I ask.

Julie hesitates before answering me, then nods. "I think it might have been good." Okay. She's wasted. But then, in an instant, her expression turns serious, and she points her index finger at me. "But don't *ever* tell anyone I said that." Her body wobbles back and forth, but she finally steadies herself and turns halfway around. "I need to use the ladies' room," she announces.

"Okay," I say. "Do you want me to come with you?" Julie shakes her head and lifts her right palm, almost smacking me in the nose.

"No," she says. "I need to be alone." I nod at her, although I'm not quite sure exactly what it is that she needs to be alone to do, and then she turns around and totters off to the restroom.

To keep the momentum going, Stacey has put on some dance music, and when I turn back around, I see that Brandi, Gemma, and Eden have joined Nadine up on the platform, where they're all dancing with one another. Dirty dancing. I watch for a minute, awed by how friggin' skinny they all are, and then I start to walk over to the deejay booth. I think that Stacey deserves some serious congratulations. I mean, if LA had a Page Six, this party would be all over it tomorrow morning. But before I can take two steps, Marley grabs my arm.

"Lara," she says. "Come on." She points up to the platform, where Nadine is waving at me and motioning for me to go up and join them.

"Oh, no," I say, shaking my head. "No way," I tell her. I vigorously shake my head at Nadine, who is nodding and yelling to me from the platform.

"It's my bachelorette party," she shouts. "You have to come up here. Did you think Julie was the only one who was getting hazed tonight?"

Well, yeah, actually, I did. I shake my head at her again. There is no way that I am going up there. I don't want to be the fat chick who makes a fool of herself next to a bunch of professional hotties. No, thanks. I would much rather have been molested by Scott Baio. But Nadine is not giving up.

"Come on," she yells. She starts walking down the steps of the platform, and then reaches down and grabs my hand. "Let's go."

I look around at the crowd of people who are watching this, and my eyes dart from side to side as I try to devise an escape plan. But Marley is behind me, pushing me up the stairs, and then, suddenly, I am up on the platform. The girls who are already up there start to clap for me, and I see Stacey in the deejay booth, laughing. Oh, I am never going to hear the end of this. Thank God LA doesn't have a Page Six.

The dance song that was playing abruptly stops, and a moment later a new song comes on. For a few seconds, it's just a quick drum sequence. *I recognize this,* I think. *What is this?* Then the guitar comes in, and I laugh. It's Van Halen. "Hot for Teacher." I look over at the deejay booth

and jokingly roll my eyes at Stacey, who is clapping her hands and shouting for me to dance. Okay. I guess I'm going to dance. I turn to Brandi
and Eden, and the three of us start dancing together. Brandi closes her
eyes, runs her fingers through her hair, and then turns around and pushes
her butt up against me.

"Are you a teacher?" she asks, looking at me over her shoulder.

I nod at her, trying to ignore the fact that she's practically giving me a
lap dance.

"Sort of," I say. "I'm a guidance counselor."

"No, way," she says, turning back around. "My guidance counselor
didn't look like you." I don't know what to say to this, so I smile and shrug
my shoulders. But this, apparently, isn't good enough for Brandi. She
points her finger over my head and yells out to everyone on the floor.

"She's a guidance counselor," she shouts. "Don't you wish you had a
guidance counselor who looked like her?" A few of the guys start clapping, and I spot Tom Collins in the corner, smiling as he watches me.

I can feel myself turning beet red, so I move away from Brandi over to
Nadine. "I'm going to kill you," I say to her as we dance together.

"Why?" she asks. "You're a great dancer. You can move, honey. If I
didn't know better, I'd think that you were a professional." She smiles at
her joke, then raises her arms above her head and turns around in a circle.
"Just relax, Lara. Have some fun for a change. Your friend did."

I am about to tell her that my friend is going to have a psychotic
breakbreak when she sobers up and realizes what happened to her tonight, when out of the corner of my eye I spot a familiar face in the
crowd. I squint to make sure that I'm seeing correctly, but there's no mis-
taking it. It's Courtney. I grab Nadine's hand.

"Courtney is here," I say, panicking. "You know, the girl Andrew flirts
with?"

"I know," Nadine says calmly. "I invited her." She spins around again,
and I have to keep myself from slapping her.

"You what?" I ask, when she turns back around. "How did you invite
her? You don't even know her."

"Well, technically, Andrew invited her," she explains.

Wait a second. What? I tilt my head to the side and furrow my brow,
silently demanding an explanation.

"I called him up last week," she informs me as she moves her chest from side to side. "I told him that I knew all about the situation with you and his dog friend, and that I thought that I could help smooth things over with the two of you if she came tonight."

She what? She said what?

"But Andrew didn't say anything to me," I tell her. "Why wouldn't he tell me that she was coming?"

Nadine rolls her neck in a slow circle and smiles to herself. "Because I told him not to, honey. I asked him to trust me, and he said that he would. He said that if I had a way to make you see that you have nothing to worry about with her, then he was willing to give it a try."

Oh, this is just unbelievable. "But why?" I ask her. "Why would you invite her *here?*"

Nadine gives me a mysterious smile. "It's all part of my plan, honey. Andrew told me everything that I needed to know about her. Now you just keep dancing, and show that girl what a sexy piece of ass you are."

I look out at Courtney again. She's wearing low-rider jeans that look to be about a size twenty-five, and a tight white tank top with one of those long-sleeved, shrug-sweater things that ties under the boobs. Her blond hair is in a loose ponytail, and her skin is so tan that I can pretty much only see her teeth. Which, of course, are as white as the driven snow, whatever that means.

As I am staring at her, Tom Collins sidles up on her right, and I feel an inexplicable pang of jealousy. I watch them out of the corner of my eye; he starts talking to her, and then he says something funny, I guess, because I see a big flash of white teeth as she laughs. He probably made a joke about how pathetic those old ladies are, dancing up there on the platform. I turn back to Nadine.

"I have to get down," I say. "I feel stupid with her watching me, and I'm too old to be acting this way."

Nadine does a shoulder shimmy into my chest. "Honey, you are the most insecure pretty girl that I have ever met. I am twice as old as anybody in this damn place, and I feel just fine acting this way. And for your information, you are the youngest girl up here on this stage."

I roll my eyes at her. "Yeah, but they all look amazing. I still have baby weight that I'm carrying. And even if I'm not older than they are, I look older." I shrug my shoulders. "I'm just not as confident as you are, Nadine. I can't help it."

Nadine stops dancing, finally, and grips both of my shoulders with her hands. "Yes, honey. You can help it. You just have to stop focusing on everything that you're not, and start focusing on everything that you are. Do you remember when I told you that you had all of those forces working against you, and you just had to figure out how to make them work for you?" I nod at her, and bite my lower lip. "Well, the forces are working for you, Lara. Now you just have to let them do their job."

I shake my head. "I don't get it," I say. "I don't understand what you're talking about."

Nadine looks at me like I'm an idiot. "You're *here*," she says. "You've got Courtney right where you want her. Make *her* be jealous of *you*. Make her think that you are so hot that she would never even have a chance with your Andrew. Make her feel stupid for even trying. Come on, Lara, look at her." We both turn in Courtney's direction. To my delight, Tom Collins has disappeared, and she is standing by herself again, nodding her head to the beat of the music and sipping a drink through a straw. "She's got nothing on you, honey," Nadine insists. "Nothing. There isn't a sexy bone in that girl's body. And in ten years she's going to be a wrinkled, leathery mess. I'm telling you, if I still had my business, I wouldn't let that girl get within ten feet of one of my clients. No way."

I glance at Courtney again, trying to take in Nadine's observations. I don't know. She looks pretty good to me. I shrug.

"I guess," I say, not really believing it.

Nadine rolls her eyes at me. "Don't *guess*, honey. *Know*." She smiles at me and does another spin. "Now, the song's almost over, so finish strong. Let's go."

I stand there for a second, not moving, and I look around me. I look at Nadine, and the girls dancing on the stage. At Tom Collins, standing in the corner. At Stacey, in the deejay booth. At Courtney.

All right, I think. *Fuck it.*

I put one hand up in the air and start to turn my wrist and my hips in circles as I slowly do a three-hundred-and-sixty-degree turn. I learned it in a dance class that I used to take years ago at my old gym in Philly—the instructor was a fortyish, flaming gay man who was way ahead of his time. He used to teach us stripper moves before anyone ever heard of *The S Factor*. Nadine watches me, nodding her approval, and I give her a coy smile as I arch my back, bend my knees, and lower myself halfway down to the floor.

When the song finally ends, Nadine holds out her hand next to me, as if to say that I deserve a round of applause. Everyone who is watching from below starts to clap and whistle, and I take a self-mocking bow.

Nadine yells out to them, pointing her finger at my head. "Four-month-old baby, everyone. She has a *four-month-old* baby."

There are some more whistles, and then a few of the guys start to yell "MILF, MILF." I feel like Stifler's mom in *American Pie*, though I can't decide if that's a good thing or not.

When the catcalls have come to an end, I climb down from the stage, where Stacey, who has emerged from the deejay booth, is standing at the bottom, waiting for me.

"Who are you?" she asks me. "I had no idea that you could dance like that. Especially in public."

I lean in and whisper in her ear. "Courtney is here," I say. But before I can explain any further, Courtney is standing next to me, tapping me on the arm.

"Lara," she says. "Wow, you are such a great dancer. That was amazing."

I fake-smile at her. "Thanks," I say. "This is my friend, Stacey," I tell her. "This is her bar."

Courtney's mouth drops open. "Really?" she asks. "That is so cool. Wow, Lara, you have, like, the coolest friends ever."

God, I never noticed it before, but she sounds like an idiot. In fact, she sounds just like some of my students at Bel Air Prep. I feel a hand on my shoulder, and I turn around and see that it's Nadine.

"Oh, Stacey," she says, "you did such a fantastic job with this place. Jimmy is going to be so thrilled."

Stacey beams at her. "Thanks," she says. "Really, I couldn't have done any of it without you."

Nadine shakes her head. "All I did was get you started," she says. "You made everything come together. And it's going to be the hottest place in town. You mark my words."

Stacey snorts. "Only if you have a bachelorette party here every weekend. I swear, I saw guys breaking out their cell phones and telling their friends to get over here as fast as they could. It's amazing what a few hot girls dancing together can do for a place."

Courtney is standing next to us, listening to them talk, and I can tell that she's starting to feel uncomfortable, so I go ahead and interrupt.

"Nadine," I say. "This is Courtney. Andrew's friend from Zoey's agility class." I turn to look at Courtney. "Nadine is the bachelorette," I explain. "She's marrying my dad." Nadine looks at me funny, and I get the feeling she's surprised—pleasantly surprised—that I have admitted this.

"Congratulations," Courtney says. "And thanks for inviting me. Andrew told me you said it would be okay for me to stop by. Maybe meet some new people."

Nadine nods. "Yes," she says, her drawl getting thicker by the second. "You're very welcome. In fact, I have someone whom I think you would hit it off with right now. Come with me, honey." Nadine steers her away from us, and Stacey looks at me.

"What is going on?" she asks.

"I have no idea," I say. "But everything that she does somehow seems to work, so I'm not going to question it."

Stacey nods her agreement, then looks around, puzzled. "Where's Julie?" she asks.

Oh, shit. I forgot all about Julie.

"I have no idea. The last time I saw her, she was heading to the restroom to recover. Or maybe to puke." I glance around, but there's no sign of her. I sigh. "Okay. I have to go find her. I'll see you later." Stacey starts to walk off ahead of me, but I call out to her before she can get too far. "Hey, Stace," I shout. She spins around.

"Yeah?"

"Great job. Really."

She flashes me a huge smile. "I know," she says. "I'm amazing."

I roll my eyes at her humility, and then I start off to find Julie.

After three laps around the bar, I finally spot her. She's sitting in a corner booth way in the back, flanked by Tawny, Brandi, and Leila. As I approach, I hear loud laughing, and then I see Tawny raise her arms in victory.

What the hell is going on here? I wonder. I walk over to the table and stand there, but none of them notices me.

"Okay, okay," Brandi says. "I never"—she pauses as she thinks about what to say next, then nods her head as she figures it out—"dressed up like a cowgirl and rode on a naked guy's back!" Tawni and Leila both raise their hands, and then they burst into laughter.

"No way, you guys!" Julie slurs.

"Driiiiiink," shouts Brandi, pointing at Julie. Julie rolls her eyes upward in resignation and takes a sip of her cosmopolitan. Okay. I think I need to break this up.

"Um, hello," I say loudly, trying to get their attention. "Hey, guys." Julie looks up at me with a huge, genuine smile. It kind of stuns me for a second, because I've gotten so used to only ever seeing the pity smile that she always has for me.

"Lara!" she yells. "Come play with us." I look at the other girls and shake my head.

"What is going on here?" I ask them. Leila smiles at me, like she just got busted with her hand in the cookie jar.

"Nothing," she says. "We're just playing I Never." The three of them giggle, and I put my hands on my hips.

"That is *not* how you play I Never," I say. "You drink if you've done it, not if you haven't." They all look at me like I'm a party pooper, and Brandi puts her fingers to her lips.

"Shhhhh," she says, as the others crack up. They're all plastered. I shake my head at them and look over at Julie, who has just figured out what's been going on.

"You *guys,*" she whines. They all laugh at her again, and Tawny hugs her.

"Sor-ry," Tawny says, in a singsong voice.

I put my hands on the table and lean down so that only Julie can hear me. "Are you all right?" I ask her.

She closes her eyes and waits a long time before she opens them again. "I don't know," she says. "Am I drunk?"

I laugh. "Yes," I tell her. "You're very, very drunk."

She nods, as if I am confirming something that she already suspected, and then she leans closer to me. "Lara," she whispers, her eyes wide. "You would not believe some of the things these girls have done. I didn't even know people *thought* about stuff like that."

Oh, great. I've gone and corrupted Julie. I need to get her out of here. Jon is going to kill me when I get her home. Although, maybe not.

"Listen," I say to Brandi. "I'm going to say good-bye to people, and then I'm going to take her home." I look sternly at Julie. "Stay *right here*," I say, pointing my finger at the table. "Do not go anywhere." I look back to Brandi. "And do not give her any more alcohol. She hardly ever drinks, for God's sake. You're going to kill her."

Brandi nods solemnly. "Got it," she says, giving me the thumbs-up.

I stand up to go, and Julie makes a pouty face at me.

"Where are you going?" she asks. "Don't go."

I put my arm around her shoulder. "I'm going to say good-bye to Nadine, and—"

Julie cuts me off. "Oh, my God, I *love* Nadine."

I nod at her. "I know," I say. "Just stay right here, and I'll be back in a few minutes to get you, okay?"

"Okay," she says. She closes her eyes and slumps back against the seat of the booth. Yeah. Jon is definitely going to kill me.

I find Nadine sitting at the bar by herself.

"What are you doing?" I ask her as I slide onto the bar stool next to where she is sitting. "You're supposed to be having fun."

She turns around to face me. "I am having fun," she says. "I just needed a minute to gather my thoughts, that's all." She takes a sip of her drink and then looks me in the eye. "Your friend was a good sport," she says. "I'll get her into that school. No problem."

"She'll be very happy to hear that," I say. "Assuming that she ever sobers up again."

Nadine smiles. "Where is she?" she asks.

"Oh, she's in the corner," I say, shaking my head. A look of concern crosses Nadine's face. "Don't worry. She's fine. I'm going to take her home now. I just wanted to say good-bye. I had a great time."

"Oh, no, honey, *I* had a great time. This was the best party I've ever had. Thanks so much for helping out with it."

"It was my pleasure," I say. "Really."

Nadine smiles at me playfully. "We've come a long way, the two of us, haven't we?" she asks.

"Yeah, considering that two months ago I was trying to figure out how to get my dad to dump you."

Nadine laughs. "Oh, honey, people always start off that way with me," she says. "But they come around." She reaches out to give me a hug, and I hug her back. "I'll talk to you next week," she says. "There are still a few things we need to do for the shower."

I look up at the ceiling. "Oh, God, that's right. Okay. Call me. Maybe you and my dad could come over again for dinner." I smile at her. "You won't believe how things have changed with Deloris."

Nadine smiles. "My plan was good?"

"Your plan was *genius,*" I tell her. I am about to fill her in on the details of the voodoo ceremony in which I recently partook, when, out of nowhere, Courtney appears in front of me. She seems really excited about something, and she's jumping up and down.

"Lara, Lara, oh, my God." She turns to Nadine. "Sorry to interrupt," she says. "But I think I just got a *job*. At a *hotel*." She lets out a little squeal. God, I can't believe that *this* is what I've been so worried about. Nadine was right. She *is* just a kid.

"Really?" I ask. "What happened?"

"Well, I was talking to that woman you guys are with—Marley—and we started talking about work, and I told her how I did the hotel program at UNLV but I can't find a job, and she tells me that she's the catering director at the Peninsula. Like, can you believe that? So I started telling her about how I'm dying to get into, like, hotel special-event coordinating— it's, like, always been my dream—and she says that she's been looking for a new assistant, and that I would be perfect and I should come by on Monday morning for a meeting. How amazing is that? It's, like, fate or something."

I steal a glance at Nadine, who winks at me. Okay, I don't get it. It's not like Courtney having her dream job does me any good. Although, I have to say, after talking to her for five minutes, I'm so over it. Please, if Andrew wants to be with this blithering idiot, she can have him.

Then, suddenly, Courtney makes a sad face.

"Oh, God," she says. "I just realized, I won't be able to take Zak to agility anymore." *Wait a minute . . .*

"Why not?" I ask, trying not to sound as excited as I feel.

She sighs. "Because most events are on Saturdays. I'm sure I'll have to work every Saturday morning."

I look over at Nadine again, and she has a self-satisfied smile on her face. *No way.*

I swear, I don't know how she does it, but she's good. She's really, really good. I shake my head ever so slightly to show her how amazed I am, and then, suddenly, it dawns on me that I've had my Mary Poppins all along. The red stilettos threw me off, but like I said, there's no reason why she can't be updated for the twenty-first century.

Nadine gives me a knowing eyebrow raise, then puts her hand on my shoulder.

"Well, Courtney, that is terrific news," she says. "Congratulations. Now, ladies, if you'll excuse me, I need to go powder my nose."

"Okay," I say, giving her another hug. "I'll talk to you next week."

She pulls back, then winks at me again. "You got it, honey." Then she turns around and disappears into the crowd.

twenty-four

When I walk into Mommy and Me on Wednesday morning, I make a beeline for Melissa, who is sitting on the floor, chatting with Amy. I stand right in front of them, holding Parker in my arms, and when they stop talking and look up at me, I smile.

"Hi," I say, taking a deep breath. "I just wanted you guys to know that Parker definitely does not need a helmet, and that my husband is definitely *not* having an affair. So if you could just, you know, clarify that for everyone else in the class the next time that you all have lunch and talk about me, I'd really appreciate it." Melissa and Amy both stare at me, speechless.

"Oh, and the blow-job thing was great. So thanks for that." I smile again, and then walk away toward the other side of the room, where I put Parker down on her blanket and hand her a teether.

My heart is pounding, and my hands are shaking a little bit. I really can't believe that I just did that. But I had to. I couldn't take the idea of them gossiping about me and my flatheaded baby and my soon-to-be-failed marriage for one more minute. I exhale, and Parker looks up at me and smiles. She has kind of a mischievous look in her eyes, like she's trying to tell me that she approves of what just happened. I smile back at her and lean down.

"I know," I whisper to her, nuzzling my nose into her neck. "Your mommy is awesome."

Okay. I feel much better now.

A few minutes later, Susan sits down on her folding chair and claps her hands to get everyone's attention.

"Hello, ladies," she says. "Good morning." The murmuring quiets down and Susan gives us a big smile. "Today we're going to talk about playing. What kinds of toys you should be buying for your child, the types of games you should be playing with them, and how to use playtime to stimulate brain development."

I glance around the room, and notice that when she says *brain development,* everyone perks up just a little bit.

Susan starts off talking about some study that showed that playing with babies during the first six months helps the synapses in the brain to fire more rapidly, blah, blah, blah, and then she starts talking about toys. Stacking toys, water toys, shape sorters, pianos, pop-up toys; all of the different kinds of baby toys that are out on the market and which ones are good and which ones aren't that good, and which ones have won awards and which brands are pediatrician-recommended and which ones are safe for a baby to put in his mouth and which ones got recalled because of some toxic dye that the company used, and which teethers you should never buy because they have a gel in the middle of them that's supposed to feel good on a baby's gums when it's frozen, but even though they're supposed to be safe, you don't really know, so why risk it. . . . I swear, by the end of this, my head is throbbing and I am so wired with anxiety that I feel like if someone touches me I might actually electrocute them.

When Susan finally stops to take a breath, Sabrina (Ashton's mom) raises her hand.

"What about the ExerSaucer?" she asks. "Is that a good toy? Because Ashton loves it."

I nod my head. I always put Parker in the ExerSaucer. It's a big, plastic, round thing—well, it looks like a saucer, I guess—and there's a seat in the middle of it, and it's raised up about two feet off the floor and is attached to another round saucer at the bottom. There are different toys around the perimeter of it, and the seat spins around so that the baby can play with each one as she turns. The thing is great. But Susan inhales and closes her eyes, like she's just heard some kind of blasphemy.

"I do not want you putting your child in an ExerSaucer," she says.

Sabrina looks upset. "Why?" she asks, sounding as shocked as I feel.

Yeah, why?

"Sitting in an ExerSaucer does not allow a child to develop the gross motor skills necessary for walking, and it prevents the legs from developing the walking muscles. Studies have shown that children who spend too much time in an ExerSaucer typically don't walk until much later than normal."

Sabrina looks as if she's about to cry. "But he loves it," she says.

Susan shakes her head. "I'm sorry. But I do not want my mommies using ExerSaucers."

For a minute I feel like I'm going to cry, too. Luthor is creeping up the back of my throat, and I can feel my eyes getting watery. I've been putting Parker in the ExerSaucer every day for almost a whole month. She loves to chew on the little steering wheel, and she always gets so excited when she figures out how to make one of the spinning things with the little balls in it move around. My God, I can't believe that I've been inadvertently retarding her gross motor skills by letting her sit in it.

As I think about this, I start to get angry with the ExerSaucer manufacturers. How can they sell a toy like that if they know that it causes delayed walking? How can such a bad toy happen to good people? But then I remember what Stacey said to me the day that I watched her have lunch.

You can't trust anyone but yourself. That's why it's so hard to be a parent.

Yeah, I think, as I redirect my anger away from the ExerSaucer makers. I'm sick of Susan and her fearmongering. It's about time for me to start trusting my own instincts.

Wait a minute, I think, feeling my burst of self-confidence wane. *I don't have any instincts.*

For a second, I am confused—*what should I do?*—until I realize that I do have them. I definitely do. In fact, I can feel my whole body tingling with them right now. I swallow, hard, and Luthor disappears back down my throat. I glare at Susan and raise my hand.

"Yes, Lara," Susan says, pointing to me. "Go ahead."

"Well, I'm sorry, but what you're saying about the ExerSaucer doesn't really make any sense." Sabrina's head snaps up, and a low murmur of surprise settles across the room.

"What do you mean?" Susan asks. "I can show you the study. Doctors have proven it."

"Yeah," I say. "I'm sure they have. But I have to believe that they're talking about *mis*use of an ExerSaucer. Like, if a negligent parent stuck their kid in it for six hours a day while they were trying to work, or something, then yeah, I can see how it would interfere with development. But none of us are going to do that. I put Parker in the ExerSaucer all the time, but she gets bored with it after ten or fifteen minutes. And I really find it hard to believe that ten or fifteen minutes two times a day is going to cause any kind of long-term damage."

Sabrina and the other moms stare at Susan, who appears to be flabbergasted that one of her disciples would dare to question her Word.

"Well," she says, blinking her eyes and swallowing, "you didn't let me finish. I was *about* to say that if you *must* use an ExerSaucer, you shouldn't use it for more than twenty minutes a day. Because that amount of time hasn't been proven to cause any problems."

Yeah, I think, *sure you were.*

I fold my arms across my chest and stare at her.

"With all due respect, Susan," I say, "you should have just said that from the beginning. Because you just got a lot of people really upset over nothing." I give her a shame-on-you look and then I sit back against the wall and cross my arms.

Susan doesn't say anything for a minute, and she looks relieved when Sabrina raises her hand again.

"Yes, Sabrina."

"So then, you're saying that it *is* okay to continue using the ExerSaucer for twenty minutes a day?"

I roll my eyes to myself. She completely missed my point. After all of that, she still wants Susan's approval. You know what? I'm so over this class. These mommunist girls are pathetic.

When class is over, I leave without saying a word to anyone. I overhear them making lunch plans on my way out, but I have no interest anymore.

I'm not one of them, I don't want to be one of them, and I don't care if I don't fit in with them. Let them make one another anxious and crazy. I have a life to lead.

Parker has fallen asleep on the way down to the garage, so I carefully lift the car seat out of the Snap-N-Go and gently lower it into the car-seat base in my car. Once I have her in place, I walk around to the trunk, fold up the stroller, and stick it inside. As I'm doing this, I hear footsteps behind me, and the Range Rover next to me lets out a beep. I turn around. It's Melissa.

"Hey," she says, as she opens the back door and lifts Hannah out of her Bugaboo and into the car-seat base. I shut my trunk as quietly as I can and walk around to Parker's side of the car, next to where Melissa is standing. I need to put the window shades up in the backseat so that the sun doesn't wake her on the ride home.

"Hey," I say back, as I roll up the shade and hook it onto the top of the window. Next to me, Melissa gets Hannah settled, folds up her stroller and places it in the trunk, and then comes back around to where I am standing and opens her driver's-side door.

"You know, it was really cool what you did today," she says. She kind of half smiles at me, and I notice that her voice is a little shaky.

"Which part?" I ask. I'm not sure if she's referring to the comment I made to her at the beginning of class, or to what I said to Susan.

"Well, everything, really, but I was talking about what you said to Susan. I don't think anyone has ever questioned her before. We all just blindly follow everything that she says, even when it doesn't always make sense."

"Yeah," I say. "I know. It's just starting to get on my nerves. I mean, our babies are almost five months old. We should be able to make some decisions for ourselves at this point."

Melissa nods, but before I can say anything else, her eyes fill up with tears, and she tries to choke back a sob.

"Are you okay?" I ask her. "Is something wrong?"

She shakes her head, unable to speak, and she sits down in the driver's seat of her car and rests her head on the steering wheel. She stays there like that for a few seconds, and then she finally lifts her head back up and looks at me. There are tears streaming down her cheeks.

"I'm pregnant," she announces.

When I hear this, I almost fall over. I grab onto her arm to steady my-self, and then pretend that I had meant for it to be a consoling pat.

Oh, my God.

I really cannot think of anything worse. I struggle with what to say next, because I'm not sure if I should be congratulating her or giving her my condolences. I decide to do neither, and just go for the obvious.

"Wow," I say. "How far are you?"

She takes an unsteady breath. "I'm already thirteen weeks. I thought that it couldn't happen if I was still nursing, and since I hadn't gotten my period yet . . . we weren't using any protection." She raises her eyebrows and looks me in the eye. "I hope you're being careful," she says.

Holy shit, I think. Andrew and I have had sex, like, five times since the bachelorette party last weekend (by the way, it's amazing what a pair of ass pants and a little innocent flirting can do for a marriage). Thank God Dr. Lowenstein made me go back on the pill.

"So how far apart are they going to be?" I ask.

"Barely a little over a year." She pauses, and I can tell that she's trying really hard not to start crying again. "I don't even know why I'm telling you this," she says. "I haven't told anyone yet. I guess I just feel like, I don't know, like maybe you would have something to say that would make me feel better."

Me? Is she serious?

"It won't be that bad," I lie. "Think about it this way: You'll get the hard part over with all at once, and they'll be close enough in age to be really good friends. My husband and his sister are less than two years apart, and they were superclose growing up." I can't tell if this sounds believable, or if it just sounds like I'm feeding her a load of crap, which I am. Andrew and his sister hated each other growing up. She told me that their mom used to leave them alone together when he was old enough to watch her by himself, and that Andrew used to chase her around the house, whispering that as soon as their mother left, he was going to stab her with a butcher knife. She still has nightmares about it to this day.

"I guess so," she says. "We were going to start trying again when

Hannah turned one anyway. It's just a few months earlier than we had planned."

"Well, what does your husband say about it?" I ask her.

She shrugs. "Oh, he's fine. He wants three or four kids, so he feels like, the sooner the better."

Oh, of course he does. If I recall, her husband was the one who left to go play poker instead of having a night alone with the baby. And I'm pretty sure that I remember Melissa saying something in the first or second week of class about how her husband went on a two-week golfing trip to Ireland the week after Hannah was born. So, yeah, I'm sure it's no skin off his back that she's pregnant again. He won't have to take care of two babies at the same time. Or three. Or four. But I'm trying to help here, not make her feel worse. I change the subject.

"And how do you feel?"

"I'm okay. A little tired, but I'm not nauseous or anything. I'm too busy with Hannah to really even think about it."

I wince. The thought of having to deal with a baby during first-trimester pregnancy exhaustion makes me shudder.

"Well," I say, "if you need anything, please let me know." *Yeah. Like if you need a gun, or a noose. Or maybe an accidental push down the stairs.*

"I will," she says. "Thanks." She pulls her seat belt down around her and fastens it into the buckle. "And Lara," she says.

I turn around to look at her again. "Yes?"

"Don't tell anyone, okay? I'm just not ready to deal with everybody yet."

"I get it," I tell her. "I won't say a word."

I get into my car and wait for her to pull out, and then I back up and follow her out of the garage. I sit behind her as she waits for the traffic to clear, and as she turns out onto the street, she waves to me in her rearview mirror. I wave back, and then turn in the other direction.

I feel like I'm in shock. It just isn't sinking in that Melissa is going to have another baby in six months. *Six months!* The whole ride home, I keep trying to imagine if it were me. How would I feel? What would I do? God, I think I would shoot myself. I'm just not ready to go through that again. I'd have to wait *at least* three years before I could even *think* about getting pregnant. You know, get one in school full-time before you have to deal with another one, is how I see it. I honestly can't even fathom trying to take care of two babies at the same time. I can barely take care of one, and I have a full-time, live-in nanny.

Poor Melissa. It's just got to suck, doing it all over again, back-to-back like that. The crying, and the sleeplessness, and the misery—and breast-feeding. She's still breast-feeding the first one, for God's sake. Ugh, and being pregnant again, and all of the crap that comes with that. I swear, just the idea of gaining all of that weight back and then having to lose it all over again makes me feel sick to my stomach.

I glance into the mirror that I hooked up in the backseat, so that I can see Parker even though she's in a rear-facing car seat. God, she's so cute when she's sleeping. I sigh to myself.

Then again, maybe it won't be so bad the second time. Maybe I'll feel different about the next one. I mean, I'm certainly not the same person I was before Parker was born. First of all, my patience level is, like, a million times what it used to be. And I would even go so far as to say that motherhood has made me somewhat tolerant of people. Please, when I was pregnant I would become positively incensed when random strangers would talk to me and ask me a million questions about my pregnancy. But now I love it when people come up to me on the street and tell me how cute Parker is. In fact, I get offended if they *don't* come up to me and tell me how cute she is. And you know, I'm really starting to think that maybe I'm not as selfish as I used to be. Maybe there isn't really any such thing as a selfish gene, after all. God, wouldn't that be a relief.

And with the next one, of course, I'll know what to expect. And, more important, I'll know what I'm getting. I'll know that the fetus making me fat and the blobby infant causing all of my misery will eventually turn into a baby that I will love more than life itself. I mean, I know I say that she's boring, and that I would never want to take care of her all by myself, but I really do love Parker so much that it hurts. Seriously, there are times when my heart actually feels like it is going to break in half and my urge to eat her becomes almost overwhelming. At least with the next one, I'll know in advance that everything will be worth it.

That's got to make it a little bit easier, right?

* * *

When Andrew gets home that night, I've already put Parker to bed, and Deloris and I are talking in the kitchen. She's been telling me about her son, who just finished his first year of medical school in Jamaica. I swear, I've learned more about Deloris in the past two weeks than I have the entire time that she's lived here. It's a little embarrassing, actually. I was so wrapped up in competing with her, it didn't even occur to me to ask her anything about her life. God, no wonder she hated me so much. I would've hated me, too, if I were her.

Andrew walks into the kitchen and gives me a kiss on the mouth that lasts just a little bit longer than usual. I get a flutter in my stomach, like how I used to when we first started dating, and I give him a you're-so-naughty smile, which he returns. Oh, I have got to find an excuse to wear those pants again.

"So," he says to me. "I spoke to Courtney this morning."

Deloris's eyes narrow, and we glance at each other.

"Oh, really?" I say. "And what profundities did Courtney have to offer you today?"

Andrew gives me a blank stare. "I don't know what a profundity is," he says. "But you'll be happy to know that she can't go to agility anymore. She got a job at the Peninsula, and she has to work on Saturday mornings." So Marley did give her the job. Amazing.

"Really?" I ask, playing dumb. He nods at me, and I smile. "That's great for her." I pause, unsure whether to ask him what I want to know. I give him a sideways glance so that I don't have to look him in the eye.

"Are you upset?" I ask. But before I've even finished getting the words out, he's shaking his head no. *Whew.*

"I'm happy for her that she got a job," he says. "And to be honest, I'm a little relieved, because she was starting to get kind of annoying. She just talks a lot about nothing. And besides, she's way too nice." He grins and slaps me on my butt. "I like my women a little bit edgier," he says.

I look at him and laugh. "That's good to know," I say. "Very good."

"Yeah, well, I thought you'd be happy about it." He takes off his jacket and loosens his tie. "I want to go change out of this suit," he announces.

"I'll be back in a few minutes." He trots up the stairs, and as soon as he is out of earshot, Deloris turns to me and puts her palms up in the air. She has a huge smile on her face. Huge.

"Does Deloris know what she is doing or does Deloris know what she is doing?" she asks.

"What do you mean?"

"What do I mean?" she repeats, sounding offended. "Didn't you just hear what Mr. Andrew said? Courtney cannot go to agility class anymore." She crosses her arms and leans back against the sink, a smug look spreading across her face.

Then, suddenly, I realize what is going on. *Oh, my God.* She thinks that this happened because of her stupid voodoo spell. I laugh.

"Deloris," I say, trying to explain. "The person who gave her a job is one of Nadine's friends. You know, my dad's fiancée? She set the whole thing up."

Deloris nods. "Yes, because Deloris put it out there into the universe," she says, poking herself in the chest. "How else do you think a job happened to be available? Nadine could not have made those stars align."

I sigh to myself, remembering what Nadine said about dealing with Deloris. *A little indulgence goes a long way,* she told me. *It won't hurt for you to play along.* I smile at Deloris and nod.

"You know, you're right," I say, as if I've just thought about it for the first time. "I never thought about it that way, but you're right." I shake my head. "That's amazing, Deloris," I tell her. "*You* are amazing."

Deloris beams at me, thrilled with the validation. "Not just me," she says. "You made the wish. Without that, the universe would not have known what to do with the energy from the doll."

I smile at her appreciatively. "Well, either way, thank you," I say. "Although, it's funny. I wanted her gone for such a long time, and now that she is, I don't even care about her anymore."

Deloris nods. "It always happens that way," she says. "As soon as you realize that you are the one with the power, all of the worrying that you have done just seems silly."

I give Deloris a surprised look. You know, underneath all of that voodoo craziness, I think that there might actually be a brain in there. God, I had it all so wrong. How could I ever have thought that Deloris would be my Mary Poppins? Deloris is no Mary Poppins. She's the Scarecrow from *The Wizard of Oz*. I smile at her.

"That's true, Deloris," I say. "That is absolutely true."

twenty-five

You're not going to believe this, but it's raining outside. In *August*. And it's not just a little drizzle, either. It's a full-fledged, windshield-wipers-and-umbrellas-required downpour. The local news channels are going crazy. They have a graphic and everything already. "Summer Storm," they're calling it, with the requisite menacing music playing in the background while some weather guy in a yellow slicker reports from Malibu, interviewing all of the shocked and disappointed would-be beachgoers. It's hilarious, actually. You'd think it was seventeen feet of snow, the way that they're talking about it.

Anyway, they're saying that it has something to do with an El Niño cycle, but personally, I think it's some kind of an omen. Like, it's God's way of telling me to just relax and stop feeling so guilty about the fact that I have to go back to work in two weeks. Oh, wait, sorry. You didn't know that I was feeling guilty. Okay. Let me back up.

So, here's what happened. I went outside to get the mail—which, not coincidentally, is when I discovered that there were, in fact, drops falling from the sky—and after I got over my urge to call up those people from the day camp where I used to work and yell, *You see, it does rain in the summer* at them, I walked back inside and found a big, fat envelope from Bel Air Prep stuck in between the bills and the junk mail. I didn't even need to open it, because I knew exactly what it was. It comes every year during the second week in August, and it's pretty much exactly the same every time. It's the schedule for faculty orientation week, which is always the first week in September, right before the opening day of school. As soon as I saw it, my stomach filled up with dread. I mean, imagine having to go to daylong sessions on the power of community, or the importance of respect, or whatever other boring theme that they pick for the year, and then to workshops on how to use the new technology that they spent tens of thousands of dollars installing over the summer, and that will, inevitably, create chaos for the first three months of school when it fails to interface with the old technology, or when it wipes out half of the English department's curriculum, or, like what happened last year, when it skips over the second-parent addresses on the mailing labels, and nobody notices until a hundred furious divorced dads start calling and demanding to know why they didn't receive a copy of Johnny's report card and why they had to hear about the D in Biology from their ex-fucking-wives. Oh, and let's not forget about the "fun" stuff that's supposed to promote faculty bonding, like the egg toss that we have to do in four-hundred-degree heat, or the scavenger hunt that instructs you to "find the math teacher who spent the summer in Ecuador, and the school administrator who worked as a bike messenger when he was in college." Anyway, you get the point. It's awful. I don't know what they think they're orienting us to, except for torture.

But anyway, back to my point. I opened up the envelope and looked over the schedule (this year we're going to be making a faculty time capsule—hooray), and that's when the guilt began to set in. No, wait—let me back up even more. You see, this morning Parker woke up kind of early, and I played with her for an hour or so until Deloris came out of her room, at which point I was starving. So I handed her to Deloris so that I could go scarf down a bowl of Grape-Nuts, and when I turned around and walked out of the room, Parker started to cry. Now, I know it doesn't sound like much—I mean, babies cry when their moms walk away all of the time—but this was a first for me. Parker has never cried when I walked away before, and I got so excited because I've been so worried that she wasn't bonded to me ever since Susan gave that stupid talk about separation anxiety—oh, right. I didn't tell you about that. Okay. I'll go back even farther.

About a month ago, the topic in class was separation anxiety. Susan was explaining what it was to us: A baby gets anxious when his mother leaves because he doesn't realize that she'll be coming back, so he starts to cry every time that she walks away from him. Anyway, then she described to us what happens during a typical separation-anxiety episode: You walk away, the baby cries, then you come back, and the baby calms down, and then you walk away again and the baby cries even harder, etc. Eventually, though, she said, your baby will learn to trust you, and he won't cry when you leave, because he'll understand that Mommy always comes back.

But while Susan was saying this, all of the mommunists were nodding and saying things like, *Oh, yeah, my baby cries if I just leave the room for two seconds to answer the phone,* and I was a total mess because, up until this morning, Parker has never so much as noticed when I leave the room. I remember that, when class was over, I called Stacey to tell her that I was having separation-anxiety anxiety—well, technically, *lack*-of-separation-anxiety anxiety—because, according to Susan, if a baby doesn't show signs of separation anxiety, it means that she hasn't bonded properly with her mother. Fucking Susan. I can't even tell you how stressed out I was about it. And I'm sorry that I didn't mention it to you earlier, but it happened before I decided that Susan was full of shit, and I just couldn't handle you thinking that Parker doesn't know who I am, especially after how I keep saying that I'm spending so much more time with her, and that I love her so much, yadda, yadda, yadda.

Which brings me back to the mail. You see, now that I finally feel like Parker does know that I'm her mother (She loves me! She really loves me!), I'm going to go back to work, just in time for her to forget about me all over again. And that's where the guilt came in. You know the drill: *Am I doing the right thing? Am I being selfish? Should I just quit and stay home with her, so that she doesn't think that I'm abandoning her three days a week? If I'm not around every day, will I be undoing all of the progress that I've made with her?* And that, you see, is when I decided that the freak rainstorm that was taking place all across the gigantic expanse of land known as Southern California was all about me, and was happening only because God wanted Lara Stone of West Los Angeles to know that she should stop feeling so anxious, because sometimes it does rain in the summertime.

And so, as would only seem prudent during a once-in-a-lifetime event such as this, I have decided to take God up on His offer by lying down on my bed, enjoying the rain, and doing nothing for the rest of the day. Or at least for as long as Parker will nap.

But then, two seconds ago, someone went and rang the doorbell, and now Zoey is going insane.

Oh, God, not again. I never thought that I would say this, but I want to kill that dog sometimes. I swear, she barks every time the wind blows, and God forbid someone should ring the doorbell; she acts like we're being invaded by storm troopers. And she's so dumb that she can't even tell the difference between the real doorbell and a doorbell on television, so whenever that stupid Pizza Hut commercial comes on—the one where they ring the doorbell ten times—I have to go diving for the TiVo remote so that I can pause it before Zoey barks herself into a heart attack.

"Shhhhh!" I yell, as I run down the stairs. "Zoey, shut up!" But Zoey completely ignores me and stands by the front door, barking incessantly. "Zoey, shush!" I lean down and grab her muzzle, holding it closed with my hand while I reach out to open the front door with my other hand. It's Nadine. Immediately Zoey stops barking, and her tail begins to wag as she solicits a pat on the head. I let go of her mouth and look at her with disgust. Damn dog. I swear, if she woke Parker up, I'm going to ship her off to a big farm in the sky, where she can run around all day and bark her head off if she wants to.

"Hi," I say to Nadine. She's wearing black pants and a white, lightweight sweater, and she's holding a long black umbrella by her side that is dripping with water. I'm kind of confused by her presence on my doorstep. She and my dad were supposed to come over for dinner tonight at seven, and we were going to put the finishing touches on the shower. At least, I thought that was the plan. Maybe I misunderstood.

"Didn't we have dinner plans?" I ask her. "Am I losing my mind?"

Nadine shakes her head and holds out an envelope with my name written on it.

"This is for you," she says. Her voice sounds funny. There's no drawl—none whatsoever—and when I look at her again, I realize that she's been crying. I reach out to take the envelope, and when I look at it, I see that it's my father's handwriting.

"What's going on?" I ask, my heart racing. "What's in the envelope?"

But she doesn't say anything. She just stands there, shaking her head. "Nadine," I say urgently. "Tell me."

She shrugs her shoulders and puts her palms up in the air. "He's gone," she whispers. "He just . . . left."

My eyes fill up with tears when she says it, and I feel like my knees are going to buckle out from under me. My head is spinning, and my mind keeps going back and forth between thinking, *There has to be some explanation; he wouldn't do this again* and, *You stupid, stupid idiot. How could you let him do this to you twice?*

I rip open the envelope and unfold the piece of paper inside of it, trying to read through the blur of tears.

Dear Lara,

Writing this letter is the hardest thing I've ever done, but I thought that I at least owed you an explanation this time. The afternoon that I spent with you and your beautiful daughter was one of the best and worst days of my life. I know that you're right about us needing to rebuild our relationship before you can love me again, but I'm not that great at relationships, and I'm afraid that you're not going to like the person you get to know. I hope that you understand that this has nothing to do with you. I love you and you are always in my thoughts. I just do better by myself; always have. Take care of Nadine; she's a great lady and I'm glad that the two of you ended up as friends.

Love,
Dad

When I finish reading, I look up and give Nadine a blank stare. She steps forward and hugs me, and I'm grateful just to have her there to lean on so that I don't fall down.

"I'm more upset for you than I am for me," she says. "I'm so sorry that he did this to you. I never thought that . . ." She lets her sentence trail off. I'm sure she realizes that there's no use in trying to defend him, or in trying to explain.

I pull away from her. "Let's go inside," I say. "I need to sit down."

I'm barely able to speak, and I'm talking so quietly that I almost can't hear myself. Nadine takes my hand and leads me into the den, and we both sit down on the couch. But before she can say anything, Deloris walks in.

"Parker is still sleeping," she informs me. "But you need to lock the dog up when she naps. We got lucky that time."

I nod at her, barely listening to what she is saying. "Okay," I say. "Thanks, Deloris." Deloris gives me a funny look—usually I spend fifteen minutes ranting to her about how I'm going to have Zoey's vocal chords cut if she doesn't watch it—and then she walks out of the room. I look at Nadine.

"Did you two have a fight?" I ask her.

But she shakes her head at me, looking bewildered. "No. Not at all. In fact, when I left this morning, he said that he was going to pick up his tuxedo for the wedding and that he would try it on for me when I got home. I was just going to get my nails done. And then when I got back . . . he was gone. All of his things were gone, and all that was left were two envelopes sitting on the coffee table. One for you and one for me." She shakes her head, and her eyes fill up with tears. "We were just saying last night that we were going to start looking for a house as soon as the wedding was over. I said that we should put down some roots here, get something more permanent—" She covers her mouth with her hand. "Oh, my God, I wonder if that scared him off." She shakes her head and makes a sad face. "Oh, Ronny," she says to no one in particular. "Why didn't you just tell me that you weren't ready?"

By now I am over the initial shock, and my anger is starting to settle in.

"He's a coward, Nadine," I tell her. "He always has been. You're better off without him. We both are."

Nadine's face is starting to get splotchy, and a teardrop slides down her cheek. "That's just what your dad said in my note," she says. "He has never understood that people love him and need him. He thinks that if he can't be the perfect dad or the perfect husband, if he can't be exactly what everyone wants him to be, then everyone is better off with nothing at all. He thinks that his disappearing will solve everyone's problems." She sighs. "But it doesn't. It just makes them worse." She looks me dead in the eye.

"I know you're angry, Lara. I don't blame you. But you're not better off without him. Even if he's not perfect, you're still better off with him, and I truly hope that someday you'll both be able to accept that."

I think about this for a second. She's right, of course. I mean, flawed or not, I would prefer it if my father were a part of my life. And I would certainly prefer it if he were a part of Parker's life. Andrew's father died fifteen years ago. My dad is the only shot she'll ever have at a grandfather. Suddenly my mind flashes to this morning, when Parker cried when I left the room.

Separation anxiety, I think. How aptly named. I suppose I had the adult version of it with my father. You know, since he showed up, every single time that I saw him, in the back of my head I thought that it would be the last time. But then he'd come back, and come back again, and come back again. This last time that I saw him, the day that he came over, I finally felt like I trusted him. I finally believed that he would always come back. How ironic that that's the day that made him decide not to.

God, I never should have been so optimistic about the rain. I mean, I was an English major. I should know that rain is always a symbol of bad things to come. I should have seen this coming the second that I felt the first drop hit me on the head.

"I just don't understand," I tell Nadine. "The last time I saw him, he told me that he loved me more than anything else in the world. He told me that when you're a parent, that never goes away."

Nadine's face contorts when I say this, like her heart is physically breaking and she's wincing from the pain.

"He said that to you?" she asks, her voice quieter than I've ever heard it before. I nod, and she puts her hand on my leg.

"He means that, honey. He really does."

I stare at her, and my throat chokes up. "I know," I say. "I know, because I know how much I love Parker." I shake my head. "But I could never leave her like this." I take a deep breath, and I look Nadine in the eye. "I would die before I would walk away from her."

Nadine nods. "That's right, Lara. You would. And you're a great mom for feeling that way. But everyone is different, honey. I'm not defending him, but everybody shows their love in different ways. And in your dad's mind, his leaving is the biggest sacrifice that he can make for you, because he would rather walk away than have you be disappointed in who he's turned out to be." She pauses, then looks down at the floor. "Honey, if there is one thing I've come to realize about your father, it's that he doesn't like himself very much. I thought that I could change that about him. I thought that I could build him up and boost his confidence, but I know now that I can't do that for him. He has to do it for himself, and obviously he's just not there yet." She sighs, and looks back up at me. I get the feeling that she doesn't know what else to say.

"It's okay, Nadine," I say. "I'm okay." And I am okay, actually. I now have cold, hard proof that I am absolutely, positively nothing like him, and it's a huge relief. I just realized, however, that I haven't even asked how Nadine is doing. I mean, the woman practically got jilted at the altar. She must be a total wreck.

"What about you, Nadine?" I ask. "Are you okay?"

"Oh, honey," she says. The drawl is back, and she smiles sadly, then winks. "Practically perfect people never permit sentiment to muddle their feelings."

I give her a funny look. It sounds strange with a fake Southern accent and not with a proper British one, but that is definitely a line from *Mary Poppins*. How weird that she would make a reference like that. I'm positive I didn't tell her that I was thinking that about her the other night.

"Is that supposed to mean yes?" I ask.

She laughs. "Yes," she says. "It is."

Okay. I just got the reference. That line is the last thing that Julie Andrews says, right before she flies away at the end of the movie. I bite my lip as it dawns on me that I'm probably never going to see Nadine again.

"So what are you going to do now?" I ask her.

She shrugs. "Oh, I think I'll probably travel for a bit. Maybe go back to Vegas at some point. I just want to get out of LA for a while. There's no use in hanging around with a lot of sad memories."

I nod at her. Somehow I knew she was going to say that. Then, just like that, she stands up.

"Well, honey, I should get going. I've got a lot of phone calls to make if I want to get this wedding stopped before next weekend."

Oh, God. I didn't even think about that.

"I'm the matron of honor," I remind her. "Shouldn't that be my job?"

Nadine shakes her head. "No, honey. Thanks for offering, but I think I should do this myself. You don't need to be explaining to people why your father left me."

Well, I didn't think about it that way. She does have a point, I suppose. I stand up and walk her to the front door, and she quickly steps out onto the porch. The rain has finally slowed down; it's just a light drizzle now, but a thick fog has settled in, making it so that I can barely see past the sidewalk. I follow Nadine onto the porch and reach out to give her a hug, but she stops me.

"I don't like long good-byes, honey. They're too sad. Just tell me to take care, and you do the same."

I can feel myself choking up again—that damn Luthor—and I know that if I say anything I'll start to sob, so I just nod at her. And then she picks up her umbrella, opens it up, and walks down the front steps of my house without looking back. I watch her as she walks away; she seems to fade into the fog, but the black umbrella is stark against the sky. For a second it almost looks likes she's floating. I smile to myself.

Good-bye, Mary Poppins, I think. *Don't stay away too long.*

twenty-six

O n the Tuesday after Labor Day, I leave my house at seven thirty in
the morning for My First Day as a Working Mother. (I'm not
counting faculty orientation week, because I skipped out on half of the
sessions and left at noon every day. Oh, please, what are they going to do,
fire me?) Of course, I was practically in tears when I woke up this morning, and then I cried during the whole commute because Parker was still
asleep when I walked out the door, and I kept thinking that this is it; this
is the beginning of me missing out on her entire life.

Anyway, by the time I pull into the parking lot at eight A.M. sharp, I
am missing Parker something awful, and I am so overcome with self-
reproach that I can hardly breathe. I'm fully aware of the fact that this
makes absolutely no sense, by the way, seeing as how most days I'm already at the gym by eight A.M. sharp, and I've never felt bad about not being with her then. But today isn't most days. Today is My First Day as a
Working Mother, and I feel that a certain amount of melodrama is appropriate, if not required.

When I step into my office, the very first thing that I do is scatter pictures of Parker on top of every flat surface that I can find, and then stare
at them and cry. But within seconds of my arrival, one of my students
comes bursting into my office. She's wearing a light blue, short-sleeved,
collared Lacoste shirt that's about three sizes too small, hence expos-
ing her belly-button ring. Gigantic, pink-tinted aviator sunglasses are
perched on her nose, and four-inch-high espadrilles are peeking out from
under her low-rise jeans, which are so long that they drag on the floor

and she almost trips over them with every step. Her long blond hair is partially obscuring her face, and she's sipping coffee from a Starbucks paper cup.

Jesus, I think as I look at her. Maybe I like babies more than I realize. The fashion plate starts in on me right away.

"Oh, my God, Ms. Stone, thank *God* you're back. I showed my English teacher an outline for my Michigan essay, and he totally didn't get it at all. He said that it's too provincial. Like, I don't even know what that means, or anything. I'm applying to art programs. They want me to tell them about my art, right?"

I wipe the tears from my eyes, compose myself, and tell her to leave it for me to look over. When she walks back out the door, I glance at the clock. It's eight-oh-three, and I already feel like I've never left.

I sit down at my desk and begin going through the five months' worth of mail, e-mails, and phone messages that have piled up, and I get a ten-minute update from my assistant—who, by the way, has assured me at least fifty times already that I look "better than ever," which I am quite sure translates into, "You look really fat, but I would never tell you that"— on all of the crises that have occurred since April and with which I now need to deal. Fourteen final transcripts never arrived at UCLA, and if we don't get them out in today's mail the kids can't register for classes. The school cut our budget for this year by fifteen hundred dollars and now we don't have the money to pay the speaker who was supposed to come to Twelfth Grade Parent Night next week, so we need to find someone else right away. The SAT dates are wrong in the standardized testing booklet that we're supposed to mail home to the entire Upper School this week, and we need to get it back from the copy guy before he prints seven hundred of them.

I reach for a pen next to my phone, and I am startled to see Parker's face staring out at me from a silver picture frame. God, I got so wrapped up in all of these details, I completely forgot about her. I glance at the clock again: It's been less than two hours, and I already feel like I never even had a baby. I decide that it's probably better if I don't stop to analyze this.

But before I have a chance to do anything, my phone rings.

"College Counseling," I answer. "This is Lara Stone."

Oh, God, please don't be a parent. I'm not quite ready for parents yet.

"Hey," says a familiar voice. Not a parent. I exhale with relief. It's Stacey.

"Hey, yourself," I say to her. "Isn't it a little bit early for you to be up?" I ask.

"Old habits die hard," she says. "So how are you doing?"

I look at the pile of paper that is sitting on my desk. "I'm good," I say. "I've been here for an hour and half and I'm already swamped."

"I was referring to your dad. Nadine. The wedding."

Oh, right. The wedding. I guess I forgot about that, too. It was supposed to be this past weekend—Labor Day Sunday.

"Oh, I'm all right," I say. "I was a little depressed on Friday, because that was supposed to be the day of the shower, and I cried a little on Sunday morning, but it was fine. I didn't really have a lot of time to think about it, to be honest. Deloris took off for the long weekend, so I was pretty busy with Parker."

Stacey sounds surprised. "So, you're fine?" she asks. "You're not upset about your dad?"

"Well, yeah, I'm upset, but what can I do, you know? I don't have time to sit around and mope about it. And really, I feel more sorry for him than anything. How sad is it to be so unhappy with yourself that you're willing to walk away from everything that you love? I mean, that's really sad."

"I guess," she says. "I'm just surprised that you're not freaking out. Because the last time he did this, you were a mess. I wasn't sure that you were going to make it through the first year of law school."

I sigh. "You know, Stace, I guess I just realize now that he is who he is, and there's nothing I can do to change him. And to be honest, I don't have the energy to get all self-absorbed about it, and to make it about me and what I did wrong. I just feel like, I'm not the kid anymore, you know? I have my own kid now, and I have to focus on being her mother."

"Okay," she says, sounding impressed. "Who knew that you were so self-aware?"

"I know," I say. "It feels weird to be so mature. But anyway, what's up with you? How's the bar?"

"Oh, I'm selling it," she says matter-of-factly.

"What?" I ask. "Why? You just bought it."

"Yeah, I'm over it. There's a guy who's interested, and he's willing to pay double what I paid for it, so I figure I should take the money and run."

"But what are you going to do?" I ask her. "You can't just retire. You'll kill yourself."

"No, I'm not retiring. I've been talking to some of my old clients, and I think I'm going to open up my own firm. You know, just me, maybe get a good paralegal or something." She pauses. "I'm a lawyer," she says. "It's who I am. The bar was fun, but it's not me. Do you know what I mean?"

I glance at the picture of Parker and smile. "I do," I say. "I know exactly what you mean."

A few hours later, as I'm in the midst of a phone call with a hysterical mother, trying to explain to her why I can't delete the F that her daughter received in Algebra II from her transcript, even though she retook the course over the summer and got a C, a deliveryman walks into my office and places a gigantic Mrs. Beasleys basket on my desk.

Who sent me this? I think. While the mother is still talking—*But if you don't delete the F she'll have no chance of getting into Stanford*—I open up the card.

Dear Lara,

Happy first day of school and thanks for all of your help with the Institute—we're in! Love, Julie, Jon, and Lily.

Well, well, well. So Nadine pulled it off. I shake my head to myself. I've spoken to Julie a bunch of times since the bachelorette party; in typical Julie fashion, she pretended like the whole thing never happened, and when I tried to bring it up, she changed the subject to her plans for Lily's first birthday party. But of course, she did remember the part about Nadine getting her into the Institute. She called me three times in one day to make sure that I reminded Nadine to call Dan Gregoire about her, and then she called me twice the next day to make sure that Nadine actually called.

But now that I think about it, I haven't spoken to her since my dad left. She probably thinks that I went to the wedding and that everything is great. Well. I guess I should call her.

After promising the hysterical mother that I will include in her daughter's recommendation a line about how she didn't click with her math teacher last year, and after assuring her that yes, of course that makes a difference (but without bothering to tell her that there's still no chance in hell that her kid is going to get into Stanford with a C and an F on her transcript), she hangs up the phone and I dial Julie, who answers on the first ring.

"Hi!" she says. "Did you get the basket that I sent?"

"Yeah," I say. "Thanks. So I guess you must be pretty happy, huh?"

"Thrilled is more like it. Jon is beside himself. Really, Lara, you have no idea how much I owe you for this. If you ever need anything, just ask. Oh, and do you have Nadine's address? Because I wanted to send her something, too. Do you think a nice bottle of champagne is enough?"

"Actually," I say, "Nadine is gone. She left town."

"Oh, that's right," Julie exclaims. "The wedding was on Sunday! They must be on their honeymoon. So how was it? Was it amazing?"

I sigh. It makes me tired just thinking about retelling this story again. "They're not on their honeymoon," I say. "They never got married. My dad skipped out on her a few days after the bachelorette party."

"What?" Julie says. She sounds shocked. "Oh, my God. So where is she now?"

"I don't know," I say. "She wanted to get out of LA. She said she was going to travel for a while."

"God," Julie says. "That must have been so embarrassing for her." She lowers her voice, as if her house is being bugged by gossipers and she doesn't want them to overhear. "Was she devastated?" she asks.

"No," I say. "Not really. I kind of got the feeling that she always knew that it wasn't really going to happen. Although it would have been nice if she had let me in on that little secret before she showed up on my doorstep with his good-bye note."

Julie makes a *tsk* sound, as if to say that she feels for me. "Lara, I'm so sorry," she says. There's a long pause, and I imagine that she's using it to gather her courage. "He left you a note?" she finally asks. "What did it say?"

I knew it. God, Julie is such a mommunist. It's so funny, too, because before I had Parker, I always thought that she was such an anomaly.

"Oh, you know," I say. "The usual stuff." As much as I do love Julie, I'm a little hesitant to tell her all of the gory details. I just don't want this becoming another juicy story for her to tell the next time she has lunch with the girls in her Mommy and Me class.

Oh, my God, you guys, listen to this. . . .

"Anyway, I've gotta go," I say, as I glance at the pile of papers on my desk. "I've got a ton of work to do."

"Oh, okay," she says, sounding disappointed. "Well, do you want to meet for lunch on Wednesday, after you go to Susan's? We could talk about it then. You know, if you want to talk about it."

"No, thanks. I'm over it. Really. And besides, I don't think I'm going back to Susan's class anymore."

"You're not?" she asks, with bafflement in her voice. "But why?"

Well, Jul, I've only got room for one mommunist in my life right now. . . .

"You know," I say, "I've finally realized that it's just not me."

twenty-seven

When I get home from work that afternoon, I am practically bursting with excitement at the thought of seeing Parker. I keep playing this movie moment in my head—I'm going to walk in the front door, and even though she doesn't move yet, she's going to start jumping up and down and smiling and laughing, all in order to convey just how happy she is that her dear, beloved mommy has returned, once again, as promised.

I blow through the front door and run upstairs to her room. Deloris is sitting on the glider with Parker on her lap, and she's shaking a rattle in her face.

"Hi," I say, enthusiastically. "Mommy's home!"

Parker turns her head to look at me for a second, and then she looks back at the rattle and tries to shove it into her mouth. No smile, no nothing. Well, so much for the warm welcome. My heart sinks a little bit as I remember something else that Susan said in her separation-anxiety lecture.

Babies don't understand the concept of "object permanence." In their minds, if you're not around, you're not just out for a few hours. If you're not around, you've ceased to exist.

Great. So basically she forgot all about me. Well, that's fair, I guess. I mean, I did forget all about her, too. Deloris, on the other hand, is very excited to see me. Deloris practically bolts out of the chair when I walk in.

"Oh, Mrs. Lara," she says. "Thank goodness you're home. I didn't know how much longer she could wait." I look at her, confused.

"Wait for what?" I ask. "What's going on?"

Deloris beams and places Parker on the floor.

"She has been trying to roll over all day, and she was finally going to do it, too, but Deloris picked her up and told her no, no, she has to wait until her mama gets home, because Mama has to be here to see the first time." She looks at Parker. "Deloris has been holding you all afternoon, hasn't she, sweets?"

I look down at the floor, and, just like Deloris said, Parker is thrusting her body upward in an effort to pull herself over. Each time, she almost makes it before falling back onto her back. On the fourth try, though, she does it.

"Oh, my God!" I yell. "She did it. She rolled over!" Deloris and I both begin to clap wildly. "Good job, honey," I say. "I'm so proud of you! You rolled over all by yourself."

Ha! I think. *The fat baby rolled over, after all.* For the first time ever, I actually wish that there were some mommunists around.

But Parker doesn't seem all that thrilled about her accomplishment. She's got a face full of scratchy Berber carpet, and she immediately starts to cry.

"Oh, she can't get back over," Deloris says, and gently rolls her back the other way. I look over at her, one eyebrow raised.

"That's really the first time she did it?" I ask. Deloris nods.

"It is," she insists. A second later Parker flips over again, then lets out a wail, and I pick her up. I can see that this is going to be a fun stage.

"Thanks, Deloris," I say. "It really means a lot to me that you waited."

Deloris smiles. "You're a good mama," she says as she walks toward the door. She steps out into the hallway, then pauses and turns around. "You learned it the hard way."

I don't know if she's referring to my problems with my dad, or with her, or just with myself, but it doesn't matter. After the day that I've just had—no, make that after the five months that I've just had—it's exactly what I needed to hear.

epilogue

I am walking down the street in Beverly Hills, pushing Parker in her new, Maclaren Quest umbrella stroller (she outgrew the infant car seat, thank God, so bye-bye Snap-N-Go), and I'm feeling really good about myself. I've finally lost that last four pounds, and just knowing that I'm back to normal has put a little extra spring in my step this morning. I'm having a really good-hair day, too—I blew it out last night and somehow, when I woke up this morning, it was just perfect. Not sweaty and frizzy and full of bends from sleeping on it all night, like it usually gets. I even put a skirt on, and I haven't done that since the day that I met Julie for lunch, right after Parker was born, when nothing else in my closet fit me. God, that feels like a lifetime ago.

I'm actually on my way to meet a new friend for lunch. She has a son who's about the same age as Parker, and we met at the mall, of all places. We were in a fancy children's clothing store; I was looking for an outfit for Parker to wear for Thanksgiving, and she was buying a baby gift for someone. Her baby was crying, and she was frantically rifling through her diaper bag, and I guess she saw me staring at her, because she gave me a dirty look. The look said, *Fuck you, hasn't your kid ever cried before?* and I recognized it instantly, because it's the same look that I give to people all the time when I'm pissed off or frazzled and I can't get Parker to calm down. Anyway, I didn't want her to think that I was a mommunist, or that I was judging her or anything like that, so I walked over to her and asked her if she needed anything.

"I forgot the fucking formula," she said. She sounded like she was going to cry. "I took out two of those packets—the little single-serve ones

that they have—and I meant to put them in my diaper bag, but I must
have left them on the counter by accident. God, I am so stupid. I am now
officially in the running for Worst Mother of the Year."

I remember that I glanced at her diaper bag, and it was a mess. There
were papers sticking out of the top, and her changing pad was just shoved
inside, not rolled up or anything.

Now this is my kind of girl, I thought to myself.

It turned out that we both use the same kind of formula, so I pulled
the travel-size can out of my diaper bag and offered her some.

"Really?" she asked. "Are you sure?"

"Yeah," I said. "Go ahead. And actually, I've already won the Worst
Mother of the Year award, so don't worry about it. She once had diarrhea
in the market, and I didn't have an extra diaper or a change of clothes or
anything, so I had to push her around in the cart naked, and I covered her
up with paper towels."

She stared at me. "That was you?" she asked, and then she laughed.
"You know you're famous, don't you? That story has been going around
for months."

I wanted to die when she said that, but then she said something else
that made me feel better. "Every time I hear that story," she said, "all I can
think is, 'There, but for the grace of God, go I.'"

And that was it. We've been meeting every Wednesday for lunch for
the last two months with the babies—we call it our Mommy and Martini
class, even though neither of us has yet to actually have a martini at
eleven thirty in the morning—and we spend the whole time talking
about everything from how much we hate Jeff from *The Wiggles* to how
worried I am that Parker is going to be obese to how stressed out she is
that Luke (that's her son) still hasn't rolled over. She's originally from
New Jersey, and she works as a bond specialist at Merrill Lynch four days
a week. Oh, and she stopped speaking to both of her parents five years ago
because she found out that they were embezzling money from a trust
fund that her grandmother had left to her when she was a kid. Erica is her
name. Erica Daniels. Stacey loves her.

Okay, that is, like, the fifth person who has stared at me and smiled.
And I don't just mean a glance. I mean a full-on stare, and then passes by

me and turns around to stare again. Wow. I must look *really* good. You know, Nadine was right. It's amazing what happens when you just exude a little bit of confidence.

I walk into the restaurant and Erica is already there, seated at our usual table. She's feeding Luke baby food straight from the jar—Susan once told us never to do that, because the saliva that gets left on the spoon after each bite can contaminate the rest of the jar. Ugh, I'm so glad I'm not in that class anymore. I hate even knowing information like that. I'd much rather just contaminate the jar and deal with the one-in-a-zillion chance that Parker will get botulism or whatever it is that she can get from baby food contaminated by her own saliva—and I smile.

"Hey," I say. I turn around to lift Parker out of the stroller, and I hear Erica chuckle.

"Nice thong," she says. "Pink is definitely your color."

What? I twist my neck around and look at my backside. *Oh, you've got to be kidding me.* The bottom of my skirt got tucked into the elastic at the top of my underwear, and my entire ass is showing. I quickly pull it out and sit down, covering my eyes with my hands.

"Oh, my God," I moan. I look up at her, and I start to laugh in spite of myself. "I couldn't understand why everyone kept staring at me. I kept thinking, 'Damn, girl, you must look superhot.' Oh, I'm so mortified."

Erica starts to crack up. "Hey," she says, "look on the bright side. At least people were looking. Imagine how bad you would feel if they all started covering their eyes and running for the hills."

That's true. I can't say I'd thought of it in quite that way.

"Ah, that's what I love about you," I say to her. "Ever the optimist."

She laughs, then launches into a story about how she drove for sixteen miles on the freeway on Saturday before she realized that she had forgotten to strap Luke into his car seat. As I listen to her, I glance at Parker, who is trying to grab Luke's hair with her fist, and I suddenly realize that I am the happiest I've been in a long, long time.

Huh, I think. What do you know? I guess I turned out to be a happy mommy, after all.

tales from the crib

RISA GREEN

A CONVERSATION WITH
RISA GREEN

Q: How much of this story is drawn from your own life?

A: Unlike *Notes from the Underbelly*, this book is not nearly as close to my own experience (no, my dad was never engaged to a Hollywood madam). That being said, I did draw on some of my own feelings about having a new baby. The crushing insecurity, the feeling of being totally overwhelmed, and even the anger at the world for not telling "the truth" about motherhood were all things that I experienced after my daughter was born. Oh, and of course, the Mommy and Me class. I took four or five different classes, and the class in the book is an amalgam of all of them. I can remember times when I would be sitting on the floor with ten or twelve other new moms, just listening to the conversation, and I would think, *Would it be rude for me to whip out my notepad right now? Because this is* really *good material.*

Q: There are some funny characters in your book that truly fit the stereotype of the high-maintenance LA mom. What are the pros and cons of raising a child in the LA area?

A: Aside from never having to zip a five year old into a snowsuit, it's kind of hard to think of any pros. Seriously, Los Angeles is a tough place to raise kids. The public school system is in shambles, but the private schools are so elitist that I live in fear of the day when my daughter will ask me why we don't fly private. Sometimes I fantasize about selling the house and moving us all to a small town in the Midwest, where my kids could run around on acres of grass and my neighbors would be farmers instead of TV agents, but then I watch *Doc Hollywood* on TBS and I realize that it would never work. The reality is that when you live in LA or in any big city, for that matter, it just means that you have to work that much harder at being a parent, and instilling values and setting a good example for your kids. And you know, I'm not sure whether that qualifies as a pro or a con. It's probably a little bit of both.

Q: What were the challenges in writing this sequel to *Notes from the Underbelly*?

A: The biggest challenge was the fact that my son was born about a month after I started writing, and I didn't anticipate how hard it would be to find the time to write with a toddler and a newborn. Or how hard it would be for me to write after getting no sleep. There were definitely days when I would write for six or seven hours straight, and then the next day I would go back and read it, and it just made no sense at all.

Q: Lara has a very difficult time adjusting to motherhood. What is your advice to mothers who find themselves in the same situation?

A: Zoloft.

Okay, okay. My real advice would be to understand that, although the birth of a child is a wonderful thing that should be celebrated, it also brings to an end a chapter of life that, for many women, is a really exciting, liberating time, and it's totally normal and healthy to take some time to mourn that. It used to be that women got married and had children right out of college and, as a result, I don't think that the reality of motherhood was as much of a shock for that generation. But now that so many women are putting off having babies until their thirties and forties, becoming a mother often means giving up a lifestyle, and we feel guilty when we miss that lifestyle. So I say let go of the guilt and realize that the reason June Cleaver was such a great mom is because she had no idea what she was missing.

Q: Were there any themes or ideas that you wanted to get across to readers while you were writing the novel?

A: My main goal in writing this book was to show that it is okay to not always love being a mother. I think that a lot of women feel that way, but there aren't many who are willing to admit it because they think that it somehow makes them a failure. I also wanted to get across the idea that, for better or for worse, our parents absolutely shape us into the kind of parents that we will become. And once we become parents, it's important to reflect on our own childhoods so that we can understand which behaviors we need to work on in ourselves, so that we don't repeat the mistakes that our parents made with us.

Risa Green grew up in a suburb of Philadephia, PA, and graduated from both the University of Pennsylvania and The Georgetown University Law Center. She has worked as a corporate finance attorney and, more recently, as a college counselor at a private day school. She currently resides with her husband, their daughter and son, and their dog in Los Angeles.